STORMBLOOD

JEREMY SZAL

This paperback first published in Great Britain in 2021 by Gollancz

First published in Great Britain in 2020 by Gollancz
an imprint of The Orion Publishing Group Ltd
Carmelite House, 50 Victoria Embankment
London EC4Y 0DZ

An Hachette UK Company

1 3 5 7 9 10 8 6 4 2

A CIP catalogue record for this book is
available from the British Library.

ISBN (Mass Market Paperback) 978 1 473 22743 9
ISBN (eBook) 978 1 473 22744 6

Typeset at The Spartan Press Ltd,
Lymington, Hants

Printed in Great Britain by Clays Ltd,
Elcograf S.p.A.

www.gollancz.co.uk

For Mum and Dad

Thank you for everything, and a little bit extra.

1

The Reaper

I realised this was a bad idea at around the time the alien bio-tech started pulsing with dark pleasure under my ribs.

Not that it had ever been a good idea, of course. When you boil it down, there're two types of plans: the ones that get you killed, and the ones that don't. When you're in the business of stealing illegal goods from dangerous people and selling them to other dangerous people, risk is part of the deal. But it was only since I'd been injected with stormtech that I'd started enjoying it. The rush of adrenaline. The thrill of danger. The heat of aggression.

The polymer atrium of the spaceport with its recycled oxygen and pallid lighting was freezing, but my skin was flushed and prickling with fresh sweat, my breathing shallow, my hands twitching by my sides. I think I was even *salivating* for some action. Moist, sticky saliva filling my mouth like treacle. I grimaced. I hated when my body did that. Twitchy hands were acceptable and sweaty skin I could handle, but I was never going to get used to a sudden mouthful of saliva. The stormtech only got this keyed up when I was walking into something no sane person would consider.

Nothing for it but to press on, keeping a watch on my body and my surroundings. Breathing hard, sweat snaking down my spine, I stepped into the spaceport terminal. It was frantic in the way only spaceports can be: people wandering around and clutching e-tickets, queuing for zero-gravity nausea meds, whirling to meet flight schedules, all while drones jostled overhead. I cut a path through the crowded chaos. No easy feat for a guy my size, though folks tended to edge out of my way, especially since I was wearing heavy armour, my face concealed behind a helmet with a wide, mirrored visor.

The humid, hot stench clung to every surface of the spaceport like a bad reputation. The stormtech had elevated my senses, letting me smell the difference between the spicy, gunpowdery stink of a suit lined with asteroid dust and the greasy odour of a suit worn by an engine-room worker. Between the familiar smell of a human and unfamiliar one of some alien species. The smells all tumbling and blending together and oozing into every pore. Didn't matter which planets or outposts or habitats you went to in the universe, all spaceports smelled like this. I'd visited enough of them, back when I was a soldier.

This spaceport was in the bottom floor of Compass, a colossal, hollowed-out asteroid. I'd never been to anything like this asteroid, and it was hard to believe, even standing in the flight terminal and seeing the geometries of chiselled rock gouged out high above, hollows sparkling with metals and threaded with girderwork and support struts like the ribcage of some giant, celestial creature.

Golden lights glistened down on tiles shiny with engine grease as I stepped into the tumultuous streets. Only now did my body-heat drop, my breathing returning to normal. Slowly, I started to think more clearly as my focus unclouded. Eyes on the corners. Ears open. Mapping escape routes and points of interest. Scanning the crowd for weapons and possible assailants.

Paranoid, perhaps. But paranoia is always preferable to a

bullet in the face. I had to assume the Jackal had look-outs and was packing surveillance gear. You don't become one of the most notorious crimelords on an asteroid of half a billion people without your own healthy dose of paranoia.

People clustered around a hexagonal viewport to watch a kilometre-long chainship soaring by, blue starlight glinting off its silver flank. Highrises towered above the spaceport, radiant with blinking lights. Multilevel shop readouts advertised ship parts, engine repairs, navsystem charts, spacesuits, cheap flights and cheaper booze in English, Chinese, Russian, Spanish and a smattering of alien and offworld dialects, bleeding stains of neon green and crimson like angry mist into the air.

A crackle echoed from the spaceport. A busted chainship engine, probably. I was the only one on the street who turned towards it. Without the stormtech bolstering their senses like mine, the average human wouldn't have heard it, or the distant warble of engines entering and exiting the spaceport, or seen the guy in a high window shooting a needle of synthsilver into his arm. Thanks to the organic blue matter shimmying down my throat, wrapped around my bones, slithering down my ribs like ladder rungs, and fused into the fibres of my organs and muscles, I could.

A sudden commslink burst filled my eardrums. 'Grim! Turn the frequency down,' I managed to growl.

The intense static quietened until it disappeared entirely. 'Sorry, Vakov,' Grim said.

'I thought we agreed you'd wait for my signal,' I said, ears still ringing.

'Yeah, well.' I could practically *hear* the ear-splitting grin in his voice. My friend's face popped into the bottom right corner of my heads-up display. He was short and weedy where I was tall and broad, pale with a shock of red hair that was the opposite of my tanned skin and black hair. We were opposites

3

in many ways. But I've found friends to occasionally be like magnets: opposing forces attract. With the emphasis on occasionally. Grim was snacking away, every crunch amplified in my ear. But telling him to stop eating would be like telling me to stop drinking. 'Everything else is ready ... and I got bored. You know how it is, big guy.'

Unfortunately, I did.

'Please tell me you're not watching me through street cams again,' I said as I brought my waypoint up. 'If *they* backtrace—'

'You worry too much. My tech's airtight, always has been,' came the hacker's easy drawl. Grim was my best friend, but in moments like these I wanted to wring his scrawny neck. 'Just making sure you don't do anything stupid. Like on Kaddus Station.'

I winced. 'You and I remember Kaddus very differently.'

Grim gave a knowing *mhm*. I changed the subject. 'Make yourself useful and watch for nasty surprises at the waypoint.'

That was our deal. I handled the physical end of the business, while he worked his tech magic from twenty floors above. Grim grumbled but eventually settled down to work. He might whine about it, but he always comes around in the end. If I need him at my side he'll be there, though sometimes the convincing gave me a headache.

He reminded me of my little brother.

I willed those painful memories away as Grim piped up: 'Vak, why are we messing with the Jackal?' The waypoint beamed a neon-green hexagon on my visor, measuring the distance as I walked. Broken glass crunched under my armoured boots. 'You know he hunts down anyone who messes with him. He takes half of them.'

'Half?'

'Half of everything. One eye, one ear, five fingers, five toes. He leaves the tongue, so they can warn others.'

4

Wasn't like I didn't already know all this. 'Your point being?'

'My point being, why are we putting our heads on the chopping block?'

One of the Jackal's less lethal enterprises was a biochem laboratory that sold experimental biotech on the darkmarket. One of our contacts wanted one of his genomes for a prototype called Hendrix – a male hormonal stimulant – enough to pay us to steal it. I make no excuses: stealing from crimelords is no less illegal than stealing from anyone else. Theft might not be my proudest work, but it's the least dangerous and least bloody kind I do.

I hadn't told Grim I only took this job to pay for his Compass residency card. He always buried the problem beneath jokes when I brought it up, but I caught the nervous flash in his eyes, worrying if this was the week he'd be deported from the asteroid.

I've not had not much stability in my life, not many people who stuck by me. Grim had. And I don't let go of my friends easily.

'Jackal boy isn't home,' Grim said over the sucking roar of a chainship departing the spaceport and punching through the hangar's electric-blue shield-barrier into vacuum. 'Probably won't be until work hours are over, so it's unlikely we'll cross paths.'

'*You* won't,' I rasped. The stormtech had slithered up to fold like wet cement in my throat, turning my voice husky and thick. I wasn't suicidal or stupid enough to break into the Jackal's biotech lab. But crimelords are usually paranoid enough not to trust their own security completely, and predictable enough to keep their closest secrets close: at home. 'I'm the one breaking into the place.'

Although, we both knew I'd partially taken this job *because* of the risk. It was a challenge. A gamble. It's no secret that my body's wired to sniff out danger for the thrill of an adrenaline rush pumping through my system. It was why I handled this end alone. I'll put myself in harm's way, but I won't risk my friends.

The chaos of the spaceport evaporated behind me as I slid deeper into residential sectors. Past colourful smears of digital ink, beneath the vertical labyrinth of jutting balconies and tangled walkways spiralling up through the buildings. I thought over the plan, my brain cycling through the risks and anticipating the possible dangers I'd confront and the kick I'd get out of them. My hands clenching and unclenching, my muscles tensing, the burning glow of adrenaline and androgen trickling through my system, feeding the alien plumbing hardwired into my body chemistry. I tried to shrug out of my body's sticky sensations and ground myself in the hard details, the schematics.

Sometimes, my body is my own worst enemy.

I passed a group of stinking drunks slumped in a doorway in one of those seedy spaceport bars that only smuggler crews visit. Glancing up, I saw a flag displaying the atom-shaped insignia of Harmony snapping in a simulated breeze up near the vaulted ceiling. Harmony was the governing body that controlled this asteroid and many others, and back when I was a soldier, that insignia had meant something to me. My body heat rocketed sky-high as I gazed at it now, stormtech clenching inside me. No surprises there. They'd injected the drug into me, after all.

I looked away, jaw hard, just as one of the drunks flicked his gaze towards me. As if despite my ash-grey armour and one-way helmet visor he knew what I was. Some folks know something's *off*. Wrong. Something down in the brain stem lets them sense the rottenness of alien biotech with no business being bottled in human flesh. Maybe he could smell me.

He threw an empty beer bottle that glanced off my armoured shoulder. The stormtech instantly flared up in response. An invitation for violence. I turned away before I was tempted to accept it. Already raring for danger like I was, walking away was harder than I liked.

I could feel my armour responding to me now. Covering me sole to scalp, the toughened nanoparticle surface was supercharged at my touch. Inside the armour, the interface tendrils shifted along my back, the electrostatic charges crackling along the nape of my neck.

I turned a corner and saw a skinnie slumped in one of the asteroid's hollows. He was birth-naked and striated with what looked like blue gills. They rippled in violent bursts along his tattered chest, his wire-thin arms, his malnourished face. Each breath sounded like stones rattling. His sweat was nearly black, oozing out of clogged pores, releasing the sickly-sweet stench of wet overripe fruit. Skinnies were stormtech addicts, some of them so consumed by their own body's sensations they'd spiralled into the deep end, beyond the point of return.

One too many missteps, I'd end up this way, too.

I swallowed hard and eased past the poor guy, glad Grim had the sense to shut up. A few minutes later, I came to the Jackal's house in the laneway below me. One of those standard living spaces you see everywhere: two storeys high, olive-green walls, largely inconspicuous. I perched on the walkway some three floors above, scanning the exterior of the building. No camera, no guards, no nasty hidden autocannons packing high-calibre armour-piercing rounds or any other fatal surprises. I vaulted over the guardrail and fell towards the roof. I landed on my feet, rolled clear to my knees. The three-storey drop should have hurt like hell, but the surface of my armour sparked as the shock absorbers cushioned the fall. So far so good.

Grim cracked his knuckles. 'Surveillance cams, sub-dermals,

alarms, thermals, laser tripwires, pressure points, and micro-detectors all off.' Hazy gold outlines of the security tech that branched throughout the building began to discolour, oozing back into their honeycombed sockets as Grim disabled them. 'Happy thieving.'

The vent slithered open and I dropped in.

I don't know what I was expecting but given the rundown surroundings, it wasn't for the place to be decked out. Ebony floors, grey angular chairs, and a huge viewport peering out to the dockyard, frantic with ships from a dozen solar systems and half a dozen alien species. I eyed an impressive gin collection sitting in a glass cabinet.

Grim gave a low whistle. 'Vak, I think we're in the wrong business.' But my body heat had skyrocketed, my elevated pulse throbbing hard and fast in my skull, warning me of the real risk. If I had been doing this for anyone but Grim, I might have reconsidered.

But it was for Grim.

I made a beeline for the Jackal's workstation, unplugged the overriding port from my suit and jammed it into the central port so Grim could get to work trawling through the mainframe while I stayed alert for visitors. A convulsion of colourful geo-metrical images and complex code flashed across the flexiscreen. Grim muttered to himself. 'Still searching ... still looking for it ... man, there's a lot of data on here ... our Jackal is busy, busy boy ... oh, oh, that's not good.' An image of a young man appeared on-screen. He was spattered with blood, missing an eye and an ear, and the fingers and toes from the left side of his body. His remaining eye was glassy and broken and full of fear. A reminder of the Jackal's work for his own private collection. My blood pressure spiked.

'Grim?'

'Almost,' he whispered. 'Almost ... almost. Found it!' A

genome sequence labelled *Hendrix* materialised on-screen as a clutter of colours and statistics. Hands twitchy again, a trickle of sweat running down my arms, I retethered the port to my suit and the transfer commenced. 'That's right, come to Grim, nice and easy.'

The screen chimed again and the Hendrix dematerialised. Finally.

'Got it.' said Grim. Sticky, hot relief flushed through my body. I'd earned a drink now. I had half a mind to swipe one of the Jackal's vintage gin bottles. As I passed the gleaming collection, the stormtech coiled in my throat and my thirst became raging dehydration. I couldn't resist. I eased open the cabinet, three dozen bottles of liquid gold glinting inside. All begging to be taken away.

I scooped up the most expensive looking one and headed to the front door. If I'd been paying more attention, I'd have heard the approaching footsteps, the conversation. So I was as unprepared for the three men ascending the porch steps as they were to see me. The echoes of their conversation withered out into stony silence.

I wasn't thirsty anymore.

All three men were about as handsome as backalley dogs, but I picked out the Jackal instantly. It was his casual slouch, the relaxed demeanour and controlled reaction that set him apart as the naked surprise on the other men's faces quickly curdled into rage. They were Sniffers, their bodies crawling with canine augmentations that helped them seek out threats and hunt down enemies. Their wide nostrils twitched and flared in unison. They'd locked onto my scent already.

'I see you have something of mine,' the Jackal said in a vaguely disinterested tone, glancing past me towards his workstation. His slender face was sharp and jagged as a mountain peak, as if the bones had been carved with a diamond-edged blade. His wavy black hair was slicked back, his moustache oiled. His soot-black eyes constantly moving, drinking in everything, missing nothing. Like me, he was half-Japanese, although I doubted that'd give me any slack. A small knife of a smile appeared on his face, as he thrust his hands into the pockets of his trenchcoat. 'And I believe that's my gin.'

'Get out of there,' Grim snapped.

The image of severed fingers and sliced ears flitted through my mind as a strip of metal unfolded in one of the Sniffers' hands. It snapped into position as a half-metre-long blade, sizzling with white-hot heat. Wielded with enough strength, it'd carve my armour into scrap metal with me inside it. He took a step forward. My muscles tightened, legs bracing in a combat position, instincts kicking in.

'Did you want it back?' I asked, and returned the bottle by smashing it across the side of the Jackal's head. Glass shattered, shards and alcohol splashing into his face. The stormtech rocketed at the fresh action and, barely hearing his growls of pain, I rammed past the two Sniffers and charged into the alleyway. I hadn't had this much excitement in months; my body was rewarding me with extra speed, hot adrenaline shooting through my veins like a turbo boost.

They gave chase, all clutching slingshivs that danced like silver fire in their hands. The Jackal roared for me to stop. I turned to look back but ripped my gaze away before I was overcome by the urge to stand my ground and fight. There was nothing stormtech liked more than a good brawl, even if it meant getting my own teeth kicked in.

I locked down my instincts and focused on how the genome I was carrying would stop my friend's deportation, letting that push strength into my legs as I ran further into the labyrinthine passageways of the asteroid. The halls blurring and smudging under sweat-logged vision. Puddles of muddy wastewater showering up my legs as I burst around a hairpin corner. They were so close behind me I could hear their ragged breathing. I cut the connection to Grim, even as he told me not to. Couldn't risk him being traced if I was caught.

One of the Sniffers closed in on me, heavy footfalls echoing. Guys like this are all meat and muscle and zero balance. I waited until a flare of chainship lights had flickered down, stabbing light into our eyes, before I jerked to a stop, tilting my body backwards and letting the man crunch nose-first into my armoured back. He tottered backwards, dazed and cursing. I slammed him sideways, into the incoming path of the second Sniffer. While he was off-balance, I hooked his leg out from under him. My fist sank into his gut, right below the ribs, my elbow slamming into his throat and sending them both crashing to the floor in a graceless tangle of limbs. I dived through a stone corridor, the stormtech *really* riled up now, stamping down on my weariness.

They knew the terrain, knew all the exits. But if I gained enough distance, I could double back and out-manoeuvre them in a wide flank. The Sniffers might be able to smell the path I'd taken, but they couldn't tell *when* I'd taken it. My legs burned as I ran on, spotting a burst of light in a narrow gap ahead. I grinned as I curved around a corner ... and my heart plummeted to my guts.

Dead end.

Two metres away, through a tall slab of hard, unforgiving, solid asteroid rock, was the spaceport. Might as well have been two kilometres.

Soaked with sweat inside my suit, I stepped back to scout for a new route as the three men stuttered to a halt behind me. They'd swapped out slingshivs for nasty-looking handguns. The Jackal's relaxed smile was replaced with a deathly-quiet expression, his cold, granite eyes dissecting me. Watching me search for an escape route. Trying to think the way I'd think. This man was a hunter, and he'd cornered his prey.

Eyes still fastened on me like restraining bolts, he spoke to his men. 'Cage him.'

Screw it. You've got to make a last stand somewhere.

I thrust forward and smashed into the first bodyguard, going straight for his broken nose. He screamed. The handgun went off as I thrust it up, the helmet saving my eardrums. I punched him in the crook of his arm, wrenching the weapon away to train on the Jackal. But I was centuries too late. A sun-bright muzzle flash in the darkness and an electranet seized up around me. Thick, chainmetal cables wrapped around my body, pinning my arms and legs, my helmet cracking against hard rock as I toppled. Rough hands rolled me onto my back. The cables crackled with voltage, getting tighter and tighter as I strained against them, my chest heaving. The Jackal's boots kicked up asteroid dust as he walked over, towering high above. He glowered down at me before delivering a series of vicious kicks to the side of my helmeted head. One, two, three, four, sending flashing lights scattering across my vision and blood flooding my mouth.

The safety of the spaceport whirled away two metres behind me as the Jackal straddled me. No one would hear me calling for help over the noise. 'Don't flatter yourself into thinking my dog-boys sniffed you out in the dark.' The Jackal pressed his sly, angular face close to mine. 'Truth is, I don't need augs to hunt a man down.'

He held the white-hot blade of his slingshiv over me, daring me to jerk away. 'What shall we do with him, boys?' His lips twitched, as if wrestling with indecision, but I know what a man who's made up his mind looks like. 'Let's crack him out of that metal shell to get to the gooey bits inside. Then flay his skin off. There's a good word. *Flay*.'

12

The stormtech pounded under my breastbone in mimicry of my thudding heart. Survival instincts kicking in for real now. I struggled in the net, but the Jackal was waiting for it. He kicked me in the head again until I slumped back down. I was vaguely aware of being dragged across the rock by one ankle.

'Business before pleasure, boys,' the Jackal said. 'First we take him home, tie him up properly and get to work. No interruptions there.'

'On it, boss,' the one with the broken nose gurgled.

A voice cut through the passageway, halting him. 'What's this? You guys picking on someone bigger for a change?'

Three figures stood silhouetted behind the Jackal. I recognised their sleek, black-barrelled marksman rifles; I'd spent too many years holding one myself. 'Harmony to the rescue, huh?' I let my head sag back against the rock.

'*Harmony*?' The Jackal's sly confidence cracked. 'How—'

'Clear off, Akira.' The trio were led by a woman, her voice sharp enough to slice bone. Her small service thin-gun remained holstered, her arms casually folded. There's power in carrying a weapon and showing you've got no use of it. 'You're lucky I don't have time for a chat about this today.'

'We were just leaving,' said the Jackal.

'Yes, you were,' she said. 'And if I ever see you harassing folks around here again, I'll find a nice airlock for you to play in. Plenty to choose from around here. You read me?'

'Of course.' The Jackal was all charm and charisma again. His sly, dangerous smile twitched at his lips, his gaze hooking mine before he and his men vanished into the smoky asteroid passageway.

I peered suspiciously at my saviours as they cut the electranet off me. 'What'd you want?'

'Harmony wants a chat, Vakov Fukasawa. A long, long overdue chat,' the woman told me as I pulled my arms free. 'I

13

don't appreciate having to backtrace your friend's feed just to find you.'

Of course that was how they'd found me. At long last, Grim's outrageous confidence in his own abilities had conspired with pure happenstance to completely screw me over.

But Harmony didn't waste time with petty smuggling. They had a galaxy to run, after all. The stormtech sparked in my chest and I had the impulse to make a dash for it. Scramble to my feet and get a head start before they caught up. Wasn't like I owed these people anything. Not after the poison they'd pumped into my body.

But they wouldn't have dug me up unless it was important. Really important. I had to find out why. So I swallowed the urge and asked, 'I don't suppose I have a choice?'

'No,' she confirmed. 'You do not.'

2

Blood, Politics and Coffee

As we walked through the brightly lit hallways towards the spaceport, I got a proper look my saviour. The shib interface implanted in my skull and overlaying my vision told me she was Katherine Kowalski, of the First Class Primer rank. While her black, one-piece underskin with its liquorice-like sheen was typical Harmony field gear, her loose leather jacket and salt and pepper scarf weren't, especially not for someone so high up the chain. She was Slavic; fair skinned with sandy hair and grey eyes that had a wild, bright look that didn't usually last long with Harmony types. At over two metres tall, she stood eye to eye with me. Unusual. Had she maybe come from New Vladivostok? No. People from my homeplanet are less forth-coming, more habitually hunched over to shield themselves from the razor-like winds and freezing temperatures.

Watching her stride in front of us, I was acutely aware of the gunrunners maintaining pace behind me, ensuring I didn't get any ideas about slipping away.

'Stupid move, stealing from those guys,' Kowalski said over her shoulder. 'The Jackal runs Tipei-Corporation. Other dark-market syndicates won't even risk selling in their territory, let alone *rob* them.'

'I'm not from here,' I told her, unwilling to explain I was only doing it for a friend.

'Tell that to the Jackal.' She slid a chrome vaper out of a pocket, breathing deep and exhaling a thick plume of scented smoke. Hardly your standard Harmony accessory either. 'He enjoys hunting thieves.'

'I'm not a thief,' I corrected. 'I'm a smuggler.'

'Don't want to hear the excuses,' she replied.

I could see we were going to get along just fine.

We bypassed the crowded spaceport and headed straight to a polished hangar bay. The metallic causeways were clustered with Hangarmasters and Shipmasters wearing flight suits. Flight schedules and docking designations for arrival ships were blaring out over the speakers. A vast viewport showed a black canvas, stained blue with stars and frantic with chainships and deepsystem spacecraft rendered in various metallic colours and swirling patterns. Their engines roared and left contrails of bright blue streaks as they shot out of view. There was even a lungship: a bulky, geometrical spacecraft several kilometres in length and built to traverse galaxies. More of Harmony's signature flags hung from gleaming walkways and observation decks. As if anyone would forget who'd won the Reaper War.

We passed through unseen and boarded a Comet-class Harmony chainship, aerodynamic in build with a vanilla-white paintjob and a black trim along the elongated flank. Antigravnets kicked into gear as we strapped in, the ship smoothly disembarking from the berth and exiting the spaceport. Holographic icons glowed across the control screens, the viewport expanding to allow an unobstructed view of space. I folded my arms, content to travel in silence as the gunrunners gossiped about me in Japanese. My face was hidden behind my helmet, so they had no way of knowing I understood every word.

'You think he'll attack us?' one asked, fidgeting with his

thin-gun. 'Stormtech screws with their heads, right? Gets them high on danger? Probably why he was messing with the Jackal in the first place.'

The stormtech swirled around my ribcage, as if it knew it was being talked about. I shifted against my five-point seat harness, tightening my hands around the shoulder straps.

'Hard to think of any other reason. He fought in the Reaper War, after all,' said the other, folding his hands around his bulging gut. 'Besides, you get that alien DNA shot into your bloodstream and sooner or later you're bound to go off the deep end.'

I knew they were waiting for me to remove my armour and expose my alien-infused flesh so they could see the blue zigzagging and looping through me. They were going to be disappointed. Stormtech increases the sensitivity of my skin, particularly my hands, feet and face, making my body temperature usually too cold or too hot. My armour was rigged up to counter this, actively scanning my biorhythms and stormtech, automatically adjusting the temperature to fit my conditions. The armour would press in on my body like an embrace, using a combination of gel-padding, thick tendrils and gritty abrasives to provide hard friction against my flesh, combating the stormtech's influence with external stimuli. Right now it was dropping the temperature to cool me, my body heat declining and the tension in my muscles ebbing away as the stormtech settled. No matter how many times I used them, the suit's custom-built functions never got old.

I exited the temperature controls as the chainship curved and the view of Compass took my breath away. The cratered surface of the gargantuan asteroid was spiked with titanic clusters of jutting, icy metal. Soaring kilometres tall, the dark spikes scintillating in the sun, it looked like the universe's biggest sea urchin. All the damaged dreadnoughts, frigates, corvettes, spacecraft, warships and ordnance from our galactic region of the Reaper War had been wilted to slag and installed on Compass like this. Harmony's final way of humiliating the self-established, bloodthirsty government that had come so close to destroying us all in the war. Some said it was the dwindling space and growing population that spurred Harvest's hand. But Harvest were only after the stormtech: the DNA remnants of the Shenoi, a long extinct alien race. Now, Harvest was forever a part of our monument to victory.

Compass. If the greater galaxy has a capital city, this is it. Home to six hundred million and counting. Between the spikes of ships, the mammoth asteroid was barnacled with entry docks, spaceports, berths, dockyards, array towers, mooring gantries, hangars, surface facilities and hubs that were home to scores of defence weaponry. Gigantic black scorches scarred Compass' rocky body like blistering skin moles. Traces of Harvest plasma artillery. We swooped closer to the pockmarked asteroid's surface, the tall skyscrapers of slag whipping by.

Six hundred million people, and my little brother was one of them, down there somewhere. We hadn't spoken in years. He'd cut me out of his life so thoroughly that when I ended up on Compass after the war I didn't even try to find him. Losing him had been hard to bear. Hoping that time might somehow have changed things between us would have been harder still. But caring for someone means doing what's best for them, even when it hurts, even when it scars.

But that didn't mean I'd forgotten how we'd lain in our shared bed as children, my brother's little body pressed against mine for warmth as our parents' arguments bounced around our tiny apartment. Or covering his ears when our father hit our mother, each strike louder and louder. Or wrapping a protective arm around Artyom's chest, the drumbeat of his heart under my palm. Or my sister Kasia leaning towards me the following morning and whispering so she wouldn't wake our father up. *Promise me, Vak. Promise me you'll look out for Artyom.*

No. Nothing good ever came walking down that path. He had his life, I had mine. And judging by present company, mine was about to get a hell of a lot more complicated.

The Kaiji ship caught my eye as I looked up. The aliens' spacecraft was elongated and angular, a bullet-shaped chunk of dark, electric-blue ice, the hull sweeping forward in great sharp curves. It hovered like a sleeping monster in the dark of space, although its long-range sensors were surely watching us, along with every heat signature within five klicks. A warning not to approach blossomed on our chainship's forward viewport. Our ship applied course-correction, veering away accordingly.

'They're here for peace talks, thrashing out some issues before they join Harmony and the Common at large,' Kowalski said when I asked about it. It came as no surprise that Harmony was expanding their reach, as all galaxy-wide governments are wont to do. Wouldn't be the first or last spacefaring alien species to join their ranks.

'Sokolav's not in charge of this outpost, is he?' I asked casually. It'd be interesting to see the guy who'd first roped me into Harmony.

Kowalski's eyes glazed over, her vision obscured by data-streams and icons from her shib overlay as she performed a quick search. 'No,' she said, the readouts vanishing. 'He's long gone. Missing.'

I leaned forward against my restraints. 'How long?'

'Seven years. He vanished a few days before Harvest surrendered.'

Harmony's outpost had come into view, sprawling steel limbs locked into the asteroid's surface like a starfish clutching a cosmic-sized rock. We docked in the auxiliary hangar and promptly disembarked before being ushered through a stream of gently lit hallways. It was the same as every other Harmony Special Service Command outpost. The same guards shelled in the same polished armour, same blur of glass offices and high-tech laboratories, same technicians and analysts poring over flexiscreens, same stench of lime-scented bleach. I picked up a few curious looks as I was brought through into a sparsely decorated office with dark marble flooring. Sitting in front of a viewport overlooking the asteroid's pockmarked curve was the Station Commander. Her dark hair was tied back in a severe bun, away from her pointed face, and her eyes were ice cubes rolled in ashes. She seemed to have adopted a permanent cynical expression, enamelled by long years of service.

She sat behind a desk of rugged black stone, typing away on a virtual keyboard. Spanish text crawled across the mid-air screen like neon liquid. A cup of coffee sat on the desk next to her. Her name, SSC Commander Juliet Kindosh, popped up in my augmented vision moments before the screen folded away, as if being tucked back into some invisible pocket.

As Kindosh's gaze skimmed over us, Kowalski stood a little straighter behind me, her hands held tight behind her back. Finally Kindosh turned towards me. 'Sit,' she said. Even in a single word, her thick Compass accent hit home.

I almost gave a polite bow of my head, but caught myself. We weren't on New Vladi. It wouldn't mean anything to them here. Forearm shakes and smiles were the standard greeting on Compass. Kowalski's men were armed and present, but they didn't file into their corners as gunrunners usually do. They remained close by her side in a protective posture.

'You can take that thing off,' Kindosh said, staring at my visor. 'I'm not talking to my own reflection.'

I seethed quietly behind my helmet. I don't take well to orders. Especially not from Harmony types, and especially when they're about my armour. But this was her station.

Her office. Her rules. She had the power to disarm me, and there's nothing people like her like more than using their power.

I took my time retrieving my palmerlog, finding the right switch and ordering my armour to release me. The chest and arms plates cracked and peeled apart, opening with a whirl of gears and servomechanisms. The air warm and muggy against my skin as I tugged the helmet off and stepped out of my suit. There was a brief, glassy click as I was severed from the electrostatic interface, the squirming tendrils along my back going dead. And there, crawling and curling and pulsing under my flesh, shining through the thick black fabric of my underskin, was the stormtech. A spool of blue circled my chest, writhing around my organs, sniffing between my ribs. Long threads coiled up my back, finding the notches in my spine and looping around my neck like a rope, as if to hang me.

Seven years since Harmony had injected it into me.

Felt like a hundred.

The men behind me shifted uneasily at the sight of it. I folded into the seat indicated, then noticed the grooves in the arm and leg rests of the chair, where restraints would clack around me if I tried anything.

They'd created me, but they didn't trust me. Good to know where we stood.

'Vakov Fukasawa.' Kindosh looked at me like I was a particularly difficult puzzle piece that didn't fit her worldview rather than a person. 'Reaper turned thief and smuggler.'

Former Reaper, I almost corrected. I was no longer one of their biosoldiers, engineered by hostile alien technology to fight their war. But telling them that would have been pointless. Once Harmony, always Harmony, as the saying went. 'What's my business to you?'

'It's illegal, for starters.'

I laughed and the stormtech in my chest seemed to laugh

21

with me. I gestured at it. 'Please. Don't tell me Harmony got an attack of conscience.'

Kindosh didn't flinch. 'You're not here to discuss the Reaper War, Fukasawa.' I couldn't help staring at her coffee-stained teeth as she spoke. 'We didn't force you to join the Reaper programme, or to accept the stormtech. That's done. We're dealing with present problems now.'

'What problems?' I tensed. Were they after the genome I'd stolen? My smuggling record? The stormtech curled around my tightening muscles, twitching in the joints of my fingers, throbbing in my armpits. I hated everyone being able to see it.

Kindosh leaned back. 'Have you or any of your contacts been involved in smuggling or selling stormtech substances, on or off Compass?'

If I wasn't used to Harmony's behaviour, I'd probably have been more taken aback. 'You must be mad,' I said. 'I'd never mess with that poison, never spread it around. You've done enough damage with it already.'

Stormtech wasn't a drug like synthsilver or bluesmoke. It was a literal weaponised virus. Experimental biotechnology that increased every physical and mental facet of the human body. It rewired our bodies with a hunger for adrenaline, dopamine and endorphins, earning their release through physical effort, risk-taking and, above all, aggression. The high others got from a good gym work-out, we got from throwing ourselves into danger, multiplied by a thousand. It made us crave the rush of fight-or-flight, the thrill of near-death and conquering opponents, let us soak up damage as fast as we could deal it out. One dose was enough to get you permanently hooked, the cocktail of your body chemicals constantly delivering the high as long as you continued giving into it.

We became addicted to our own bodies.

So it wasn't exactly a surprise that we fared well in battle.

We smashed Harvest to pieces, reclaimed our fallen planets and won the Reaper War because we didn't know when to stop fighting.

We still don't.

Once stormtech worms its way into your system, it's there to stick around. It had fused with my nervous system, in every blood cell, wrapped around every bone. Even now, I could feel the hunger for danger zigzagging between my ribs, my mouth coated with sticky saliva, hands twitching. My eyes wandered to the autorifle dangling loosely in the nearest guard's hand and I quickly tore them away, squashing any thoughts about making a lunge for it. There's no such thing as a fantasy for me. If I think about doing something for long enough, I end up doing it.

Harmony knew all this but they wanted to win the war desperately enough to pump us with bleeding edge alien bio-technology. I hated their guts for it and always would. And I'd rather step into open vacuum than spread that stuff into other people's bodies.

Kindosh gave a sage nod. 'Good to know. Good to know.'

There was something they weren't telling me. 'What's this about?' I asked. 'You can't honestly think I'd be peddling stormtech around Compass.'

'Why not? It's the biggest drug on the market,' Kindosh said. 'The current craze. Hundreds of years ago it was alcohol. Prohibition period, you ever hear about that? Nucky Johnson and Al Capone – look them up. Then it was cocaine. Then synthsilver. And now this. I can imagine you wanting a slice of that very profitable pie.'

You'd think people would avoid stormtech like the plague the moment they heard horror stories from the Reaper War. But humanity's greatest vices have always been the ones most likely to kill you. Besides, we don't exactly have a history of playing

23

smart with things we don't understand. Some people who tried stormtech were just sniffing out the next high. Others were simply curious. Others had run their full course with other narcotics and wanted the peak of the psychotropic mountain. But most who voluntarily took stormtech liked the idea of tweaking their physiology. Of being rewired to crave tension, excitement, danger. They wanted their biochemistry to reward them for taking risks, for pursuing excitement. Stormtech didn't just enhance those cravings. It made them addictive; it made people *enjoy* being addicted. Maybe they wanted to add some colour to their lives. Or escape depression. Or have the stormtech eat some yet-incurable sickness out of their bodies. Or have the courage to do what they'd never do without alien biotech urging them along.

There were as many reasons take stormtech as people who took it. But the results were always the same.

'You want a likely candidate, ask the Jackal,' I said. 'Don't waste your time with me.'

'We've got our eye on him,' Kindosh said in a tone that revealed how little she liked being told how to do her job. 'But I like to cover all the angles. Right now, we're fighting an uphill battle and losing.'

At the mention of battle, a strand of stormtech split apart, threads chasing each other up and down my forearms like turquoise stormclouds in fast forward. 'Are you surprised? You created that drug market the moment you shot stormtech into us.'

'We did what was necessary,' Kindosh said crisply. 'We won. Now we're dealing with the fallout.'

'We get Reapers and skinnies coming here every day,' Kowalski interjected from behind me. 'We've set up a dozen rehab facilities to help. They can get everything they need to get clean. Like you did. Ritalin, sedatives, muscle relaxants,

24

emotion-suppressing stims, all of it.' She paused, as if to compose herself. Kindosh gave the tiniest of frowns. 'Only there're two dozen stormtech products on the market, and we've got more people Bluing Out every week.'

Bluing Out. I managed a dry smile. Hundreds of years ago, when computers crashed they called it the Blue Screen of Death. Now human beings crashed. Only difference was that there was no rebooting them. The phrase had been Reaper gallows humour. A way of coping with the torture chambers our bodies had morphed into. Now it was common usage. Wasn't too sure what to think of that.

'Only they're not just Bluing Out,' said Kindosh. 'They're contracting some sort of hostile biovirus.'

'Biovirus?' I asked before I could stop myself.

'First our stormtech shipments have been going missing.' The wrap-around flexiscreen monitor flickered back to life and expanded in a semi-circle. 'Then someone broke into our rehab centres. We thought it was a failed robbery. Wouldn't be the first addicts who've broken in. Now we think they deliberately tampered with our suppressors and chemical stockpiles, since *everyone* who took them Blued Out. We think it's the same story for our stolen stormtech: it's being poisoned, altered to be lethal.' On the flexiscreen, whirling, multicoloured fragments coalesced into an image. A tall, black-skinned man with a shaved head. I realised with a cold jolt that I knew him. It was Alcatraz. He'd been in my squad, my fireteam. We'd survived the Reaper War together. Now he was sprawled out on hard concrete. His veins were a dark spiderweb, his skin rippled and his eyes a glassy blue-black that told me he'd died in agony.

I felt an instant flare of anger for my friend. Crushed it and tried to think. Harmony weren't showing me this by accident. They knew about our friendship. Our years of hard service together. They were manipulating me and I didn't even know why.

'The ex-Reapers Bluing Out is what tipped us off. They either drop dead or go on a rampage,' continued Kindosh. Kowalski had her eyes averted from the image. 'No visible overdose, no warning signs, no prior evidence of self-destructive behaviour. The only thing they had in common was their visits to rehab and taking suppressors.'

I saw what they were getting at. Harmony's reputation, both as a galaxy-wide government and military force, had been shattered once the sprawling systems and species in the galactic community comprising the Common figured out just how we'd won the Reaper War, and Harmony was desperate to rebuild it. I wasn't about to forgive them, or forget the friends I'd lost as Harmony's untested, experimental drug violently fused with their systems on a molecular level. We'd taken losses without even hitting the battlefields. Their tortured screams as they thrashed in their restraints around me still echoed in the back of my head.

Our rehabilitation was one of Harmony's major point-scoring PR campaigns. Harmony couldn't let thousands of biosoldiers wander the Common ready to explode into action at the slightest provocation. So they'd introduced the rehab centres, which had worked a charm. Going through withdrawal – Shredding – had nearly killed me. It's a hell of a difficult thing to deprogramme a human body. It had taken endless rehab, discipline and training not to slip into the vortex of using aggression as my primary method of solving problems. Gradually, the stormtech's control over my body had weakened, as had my additional strength, healing and pain tolerance. Not completely gone, of course. The alien biotech's as much a part of my anatomy as my nerves, my musculoskeletal system. Combating my body's most dangerous urges is an active, daily battle. But rehab had made it a winnable one. What had also stuck around were the dozens of micro-effects the stormtech had on my body. It accelerated my pheromones, the growth of my body hair and nails, bloated my sweat and saliva glands, hammered me with skin rashes.

Compared to others, I'd got off easy.

Kindosh poured herself another coffee, her black three-dee printer whirling as it conjured up synthetic brown sugar. 'Any drug can have a bad batch. But if people stop trusting the rehab centres, they'll go to street stormdealers instead. Then the addiction will keep spreading and spreading. There'll be more people shooting all we have left of the Shenoi into their veins and turning themselves into ticking time bombs. We'll have an epidemic on our hands. And if no one trusts the treatments, we won't be able to stop it.'

I swung my gaze back around to Alcatraz. We'd promised each other that if one of us fell in battle, the other would get their body sent to their homeplanet to be buried. But we'd said nothing about *after* the war. I looked at the blue foam oozing from his gaping mouth, stormtech slicing his chest open from the inside. Someone had done this to my friend. To a man who'd saved my life as many times as I'd saved his. Who'd got me through the worst war can throw at you, as all my fellow Reapers had. I'd be hacked to pieces and buried in the mud on some war-torn planet without them. We owed a life debt to each other in more ways than we could possibly count. We weren't just soldiers, we were brothers. Family. And now someone was poisoning the drugs which kept ex-Reapers sane. Trying to turn us into trigger-happy, walking stormtech time-bombs, a threat to themselves and everyone around them, all the while driving us to the brink of insanity and death.

We'd saved the Common. And this is how we were being repaid.

A marrow-deep rage I hadn't known I was still capable of

27

built up in my chest. The white-hot anger at whoever was doing this eclipsing my distrust and dislike of Harmony and their manipulative games.

'You want me to hunt down the people doing this?' I asked levelly.

'You're the best candidate for the job.' I followed Kindosh's line of sight out the viewport towards the alien dreadnought as she spoke. 'And timing couldn't be worse. The Kaiji always insisted tampering with stormtech was too dangerous. Their entire species, their entire civilization, joining the Common depends on us killing this at the source. Their Ambassadors come here regularly to inquire about our progress. I intend to show evidence of it.'

I had to ask. 'Why me?'

'Two reasons: because you're a Reaper who has their stormtech under control. You were even captured by Harvest and escaped.'

I shouldn't have been surprised she had that knowledge tucked away. Harmony knew my muscles' density, my blood pressure, the pH of my saliva, so she'd clearly pulled my records.

'And because we already have a suspect.'

My fingers went bone-white around the armrests. 'Who? Who's killing Reapers?'

'We have some swarmbot footage. It's inconclusive from the break-in' – the flexiscreen brought up a hazy shot of two men, faces averted – 'but we've got something much clearer from a stormtech theft down near Limefields.'

'Don't know where that is.'

Kindosh took a slow sip of coffee and meticulously savoured the taste. 'Of course. I forget you're not a local. It's on the eighty-second floor of Compass.' Another still image grew on-screen to show the same figure hunched over the stormtech canisters. It focused with crystalline clearness on a young man with the same black hair, tilted dark eyes and bulky, muscular build as mine.

It was my brother.

Artyom.

All the staring, the guards and weapons, suddenly made sense. A tsunami of stormtech rolled down my chest, crashing down into my stomach and washing away the rage working up inside, leaving me with sour, hollow dread.

'Artyom could have stumbled across it. He might not have known—' The words became ash in my throat and I knew she had me.

Kindosh held my gaze long enough for me to feel uncomfortable. 'Artyom Fukasawa works at an alehouse in Limefields and leaves each night at around the same time this image was taken. We need someone to poke around, find out the details.'

'We've barely spoken in years,' I managed. I was grasping for anything but the obvious explanation. I thought back to our last happy evening together. Sitting by a campfire on the mountain, the logs in our makeshift fire crackling and spitting scintillating orange sparks as we traded stories over a bottle of vodka. What was my brother doing with a stolen canister of the universe's most dangerous drug?

Kindosh shrugged. 'Saving Reaper lives matters to you. I suspect keeping your little brother out of prison does, too. If there's anyone who can navigate both sides and help deliver a solution, it's you.'

The rage began trickling back, but this time it was channelled in a very different direction. Beneath this veneer of sincerity and smiles, Harmony was just as manipulative as ever. Using Alcatraz against me. Using my brother against me.

It was clever. And it was Harmony to the core.

Except, Kindosh had made one tiny, crucial mistake.

She didn't know me. And I don't play ball with people like

this. I've got zero patience for Harmony's crap. I wasn't about to be another cog in their meat machine. I desperately needed to talk to my brother, unravel whatever he'd got tangled up in. I'd try to protect my fellow Reapers. But not on Harmony's terms. I'd find my own.

'Allow me to put this as delicately as I can. I'd rather eat a bucket of razorwire than do anything for you.' I held Kindosh's gaze as I stood. I spread my arms, displaying the writhing electric blue. 'Harmony has done enough damage to the universe. I'm done taking orders.'

I expected disappointment. Perhaps anger. Instead, Kindosh's lips twitched into a smile colder than a New Vladi winter. 'Well. We'll have to find a way to convince you, won't we?'

That sounded unpleasant. 'I don't do charity,' I said, as haunting images of Blued-Out Reapers tumbled away on the flexiscreen. So many good men and women, all wasted flesh.

'There are many alternative provisions we can make for our allies.' There was subtle emphasis on the last two words. 'Nothing so ... trite as money.'

It was good to see Harmony hadn't lost their inability to take no for an answer. I don't think Kindosh understood the notion. 'You've got nothing I want. Nothing of value.'

'Really, Fukasawa? What if we can offer information? Answers. Solutions. Things you cannot find on your own. Surely, when it comes to your brother, those become of value.' She traced my gaze as the images swapped back to the shots of my brother, caught in the moment of his crime, again and again on a loop. She set her coffee down with a final, deliberate tap. 'Or perhaps that Harvester friend of yours. What's his name?' She continued without waiting for an answer. 'I believe he's lacking in a Compass residency card. That can be easily remedied. As can all those charges of smuggling. I don't imagine you'd want to him see him arrested or deported.'

My face split in a humourless, dour grin. This was the Harmony I knew. Nothing so low it was beneath them, no act of extortion too undignified. I opened my mouth and prepared to say something I'd later regret when Kindosh talked over me. 'Think on it, Fukasawa. In the meantime, I think it's best if Kowalski acts as your liaison. With Reapers dying, we can't very well have you wandering around without protection, can we? She'll make sure you don't run into trouble. Perhaps even help you along the way.'

'What?' Kowalski spluttered as a sinking frustration plummeted through my gut. It wasn't enough for Kindosh to corner me into doing her work; she had to lock me out of any other options, too. 'We never discussed this.'

'I'm sorry,' Kindosh said in the least apologetic of voices, 'that wasn't a request.' Behind me Kowalski's men shifted in their suits, but none of them said anything. Kindosh turned back to me, all business. 'We reward cooperation, we always have. But don't take too long to think about it. It'd be quite unfortunate if your brother found himself in deeper trouble in the meantime.'

I swallowed back two dozen venomous replies and looked between the image of my dead friend, killed by poisoned stormtech suppressors, and that of my long-lost brother, caught in the act of poisoning the stormtech.

3

Hand Covers Bruise

We rode the clatterlift alone in silence.

Built along the spine of Compass, the lift is the quickest method of accessing each floor and subsector of the asteroid. Kowalski was to escort me to my apartment in Starklands and accompany me wherever I went. Supposedly for my protection, but no doubt meant to encourage some co-operation through her mere presence. I know how these people work.

The awkward silence stretched on as we plummeted down through kilometres of space. To my credit, I held out. She broke it. 'Please, make both our lives easier and stay out of trouble.' She took out her vaper and sucked deeply. Tendrils of sweetened smoke curled around her like ghostly fingers. 'I've got dozens of unidentified skinnie deaths on my plate without dealing with this, too.'

'Got it.'

I didn't intend to make trouble, but the stormtech frequently had other plans. On the one hand, it didn't have a strong enough hold on me to be overpowering, and if I clamped down on the urges hard enough, they faded. On the other, I could be triggered by something as simple as getting looked at the wrong way on the street. Reapers' bodies demanded a continuous release of adrenaline, which was almost impossible to stop once we got going. I'd seen a Reaper get his arm blown off in the heat of battle, still roaring as he slaughtered two dozen Harvester infantry in a rampage. It was hours later that he camedown and realised his arm ended at the elbow joint.

I held my hands behind my back, the vambrace plates grinding. I'd expected Kindosh to take the Hendrix, but it must have slipped her mind and I was still smuggling the genome in my suit. I'd shot Grim a message the moment we'd left Kindosh's office and he'd responded that he was okay and would be swinging around later to talk shop. A small victory, but you've got to celebrate them where you can.

I'd shrugged back into my armour before we left, but the plates weren't connecting. My left side was exposed, revealing blue strands flickering around my ribs like seaweed in an ocean current. Kowalski watched it with something between fascination and unease.

'What does it feel like?' She stared, but didn't try to touch it, like so many people thought they had the right to do.

'It tickles,' I said quietly as the plates finally slid into place, covering me up. She nodded slowly and I felt the stormtech strumming through my muscles. Tonight's excitement had riled it up, and now it was eagerly awaiting the next adventure.

On the clatterlift's panel was a layout of floors, subsectors and docking levels positioned around the asteroid superstructure like a nervous system. Several nodes were blocked out with a bruise-coloured label. 'They're Void Zones,' Katherine Kowalski explained when I asked. 'Floors damaged in the Reaper War, some still exposed to vacuum, too unstable to enter.'

I found I was making a mental note of them as she spoke. I've had boots on enough alien planets in far-flung galactic regions of space to know you should never be a stranger to your surroundings. Especially not when your enemies know it better. I began snapping images of floors, levels, subsectors closed to the public, zones that led out to the asteroid's surface for EVA work, floors wired with life-support systems conditioned for certain species. A minute later, our clatterlift coasted to a smooth stop on Starklands.

We spilled out into the sprawling streets. The rocky ceiling had been covered with pixelsheeting, the display set to the black canvas of a night sky, scattered with blue stars and the steely reds and greys of planets and moons. But if I zoomed in, I could see some of the sheeting flickering, superconductor cables and loose wiring dangling through holes in the fabric.

'Look.' She nodded to a trio of figures making their way to the Harmony Station. It was the Kaiji. Just over two metres tall, barrel-chested with slender, ash-coloured bodies. Heavy, hooded clothing obscured the aliens' features. These had to be the Ambassadors that Kindosh had mentioned. I remembered sitting in a cozy little New Vladi noodlehouse one evening, hunched over a bowl of steaming ramen, listening to their interstellar broadcast urging humans not to use stormtech.

We turned into the main boulevard. Overhead lights painted the streets a constellation of gentle blue-whites and neon purples. The sharp minerals of petrichor scented the air. Bustling restaurants, lively bars, film theatres, glass libraries, multilevel arcades and shops crowded every cubic metre of the street as close as breath and heartbeat. Streams of aerial traffic navigated between opulent penthouses, rooftops and blinking skyscrapers. Buildings loomed over us, done up with layered glass and angular edges, wide as small mountains. Side streets led down towards sweeping hotel lobbies, galleries and showrooms displaying the latest tech or artwork. Silver-flecked ivy crawled up latticework walls and lush green gardens spilled down from balconies. New Vladi had never been this open, this loud, this extreme. I stood and breathed the madness of the city into my lungs. I had a buzz in the back of my skull, a feeling that something bizarre and new was around every corner, down every alleyway.

Only the chiselled walls of the asteroid told us we were not planetside. Chunks of the bare, exposed rocks were scorched black. Fingerprints of war. But Compass had been lucky. I'd seen entire worlds blasted to smoking ruins when Harvest was done with them.

New Vladivostok's population was mainly Russian, Japanese and Korean with a smattering of Poles, Ukrainians and Kazakhs. Compass is infinitely more diverse. We walked through a mix of Africans, Hispanics, Indians, Nordics, and races completely new to me. There were enough other folks equipped with armour, hardsuits and varieties of exoskeletons that I blended in easily enough.

As we walked down the streets, we passed one of Harmony's rehab facilities. One of those polished, angular designs, desperate to stand out amid the throng. Looked like the place where I'd had stormtech violently detoxed from my body, stripping away my strength, enhanced senses and ability to heal. Advanced self-healing was one of the most valuable assets of stormtech; short of a decapitated arm or getting your skull split open, our bodies could patch up almost anything. But that ability had been wrung out of me along with everything else the stormtech bolstered, in exchange for being free from stormtech. Or as free as anyone could be. A sign outside was displayed with hotline numbers for all types of addiction and violent or suicidal thoughts.

'When did you come here?' I asked Kowalski as we picked up our pace through the rush hour. I glanced over my shoulder in case the Jackal really was stupid enough to attack me despite being under Harmony guard.

'When I was a kid,' she said over the roar of overhead chain-ships. 'Dad worked on a mining colony on an asteroid belt in the Fernik Sector. Horrific conditions, even before the Reaper War. He hit it big one day and got the whole family over here. Joined Harmony when I was sixteen, working in narcotics. Kindosh took me under her wing.'

There was clearly more to it. Spend enough time with Harmony types and you learn to read them. I remembered her rigid posture in Kindosh's office. There was definitely something she wasn't telling me.

In the middle of a concourse was a colossal statue of a Reaper. The marble had been chiselled to the nanometre, from its bulky armour, helmet and autorifle to the heavy boot planted square in the squealing, mud-caked face of a Harvest insurrectionist with anti-Harmony slogans plastered on his armour. We had something similar in New Vladi, only ours was modelled after an axe-wielding *bogatyr*. Medieval warriors from the windswept tundra of east Russia, like my ancestors. A terminal underneath the Compass statue detailed the bloody statistics of the war. I didn't need to read it to know how many habitats, planets and stations Harvest had levelled, how many civilians we'd lost: I'd lived through it. People gathered around the heroic statue in awe, remembering our fight. But they'd never built a monument to the battle we fought daily against stormtech. They'd never make a statue out of the dying man in the alleyway.

Kowalski must have sensed my thoughts as she carefully guided me back into the main road and away from the marble Reaper.

The conditions of the streets worsened as we approached the Southern District, the grimier part of Starkland. Squalid tenements hunched over crowded shopping plazas, neon blinking behind grimy display windows, the walls infested with jungles of exposed wiring. The streets were less streamlined, more haphazard, with industrial yards, smoking workshops, coffeehouses and street stalls weaving into the dermis of the floor like sweat glands, blood capillaries and nerve endings.

These areas were populated with skinnies. I saw at least three at an outdoor eatery, blue fluctuating down their arms as they slurped broth. It was clear that other people were avoiding them. To many, stormtech meant you weren't entirely human anymore. You were tainted, transformed, infected. A younger man squatting in the alley was so far gone that the ropes of saliva drooling from of his mouth were blue.

My apartment building was the same ubiquitous gunmetal grey as the dozens of serried buildings around it. A quick scan of my palmerlog at my door at the third floor and we were inside.

'What the hell?' I froze in the open door as the room morphed around us. Tables, chairs, kitchen counters and wallframes folded away as the room expanded backwards, creating more space. Furniture melted into the walls or floors, only to snap back into position as if nothing had happened, upgraded and new. The nanoplastic dining table was now rich granite, the battered lounge now black leather, draped with wool blankets and pillows, the coffee table made of rich oakwood. The dingy kitchenette had dissolved into a marbled galley kitchen with state-of-the-art appliances. The whole room had adopted a polished, showroom sheen. Even the air was fresh with the smell of smoky wood and wet stones. The luxurious coffee machine pinged as we walked in, fresh beans grinding away. An elegant wine carafe filled with some local vintage sat waiting on the tabletop.

'I take it this is your boss's doing,' I muttered. Kowalski didn't say anything, and she didn't have to. Harmony might be the same, but using bribery was certainly new. 'Even a dump like this comes with upgradable living space?' I asked.

'Everywhere on Compass does. You can live somewhere

like . . . well, like *this* place, and still have the most luxurious living space inside. Or the other way around.'

That explained the Jackal's home, at least. I grinned at the absurdity of it all. I'd heard how defiant Compass could be. They'd carved out an asteroid and stacked cities atop each other inside it. Why stop there? And, of course, what was given could as easily be taken away.

'Good evening,' came a sniffly voice, like that of a classic butler. There was a gratuitous puff of smoke as a lazy-eyed black rabbit the size of a coffee table and eerily lifelike, was projected in front of us. The rabbit's mouth moved as the building's Rubix, an AI caretaker, spoke. 'Can I be of service to you this evening, Vakov Fukasawa and guest?'

So they'd upgraded the intelligence level of the Rubix, too. The previous Rubix could barely hold up its end of a conversation.

'Why the hell are you a giant rabbit?' I asked.

'This is the form I prefer,' the AI replied with swift finesse, whiskers twitching. 'Now, is there anything you require?'

'That won't be necessary,' I said.

'Surely there is something I could do?' the Rubix persisted, anxious to please. I reassured it that I was fine. The rabbit gave a sad sigh and vanished back into smoke. A couple of minutes later I discovered that I had a security upgrade by way of an autocannon that folded out of the walls on verbal command. Wasn't too sure what to think about that.

'I'd suggest you help me finish that wine, but it's been a long day.' I stretched my arms and felt the stormtech roll from one shoulder joint to the other.

Kowalski shot me a questioning glance. 'Kindosh will manacle us together if you try anything related to the case without telling me first.'

'I'd like to see her try.' Kowalski didn't smile. I sobered up. 'I don't intend to make trouble,' I told her.

She hesitated, then the pressure seemed to puddle out of her. 'I'll come for you tomorrow. I don't have to tell you how important this is, Vakov. Think on it?' Darkening skies framed her as she lingered in the doorway. 'Everyone in the Common is alive because of you Reapers. My sister and all her kids are still here because you put yourself in the line of fire. Nothing changes that.'

My helmet obscured my semi-smile as I waved her goodbye. I was starting to like her, and I honestly *did* feel a little bad as I slipped out the window and dropped four storeys into the dingy alleyway, the stormtech thrumming at the unexpected rush of danger.

Kindosh might feed me my own guts for this. But my little brother was involved with drug syndicates and Reaper deaths, and he clearly wouldn't talk to Harmony.

Only one way to find out what was going on. Ask the man himself.

Kindosh had made the mistake of telling me which floor Artyom was on. There was only one alehouse on it, so it was an easy find. Like most levels of Compass, Limefields wore its own aesthetic. I couldn't place it until I plugged a few queries into a search engine and discovered Limefields was meant to replicate a 1920s city square on Earth. Low, broad buildings in red, brown and white rose up around the boulevards, showered with golden light from nearby streetlamps. Wooden planks bounced under my feet as I strode along a lengthy boardwalk packed with vaudeville street performers, drinking clubs and gambling parlours. Curlicue twists of stairs curled up to antique libraries, burlesque theatres and domed pavilions, where crowds in era-specific dress flocked to parties.

I walked along until I found Artyom's alehouse: an exclusive venue called *The Wild Hare* with a distinct cinnamon smell. Columns of carved mahogany supported the high, ornate ceiling. Low conversation drifted like smoke between the leather armchairs, marble-top tables and Tiffany lamps. Faint music spilled from an antique gramophone. Over a hundred bespoke brews stood behind the rhodonite counter, connecting to a complication of bronze pipework. But it was the impressionist paintings of the Shenoi that stood out.

Since all we knew about the Shenoi was their biotech, usually found buried deep underground or in asteroid rocks, we had no way of solving the mystery of the aliens' origins. What they'd been, what they'd looked like. Didn't stop people from guessing, though. The artworks ranged from towering, tentacled monstrosities to quiet hooded figures to ethereal beings of pure energy and everything in between.

Their entire species was extinct: what did it matter what they looked like?

And then I saw my little brother. His mouth pursed as he sopped up ale spills on the counter. I took a moment to watch him from the shadows. He seemed so distant and familiar at the same time, like a distorted reflection of myself: the same mixed features, glossy black hair, dark eyes and angular jaw as me.

I almost backed off and left him undisturbed. Like he wanted. I don't break my promises lightly, and I'd already broken the one that mattered the most to him. He'd come to Compass for a fresh start, after all. But my brother was in trouble, and this needed doing. Connecting my palmerlog to the alehouse's menu, I ordered a bathtub gin and tonic, garnished with mint and rosemary. I ducked into a discreet alcove seat guarded by a mural of a stork in midflight. I tugged my helmet off, placing it on the table beside me, and waited until my brother brought the gin over in a chilled copa glass.

He froze the moment he saw me.

'Hey, Artyom,' I said in Russian, my voice carefully level. 'How're you holding up?'

He set the glass down with a bang on the table. 'What are you doing here?' was all he would say.

At twenty-four he was three years younger than me, a little shorter and leaner, but in the right light we could have been twins. I saw the way he unconsciously hunched and turned away from me. Uncomfortable in my presence. Angry. An unexpected tightness built up in my chest.

'We need to talk.' I hoped no one in the vicinity had inbuilt translators. The last time we'd spoken he'd refused to use Japanese anymore, and I wanted to respect at least one of his wishes. I gestured to the seat opposite me.

I'd expected him to refuse, but he slid into the booth, hands folded on the table. 'We've got nothing to discuss.' He was talking to me. Progress.

'We do when Harmony arrest me to talk about it.'

'You should leave, Vak.'

I couldn't remember the last time he'd called me that. I held out the arrow-shaped pendant he'd given me all those years ago on top of that mountain. 'Does this mean nothing to you?'

My heart squeezed as I saw a spark of emotion in his eyes. As if he wanted to speak, but something greater was stopping him. He had started to move away when I grabbed him back. There was a series of deliberate slashes across his forearms and wrists. Some were only the residue of scars, like the ones he'd made by the frozen lake after our father had punched out one of his teeth out in a rage, and he'd seen no way out of our domestic nightmare. He'd have bled out if I hadn't patched him up. The other scars were fresher. A crisscrossing, bloody tapestry.

We shared a long look. He snatched his arm back and tugged his sleeves down.

41

'You promised me you'd never do that again.' There was more heat in my voice than I intended. My brother brings out the worst in me: I'm both too emphatic and too angry with him.

'Yeah.' He couldn't meet my eyes as he picked at a wood splinter on the table. 'Well, we both made promises, didn't we?'

The images of Artyom rolling the stolen stormtech canister and Alcatraz's broken, mangled body spliced through my mind. 'I'm trying to help. Harmony knows you're stealing stormtech. You're done.'

'My life, my business.'

'You're not stupid enough to believe that.' I leaned forward. 'I can help you, Artyom. I can get them to protect you. Whatever it is, we can make it work. I can get you out. Help me help you.'

I expected quiet, brooding anger, the sort I usually got from him. Instead, he cast me a sad, tight smile, as if I couldn't understand. 'It's too late to stop this. I—'

'Is someone forcing you, Artyom?' They must have something on him, something dark. 'Talk to me.'

'Now my big brother wants to protect me? That ship sailed, Vakov. It sailed when you went to fight your stupid sodding war. You left me with Dad, knowing you'd promised to stay, knowing what he'd do while you were gone, and then you came back full of that ... *stuff*.' His mouth twitched into a pitying, mocking smile. 'Was it worth it, Vak?'

'I sent money every month.' I was feeling more and more uncomfortable, and more and more determined to break through to him. 'I made sure you got a share of everything I earned.'

'You really don't get it, do you? Nothing you *sent* could make up for you leaving me.'

'But I came back,' I said, lowering my voice. 'After everything that happened and everything that war threw at me, I came back home.'

Artyom's chuckle was a throaty, raw sound. 'What, and you

thought we'd all just pick up where we left off? Pretend it never happened? No. No, it doesn't work like that. I've got my own life now.'

I could feel the stormtech wrapping tight around my chest like nanosteel as childhood memories crashed on the banks of my mind. I locked gazes with him, searching for a connection. 'Remember when we used to go behind the observatory and stargaze? Just lie there and forget the rest of the world? It was just you and me up there. You picked a different soundtrack from your collection every night. You wanted every night to be different. You'd spend so long searching, because you wanted to get it right. Remember?'

Artyom's eyes seemed to glaze over, as if digging up the bones of an old, old memory. 'That was a long time ago.'

'We got through so much together,' I offered. Even if the memories hurt, even if they scarred, even if I had to reopen all our shared bruises and wounds, I would do it to reach him. I loved him too much to walk away. Because beneath the pain were the moments that had bonded us together and made us who we were. Maybe, just maybe, they could again now. 'We can work this out, Artyom. We can fix this. We always do.'

He blinked slow and hard, as if it hurt to see the world again. For a moment, I thought I'd won him over. Then, ever so gently, he said, 'Vak, I don't ever want to see you again.'

It was the worst thing he could have said.

The stormtech clawed up in my chest and I imagined slapping him. Hand cracking across his face, splitting his lip. The horrible urge departed as fast as it came, but the new steely, distant look in my brother's eye didn't belong to the boy who'd grown up with me. The boy who'd walk the city streets with me, exploring underground pubs and concert halls until dawn.

But we weren't children anymore.

'Mr Fukasawa, is this man bothering you?' The inquisitive

voice came from the bar's Rubix, acting as manager. He'd manifested as a tall gentleman in a crisp tweed suit, a blue cravat and a ridiculous bowler hat. Only heavy-grade AIs are allowed to physically roam around, even in a limited capacity.

'Yes, he is,' Artyom said in English. He stood. People were staring despite the privacy of the dimmed alcove. 'I want him to leave.'

'Very well.' The Rubix's grin was wide and perfectly polite as it turned towards me. 'Sir, please vacate the premises immediately.'

I ignored it. 'Artyom, we could—'

He wouldn't even look at me. 'You had your chance.'

'Artyom—'

'Don't, Vakov. Just don't. Go out with a bit of dignity, why don't you?'

'Sir.' The Rubix's voice had sharpened. Eyes bulging with exaggerated anger. 'You *will* leave.'

'Not until I've finished talking to my brother.'

'For god's sake, Vak, for once do as you're bloody told.'

'*Get out of my bar.*' The handsome Rubix face had melted into a nightmarish monster, its voice becoming thick and barbed. A crown of horns protruded from its misshapen, bloodstained head. A mass of needle-sharp teeth growing out of its mouth. The tweed suit was beginning to blacken and sprout poisonous thorns. It didn't scare me, but I couldn't say the same for the other patrons. '*Leave my bar and never come back.*'

The Rubix would get shut down if it hurt me. But it could summon security, and then I'd have Kindosh on my back. My body told me to squeeze Artyom, see how far I could push this before I was thrown out. I had to physically swallow the urge as I stood. 'You can't push me away. Not over this,' I told Artyom, my voice hard and brittle.

Every eye was trained on me as I left. There was a wet

44

slithering and the Rubix's voice, and presumably its face, returned to normal as it spoke to the startled patrons. 'I do apologise for that, everyone. May I offer you a free round of drinks—'

My knees shook as I took the stairs to the thoroughfare, a thin sheen of sweat coating my skin. Had I really turned my brother into this angry, bitter young man? I tried to shrug off the weight of memories before setting foot on the street. Only someone was blocking my path.

It was Katherine Kowalski.

Oh hell.

4
Noodles

'How did I know?' Kowalski laughed, lacing her hands across the nape of her neck. 'It took you all of ten minutes to go behind my back. Ten. Minutes.'

My maelstrom of emotions deflated like a popped bubble. 'Sorry?' I offered.

'No, you're not,' she mumbled as she vaped, plumes of smoke disappearing into the air. 'You're not sorry in the slightest.'

'That stuff isn't good for you,' I told her.

She fixed me with a glare, then pushed out a sigh. 'We should talk. But not here. It's late and I haven't eaten and you probably haven't either. Should we find somewhere?'

I'd expected to be arrested then and there and have my arse dragged back to Harmony to be thrown headfirst into a stinking cell for the week, so I wasn't about to decline dinner.

We took a switchback stairwell out of Limefields to a floor strung with a vertiginous boulevard of multicultural bistros and eateries. Kowalski picked a Japanese restaurant out of the selection. The rich scent of sake and rice vinegar whirled me back to the noodlehouses on New Vladi I'd visit on wet, dreamy afternoons: cupping my hands around a hot bowl of miso soup and inhaling the steamy aroma. Listening to the quiet spatter of rain on the breath-fogged viewport, chainships glowing green and red as they soared over the mountain ranges.

There was a Torven watching the restaurants. I'd seen the aliens over vids, and knew they made up a small percentage of Compass' population, but I'd not been here long enough to *see* one before. It was almost as tall as me with skin the colour of dirty sand. Its sharp, pointed face was vaguely avian, with large eyes and small nostrils. Bony arms sprouted from broad shoulders, digitigrade legs bound tight with muscle, dexterous-looking hands equipped with four fingers. The alien had the spicy smell of cloves and pine-needles, and wore a grey one-piece suit that had the appearance of dolphin skin.

'How long have they been here?' I asked.

'Almost since Compass was built. They were the first space-faring species to become a part of the Common. There's the fifth, maybe sixth generation of Torven living and trading here.'

The alien watched us as we passed, narrowing its dark eyes in what seemed to be an expression of mild irritation, as if we'd blocked its view of the eateries.

We were about to enter the restaurant when the Rubix at the entrance stood in front of us. 'All exoskeletons and armoured suits must have shutdown mode activated,' the AI told us with an air of self-entitlement. Its gaze swung over to Kowalski. 'Nor can you bring weapons.'

She rolled her eyes, but parted with her service thin-gun and glanced at me. I sighed and thumbed the option on my palmerlog. The exterior lights pulsed a tepid green, the suit's systems stepping down from combat-readiness. My helmet had already slithered back into my neck joint, the armour along my hands doing likewise. Wasn't too happy about it, but I wasn't in the mood to get into a shouting match with another Rubix.

I picked an alcove on the fringes of the restaurant, trying to expose my stormtech to the minimum of people. A wall-spanning viewport peered out at the rest of the sprawling floor. The restaurant was garlanded with hanging lanterns and mini sculpted bonsais, the walls heavy with kanji calligraphy and swirling designs of bloody samurais. Mumbled shreds of conversation from other patrons echoed around us. A low soundtrack, by a group that my shib told me was *The 5.6.7.8s*, played softly in the background.

Kowalski caught me staring at the kanji. 'Can you read that?'

'I'm from New Vladi. Everyone there knows their parents' ethnic language as well as English,' I said. 'Got Russian and Japanese up my sleeve. At least the dialects we speak. You?'

'I'm Polish, but I'm too lazy to learn it.' Her fingers twitched for her vaper. 'Must be nice, communicating in another language with family and friends.'

It might be nice for others. I opted not to mention that Artyom had refused to speak Japanese for years. It was our father's language and culture and my brother had long pretended that part of him didn't exist. As if he could just deny it out of existence. I know better than most people how permanent genetic makeup is.

I didn't get as many glances as I'd expected from the three dozen customers, though a scattered few were not so subtly staring at the stormtech that was busy curling up and down my forearms like jellyfish tentacles. Live with this blue stuff plugged up into you, and getting side-glances and double takes becomes the norm. Not that I was anything special; there were plenty of Reapers around here, and even more skinnies. But the fascination with glowing alien DNA twitching inside human flesh never went away, and their glances made me squirm in my seat. I wished they'd just gawk. At least they'd be honest about it.

I weighed up how much to tell Kowalski as I ordered. I was a long way from being friendly with Harmony. But my brother's rejection still stung and something was off about his behaviour. To Kowalski, he was a lowlife suspect, a drug trafficker. I kept that in mind as I related our conversation, his refusal to talk, and my own theory of him being blackmailed. She folded her hands under her chin, taking a few quiet moments to process this new information.

'If he's involved with the theft and sabotage of Harmony property,' she said finally, 'even at a minor level, we need to take action.'

'You don't know that he's involved in anything bigger. Not for sure. Not completely.'

'Which is why we're having this conversation. You're as much at risk as anyone else.' She flipped open her palmerlog and glanced at a newsfeed. 'While we've been here, a Reaper Blued Out a few floors up, right in the middle of the town square at rush hour. She was in rehab, taking our suppressors.'

I almost didn't want to ask. 'What's the damage?'

'Bad. She killed four pedestrians, one a husband in front of his wife and kids, before she went down.'

'Oh, hell.'

'Yeah. She'd already shot and injured five more. Worse, one of them was an offworld Torven, not native to Compass. So the Alien Embassy's become involved. They say she tried to blow her own brains out in the end, but she started convulsing with a seizure before she could finish the job.' Kowalski eyed me over the flickering, membrane-thin screen. 'No kid should have to see their parent murdered in front of them. I want this plague stamped out of my city, out of my asteroid, and I want it done now.'

'And you think this incident is connected to the other deaths.'

'I don't see how it could be a coincidence. Even if it isn't con-nected, it's doing the same damage to people, and to Harmony. These deaths have been escalating, occurring more and more

49

in public places and harming civilians. It's deliberate. Vicious. Because the Reapers will get their suppressors, and the skinnies and party-goers are going to get their fix either way. If the Reapers don't trust us, they'll turn to the streets. And that stuff is lethal, unregulated, cripplingly addictive.'

'Let me hazard a guess: stormdealers and other drug-trafficking syndicates are your top suspects.'

'We don't want to jump to conclusions, but it's hard to imagine anyone benefiting more than them.' She drummed her fingers on the table. 'We captured a mule a little while back. He'd crammed five phials of stormtech down his throat. His stormdealers had a sharpshooter take him out within minutes, clean through the heart. This isn't just about saving Reapers; it's a war against drugs from a source that's not even *human*. And we're losing.' She rubbed her eyes, bloodshot with the residue of too many sleepless nights. 'We can't even call it a war.'

'Why's that?' I asked.

'Wars end.'

'No, they don't. Wars last as long as there're people to remember them.'

The awkward silence was only broken when an octodrone brought our steaming food over. Its gangly electromuscles, thick as my arm, served our ramen while our chopsticks autoprinted.

'Even for a guy your size, that's a heavy serving.' Kowalski nodded towards my bowl, filled with karaage ramen, boiled eggs, spring onions, and sides of tempura and gyoza.

I sprinkled chilli seasoning on my meal. I'd never much liked the stuff before the stormtech, but now I had a perpetual craving for it, along with acids, sodium, spices, dairy. Anything with a kick, and the stormtech liked it.

I pointed with my chopsticks to the knots of stratospheric cerulean climbing down my arms. 'I'm eating for two. The blue boys need fuel. It's like being pregnant for ever.'

'Very funny.'

The food wasn't up to New Vladi standards, of course. But the chicken karaage was juicy and the ramen soup was filling enough. The green tea Kowalski had ordered melted into my stomach with a pleasant, warm glow.

When our bowls were scraped clean, Kowalski leaned towards me again. 'So. What's the plan?'

'Artyom won't talk to me,' I told her.

'Reapers are dying every day, Fukasawa. And Artyom is the only lead we have. The only reason he's not in a Harmony interrogation cell right now is because we're giving you a shot. We know he's not acting alone. Arresting him will tip our hand. You're our best shot at doing this cleanly.'

'You have an idea who's behind this, then?'

'I've told you about the mule we picked up. We've also picked up stormtech distributors, xenochemists, even top dogs among the more dangerous stormdealer syndicates, the ones who control the trade and practically *own* floors. So we know a little about their security. The low-key guys get installed with a bioleash. It messes with their brain chemistry, makes them activate a suicide trigger in their molars if they're caught. Sometimes that's combined with a smelter-bomb wired to their vitals. They like taking a few of us out too, if they can.'

A sour knot tightened in my gut. 'And you think Artyom's wired with one.'

'We'd be naive not to assume it's a possibility. It might explain his reluctance to talk. Even assuming we take Artyom by force, and assuming he makes it into interrogation alive, there's no way in hell they won't be tracking him. The moment he's compromised, they'll pack up and vanish. Our only lead disappears and Artyom needs armed protection for the rest of his life. We've played this game too many times not to know the rules. We'd risk grabbing him if there was no other choice.

But now we've got you, and you being a Reaper means there's a chance to fix this.' A steely look came into her eye. 'Every minute this problem exists on Compass, more people get hurt. We're gambling a lot of lives on giving you and your brother this chance. My advice? You use it, and you use it wisely.'

'Forgive me if I'm not glowing with gratitude.'

'It doesn't matter what you are as long as you get him to come clean.'

'If he won't talk to me, he sure as hell won't talk to you.' My little brother's infinitely more stubborn than I am. No easy feat.

'Don't be naive. Harmony always gets the answers it wants.'

I understood the veiled threat. Commander Sokolav had said as much when I'd served in his Battalion. He'd been merciless with the Harvest soldiers we'd captured. I'd never known his methods. Didn't need to, because he always got results. I shivered as I imagined Artyom, strapped to a chair with a distortion-mask wrapped around his face, an interrogator standing over him with pliers.

Kowalski slid a thumb over the sweeping engravings on her ceramic mug. 'Artyom tried to sign up for the Reaper programme too, didn't he?'

Of course Harmony had dug that data up from somewhere. 'The chances of your body rejecting stormtech are astronomically low,' I said quietly. 'Artyom never got over the disappointment.'

When Harmony asked, I'd said I joined the Reaper programme because I couldn't sit back as habitats and moonbases and whole planets got blasted to rubble and ash by Harvest warships. I'd never admitted I had to escape a violent father ... or that one of us would have ended up dead if I'd stuck around. And if I'd killed him, his colleagues in high places would have ensured I'd been dumped in prison for killing a good man and Artyom would have ended up in foster care. Not exactly material you can scribble across the dotted line.

I changed the subject. 'Why did Kindosh put you on my tail?'

Kowalski gave a hard sigh, as if it was inevitable I'd find out. 'Remember I said I'd joined Harmony young? I was on the Narcotics Squad. Not just stormtech, but grimwire, synthsilver, bluesmoke, cloud, devilweed, whatever's fresh out of the labs. One day we raided a junknest, where they manufacture drugs. Found a woman injecting her three-year-old kid with synthsilver from a second-hand needle. Thought it'd get her to stop screaming.' Kowalski's hands were tight and twitchy on the table. 'I shot that woman seven times.'

I was silent for a moment as the restaurant clattered around us. 'I might have done the same.'

There was a flicker of gratitude in Kowalski's eyes, that I hadn't judged her, hadn't condemned her as others had done. I felt some of the tension deflate. 'Not everyone at Harmony felt that way,' she said. 'My unit didn't want a bar on me. It should have killed my career, but Kindosh pulled some strings and got me reassigned to her. And now I get babysitting jobs like this.' She gulped down her steaming tea. 'And you know the funny thing? My nephew Andrezj is a skinnie. I can rescue a whole shipment of stormtech at any dockyard, I can crack down on a stormdealer, I can wring a confession from a distributor. But I can't stop my own family from using the stuff.'

The Reaper War had ended in 2429, two years ago now. It still didn't feel like we'd won it. We'd just swapped one enemy for another.

'You know why they call us Reapers?' I asked her. 'Because we were the only ones who could stop the Harvest from digging their roots in like weeds and choking everything. It's a wonder they didn't give us scythes instead of rifles. "Reapers to

clear the Harvest away." That's what we'd chant before battle.'
I sipped at my tea, cooling my dried throat as I stared down at
my arm where the stormtech had pooled, flickering like tongues
of flame along my fingers. 'No one thought about what happens
afterwards when the Harvest is clear but the Reapers remain.
No one had a chant for that.'

I was suddenly whirled back to the laboratory where I'd
been transformed into a Reaper. Metal walls, white tiles, churning machinery. Plugged up to life-support systems, flat on my
back and strapped to an operating table and listening to my
friends scream and thrash around me as stormtech shredded
their organs, poisoned their blood vessels and twisted their
muscles. You can leave a battlefield behind, but you can't do
the same for your body. And that's where the real, unwinnable
war was being fought. Where we all kept fighting until we
couldn't. How many Reapers and skinnies had passed through
the rehab centres in the hope of taming this addiction, only to
end up killing both themselves and the people around them?

How much of a hand did my brother really have in this?

'Local, small-time dealers initiating a turf-war or selling
their product to a Common Official is one thing.' Kowalski
elbowed her way through my thoughts, as if she could read
them. 'That we can handle. But this is beyond dealing a tainted
product when we're seeing Reapers being poisoned – brutally,
publicly killed, and framed as the villains – all over Compass.
Poisoning the suppressors is methodical, deliberate, and it's got
force behind it. They're attacking Harmony and laughing in
our faces. That's not something we can ignore, just as we can't
ignore your brother's involvement.' The edges of Kowalski's eyes
were ringed with exhaustion, frustration. 'I'm at my wits end
here, Fukasawa. We all are. So I'm asking you again, to please
help us out. You want to help Reapers? You want to help your
brother out? Then work with us.'

For years, I'd known I should have stayed with Artyom. Done my duty as the older brother, as I'd promised. I'd failed miserably. Maybe this was my shot to correct that mistake.

'There are some things I'll need in return,' I said slowly.

Kowalski gave a small laugh. 'Kindosh isn't the flexible type.'

I knew exactly what type Kindosh was, which was why I was negotiating with Kowalski instead.

'She's made me promises. She'll give me some leeway.' I took Kowalski's silence as an invitation to continue. 'So: this won't work if Harmony is breathing down my back, or if I keep being summoned to Kindosh's office like an errand boy. I'll work with you, no one else. You can pass along my updates. Once this is done, I'm out. I'm not going to owe her any surprise favours in the future, nothing hanging over me.' She nodded. So far so good. 'And if ... *if* my brother is involved, he gets immunity. No one coerces him, no one talks to him before me.'

She stopped nodding. 'That might not be possible.'

'Tell Kindosh to make it possible. If there's any misunderstanding, if he's held against his will or being blackmailed, I won't risk him getting lost in the bureaucracy because Kindosh needs a scapegoat.' My armour creaked as I settled back into my seat. I hadn't realised I was leaning forward. 'We're talking about rehab centres being targeted, Reapers being murdered in public. You don't pull that off without a hell of an organisation backing you up. These people would have years, decades worth of work behind them. Artyom hasn't been on Compass long enough to be anything but a part of someone else's plan. I don't want that forgotten.'

Kowalski gently twirled her mug, the motion reflected in the viewport. 'I'll talk to Kindosh. She's not going to be happy, but I think she'll find your terms acceptable.' I had no doubt she would. She wanted me involved badly enough to make allowances. 'What matters is that we get this solved.'

'This isn't for Kindosh,' I said. 'It's not for her alien buddies or her career or Harmony. That's your screw-up. I'm doing this for the Reapers I fought with. I'm doing this for my brother.'

It was ironic that it had taken a stormtech outbreak that threatened thousands of people, the very thing that split my brother and I apart, to bring our lives crashing together again, but you don't choose the cards you're dealt. I'd hoped that time would have eased things, or that Artyom might have forgiven me, even if I hadn't forgiven myself. This was far from how I'd envisaged reuniting. But while Artyom's view on me hadn't changed, the situation sure as hell had. Ugly as it was, I had to follow this problem to its roots, even if I unearthed things I'd rather leave buried.

Of all people, it had to be *my* brother.

Kowalski nodded. 'You're doing a good thing, Fukasawa.'

I wondered.

Whatever hells the war had thrown at us, it had created an ironclad, unbreakable bond between Reapers. We stuck together no matter what, because no one else understood how it felt to have an alien organism slither up your backbone and into your brain. What it was like to be *excited* at the prospect of charging head-on into a maelstrom of Harvest gunfire and Berserker killsquads. How your adrenaline spiked when enemy sniper rounds began chewing your cover away. Or what it felt like to be struck with a stormtech-induced seizure in the middle of a tactical operation, your hands clenching with the urge to kill every living thing on the planet, including the members of your own Battalion.

No one who's not been there themselves can wrap their heads around a nightmare like that. No one but the men and women who stood by your side and survived it with you.

I'd been badly injured in my first skirmish with Harvest, a plasma blast searing across my thigh, leaving a scar I still have.

Our intel was compromised, the terrain unfamiliar and access to SSC aerial support jammed. My armour had been fried, my weapons lost in the fray, my leg broken. I was dead in the mud. Alcatraz, multicoloured artillery fire glaring off his armour, scooped me up and carried me over his shoulder for three hours, blasting Harvesters one-handed like something out of a Harmony propaganda piece, until we reached the safety of our buffer-zone. I lay panting on the cold floor as he unstrapped me from my armour and asked him why he'd risked his skin for someone he didn't even know. He looked at me for a long time before saying we were both Reapers. That made us brothers. 'To Harmony, to the Common, we're nothing,' he'd said, sinking down on his haunches next to me. 'A bunch of freak experiments, fighting their war for them. And if we don't look out for each other, who will?'

Wasn't until he'd limped away I'd seen he'd been shot in the shoulder. He hadn't breathed a word about it.

We didn't survive because we had better guns, better wartech, better tacticians, better orbital dogfighters. We survived because we trusted each other with our lives, through every bloody step of the screaming, unflinching darkness of the Reaper War. You don't survive the traumas we'd endured and the horrific, gut-wrenching things we'd seen without being scarred. Without forming a bond. So, no matter what battlefields we faced, no matter what horrors Harvest would throw at us, we relied on each other. We shared an unbreakable loyalty and honour that every Reaper would shoulder for the rest of their lives.

And now, in order to save them, I had to turn on my brother. Believe that the boy who'd been beside me and Kasia since we were children was involved in their murders. It felt like a betrayal. Worse: the soldier in me shouldn't have thought twice.

I was dead to Artyom. My fellow Reapers had been my only family for half a decade.

But that's the burden of being human – doing right by the people you love, long after it's stopped making sense.

5

Grim

We got as far as the Starklands Central Station before I was sure someone was following us.

The stormtech sharpens your senses with a permanent extra edge, so I was distinctly aware someone had kept pace with us since the restaurant. I almost mentioned it to Kowalski, but by the time we got back to my apartment complex there was no one in sight.

I unlocked the door, only to find the turret had unfolded from the wall and was spinning around like a disco ball, gears whirring. Kowalski swore and was reaching for the thin-gun holstered at her hip when I stopped her, seeing a figure sprawled on my couch, chomping away at a bowl of cereal. There was only one person who'd dare to pull something like this.

I sighed. 'Grim? What did we say about locked doors?'

'Hey, Vak! Your place is nicer than I remembered. Good to see you made it out, by the way.' His sly, foxy grin died when he saw I had company. He tumbled off the lounger, his gaze on Kowalski. '. . . and you are?'

'How did you get in without triggering the alarms?' Kowalski spluttered, bringing her palmerlog up. 'This security system is airtight. And what the hell did you do to the turret?' Knowing Grim, I was glad he'd not chosen to test its firing capacity.

'Oh.' He had the decency to look a little embarrassed as he flexed his spindly fingers. 'I disabled it. Couldn't have it stopping me from getting inside.'

For the first time, I noticed the AI rabbit in the corner of the room, reared up on its hind legs, its eyes engulfed in burning flames, stamping its foot and issuing clouds of smoke. 'This vagabond has locked me out of my system!' The rabbit sniffed. 'He's tearing my mainframe apart.'

'Shut up, furball. I hardly did any rerouting!' Grim protested.

'Furball?' the AI spluttered indignantly, holographic flames jetting from its eyes, nails extending from its paws. 'I'm a Nova-Class, Pure Core Rubix with a platinum substrate rating, and I will—'

'Oh, shut up. It's not my fault your safeguard software sucks.'

The rabbit puffed its chest up. 'You shut up, and you listen here; I'll have you know—'

I interrupted before the argument spiralled out of control and told Grim to quit it. Grim gave me a cheeky, innocent smile I knew all too well and deactivated something remotely in his shib. The autocannon above me stopped spinning. The AI levelled one last demonic-looking death stare in Grim's direction before vanishing in a puff of angry black smoke.

I strip-mined my brain for an appropriate response, but returned empty handed. I turned to Kowalski and mumbled an apology instead.

'That's top-tier Harmony security software. Supposed to be unhackable.' She rubbed her face with the air of someone who doesn't want to know any more. She threw me one last look as she steered for the door. 'Get some rest, Fukasawa. I'll see you tomorrow.'

'Oh boy.' Grim sucked air through his hacksaw teeth and scraped both hands through his wild hair, tangled in a permanent mess. He was habitually seeking out weird new gadgets

60

from across the Common. Today, he was dressed in an under-skin with a nanoweave stitching that turned him into a neon skeleton from the neck down, his ribcage stuttering red and green like an adboard. 'Man, I leave you alone for a few hours, and you get in bed with Harmony?' he asked, slapping my arm.

'It's not like that,' I protested.

'What's it like, then?'

'They only found me because of you.' Grim's cheerful face turned pallid. 'Yeah, they traced your untraceable feed back to me.'

'That means—'

'That means they know who you are, and that you don't have Compass residency.'

Grim groaned. 'Oh god.'

'I'm handling it, don't worry.'

Grim rubbed at his eyes with his knuckles. 'Do you have the genome at least?'

'Smuggled it out right under Harmony's nose.' I grinned as I extracted the datapoint from my suit sleeve and tossed it to Grim.

A scattermash of HUD icons and multicoloured overlays grew over Grim's retinas as he used his shib to send the genome to our buyer. 'Done. They're not too happy about us being late, but we're in the clear.' Grim scratched at a scab on his temple. 'Now we've only got the Jackal to worry about.'

'What about him?'

'Well, word is, he wants to strangle you with your own guts.'

'I'm well aware, Grim.'

'But he's the Jackal. Most crimelords get their blademen to take care of loose ends. This guy does his own dirty work, does his own finger and toe slicing. Up close and personal.' Grim sniffed. 'He *enjoys* hunting people down around Compass. Makes a game of it.'

My body remembered and tensed, expecting incoming danger. I clamped down on the sensation and focused on peeling out of my armour before pinching into the seat next to Grim. There's only so many times you can be creatively threatened in a day before the novelty starts to wear off. 'If selling the genome isn't enough I can get Kindosh to get you Compass citizenship as part of our deal.'

Grim stopped scratching his head to stare at me. He must have realised the real reason I'd taken this job. 'Wait. You'd do that for me?'

'Consider it done,' I said.

'While you're at it, get Harmony to upgrade my place, too?'

'Now you're pushing it.'

'Can I move into yours, at least?'

'Not if you keep breaking into it!'

'It won't happen again,' the Rubix interjected in its usual sniffy voice. 'I'll do my utmost to keep this horrid ruffian away.'

'Oh, good. I love a challenge,' Grim shot back, wearing that infuriating grin of his that had nearly got us killed at the wrong checkpoint.

I went for the liquor cabinet to make us drinks to celebrate. The stormtech negates the effect of alcohol, meaning I could drink every drop of booze on the asteroid and not get tipsy. Doesn't mean that I don't enjoy the taste of alcohol, though.

The glass shelves were stocked with the classiest labels, courtesy of Harmony. And they'd stocked the bar with everything: whiskey, bourbon, vodka, gin, rum, genever, brandy, tequila, many bespoke Compass varieties. A terminal listed the botanicals and recommended mixers for each drink. I went straight for the gin. I always like to try the local colour so I settled on an unfamiliar label from a small distillery a few floors up from here. I built a cocktail called Reaper's Bane. Three measures chilled gin, berry liqueur, a squeeze of lemon, a good splash of blue Curaçao. It was the drink me and Grim had discovered the night we'd met in an offworld spaceport bar. Grim had been caught hacking a gambling terminal. I'd flashed my Reaper credentials, saved him getting his face caved in by a bloodthirsty bodyguard. However people might look at us on the street, Reapers are widely revered for standing on the frontlines of our besieged planets and making a difference in the war. Doesn't matter where I show my credentials, I've got some pull. No one wants to get in a fight with us, not if they want to keep their teeth. Grim's assailants backed down. He'd bought me the first Reaper's Bane in gratitude. I liked the guy enough to buy the second round. By the time the fourth swung around, we were partners.

Grim apprehended the square-cut glass with a skeletal hand. 'Spill the beans, Vak. What's going on?'

I told him. Harmony hadn't sworn me to secrecy, and Grim was the only one I could talk to about this mess.

'Don't know if I like this,' he said when I was done.

'My take? It's a takeover bid by a drug syndicate. In the end, I'd rather have Harmony control stormtech than let someone new monopolise the market. They're the lesser of two evils.' I thought of Alcatraz's broken body, poisoned and mutilated by stormtech my brother might have helped move, and a chill trickled down my spine. I sipped the gin, the pungent liquid giving my throat a warm, pleasant glow. 'Got no choice but to trust them.'

'I wouldn't,' muttered Grim.

'You're hardly unbiased.'

'Harmony bombed my homeplanet, Vak.' Grim was serious for once, his thin shoulders slumped. 'They tore families apart. They took children.'

It was an unspoken truth that Harmony had targeted under-privileged families on backwater planets during the war, pitching the Reaper programme as the most innovative technology since spaceflight. They'd found prime candidates as young as fourteen and all but kidnapped them. The ones their psychoanalysts believed were the best match got put through their stormtech experiments. They called it conscription, but in my book it was evil no matter what you called it. Sure, the Intelligence Officers and xenochemists responsible had been court-martialled, but that didn't undo damage they'd done. But I'd been furious about it half a hundred times in the past. I didn't need to rehash it tonight. 'I know, Grim. But circumstances change.'

'It's your choice, mate. Not like I could dissuade you anyway.' He reclined against the soft leather, legs folded beneath him. 'Did you watch the films on that memorycrystal I gave you?'

Grim had an unabashed love of cult films and serials, particularly the ones that had originated on Earth, with several libraries' worth stored up. He had a side-business selling them to people looking to be entertained by something on the weirder side. Occasionally, he passed them to me. Not all of them were terrible.

'No,' I said. 'I've been too busy being kidnapped by Harmony.'

'Maybe you've earned some R&R.'

'Can't see that happening any time soon.'

He dropped a hand on my shoulder where it blinked between gold and purple. My knee-jerk response was to shrug it off. The sensitive, overloading nature of the stormtech means Reapers don't like being touched. But this was Grim, so I overcame the sensation. 'Then if you have to play with fire,' he said, 'let me share the heat.'

'Grim, I don't want you to get hurt.'

'It's never been a problem before.'

'This is Harmony, Grim. Not darkmarket smuggling.'

But his mind was made up. Grim's as loyal as a dog, and whatever I was going through, he'd refuse to let me do it alone because he knew I'd do the same for him. He gave my shoulder a final squeeze before downing his drink and heading for the door. 'Don't worry about your brother, yeah? He'll come around eventually.'

I downed my own drink as the door closed behind him, then stripped my sodden underskin and padded to the bathroom to shower. I stank with an overripe, sickly-sweet stench. The stormtech doesn't just change the way you smell, it makes your pheromones sharper, more powerful. Skinnies have been known to lick blue sweat off their own bodies, getting high on the sweet-sour toxins secreted from their pores.

My freshly upgraded bathroom was decorated with black and white marble and equipped with an immense steam jet-shower. Fibres in the floors warmed up against my bare feet as I examined my latest collection of wounds and bruises in the curving mirror, stark against my patchwork tapestry of old scars, burns and lacerations. Stormtech might heal the flesh, but it's going to leave a mark. Thick ropes of stormtech swirled down my stomach and streamed up my breastbone like a comet. I bunched my fist, watching the blue strands flare up along my arm in response. A layer of sticky alien circuitry forever fused to every part of my anatomy. I'd done the best I could not to hate it, try to live with it. Others had fared far worse when trying to adapt to it. If they adapted at all.

I knew some Reapers who'd spent years in rehab as Harmony tried to weaken the stormtech's grasp on them, reconditioning them to resist their body's visceral urges, rewiring their brains against their addiction to their own bodies. Others had slipped off the deep end, caving into it. They were Husks, their minds broken, swallowed by the sensations of their bodies, even if it meant hurting themselves just to feel something. They were beyond saving.

I unclenched my hand and stepped into the shower. Usually, the apartment complex Rubix warned me not to use too much water, but those restrictions seemed to have been lifted with the upgrade. I let myself be blasted by scalding jetstreams of water, feeling my muscles slowly, slowly unwind, the tension leaving my body as I breathed the steamy air. I allowed myself a luxurious half-hour before towelling off and heading into the bedroom. I cranked up the aircon and sprawled naked on the king-sized memory-foam mattress, sinking into its body-moulding softness. The bed released a calming scent and I sighed deeply into the cool darkness. Listening to my rapid heartbeat, the rhythm of my breathing, trying to decompress and compartmentalise the day. But the image of my brother with that canister kept churning over and over in my mind. After an hour of tossing and turning I gave up any attempt at sleep, returned to the liquor cabinet and poured myself a tall glass of the same local gin.

I leaned out the fogged window to watch the flickering cityscape. Roads winding over neon-stained alleyways and streets, past the hunched shoulders of tenements and apartment complexes to the mesh of the sprawling city beyond. The constant flow of aerial traffic formed a multicoloured strip between the megastructures and soaring highrises. Branching passageways tethered the bones of the cityscape together like joints. Organic art installations oscillated over galleries, clubs and expansive parklands. Glinting clatterlifts and traveltubes thrust into rock, plunging towards adjoining Compass floors and punctured with apertures leading towards parking bays and other hidden areas. Chainships and quickships peeled out of the traffic flow, swooping around overpasses and towards spaceports and massive circular tubes jutting from the ceiling

66

that acted as elevator shafts for ships between floors. The concentric rings blinked white and red in the darkness, ships slipping in and out of its wide mouth. City lights glittering like stars from a million sources.

Maybe I'd have marvelled at it all some other time. Now, it was a poor distraction from my thoughts.

Blinking neon adboards four storeys high shattered through the prism of my glass, turning my gin into molten liquid fluorescence. I slammed half the drink down in a single hit, wishing the booze would dull my senses as the seething metropolis whirled on into the night.

As hellish as our father had made our childhood, Artyom, Kasia and I had always had each other. In a way, it had tightened our relationship. No matter how hard someone tries to knock you down, having someone to lean against, someone who's got your back, makes it possible to stand up again. When I was twelve, I'd come down with pneumonia, the kind that clogs your nose and turns your lungs into sandpaper. I'd lain in bed, sniffing and miserable and beyond frustrated when Artyom came into the room and sat down on my bed next to me. 'Leave me alone,' I'd grumpily told him at some point, a soggy tissue pressed to my leaking nose.

'Someone's got to take care of you,' he'd said with a small smile. He'd cut school to keep me company the whole day. He'd brought his portable speakers with him and the two of us sat there, drinking coffee, talking and listening to music and watching the snowstorm whirl outside. It was one of the most uneventful days of my life. But for some reason, it was also one of the best.

In a blink of a bloody eye, we'd gone from that to here.

We never see the important moments as they happen. Never realise when things start to change. It's only when we look back on those years and see all the tiny, inevitable steps we took.

67

The things we wished we said. The things we wished we hadn't done. The opportunities we watched go past.

Maybe it had started when my sister had been killed. When rage for her and fear for my brother had driven me up the windswept mountain to the old observatory. When I'd asked permission to do something I knew couldn't be undone. Even if I survived, I knew it'd change me. Was that when we began drifting apart? Even before I started rifling through the Reaper conscription benefits, and believing the interstellar progress reports about Harmony using alien biotech to repel the Harvest invasion fleets? Before I started looking for a way off the miserable, backwater planet I'd been trapped on my entire life?

Didn't matter, now. This was the hand the universe had dealt us and I had to do right by the people that mattered to me. I drained the gin, images stabbing through my mind. My brother getting caught with those stolen stormtech canisters. Reapers going viciously insane, dying on the street because they'd trusted Harmony's suppressors. Harmony dragging Artyom to a dark cell and cutting away until they dug out the truth.

Unless I found it first.

6

The Unforgiven

The early morning bells chime as I pick my way up to the observatory, the wind howling around the ragged edges of the mountain, slicing on rocky teeth. Snowdrifts are piled around me on the stone steps. Snowflakes rush into my eyes. I wipe them away with trembling fingers that come back wet with tears.

I can't let her see this. Otherwise she'll see me for the child I am, not the man I want to be. Not the man my sister made me.

The observatory looms over me. Onion-domed, crimson-red and decorated with paper lanterns. Kanji, Hangul and Cyrillic flowing into one cohesive mosaic. It was an old monastery before she took over. Wild animals still roam these parts, old skeletons peeking out of the snow. I close my eyes and imagine hundreds, thousands of footsteps crossing these timbers, coming to demand the impossible, the unforgivable.

I pause at the top. My chest heaves as I peer out at New Vladivostok, flanked by the primordial blue mountains as if sheltered from the rest of the universe. Watery sunlight glints off windswept cliffs of black rock. Thick, dark forests stab upwards like swords on the horizon. It is everything I have ever known. Looking at it, I feel so small and alone.

I steady my hands, breathe deep, remember my purpose here and enter.

Two guards stand in the atrium like samurai. Arms crossed, they're wearing traditional dress over their thermal suits. All they need are katanas and sangu armour to become ancient warriors. They're silent as statues, but I know they're not here for show.

I slip my shoes off in the genkan as is custom, then spread my bare toes on the warm, comforting timber. I'm hot inside my thermal suit, but I don't unzip it. I won't be staying long. The reception is minimalist and stripped of all but the essential life-support technology. Edo-style ukiyo-e prints sit on the wall. The first showcases the evolution of human space travel across the ages, ending at our establishment of the colony on this frontier planet. The second portrays the Russo-Japanese war back on Earth, hundreds of years ago. Artyom always thought it funny that so many of us are a mix of ethnicities that wanted to kill each other not so long ago. But my brother hasn't laughed or smiled in a month now. I don't think he even listens to music anymore.

A painted wooden door opens silently, and I go to see the Babushka.

She doesn't look up from her papers as I seat myself on the hard, wooden chair opposite her. Smoky incense drifts past over-flowing bookshelves and relics from Earth. The room is silent for what feels like an eternity before, with her head still bowed, she asks, 'Do you understand what it means to come to me, Vakov Fukasawa?'

I nod slowly. She knows why I am here. She would not see me otherwise.

'Good.' She looks up for the first time. She's still young for this position. Most are at least sixty when they are chosen by the previous Babushka on her deathbed. Her blonde hair is faded. Her skin is as pale as the papers she reads, her eyes grey like my mother's, but there's a tilt in the edge of her eye that hints at an Asian grandparent. She is the average, everyday face of New Vladi. But there's solidity underneath those bones. Like hard, jagged stone underneath a thin layer of snow.

'I heard what that Szymanski boy did to your sister,' she says.

'Kasia.' My voice is raspy and hoarse. I clear my throat and try again. 'Her name was Kasia.'

'I know, child. I know.'

Joon Szymanski is infamous across New Vladi. The boy who, at age twelve, had cut open a pregnant cat's belly and pulled out its unborn babies to see what they looked like. After he began chopping their heads off with a shovel, people stopped pretending it was a childish phase. But his rich, privileged family protected him then. And again when he threw acid in a girl's face for mocking his height. She is scarred for life. The memory will haunt her every time she looks in the mirror. But at least she is still alive.

The Babushka creaks back in her chair. 'Are you sure you do not wish to seek an agreement?'

'I'm sure,' I say, the words brittle. I will not settle. Not after he killed my sister.

'Very well.' The Babushka's voice doesn't change, doesn't betray any emotion. 'No direct action will be taken by my office, but you have permission seek justice as you see fit. The Five Courts of New Vladivostok will protect you. No punishment will befall you, so long as you do not harm any other party.'

My hands tighten on the arms of the chair. My sister had been nothing to that Szymanski boy. All her promises, her spirit, her laughter, dying out like lonely echoes in these cold mountains.

The Babushka places a number of objects on the table. A tube, connected to a series of wires. Hypodermics. A vacuum-sealed bag of liquid silver. An untraceable thin-gun.

'Do what you need to do,' she says. 'And do it freely.'

Heart pounding in my chest, I collect each item. I don't feel the cold as I carry them with me down the mountain. With every step my anger and resolve hardens. And by the time I reach the bottom, I know not just what I have to do, but how.

7

Claws

I must have finally dozed off, because I woke to my palmerlog ringing. Kowalski had sent me the details of the latest Bluing Out incident. I was to analyse the scene and circumstances around the death. What the victim had been doing at the time, and before, their death. Dig up any enemies or reasons someone might want her dead. Damage control, if necessary. There was a *thanks* attached to the message. I sighed and blinked at the shavings of pale dawn light angling through the louvred windows. *I'm really doing this,* I thought as I dressed. When I got outside, I grabbed a bacon and egg roll from a street-vendor and hurried over to the traveltube station, heading for Kirribuli.

It was a resort highfloor, the kind tourists and rich people frequent. The asteroid was a little wider in this sector, allowing the floor to spread outwards, big enough to construct a multitude of linked seas, rivers and beaches across this colossal space. Great stalwart cruiser-liners were constantly setting sail across the waters, sometimes taking days to do a complete circuit of the level. I'd barely had a chance to take it all in before being led past the security cordon to a cruiser-liner, docked in its berth, the corpse waiting for me at the sundeck cafe on the ship's top floor.

72

I don't think I realised how much of an emotional marathon this was going to be. Not until I recognised who the body belonged to.

Samantha Wong had always insisted we call her Sam, but it had never quite stuck. I'd last seen her a few days after Harvest surrendered, her loud, throaty laughter filling the room. Now her cold body was stretched out on the stone floor, and she'd never laugh again.

She'd died hours ago, though the stormtech was still active in her body. Blue squirming under her lifeless flesh, attempting a post-mortem reboot. Stormtech needs a living host, and it'll do anything to ensure it has one. It was still frantically tunnelling through her veins and ligaments, searching for any spark it could use to jumpstart her like a chainship engine. But humans don't work that way. There was no bringing her back.

Like Alcatraz, Wong had been taking suppressors from Harmony's clinics. And if the furious articles popping up on my shib newsfeed were any indicator, Harmony was already copping the blame for her death.

I'd already viewed the security footage of the incident. She'd been sipping a coffee by the viewport when she'd collapsed, twitching and spasming on the floor. There were vivid, raked gouges along her arms where she'd tried to claw the stormtech out. When that failed and it overwhelmed her, she'd turned on the people around her. Leaped at a man twice her size, slamming his face against the glass so hard she'd broken his nose. The security robot had been forced to shoot her, or risk her killing someone.

First Alcatraz. Now Wong. How many more of my friends would I have to stand over, staring at them like broken puzzle pieces? I remembered Wong sitting next to me after an operation went sour. A smelter-grenade had just blasted good men and women into a pile of guts and gristle. She told me we'd get through this, that we'd look back on it some day like a distant nightmare, realising how far we'd come since. Looking at her corpse spread in front me now, the memory almost felt cruel.

A cool salt breeze drifted through the cruiser-liner's porthole. An artificial beach stretched below us, aquamarine waves crashing on a curve of golden sand, scattered with sunbathers and people striding along a sun-bleached boardwalk. Even the air smelled salty and fresh, the way the real thing was meant to. I rubbed my neck. I'd left my suit charging at home, thinking it probably wasn't a great idea to show up to a crime scene armed to the teeth, especially in this district. No need to freak these people out even more. It meant that the alien plumbing zigzagging through my flesh shone through my clothes, but it was no secret I was here on Harmony's behalf.

The owner of the cruiser-liner was a soft-spoken giant with a sharp jawline and purple bags under his eyes. Probably hadn't slept since the incident last night. 'Did she come here often?' I asked, remembering how Wong would give someone a piece of her mind if they stepped out of line, but would give them the shirt off her back if they needed it. You couldn't hate her if you tried.

'All the time.' He pointed to a stool in the corner. 'She'd sit there. Liked three sugars in her coffee. Full-cream milk, always. And yesterday she just . . . snapped.' His Adam's apple bobbed and he shook his head. 'She was good. Wouldn't have hurt anyone. Offered to help clean up a few times. This isn't right.'

'You don't have to tell me,' I said. Reapers didn't *just snap*. Not when they were clean. She'd been targeted like the rest.

'Was she with anyone?' I asked.

'No. Always came alone.'

'She ever talk of family? Friends? Anyone she was seeing?'

'She wasn't chatty. Not like that. She seemed lonely, if I had to guess.'

74

'Do you know where she lived?'

'Sure. Got to have an address to sign on for a cruise.' While he went to check his records, I stooped down to examine Wong's hands. The fingerbones seemed to be moving, curling back and forth, subtly enough you'd never notice if you weren't looking. She'd had machinery installed inside her hands. The cheap kind, if they were malfunctioning like this. She definitely wasn't wired up when I knew her.

Brushing the thought aside, I rifled through Wong's sparse belongings, found nothing of interest until I happened upon a small, magnetically sealed phial in her handbag. Empty, from the weight. I popped it open and sniffed. Sweat broke out on my forehead as I raked in a desperate breath and feverishly snapped the lid closed. My body was all too familiar with the smell of raw stormtech. The stormtech in me writhing in response to it as I tried to think. This phial would have contained the crystallised essence of stormtech, ground down into blue particles the size of salt crystals for oral ingestion.

Stormtech might be locked permanently inside us all, but like any muscle, it doesn't strengthen overnight. It takes time and training to reach the higher levels of ecstasy, building a tolerance for the drug. Training. But, like a shot of anabolic steroids, if you wanted an immediate, supercharged burst of stormtech-induced bliss, you could ingest the stuff. Most people were already overwhelmed by the stormtech inside them. Those who took additional shots were usually recovering addicts, desperate to reclaim their highs, even temporarily.

It seemed Wong had been one of them. I found I was disappointed, although I'd known plenty of Reapers who went down this toxic path, knowing would it'd do to them. The tube was cool in my sweaty palm, my body daring me to prise it open again. Get another whiff. I stuffed it firmly into my suit pocket as the owner returned with Wong's address. It was almost a hundred floors away, scraping the bottom of Compass' barrel.

Stepping from the cruiser onto the boardwalk, I swept a tumble of black hair out of my face, slicking it to the back of my head. The stormtech accelerates cellular growth, which means hair and nails grow faster. I hadn't trimmed it in almost a week and it was starting to fall down to my neck in blue-black waves. I strode past rows of hotels, apartments, restaurants, libraries and attractions fashioned in the style of an open-air city harbour. Cafes advertised unique coffee blends and cocktails, while music and the scent of seafood wafted from open windows. Glass galleries, sculpted in the shape of animal skulls, loomed overhead.

That breakfast wrap hadn't been enough, so I grabbed another and watched the early morning swimmers dive and swim in the swell and curl of the whitecaps. Yachts bobbed on the glistening green water, families playing in rocky lagoons in the distance. A ruby-red tree with silver leaves released the scent of cinnamon and lemon as I approached, the branches sensing anyone in the proximity and unfurling towards them. I licked my fingers clean of barbecue sauce and headed in the direction of the Travel Depot, where chainrails, traveltubes and transit hallways would take me to Wong's floor. Light rain scattered down from hidden sprinklers in the asteroid roof. Warm water soaked into my hair and trickled down my back. Bruised thunderheads curled overhead, a pixel storm gathering its breath.

I walked a little quicker, past the various Alien Embassies and Processing Datacentres where arriving travellers of various species stated their business: to trade, visit, or permanently migrate to Compass. Not every species had the best of intentions, especially after the war ended and they'd cottoned-on that humanity's position within the greater galactic community was indeed vulnerable.

Past the harbour area and towards the outskirts of the central city area, I could see the Compass Academy Building, where they studied xenobiology and xenoarchaeology. We've been interested in aliens from the moment we made contact with the Torven four centuries ago. The civilisation had been in its spacefaring infancy when they happened upon and rescued a lone human lungship in deepspace, its engines leaking and life-support on the verge of collapse. In return, Harmony provided living space and a cultural foundation in Compass. No surprises that it helped strengthen the Common politically. Somehow, the word got around to other spacefaring species and they came calling. Some points of contact resulted in skirmishes that didn't end well for either side, while others saw more species joining the Common.

I slowed a fraction and turned away from the rain-streaked Travel Depot terminal to study the Academy building, confirming that I was, as I thought, being followed. Reaper intuition was enough, but a glance in a reflective gable window confirmed it. I got a flash of a slender, pale figure under heavy, hooded clothing. One of the Jackal's men, I suspected, which meant trouble. Couldn't let them know what I was up to.

Time to take them on a little tour.

I casually turned down a rain-slick street and pretended to browse storefronts selling translation software and cruiser-ship passes as I threaded through the stream of recent arrivals bleeding out of the Depot. I had to set a trap for my stalker. But, amped-up by that whiff of stormtech, my body began to itch for a confrontation. My muscles were tightening and my mouth was already thickening with eager saliva. I stamped down on my rising urges as best I could, but after another few blocks I was getting sick of this damn idiot and I couldn't have him breathing down my neck all the way to Wong's place.

Got to love it when the number of options shrinks down to one. Really speeds up the decision-making process.

I turned into an alley clustered with garbage bins and flattened my back against cool brick. Positioning my legs into a fighter's stance, body angled forward. I counted the footsteps and whipped my elbow out. It sunk into my follower's stomach, sending him reeling backwards with a curse.

'You looking for me, mate?' I asked.

Whatever exposed flesh I could see was completely hairless. His skin was pale as bone and covered with smooth glistening scales, like a reptile's. Dark, beady eyes flickered down my body, assessing me. His hands twitched and taloned claws slithered out from the ends of his fingers, glinting in the light. A result of some wacky experimental surgery, recreational augmentations. A moonmetal slingshiv glinted as it danced between his claws. He meant business – which meant he hadn't been sent by the Jackal. That bastard liked to play with his food.

His expression remained stoic as he lashed out with the slingshiv. I parried the first blow, grabbed his arm on the second, dragging him forward as I hooked his leg out from under him and smashed him into the brick wall. I punched the crook of his arm, tried to twist the weapon away, wrapping my arm around his neck. He snarled and crushed me against the wall. My back scraped the bare brick, his slingshiv darting back over his shoulder, aiming for my throat and tearing bloody slashes into my shoulder. Agony and stormtech burned through me as I locked my arm around his throat in an iron grip and pulled. He spluttered, struggling for air as I pulled harder, harder, his legs flailing, our muscles straining, saliva flying from my teeth.

He must have been seconds from blacking out when he slammed the back of his head into my nose. The momentum sending us twisting away, legs tangled, my grip loosening and him slithering away and kicking me backwards into a stack of garbage disposals. Food waste and stinking liquid exploded into my face, sticking to my clothes. I spat out something foul, my hair matted and sticky. Gritting my teeth, I hurled one of the small plastic bins at my assailant's face and it smashed into his chest, garbage spattering out. The stormtech strummed through my nerve centres as I swooped in to deliver two iron-fisted blows to his stomach, sent another smashing across his head. He ducked under my third blow, swiping sideways at me with his claws, digging into the skin and leaving burning gashes down my sides. I growled, threw my hand up to protect my throat and earned a searing claw slash across my forearm. I hunched forward, taking the blow with my shoulder, ramming into him and sending him reeling backwards. I slammed my open palm into his nose with a wet crunch, breaking it. He skidded backwards, still clutching the slingshiv. Blood and hot garbage soaked my stinking underskin. I knew his style now. Fast and shallow. Death of a dozen cuts, they called it.

I circled him, arms held up in a defensive position, ensuring my back wasn't to the wall. Chest heaving, squashing my body's urge to pounce first. Half the fight is trapping your enemy, tricking him into making a move he can't resist before turning on him.

Wait for it. Wait for it.

He went for me, just as I'd hoped. I sidestepped, chopped a blow into his sternum, clapped a cupped hand on his ear, and finished with a vicious strike at his windpipe. He coughed and spluttered as I ripped the slingshiv out of his claws.

He froze.

I realised I was holding it against his jugular. White-hot blade ready to slice. The black gel of the grip vibrated against my touch, readjusting to my hand. The stormtech thrashed in my chest like a livewire. One flick of the wrist was all it would take.

I imagined blood jetting out, spraying the brick walls red. The thought jolted me and I mentally backed away. Questions first, then I'd decide what to do with him.

'Who are you?' I wheezed, keeping him firmly in place and making sure his claws kept their distance from my eye sockets, 'and what the hell do you want?' No answer. Only his equally laboured panting. I squeezed harder and leaned close to a pale ear. 'You're wasting my time. That makes me unhappy. When I'm unhappy, I do things I shouldn't. So: what do you want?'

His only response was a sneer. As the artificial sun peeked out from behind thick clouds, its rays streaked down to knife across my face, blinding me. He used the advantage to go limp, dropping to the floor like a boneless fish and propelling himself out of my range. We faced each other across the stinking alley, chests heaving. My body gurgling with the rush of adrenaline, my hand clenching his slingshiv. Sweat stung my wounds. Part of me hoped he'd rush me, body hunched forward in combat-anticipation even as the other part of me clamped down on the feeling.

He flexed his claws as he backed away, bloodied nails extending with the sound of his knuckles cracking. I spat on the pavement, my eyes never leaving his. *I'll be back for you*, his expression said as he ducked out of the alleyway and into the crowded Travel Depot. I sank down, breathing hard and fast, as if a switch had been thrown and snapping me out of combat-mode. Because my job wasn't hard enough, now I had an augmented stalker on my back and I knew zero about what he wanted from me.

At least I could go to Wong's place unmolested now. I double-checked my nose wasn't actually broken, and that's when I noticed the rivulets of blood dripping down my arms and spattering at my feet.

*

I burst into my apartment, ignored the Rubix's chirp of *Welcome home, Mister Fukasawa,* and shouldered the bathroom door open for med supplies.

That bald bastard had cut me in half a dozen places, knowing exactly where to make his mark. No arteries nicked, though not for a lack of trying. The wounds sent sour shivers up my body. Choking down the garbage fumes, I dumped the sealed bags of medical equipment into the sink and sifted through them, the effort of resisting my churning stormtech leaving me in a cold sweat. I found a hypo for the pain, antibodies for infection, and a Sealer to cauterise the wounds. I shrugged carefully out of my soiled underskin to treat the first wound.

Only I didn't have any.

Nothing on my chest, nothing on my hands. Nothing on my forearms, nothing on my shoulders where metal had cleaved deep into my skin. I had dozens of knife-thin slashes to my underskin and clothes, but no cuts in my flesh.

I leaned back against cold marble and peered down my torso. Blue streams of stormtech were twisting across the ridgeline of my breastbone, over my muscles and between my ribs. Between the alleyway and my apartment, the stormtech had sealed up the lacerations, only an echo of the stinging pain remaining. I'd been so unused to the stormtech doing anything like it I hadn't even noticed. Shouldn't even have been possible. When I detoxed the stormtech's influence over my body, the ability to self-heal had gone with it.

Or not.

I ran my hand over my chest. Half an hour ago I'd had a deep wound right above the breastbone. Now the skin was unbroken and ivy-like strands of blue were whispering over the length of my ribcage, weaving deeper into my system, stirred up by the adrenaline and danger. I squeezed my eyes shut. I'd come so close to killing that man. I shuddered, but something inside me relished the idea. Addiction to bottomless aggression and desire to conquer and destroy had been threaded into every single Reaper. I'd spent years trying to rip it out.

I sprawled against the cold tiles. Wong had still being taking stormtech after all this time. Had it killed her? Or she was targeted like the rest because she'd been a Reaper? Had Artyom known what the poisoned stormtech would do to her? If he had, how could he possibly justify it?

Whatever he was doing, whatever path he wanted to walk in life, it was his own. If things had been different, I'd have let him go his way and I'd go mine, as he wanted. Let Harmony deal with him. Even though the threads of our lives were too tightly entwined for me to slice him off without tearing a part of myself away, too. But our sister had always been the cord that truly tied us together and I couldn't let her down. *Promise me, Vak*, Kasia had said. *Promise you'll take care of him.*

I'd failed once. Now, though I couldn't stand by and let Reapers get killed, I couldn't desert Artyom, either. No matter what, he was my brother and a promise, even a broken one, is a promise.

I exhaled and clenched my fist. Bone-deep biotech spread from my chest, down to my arms like cold fire. And I wasn't entirely sure that I did not welcome it.

8

Don't Breathe

I'd never believed Compass could really function until I arrived here. Cities stacked on top of cities on top of *more* cities, squeezed inside an asteroid. It sounded like one hell of an eyesore, and a complicated one at that. Only when I'd been here for a month and had done some exploring did I understand how wrong I'd been. The floorplan had been meticulously designed from top to bottom. The architects hadn't been messing around. Turns out, they did exactly what countless habitats, orbitals, moonbases, stations and planets did all over the Common: developed economic infrastructures.

The poorer, less privileged folks live towards the lower levels of Compass, typically on floors infested with industrial centres, dockyards, factories, printing farms, flophouses and slums that are just as shabby as they were in the Construction Era, when Compass was first formed. A little further up the social ladder are lowlevels teeming with marketplaces, seedy hangouts, space-docks run by crimelords, and crowded metropolitan streets. Go higher and you'll find the majority of Compass inhabitants on midlevels, cleaner cities containing coffeehouses, bars, sprawling apartment blocks, lively entertainment, trading centres, shopping plazas, areas of community living. Higher still are the central business districts, townhouses, opulent spaceports, theatres, waterfront restaurants, and well-off suburbs. The pinnacle of the asteroid is honeycombed with floors terraformed with beaches, parklands, forests, snowy mountains, vacation resorts, private hangar bays, hotels, and extreme superstructures only the stinking rich could afford. Scattered between them are smatterings of private spaces, subsectors and random floors no one quite knew what to do with or how to place. Alien species can be found either living in their own designated spaces rigged with species-appropriate life-support systems, or spread throughout the infrastructure. Nothing is quarantined or as strictly defined as people like to think, with the ecosystem of lifestyles, micro-societies, peoples and species bleeding and meshing into each other. You'd need a lifetime to explore all of it, let alone the several, kilometre-long empty spaces still under construction. Not to mention the Void Zones, still sealed off and under repair after Harvest artillery fire had shredded any chance of them being habitable.

So, when I emerged from a winding maze of stairwells, access tunnels and transit hallways to arrive on Changhao, one of the lowest levels of Compass, where Wong had her apartment, I knew what to expect. Cubed, windowless compartments had been stacked six or seven storeys high like discoloured boxes. Mostly shipping containers from the dockyard, retrofitted into living spaces. Purple smoke slithered from burner stubs and up through crisscrossing stairways and balconies jutting like rusty ribcages. Powerlines and pipes thick as my arm scaled buildings, a good half of them frayed or leaking onto the streets. Hippomechs, used for transporting heavy objects, rested on polished bogies. Neon words writhing in mid-air advertised cheap accommodation, clubs, vidgame arcades and sensory simulation cubes. Thick steam billowed from grimy kitchens and street stalls. Only a little of the atmosphere's damp, hot scent leaked through my helmet filters, but it was enough to make me gag.

Amateur stormdealers and drug lords weren't even bothering to hide here. Every second corner had sellers lingering on the streets. Customers swapping cards filled with Commoner-credits for sealed bags. Grimy drug-dens and distribution centres sat out in the open in alleyways, the chemical reek spreading like fog, their presence fused to the infrastructure like cancer clinging to the bone. If you worked out in the open, you were either stupid, or knew there was no chance of getting caught, because you owned the floor. I'd missed the warning in my shib alerting me that I was in dangerous, controlled territory. I'd probably already been spotted. Just as well I was fully suited up in my armour again. If they wanted to take me on, they'd have one hell of a time.

My palmerlog chimed, a message from Kowalski growing in blue text across my overlay. Scattered water droplets punched through the visualisation. I was afraid she had another Reaper death for me, but she was just fishing for an update. I replied I'd examined the body and would keep her informed on any leads I followed up. Mentioning the fight would only invite questions, and I wanted to take all factors into account before I made a move.

The message disintegrated into space. I passed by two over-sized robots standing guard outside a building covered in gang glyphs. Their cinderblock heads, black metal bodies and claw-like hands were beaded with oily water like thousands of tiny liquid eyes. Behind them, a creaking staircase led down to a fighting pit, yells and cheers echoing up the stairwell. Grim had dragged me to one of those on my first day here. 'They've just managed to make them legal,' he'd screamed over the tumult.

Sweat and death had hung in the air like a weight on our shoulders. I'd heard about null-gravity knife fighting arenas, but never seen anything like that. People would bring robots, custom-built droids, even exotic creatures captured from all over the Common. The rarer the creature, the bigger the bet. I'd stared at the cages and a freak show of claws, oily feathers, scales, clacking mandibles, hissing fangs and bulging eyes stared back. The nearest cage had housed a little monster with a leathery, carmine-spotted hide and a retractable jaw. It went berserk when it saw me. The owner, a cowl-wearing Torven, had shoved me away and tried to calm his pet down.

But the real attraction was human fights.

'Bets double when they've got stormtech,' Grim told me as two men battled it out in the pit below us while people cheered them on in a dozen languages. 'They've been trying to get the ban lifted since the Reaper War ended. Said it was insensitive while the war was going on, but now the war is over ...'

My hands were sweaty and tight now as the sound of fists striking flesh reached me on the street and the stormtech leaped up inside me. I'd forced the sensations back then as I did now, the crowd's roars echoing behind me as I homed in on Wong's quarters. The waypoint took me through a flashy club to get to the housing blocks, all other access points blocked off. Done intentionally to drum up business, of course. Wasn't like anyone would be swinging by to change it.

The club was packed, people crowding around stained tables cluttered with drinks and nasty-looking stains. This floor was known for its body augmentations, with plenty of its participants gathered up here. I saw chrome and alloy hands gripping glasses and tumblers. Arms and legs that were whirling meshes of gears, tubes and artificial nerve joints. Bionic eyes twitching in metallic faces and torsos crawling with internal machinery. Subsurface lighting scattered reflections across flesh injected with skingrafts, turned scaly and leathery, growing horns and antlers and wings or sprouting silicone feathers. In the smoky glow, it looked like I'd stumbled into a nightmare, like a demented child had stitched together random parts of animals and machines and people. Most of these people were unable to afford to have fingers or limbs reprinted in a medclinic, so they had volunteered to be experiments. They'd let scientists and cyberneticists test unorthodox and bleeding-edge procedures on them, either for their own personal fascination or so they could be perfected for those who could afford it.

Like that was ever going to go well.

Several rotated to look at me. The only defence I had was a metal projectile I could shoot out of my armour's sleeve, but I'd hoped not to use it.

The bartender was a skinnie, the blue thrumming up and down his chest as he mixed expensive drinks from cheap ingredients. The bright-red pockmarks along his arms were tell-tale signs of a synthsilver user. The liquid was meant to be squeezed into the eye, but hardcore addicts always went for the veins. Hunched on a battered couch next to me, a man rubbed a smear of dark-grey grimwire along his stained gums. His body shuddered, eyes rolling back as the hit spread through his system. He'd have hallucinations for hours.

Doesn't matter where you go in the universe, places like this are going to exist.

I could feel people watching me as I exited the club and climbed a rusty stairwell through the guts of tenements plastered with neon. Beyond grimy and smashed windows, the floor stretched into a rabbit warren of makeshift housing and prefab metal cubes, crisscrossing staircases and ladders snaking through the fissures between the building. The clanging of metal and revving of engines echoed through the network. I felt like a rat trapped in an endless metal maze.

I passed by at least a dozen more stormdealers selling their wares from dimly lit storage units, before I found Sam's door. I swiped her card and stepped in.

The smell slapped me like a soggy towel in the face. A sweet, syrupy smell like wet hot glucose crusted on skin, triggering my stormtech. I snapped off my helmet filters and flicked my rebreather on, chopping the smell off. Cool, clean oxygen flooded my lungs. I swallowed and reached a hand to the wall to steady myself.

Wong might have been doing Harmony's rehab, but she hadn't been quitting by a long shot.

The room was practically dripping with stormtech. Constellations of chemical attributions popped up on my HUD. Her furniture was overturned and smashed apart, mostly stained with grimwire and synthsilver. Empty phials and hypodermic needles crunched under my heavy boots. Almost everyone who Shreds turns to some other vice to achieve the same high. I knew first-hand it never works. Because nothing's ever, ever good enough.

I still remember surrendering myself to rehab. The wet, skintight fabric of the sensory-deprivation suit sealing around me. The tendrils and inner abrasives stirring to life against my flesh. The multitude of buckles and full-body restraints biting into my skin as they strapped me down, secured blinders and mufflers over my eyes and ears. The algae stink as they lowered me into the soundproof tank and pumped me with anti-stimulant chemicals to combat the stormtech and ease the withdrawal symptoms. No matter how I begged or thrashed, they wouldn't untie me, wouldn't free me from the tank. If they had, I'd probably have killed myself.

That was Stage One. Stage Two had been a series of training and rehabilitation exercises, working my muscles, psychotherapy, counselling. Reconditioning my mind and de-programming my body, freeing me from seeking physical exertion. Prying free all the instincts the stormtech had hammered into me until I had a grip on my urges again.

If I opened my suit one crack, breathed the air in this stormtech-drenched room, years of agonizing work could be undone. My skin itched and demanded it with pheromone-induced hunger. But this mattered more. The Reapers mattered more.

I quickly sifted through the gutted room. Harmony couldn't have realised it was this bad or they'd never have sent me here. Too great a risk of losing me down the gravity well.

Sam's sanity levels were scrawled across the room. The scratches and fist-sized dents in the walls. The dry blood in the bathroom. The sweat-stained bed sheets. I could almost see her in here, screaming and weeping and slowly driving herself mad, knowing she'd kill anyone who walked through her door and probably then herself. There are a million symptoms that come with Shredding, none of them pretty. Rehab had been her last resort. Someone had noticed she'd relapsed into taking stormtech and used her weakness to murder her.

If that person had been standing in front of me now, I'd have my own murder to explain to Kowalski.

Unless I found the source, Wong wouldn't be the last Reaper or skinnie to die like this. At least I now knew why Wong had machinery jammed inside her hands. She'd volunteered for human-modification experiments just like the people outside. Some cyberneticist in a backalley clinic had used her as a human lab rat in exchange for some meagre drug money.

The only source of luxury in the room was a small curving viewport that peered out into a star-speckled space. Wasn't a real view of space, of course, only a live-feed. Most of Compass was buried deep inside the asteroid; only a lucky few apartments on the fringes got a direct view into space. I switched it off and searched through the drawers and compartments built into the walls to conserve space, trying to be impersonal as I rifled through my dead friend's possessions. I wasn't sure what I was looking for until I found it. A small case tucked under the bed, filled with half a dozen empty stormtech phials. It hadn't been the suppressors that had killed her. Poisoned stormtech had done the same trick.

At the bottom of the case was a small strip of paper with a number and code punched into it. I angled the paper in the light and caught the words *Upper Market* in iridescent small print. I had no idea where the hell that was. Kowalski would. A white window expanded on my shib, filled with glowing blue text as I sent Kowalski the details. No response. It was well into the night and she was offline at this hour. Couldn't afford to wait around. Grim had to know where this place was.

There was also a small metal tag, hanging by a length of chain. It was emblazoned with the Reaper symbol: a crossed pair of arms, forked with blue lightning. Couldn't believe Wong still had hers. In the field, we were always sealed up in full armour and rarely removed our helmets. So we'd improvised with crossing our arms over our chests gesture. The rest of the Common thought the gesture was a salute, a greeting. But they'd never understand. It had been how we recognised family. A sudden lump surfaced in my throat. Wong had been a Reaper until the very end. Like Alcatraz. Like all of us.

My armour creaked as I stood. My ragged breathing echoed in my helmet, sweat running in rivulets down my arms. My heart was beating unusually loud and fast against my ribs. I placed my hand on the wall, soaking up the last, miserable memories of my friend. She had deserved so much better.

Why would someone do this to you, Wong?

9

Needle in an Asteroid

The Upper Market wasn't just a few shops. That would have been too easy. It was an entire floor of Compass *dedicated* to them. It was never closed, never empty. It formed a honeycomb of thousands of shops, stalls and alleys, access tunnels and looping passageways, stairwells and multilevels. An urban jigsaw, all its pieces twisting and bleeding into one another, squeezing the geometries of their architecture into the space. I could spend hours exploring.

At any other time.

'You weren't kidding,' I said to Grim as we entered the floor. 'It's huge.'

His grin ate up his whole face. 'Told you.'

Grim had insisted on wearing his neon skeleton underskin, and I'd long learned that you can't talk Grim out of something he's into. So we made a hell of an odd couple: me a two-metre tall guy covered in heavy armour, walking beside a skeleton flickering with colours. Following the attack yesterday, I kept scanning our surroundings. It didn't escape Grim's notice. 'If you're trying to make me feel safe, it's not working.'

'Just being cautious,' I told him.

'What'd he look like, anyway?' Grim asked as we entered the network of shops.

'Well, he was hairless.'

'Did you check everywhere?' Grim asked breezily.

'Sure. Got him to strip down for inspection when he wasn't trying to stab me in the face with his big, ugly claws.'

'Claws, you say?'

'Yeah. Looked like he'd escaped from a body-splicing lab.'

'Almost. He was probably a Shifter.'

'A what?'

'A Shifter, Vak.' Grim threw two bone-arms up into the air with strained patience, as if this was common knowledge. 'They're into cybernetics. You know, tweaking their physiology and biochemistry, trying to become human-animal hybrids.'

'Very interesting. Maybe we should focus instead on the part where the tosser tried to kill me?'

'Why didn't you take this to Kowalski?'

'I don't want it getting to Kindosh just yet,' I said. 'Not without knowing for sure why I was attacked. Same goes for Wong's death being stormtech-related, not a result of poisoned rehab suppressors – I want to know for sure what happened before going back to them.'

That was part of it. But these were also Reapers, and I was going to do right by them. The war was over, so many of the good men and women I'd fought with had turned to ash and blood in the wind, buried in an unmarked grave on distant planets. But that didn't mean our debts to each other were gone, or forgotten.

A million Upper Market smells swirled around me: the earthy bite of burnt coffee and freshly brewed sticky chai, spices and sizzling chicken, sickly-sweet candies and dairy. Around-the-clock eateries spun food and drink for the crush of people, offering delicacies from faraway locales. The display windows of booths and stalls were lined up one sweeping row, showcasing tropical fruit and dripping green noodles, sweet pastries and sticky rice, bubbling vats of meat marinating in their own juices, as well as less tempting fare like spongy red moss, deep-fried insects, vacuum-sealed meats from offworld colonies, and a squirming jelly that looked about as appetising as nutrition cubes.

We burrowed down the narrow, tangled streets, pipework and ribbed cabling squeezing past the crowd. The pixelsheeting above us had been set to mimic multicoloured tent-cloth, snapping and billowing in an imaginary breeze. On New Vladi we'd had big, sprawling markets like this on the first day of each month. No matter the weather, you could guarantee that wizened old babushkas and young smokeheads alike would be setting up and selling everything from robots that could shapeshift into different animals to replicas of old samurai weapons. I'd taken Artyom to one a few times, on weekends. Though once I'd turned my back for three seconds to look longingly at a katana I'd never afford, and he'd disappeared. Just vanished. I'd scoured the crowded market for him for hours, terrified he'd been picked up by one of the gangs. I'd imagined them holding him down and pouring lye into his eyes like they'd done to a girl the previous month.

I'd eventually found him sitting by the water fountain, watching a three-dee display. I'd been relieved and wanted to pound some sense into him in equal measure. I probably would have, if Kasia hadn't taught me better. He'd seen me and grinned his cheeky grin before asking if I'd buy an album for him.

He seemed so different now. Could Kowalski be onto something, suspecting he was laced with a biochemical targeting agent or suicide trigger? Could it be he was trying to protect me? Or was he in it with both feet, and genuinely wanted nothing to do with me?

I wouldn't find out unless I kept investigating.

People and aliens from across the Common filled the network of shops around us, text in over a dozen languages vying for our attention. Everything was on sale, from home decor and designer underskins to Rubix upgrades and the latest hardware. A squinting, grumpy woman sat buried in a nest of squirming wires, fibre-optic cables and multi-adapters. Children squatted atop teetering piles of storage crates, sneaking baklava and halva from the Middle-Eastern grocery, while a nearby Torven claimed to offer the best prices on lungship modifications across Compass. Graphic designers sketched paintjobs for chainships and men tinkered with hardware at cluttered workstations. A Torven wearing protective optics and a thick utility harness used a laser chisel to sculpt asteroidal debris into jewellery. Everything was in motion, every available square inch filled.

'There're a lot of Torven here,' I said. I'd never been so surrounded by aliens before.

'They have a nose for business,' Grim told me. 'When they first made contact with us, one look at our shipyards and spaceports and they knew there was money to be made that they'd never get from trading with other species.'

Something caught my eye in a shop. Someone was *actually* selling figurines of fully armoured Reapers, replica Reaper weapons, and what I could only assume were Shenoi plushies. I shook my head and glanced through the frosted glass of a Rubix mindmeld station. People sitting in uncomfortable-looking chairs, neuragel readers plugged into their skull sockets. Building AI was one thing, but every smart Rubix had a human mind behind it: their personalities and kinks were copied directly from human brains. It was living on after death, in a way. Grim had pondered doing it and I'd said that one of him was more than enough.

We reached the central market plaza, its full weight and scale almost crushing. Somehow, we had to find one seller in all *this*. We might have a stand number, but half the stalls had their tags torn off or faded away with use, and Grim had been unable to find any coherent system. With multiple levels, sub-flooring, and the haphazard geometry of the plaza, I didn't know how the hell anyone functioned.

We paused so Grim could pick up some films in a shop dedicated to them, while I tried to get our bearings. Even the shop was a maze. A shoddy staircase spiralled up through multiple floors of towering shelves and platforms. Each platform was an access point for films, soundtracks, collector's items, records, framed posters, and memorabilia from specific decades of Earth's history, each shelf sagging under the weight. I asked the owner for directions while Grim was busy, but he seemed as mystified as us by the system. 'I've been looking for these *everywhere*,' Grim said when we finally left, a bundle of discs in his hands. 'Didn't think they even *existed* anymore.'

That was our only success. The maze of cluttered corridors and stairwells began to smear together. I swear the only thing we *didn't* see was the stall number I was looking for. After walking past endless software stations, budget beauticians, shib installers, snackbars, parlours where aliens of multiple species lounged in micro-massage cradles, graphic designers for chain-ships, and tailors selling nanothreads that changed fabric and style by the hour to match the latest fashion, I was fed up. At this rate we'd still be searching as the next Reaper Blued Out on the streets.

Sometimes, you've got to grab the bull by the horns.

'Grim,' I said, 'could you do some slightly illegal hacking for me?'

Grim wolfed down the last few bites of the crepe he'd been eating, smearing a thick glob of cream from the corner of his mouth. 'For you, Vak, anything.'

We found a terminal sitting in a quiet alley of souvenir shops, the dimpled walls covered with graffiti. Grim swatted away the gaudy holos about daily offers, remotely hacking into the terminal mainframe with his shib. His visual cortex glazed over with flitting icons as he did his Deep Dive, digging through the composite layers of virtual worlds. 'If there's a shop with that ID registered with Compass, it'll be in the mainframe,' Grim said, his voice distorted from accessing the hardware, as if coming from a ghostly commslink signal.

'And you couldn't do this remotely?'

'Hell no. Need to be directly in the terminal if you don't want to get locked out. Watch the projection.' A phantasmagorical riot of colours erupted around us in a wild blizzard, like an explosion of paint frozen in time. Membrane-thin strands grew between them like a nervous system in fast-forward, spiralling away in bewildering complex geometries that hinted at a larger world beneath the surface. A small cube, presumably Grim's presence, navigated among them. I guessed we had a minute before someone spotted us. 'Got to do a little virtual hunting is all.'

'And we'll find it? Just like that?'

His body twitched with convulsions, arm hairs all going stiff and rigid like bristles. Looked like he was having a seizure, but I think the little guy *liked* doing this. 'Not so simple. Got to get the Rubix's attention, make a few purchases to show we're in the market.'

Before I could stop him, Grim had already purchased a massive fish tank, an antique diving suit, a vinyl record player, three Rubix skins, five buckets of nitromethane, seventy kilos of Torven snacks, and a year's worth of rental space at the dockyard.

The virtual projection around us chimed with orders, the sum total reaching offensively expensive heights. 'You're in trouble if I end up paying for any of this,' I warned.

'You worry too much. It's all going on a stolen account.'

'You do this often, don't you?'

He grinned, his head lolling backwards. 'Would you believe me if I told you no?'

The colours abruptly exploded with counterintrusion icons, the lines between them pulsing red with fury. A series of torpedoes appeared, swiftly homing in on Grim's presence. He seemed unfazed.

'Ah. The security Rubix isn't too happy we're messing around in his mainframe,' Grim muttered, his virtual presence darting away. The flashing torpedoes followed like sharks sniffing out blood. 'It's already started a countdown. Why can't they just let guests tamper with them every once in a while?'

'What happens if they catch you?' I asked tentatively.

Muscles twitched down Grim's legs. 'Alarms go off, security drones get called, and we get sprayed with tracking pheromones, chased down and arrested. The usual.'

I felt my teeth gritting. I decided to trust Grim's judgement and watched him play a cat-and-mouse game with the security Rubix, the AI getting more and more outraged, with its icons flashing so frantically I suspected Grim was moments from triggering an alarm. Knowing him, he was seeing how far he could taunt the AI before it turned on him. 'Aha! Found our shop!'

He disconnected from the system, his body twitching, hands shaking, eyes bloodshot and sparking with shib warning icons as the projection around us disappeared like mist. 'You okay?' I asked. Never knew how much these Deep Dives messed with his grey matter.

'I enjoyed that, actually.' Grim clapped me hard on the back. 'Now. Let's pay a little visit to your drug dealer.'

Turned out the shop was at the very back of the Markets, built into the concavity of the asteroid. Little wonder we'd never found it. A figure blurred beyond the red-tinted window frames, a chime sounding as the door dilated open for us.

It was a robotics hire and parts shop, crammed with enough stock to last a century. Hippomechs, broken drones, and droid appendages were scattered like discarded toys on every available workspace, as if the owner was allergic to throwing anything out. The room smelled musky, like burnt tea leaves. Chunks had been carved out of the asteroid, connected to a nervous system of chutes that wormed through the rock and allowed deliveries across Compass.

The owner was a Bulkava. He was wearing a black and red suit with a helmet, elongated to fit the alien's skull shape. I heard the quiet hum of a rebreather system built into the alien's suit, thick cables extending from internal machinery and plugged into the base of his helmet. Two large eyes darted around in a furry, mammalian face, the slender creature a good half-metre shorter than me. I'd spotted the aliens around Compass, but never seen one up close before.

'They're not dangerous,' Grim murmured to me as the door snapped shut, cutting off the noisy chaos. 'They just can't tolerate our atmosphere. Outside their dedicated biospheres they have to wear suits and helmets rigged with a life-support system at all times.'

'Customers!' The alien had a high-pitched, strained voice. He had two pairs of arms, each sporting four fingers, all four lifted in greeting as we approached. 'Oh, it's you again!' It took me a second to realise he was speaking to me. I cocked my head, took another step. 'Oh! No, no, no. My mistake! So sorry!' He gave something resembling a bow. 'I am Aras. How can I help you? Do you have an order? Anything you like?'

I slid the e-stamp across the scuffed counter. 'Got a pick-up to make,' I said, hoping Grim would be smart enough to play along.

Aras swept some clutter on the counter aside and turned the stamp around towards him. 'For who?'

'Samantha Wong. She needs her delivery today,' I said.

'Of course, of course,' the alien said, lower-left arm reaching behind the counter while his other scratched his chest. 'Hmm. I do not believe she's placed any new orders...'

'Orders for these?' I asked, swallowing a lump of anger and holding the phial up in front of Aras' face. 'Look familiar?'

Aras recoiled as if I'd shoved a particle gun in his face. 'I... I... yes. No!' He began to scurry away. 'I think its closing time. Do excuse me...'

I blocked his escape route. 'Where are you getting this stuff from?' The picture of Alcatraz flickered in my mind and I had to physically squash back the anger, stormtech squirming like tentacles inside me. Aras didn't answer, but maybe he was finding it hard to speak after I'd grabbed him by the chest straps of his harness and hoisted him against the wall. The alien flailed at me with all six limbs, but said nothing. 'Don't want to talk to me? Fine.' I made to drop him. 'You can talk to Harmony instead.'

I wasn't about to hand him over, of course. But Aras didn't know that. The alien made a throat-clearing noise before squeaking out: 'There's an offworld supplier! They supply me and I have to sell to humans here and send the money to my family!'

I'd scanned the room. No chemical evidence he was manufacturing the product himself. Certainly not here. 'Who's your supplier? Where are they based?'

'On Vilanov.' It was a shipping moonbase, one of the many that clustered within serviceable shipping range of Compass. 'We have an exclusive contract!'

'And they're Bulkava, too?' I was guessing, and Aras hesitated before nodding.

'How long have you been dealing?' Grim butted in.

'Two months.' Aras shrugged helplessly with his upper arms

and held up one finger on each lower hand. 'Ever since I came here.'

I tagged the intel as high-priority and sent it over to Kowalski, although it was tenuous at best. These incidents had kicked off almost a year ago. There were networks of stormdealer syndicates and narcotic manufacturers threaded through Compass, many likely based on this very level. If Aras had any involvement, it was minimal. He likely didn't even know his product was tainted. Whoever I was hunting wanted the chaos spread wide. They'd probably supplied it to third parties to throw us off their trail.

I might have all I wanted from him, but he still had a direct link to Wong and we'd have to turn him over to Harmony. Doesn't matter why they're doing it, I've got zero patience for drug traffickers. I set the struggling alien down, and he made a great show of readjusting his harness and smoothing down his creased suit. 'Are you—' he gestured helplessly '—one of them?'

I was going to deny it, but the lump moving along my breastbone seemed to discourage lying. 'Yeah. I'm *one of them*.' A sudden idea struck me. 'When I first came in, who did you think I was?'

The alien cocked his head. 'You look . . . very similar to another customer of mine.'

Grim adopted an expression of mock offence. 'Oh right. All humans look the same to you, that it?'

I rolled my eyes as Aras made that desperate gesture again. 'No, no, no.' He nodded at me. 'He has the same hair, the same looks—'

'This man?' I thrust my palmerlog with the picture of Artyom in Aras' face. There was no way to gauge the alien's reaction as he scooped up the palmerlog with his lower right hand and studied it.

'Yes, that is him,' he said.

I took my palmerlog back and snapped it shut. 'Does he buy stormtech from you?'

'No, no! Legitimate customer!'

'Customer for what?' When Aras didn't respond, I leaned closer. 'Selling stormtech is one thing, Aras. Down here, someone might turn a blind eye to it. But what you've been selling? Your customers end up dead, hours later. That's bad. And selling your lethal product to Reapers? That's even worse. Now, you can answer my questions, or you can answer to Harmony.' I locked sights with the alien's dark, fearful eyes. 'Do you understand?'

Aras fell apart like a disassembled rifle.

'He rents a Hippomech!' Aras skirted over to the bulky, four-wheeled robot and patted its triangular head with affection. 'There's nothing wrong with that!'

'How often?' I asked. The stormtech had started to fold into my thorax again and all my words came out raspy and sandpapered. 'What for?'

'Once a week,' said Aras, tugging at his suit. 'Most weeks.'

'You only need Hippomechs if you're lugging something chunky,' said Grim slowly. 'Or something you don't want seen.'

They'd snapped that picture of Artyom a week ago. The same day he routinely left the alehouse early. 'He's renting one again tonight, isn't he?'

'Err, yes?'

'Where's he collecting it from?' I asked, voice still coarse with stormtech-induced thickness.

'From the Warren,' Aras muttered. 'In the Hovergardens.'

'That's at the back of Level Forty-Seven,' murmured Grim, turning over an expensive-looking component. 'It's a dump. Whole place smells like a nursing home.'

We were finally zeroing in on him. I couldn't take the risk of going back to the bar – not after Kowalski's tip that every cog in the stormdealer's machine was under scrutiny. But if knew where he *would* be, I could pick up his trail without the risk of triggering any biochemical hardware in his head. It was a slim lead, but if it took me to the rest of the organisation then I could keep Artyom out of it. Maybe even stay away from him, as he wanted. I took a step back from Aras.

'Luckily for you, you've been helpful,' I told the anxious alien. 'So, here's what's going to happen. You're going to pack up shop and leave Compass this week. You can take your robotics business all the way out into a deepspace spaceport for all I care. As long as you're not on Compass. Do that, and I won't turn you in to Harmony. If you ever *breathe* the word stormtech again, let alone sell it, you'll be hearing from me. Do you understand?'

He nodded feverishly, wringing all four of his hands together. 'Of course, of course, of course. I'll leave today! I promise.' He gave me a final parting glance. 'You really do look like him, you know. Do say hello for me!'

'Don't worry,' I smiled, stormtech leaping through me, 'I will.'

10

The Warren

Grim hadn't been exaggerating about the Upper Markets, and he wasn't exaggerating about the Warren either. The streets were broken and cracked landscapes of asphalt and concrete, caked with ash and grime. The rooftops were nightmares of warped steel and exposed rubble, spilling down into dark alleyways. Turgid wastewater dripped down rusted stairwells. The temperature-regulating systems were broken, leaving the level freezing and stinking like damp, rotten leaves. It was cold even by New Vladi standards, cold enough to form a thin layer of frost on my armour. Blocks of derelict buildings were long abandoned, windows like dead eyes, doors boarded up with electromagnetic seals, chainlink fencing with *DO NOT ENTER* signs in floating, blinking letters. As if anyone *wanted* to come here.

The Hippomech had already arrived, and Artyom could be here at any moment. I couldn't risk missing it and bolted straight here from the Upper Markets. Although I'd barely slept since Harmony picked me up, the stormtech was feeding me energy, combating the exhaustion. Back when I was all Blued Up, I could go full speed ahead without a wink of sleep for days. Great if you're besieged by Harvesters, or have an assault charge to lead or an outpost to recapture. But what the stormtech gives, it'll eventually ask back, and I was waiting for the Crash Down to smash my system like a tonne of bricks.

The faded remains of adboards indicated this had been the old Latin Quarter. Digi-art murals of sun-baked Sicilian landscapes and Mediterranean beaches adorned the walls of open villas and espresso cafes, digital renditions of waves crashing on sandy shores on an endless loop. The Reaper War had left scorch marks where the fighting had been especially savage, leaving shelled-out highrises and streets across this section of Compass. They said they'd dug out all the bodies from the rubble, but I've seen what smelter-grenades do to human flesh. This floor was a graveyard. Always would be.

Nominally, the Warren was sealed off, but you'd always find skinnies holing up in hideaways called ratnests. I could hear them twitching under rags. Scampering in the dark, their rattling coughs echoing through the tenement halls and dilapidated warehouses like gunshots. Thousands of people, hiding away and left to rot in this miserable place.

Grim waited on the other end of the commslink, sitting in his technest for backup and auxiliary support. He'd already combed the Warren for any surveillance tech that might track Artyom's movements. He'd turned up empty, but remained on watch as a contingency. If my brother was under scrutiny, I'd stand down. I didn't want Artyom to be at risk just because I was tailing him.

I'd set myself up in the shelled remains of some kind of office building. A bank, maybe. I peered through a grime-smeared window into the heart of the Warren's spider-webbing of blackened streets. The Hippo was stored for collection mere metres away. I flicked on my HUD's spectral and thermal amplifiers and the world flickered into an overlay of cool colours and sound. My readouts scrolling with stats. Assuming our alien drug dealer hadn't been lying through his teeth, Artyom would be along soon, and it'd be impossible to miss him.

I squatted on a mouldy old couch, rolling my shardpistol in my hands. Shardpistols fire crystals that punch into human skin. The more lethal versions detonate on impact, burying toxic-coated shards into the target's body. Both are illegal, of course, the latter more so. I'd asked Grim to get one for me and, never one to let the tedious complications of legality bother him, he'd passed me one fresh out of its foam casing in less than two hours. I wore it like a knuckle duster, and when I flicked a button the weapon coalesced into my hand like millions of shiny insects scrambling over each other. Standard carbon-black stock. Long, thin barrel. Red holographic sights. No ammo. Like all ranged weapons, shardpistols autoprinted projectiles, something that had given us a monstrous advantage over Harvest. It varied on the calibre and weapon, but you could generally fire over two-hundred rounds before inserting a cartridge of quickmatter – the baseline material all printers used.

I flicked the shardpistol on and off, on and off, on and off. A habit I'd had ever since I was issued one, a year into enlisted duty. I'd still struggled to wear my bulky armour in the higher gravity. My fireteam had been deployed to a small city on the broken outskirts of a wasteland, rescuing stranded civilians and securing outposts abandoned by Harvest. We knew something was wrong the moment we entered the city outskirts, unease rippling from man to man. 'Weapons up, eyes open,' Alcatraz had said while following Ratchet, our quick-footed scout. Cable and Myra had my flank as we moved through abandoned concourses and desolate streets. There was a rank, sour stink in the air as we followed the shattered storefronts. Splatters and smears of dark blood congealed across the pavements. It was the silence that got to me. Like the quiet after an avalanche: total, complete, utter silence.

Didn't take us long to discover everyone in the town was dead. Men, women, children, the elderly, everyone. Gunned down, dragged from their homes and into a flaming pyre in the middle of the town square. Dirt had been kicked up in a likely struggle, showing that not everyone had been dead when the burning started. On the edge of the pyre was a small, withered husk that could only be a child, the outstretched, skeletal hand of a parent reaching out one last time. The smell of burnt meat was still in the air.

I gagged, hoping to be sick, but the stormtech stuffed the sensation back down my body, keeping me alert to danger. I stood there, guts roiling and acid tearing up my stomach and chest.

'No,' Cable groaned beside me, his voice choking up, his heavy assault autocannon sagging in the dirt. He was always hit hardest by the horrors we encountered. 'No, no, no.'

Myra, our sniper, was always more callous. 'Stop it,' she hissed. 'We don't have time for—'

'*They were just children*!' Cable all but roared. 'They were just children.'

I put a hand on his shoulder, feeling the tremble in his bones through the armour. I wasn't sure if the stormtech or paralysis was stopping my legs from buckling. Even Ratchet was just standing there, frozen at the sight. And that's when Alcatraz pinged us on the commslink.

The Berserk killsquad of Harvesters who'd carved up the town had set up a temporary camp in the remains of the bombed-out schoolyard. Chatting, sitting around and eating from nutrition packets. Swinging from a tree next to them by a length of rope were two teenagers, riddled with bullet-holes. They'd been using them for target practice.

Any other type of soldier in the SSC would be trained for this. To follow protocol and procedure, neutralise the enemy and bring them in for questioning.

But stormtech was designed to react to our emotions. Harvest had reduced cities to rubble, shot down evac ships, set forests on fire, trained their soldiers to hunt Reapers like animals across the planet. Now we'd walked through a civilians' pyre, the stormtech swiftly converting our grief and horror into blinding fury.

We all moved as one.

Alcatraz blasted the squad leader in the back of the skull with his shardpistol. Cable grabbed a man, dragging him across the ground and smashing his head against a rock. Ratchet blew a sniper's hand off at the wrist before following up with a headshot as Myra and I each throttled the trigger of our marksman rifles. I don't remember how long I fired or how many I hosed down. Only that we fought until the echo of gunfire stuttered to a halt and the Harvesters stopped moving. That silence descended again. The rage leaking away as we glanced at each other across the smoking camp of dead Harvesters. Realising what we'd done, what we'd carry with us for ever. Alcatraz placed a hand on my shoulder, breathing hard.

There was a scampering noise from the schoolyard. We snapped around as one, weapons readied. A young girl, caked in ash and dirt, streaked from her hiding place, running away from us. Cable reached her just as she tripped and sprawled in the mud. We watched as he knelt down and gently scooped her up in his powerful arms while she spluttered and sobbed into his chest. Cable whispered to her in her own tongue as he hugged her, her cries dying down to moaning whispers. Although I didn't understand a word, I didn't need to. He clutched her to his chest, not letting her see the devastation as he carried her past the massacre, past the burned pyre, past the burned bodies, all twelve kilometres to our fallback point. Each of us automatically watching his flank as we walked.

You can't explain to people who weren't there the bond from being stuck in that hell, your fireteam the only anchors to sanity in a hell gone mad. A reminder that life and goodness still exist somewhere in the galaxy. How that sense of friendship and unity draws you closer together.

My radar chimed, dragging me out of the memory. Someone was trotting down the blackened steps. A skinnie, wrapped in stained clothes and pushing some kind of shopping cart, his body streaming with violent blue bursts of lightning. He scratched at bulbous growths protruding from his arms and legs. Probably couldn't even feel the stimuli, his skin was so scabbed and scarred. His bloodshot eyes darted back and forth, like the shadows couldn't hold all the ghosts he was seeing. He was picking through mounds of trash when a trio of skinnies peeled from the darkness towards him. He jerked upwards, running away with his cart as they chased him with makeshift weapons, screaming. Their feet slapping on the pavement as they disappeared into the network of alleyways with the rattling of metal.

Half a dozen more skinnies shuffled past before Artyom came along. I sat up as he keyed the code on a datapad set into a secure lockup. Blackened shutters rolled back to reveal an armoured door that groaned open as alloy bolts shuttered back. The Hippo was lifted out of a subterranean storage compartment, bogies whirling as it rolled out to meet Artyom.

'Got him,' Grim whispered.

'Stay sharp,' I told Grim. I raced down the crumbling stairs, hugging the scissoring shadows of the piazza, stormtech roiling down my hamstrings. My thermal vision had turned Artyom into a humanoid coal through the plasma-punctured walls. His gait was slow and casual as he led the Hippo across this forlorn, forgotten chunk of Compass. My jaw clenched as I closed the distance over debris and the skeletal spines of rebars. However he was involved, I'd find a way to get him out.

He zigzagged down a staircase into the courtyard of a ruined mansion. A thin, cadaverous figure was leaning casually against a retaining wall, hands tucked into the pockets of his leather jacket. Middle-aged with a blonde beard streaked with grey. No visible weapons. I tensed, actively combating my body's urge to go for my shardpistol and end this now. I snapped off my thermals to get a better look and cranked up my audio amplifiers. Voices materialised as stuttering cyan soundwaves in my HUD.

'Hey, Mueller,' said Artyom, 'you're early.'

'You have it?' Crystals were embedded in the man's stained teeth, catching the light as he spoke.

'As always.' Artyom spoke casually, his posture showing the ease of someone who'd done this many, many times.

'Have to check. You know the drill.' Mueller scanned his palmerlog and the belly of the Hippo spilled open. Even if I hadn't expected the contents, the jackhammering of stormtech against my chest would have told me what it was. Stormtech canisters. The Harmony symbol etched on the metalwork.

'Four?' He gave a low whistle, checking each canister.

'You ask. I deliver.'

A grin split Mueller's face. 'Great job as always, Artyom.'

'Had them stolen ages ago. Couldn't risk moving the supplies, the heat's been on me. Better to wait until we're in the clear, you know?' Artyom leaned against a scorched column. 'You know how it is.'

'Remember, the long game is what counts. You stay out of owned territory and meet your quota, you're good.'

'I'm hitting it, no problems there. I might even have a little extra this month.'

'Good man, good man.'

It felt like my guts were being sucked out of me by hard vacuum.

'Do you have to head straight off?' Mueller asked as they turned towards a door, the Hippo lumbering behind them, its wheelset whirling.

'I've always got time for a drink.'

Mueller clapped a friendly hand on Artyom's shoulder. 'We got a special of offworld vodka shipment today. Thought you'd like to try it.' Their voices died down as the sliding door clanged shut behind them.

'Vak,' Grim whispered on the other end. 'I'm so sorry, man.'

I barely heard him. My brother was dealing the most illicit drug of the last century. He was part of an organisation that was poisoning stormtech and killing Reapers. And not because he had to. He was a major, long-standing cog in their machine. And he clearly had no plans to stop.

There's something that every stormtech user experiences at least once. The Non-Reversal Crisis, the xenobiologists call it. It's the moment you realise that this biotechnology from a long-extinct alien species is now locked inside your body for ever, because *you* put it there. It's fused to your blood cells, your flesh, your pheromones, your nervous system, and it's never, ever coming out. No unringing the bell. I'd had it at the end of a long day of training during the Reaper War, when I'd caught a glimpse of my reflection and not recognised myself with the blue lashing through my chest, arms, and legs. I'd sunk to the cold floor of my quarters, my entire body racking with sobs. Unable to breathe, unable to even raise my head, fighting back the urge to rip it from my skin and nerves.

This felt similar. I'd been so very wrong about my brother. My memories – my guilt, my determination to protect him – had blinded me. Even when he had practically told me.

110

Stupid. So sodding *stupid*.

I mentally picked myself up, gathering my thoughts together. The shardpistol gave a little whine as I snapped it into combat-ready mode. 'I'm going after them,' I told Grim, the tugging in my gut egging me on. 'You know the score. I'll be in touch.'

I cut him off before he could protest.

Keeping to the shadows between the columns, I followed their pathway across the derelict courtyard towards the mansion. I don't go anywhere without knowing where the exits and blind spots are. I kept an eye on my flank as I advanced, scanning for tripwires Grim might have missed. Nothing. Broken ventilation clanked and crunched high above me. My comms spluttered and vanished as I walked. Signal jammer, and a strong one at that. Guess I really was on my own. I glided out of the darkness and made a beeline for the doorway, eyes peeled for secondary entrances and surveillance gear. Up a short flight of scorched stairs, heading for the shadow of a crumbling balcony. I'd almost made it to the mansion when there was a dull, familiar *click* behind me.

There's only one thing in the universe that sounds like that.

'Well, well, well,' said a voice, barely above a whisper. He must have been watching over the deal, only to catch me. 'Who the hell are you?'

Of course. I was fully suited up in armour. He couldn't see me. Couldn't guess Artyom was my brother. Had to keep it that way for his sake.

I tried to turn my head. 'I—'

The weapon nudged my helmet, hard. 'Eyes straight, mister. Eyes straight.'

I'd already seen what I needed to see. His handgun was retooled for high-calibre, armour-piercing rounds. They'd punch clean through my helmet and splatter out my visor, dicing my brain into fish meat. I'd no doubt he'd do it. Some guys think a ranged weapon makes them the boss of the room. Others understand that a gun is a tool. It only matters if you're willing and able to use it correctly.

This guy was the latter.

My shardpistol was torn from my hand. Screwing the handgun to the back of my neck, he marched me down a series of miasmic hallways, infested with leaking plumbing. My comms were still dead. Minutes later, we reached the shelled-out remains of a compound. The words *Crimson Star Industries* were trapped in a glass frame above the lintel. The door dilated open and I was shoved into the vestibule. 'Got a visitor,' he shouted as the door slammed shut, heavy bolts thudding home.

Workstations, flexiscreens, storage cabinets and sofas sat atop a stained rug covering a spacious room. My visor picked up greasy smears of food and the powdery glimmer of grimwire on the glass desks. Place was lived in. A cracked viewport peered out into a small garage, the curving walls a smear of crumpled service machinery. The sort of place where they'd construct customised chainships and small spacecraft, outfit them with tattoo-like paintjobs. The skeleton of a black chainship, as if chiselled from space itself, was still suspended in front of a colourful catalogue of decals. Thigh-thick powerlines and rusted docking tubes jutted from scuffed decking like broken spinal cords. Long abandoned, the war had turned the whole place to a crumpled shell.

And now it was a base of operations for a stormdealer syndicate.

'Lasky? What is it?' A woman wearing an underskin with an arterial pattern trooped into the vestibule, chewing gum. Her long black hair dripped around her head like a stream of crude oil, her collarbones festooned with tattoos. She swore in Korean as she saw me. 'Who's this?' she rasped. Her coal-dark eyes flickered over me like a butcher inspecting a cold slab of raw meat. It was the same calculating look I'd seen on a girl on New Vladi as she ran a kitchen knife down another girl's face because all the boys said she was prettier.

'He was following Artyom and Mueller,' Lasky said, handgun still fixed against my neck. The little runt had dirty blonde hair, slicked back from a strangely childish face. He was a head and a half shorter than me, but a weapon's got a way of equalling the dynamic.

She tilted her head back to call out without unlocking sights with me. 'Hausk! Lyndon! Get in here.' Lead-heavy footsteps echoed as two more men approached. They both wore armour, engraved with markings that placed them from some installation or wayward spaceport far from Compass. They were twins, ugly as each other, though one had dyed his hair a fiery red, and the other had a face crisscrossed with so many pockmarks and scars it looked like a butcher had used it as a chopping block. I decided the ugly one was Lyndon. 'Hideko, what's going on? Are we blown?' he asked.

'I'm handling it,' Hideko snapped. Both men shut right up. She was evidently the boss around here.

Hausk was squinting at me, as if he could somehow see through my visor. 'Who the hell is he?'

'What an excellent question.' Lasky moved around in front of me to thrust the handgun under my chin, tilting my head upwards. 'You heard the man. Who are you?'

I was increasingly sure these guys were the ones dealing poisoned stormtech, torturing and murdering my friends. If they found out I was with Harmony, they'd bury me alive. If they thought Artyom had double-crossed them, they'd bury him with me.

Lasky jammed the handgun harder. 'Who are you? Why were you following us?'

'Which one you want me to answer first?' The words were barely out of my mouth when I realised my mistake.

A grin spread on Lasky's face. 'That's not a Compass accent. He's not from here.' The grin widened as he patted my shoulder. 'We progress.'

'Cut him out of that armour,' grumbled Hausk, 'or put a bullet in his face.'

Grim would wait twenty-four hours to hear from me before alerting Harmony. If they took him seriously and acted fast, maybe they'd find me, but not before these guys got the cutters and electric grinders out.

'Oh, I'd like to,' said Lasky. There was a glimmer of cruel curiosity in his child-like eyes, as if he wanted to start hacking and sawing away at my body, just to see what fluids would leak out. 'If only we had the tools to do it without killing the sod. But she'll want to talk to him. You don't wear this sort of gear for a stroll in the park.'

The temptation to butt him in the forehead, hear the crunch of his nose breaking, swipe the shardpistol from his hand and blast away was so strong I could feel my arm almost swinging into motion, the muscles twitching.

Lasky rapped my visor with my own shardpistol. 'Someone sent you here. And you're going to tell us who.'

My neck flushed hot with stormtech and the words came spilling out. 'They'll come for me,' I rasped. I glanced about for exits, blind spots, tunnels I could dart into. Nothing. Hausk and Lyndon were already moving behind me, hands flexed and drawn into a fighting stance, as if waiting for me to try. 'They'll come here and mow you all down.'

'Bleeding stars, just shoot the bastard and peel him apart afterwards,' grumbled Lyndon. 'Get it over with.'

But Lasky only grinned. 'Oh, haven't you heard? People are

going to come for him.' He stuck his face inches from mine. 'Who is?'

I clamped down hard on the stormtech, glued my mouth shut. Put my two objectives at the forefront of my mind: not, under any circumstances, taking my armour off and risking Artyom, and getting the hell out of here.

Lasky's grin was hungry. 'All right, tough guy.' He gently patted my chest. 'I want you to remember you had a way out. You could have talked to us at any time. No one to blame but yourself for what's coming.'

Hausk and Lyndon moved towards me. I jerked away on instinct, but they cornered me, grabbed one arm each, kicking my legs out from under me and slamming my helmet back against the concrete. My body pressed up against the wall, I watched Hideko toss Lasky a matte-black gizmo the size of a fist and slap it against the side of my head. Spindly needles going *rat-tat-tat* against my helmet as it secured itself. My HUD scrambled, readouts and icons flaring in and out like neurons firing, all devices and security dying. Overriding and shutting down my suit. I couldn't get it off now, even if I wanted to.

Hausk and Lyndon jerked me to my feet, twisting my arms behind my back and marching me down a series of shadowy hallways. With the device fizzling against the side of my helmet, walking felt like I was encased in wet cement. Hideko walked in front and Lasky from behind, heavy footsteps echoing across the scuffed floor. Reaper training teaches you to suppress fear, to channel it into something proactive. Formulating an escape route, clawing up a weapon, getting an emergency signal out. Anything that'll keep you breathing long enough to fight back. But coldness was starting to fester inside me, born of Lasky's smile, and I'd realised the types of people my captors were. It would be so easy for them to kill me, as they had Alcatraz and

Samantha. Leave me Blued Out on hard concrete. Another dead Reaper on the pile.

Would Artyom even care, when he found out?

At the far end was an image on the wall, like a tattoo stamped in concrete. A thick, matte-black shape, the edges entwined together and vibrating with an outline of dark energy.

Tried to get a better look, but the world kept sliding in and out of focus. The gizmo crackled against the side of my helmet again. I just had time to recognise the whining prime of an EMP before it exploded in my skull. The world glared hot white, shadows spearing through my head. Blood and metal filled my mouth.

'Is the son of a bitch down?' one of them asked from a hundred light years away. My knees gave out under me. 'Good. Get him locked in.'

The concrete floor came rushing up like a kick in the face.

11

Nightware

I emerged from deep smothering darkness to find myself strapped into a metal cradle. Thick, titanium restraints clamped tight around my wrists, ankles, thighs, between my legs, over my shoulders and crisscrossed my chest. Metal shackling had been secured along my spine, locked around my neck. The reclined cradle was deep and sturdy, built for carrying fully-armoured men in chainships, now retrofitted to secure prisoners. I tried to move, but I might as well have been wrapped in concrete. The cradle registered even my feeble struggle and all the restraints tightened with bone-crushing force.

I settled back, sweating and raking in lungfuls of air, my hands clenching, the cradle hard and humming against my back. They hadn't carved me out of my armour. Not yet.

The minutes trickled by, the whole situation horribly familiar. Unwanted memories of being captured by Harvest surfaced. At least then I'd been brimming with stormtech, letting me hold out against advanced torture techniques that would have broken most men. Now I had nothing. My stormtech was wild and unharnessed. It did nothing to suppress the sour dread growing in my gut.

I was being held in a server room. Humming mainframes and cabinets lined the membrane-patterned walls. Ribbed cables fed into the dermis of crackling substrates beneath me and the stink of supercooling fluids hung heavy in the air. A winking red terminal connected to the cradle caught my eye, but when I tried to lean in for a better look the restraints crisscrossing my chest pushed back, holding me tighter. My comms were dead, like my suit, access to the net cut off. No, I wasn't going *anywhere*.

I don't know how many hours they left me strapped there, but it was long enough for my arse to turn to rock before the door crashed open and my two least favourite people in the world strolled in. Lasky had a lanyard draped around his neck, a keycard at the end.

'Comfortable?' He rapped my armoured shoulder, as if it might echo. To me, it felt like he was touching my flesh. 'You better be. These cradles are built to take damage.' He held up the keycard around his neck. 'Only way you're getting free is with one of these.'

Hideko rolled her eyes. 'Just tell us who sent you, we can go from there.' She unwrapped another stick of gum and slid it into her mouth. 'No need to die for people who don't give a toss about you.'

Me and Harmony didn't see eye to eye, no. But they weren't my enemies, either. Whatever their broader motives were, they wanted to stop stormtech spreading on the streets, stop more people from dying, stop it from becoming a destructive, franchised drug. Hard to argue with that. Made them the lesser of a million other evils in my book.

These people didn't know I was onto them, or that Artyom had been my way in. Had to keep it that way. Vital battlefield intel isn't always about what you know. It's about what the enemy *doesn't* know.

Lasky made a little choking laugh that sounded like someone trying to give birth to a tractor. 'We've got time.' He clutched my shoulders as the stormtech leaked through the cracks in my common sense. 'You don't. I wonder, how many days can we leave you sitting here without food and water? Without sleep?'

I said, very quietly and very calmly, 'Listen here, you stinking sack of stupid, you touch me again and I'll break your hand.'

Lasky smiled. Then slammed a wrench into the side of my helmet – once, twice, three times – square on my ear. I choked on my own breath as white-hot pain went rattling through my skull.

'I'm sorry,' the little sociopath said, 'what did you say?'

'Just tell us who you are.' Hideko sounded bored to tears. 'It'll make all our lives easier.'

But the stormtech was whiplashing me into a frenzy and I wasn't about to cave now. 'Go rot in hell, you insufferable waste of oxygen,' I snapped, breath burning in my throat.

'This is pointless,' Hideko sighed, twisting her gum wrapper.

'Then we use the nightware.' Lasky stooped down next to me with a smile I really didn't like. 'Torturing another human is draining stuff, you know. There's the screaming. The long hours. The broken bits everywhere. Worst of all: the empathy. After a couple of hours of blood, broken bones, smashed fingers, screams and pleas for mercy, people start to go easy. They might slow down. They might take pity.' Lasky's stale breath reeked as he stared at me through my visor. 'A nightware Rubix won't.'

Lasky reached behind one of the mainframes to bring out a fat armoured case and pass it over to Hideko. Inside was an array of blinking knobs connected to a cluster of powerful processors I really didn't like the look of.

'It'll infect every inch of your suit's circuitry. There's no pleading or bargaining with this,' Lasky said, savouring every word as Hideko began jacking the nightware into my armour. 'It's not programmed to have morals or limits. These Rubix

119

AIs were built up from the brains of psychopaths and serial killers. And that's *before* they were tweaked. Mercs and pirates in deepspace use these suckers for advanced interrogation. Most folks are lucky to survive an hour. The AIs need to be kept in a constant state of perpetual pain, to keep them fresh and eager in the tank.'

He turned to Hideko, drumming his fingers across my knee. 'What do you think it'll do first? Raise his temperature? Crush him inside? Start the internal wiring and cables growing through his skin?'

Hideko's gum bubble burst like a gunshot. 'Difficult to say. Who knows, maybe all three at the same time?'

These people were not in charge. They were bullies who hid behind others, who took as much pleasure in sadism as in knowing they were untouchable.

I knew these types all too well. And knew they meant every word of what they'd said.

'If it were up to me, I'd put a bullet in your face and be done with you, let someone else play with your corpse,' Hideko told me, stooped over the nightware case. 'But not until we know who you are and who's coming after us. Since you're not in a talking mood, we'll get you nice and loosened up for some friends who'd like a chat. See how communicative you are after the nightware's done its business with you.'

'How long shall we give him?' I couldn't help but watch as Lasky reached for the dial. Cranking up, up, up, past ten hours, past twenty, all the way to thirty. 'There. Thirty hours sounds like a good round number.' Lasky patted my chest, pressed his face inches from mine. 'Don't worry, big guy, it won't kill you. We need you alive. But then, *alive* has a pretty broad range of conditions, doesn't it?'

The Rubix at Artyom's bar had been a caterer, working in a public space. What would a Rubix designed for torture and advanced interrogation do to me, given complete control of my suit?

I held my silence as the switches were flicked, snapped and locked into position. Was there anything I could tell them? No. Every piece of information led back to Artyom. And the moment they realised the connection between me, him and Harmony, we were all dead. I'd protected him from our father, from gangsters. I was going to protect him now.

My shib display flickered as my suit jumped to life, ghostly warnings squirming along the voxels. The readouts of my HUD disintegrated into dust. Instead, the surfaces were oozing with black mould, growing thorns that glistened wet with toxins, icons reforming into cracked skulls. The nightware was already inside.

Lasky's fingers danced over a panel. Additional straps shot out of the cradle, clamping tight around my elbows, waist and knees. Going tight, tighter, crushing me down. I gritted my teeth, twitching hard in my restraints. 'No need to be tough in here.' Lasky tapped the wall. 'Soundproof. Scream as much as you like. You're on your own, big guy.'

They were about to file out when Hideko pointed to the chair's keycard. 'Hey, sling that around his neck. He'll go bonkers trying to get at it.'

'Good idea!' Lasky carefully draped the lanyard around my neck, leaving the keycard resting on my heaving chest. Their footsteps echoed away and I was left alone with the nightware.

I couldn't break out of my restraints, but I wasn't going down without a fight. I worked up a feverish sweat as I struggled in my cradle, breath sawing in my throat. The stormtech lanced from rib to rib, battering against the closed cage of my chest like it was trying to smash through. The keycard drew my gaze like gravity. I made a desperate attempt to wriggle out of my wrist restraints and grab it, but what the hell was the use? I went limp in my cradle.

I was utterly and completely screwed.

I choked out a laugh. Earlier today I'd been browsing a shopping plaza with Grim and arguing about what to get for lunch. In following my brother, I'd made one hell of a misstep. And the worst part? No one was coming to save me. I'd be screaming insane by the time Grim alerted Harmony. Assuming they even *found* me in the broken maze of the Warren.

I could only try and hold out. If I survived the nightware, maybe I'd find a way out of here.

My HUD thickened with dark smoke. The server room walls peeled back, as if they were a mere illusion and the true, bleak reality of the world was being revealed, some place I'd never escape. I was in the decrepit hallway of some abandoned house or mansion, full of rotten timbers and flaking walls. I could see the mangled remains of animals, piled up in the corners. Razorwire and creaking cages dangled from the ceiling, full of slithering, unrecognisable monstrosities. Behind me, something skittering, writhing, feeding in the darkness. Fresh sweat broke out on my forehead, my chest and neck, but it wasn't until I gasped the warm, muggy air that I realised my armour was heating up, my rebreathing filter lowered, cutting off fresh air.

The smoke coalesced, with agonising slowness, into a twitching figure. The monster was a grotesque amalgamation, as if parts of different predators had been grafted together in a horrific experiment. It stalked towards me on four mangled legs, claws scraping wood, a blood-curdling growl building in its massive chest. Yellowed bones jutted out through torn, muscle-bound fur. A rotten spine peeked through the mottled skin like the ridgeline of a mountain. Parts of its body were violently fused in a gristle-coloured exoskeleton. The monster's mouth was locked behind a rusted metal cage, stitched into the flesh.

Behind the wide bars, jagged lips peeled back, revealing rows of black, tombstone teeth. Its torn nostrils flared as if smelling my scent while small, furious eyes rattled inside a hollow skull. Its jaw opened wide with a sickening oozing sound. Acid, gristle and ropes of bloody drool blasted through the cage and into my face.

Nothing more than a cheap visual effect, cooked up with a few lines of code.

It wasn't real. It wasn't real.

The monster's eyes glinted as I went rigid with tension, restraints working hard to keep me cemented in place. The temperature was rising and rising, breathing becoming harder and harder.

It was turning my suit into a furnace.

The nightware construct burst into a raging fire. Thrashing flames blazing up its twisted body, its flesh and fur burning, bones crackling. It hunched over me like a towering inferno and pressed its dripping, burning face inches from mine. Locked my gaze before roaring out an evil, ear-splitting shriek, smoke streaming out of its mangled jaw and into my lungs. I jerked back on panicked reflex, away from this blazing world of smoke and fire. In my augmented vision, my armour was beginning to melt into my flesh with the heat, as if to prove it was real.

My chest tightened, stormtech rolling inside me and any shreds of thought evaporated as I battled to breathe, my throat and lungs burning. The Rubix was testing how little oxygen I could survive with, how fast it could dehydrate me. My body churning sweat out like a pump as I fought for breath.

Then the noise started. Talons raking metal, the shrieking of tortured animals, punching through my ear drums. Growing louder, louder, until I didn't think there could be any louder sound in the universe, then louder still. I thrashed helplessly, aware that I was screaming, though my own voice was drowned out, cocooned in this infinite sound. A vibration kicked into my suit. Crawling up my spine into my nervous system. Every centimetre of my inner suit was shuddering, sandpapering my skin. Shaking me until my vision blurred and my teeth rattled together. I tried to set my jaw. I wouldn't beg. I'd won the Reaper War. I'd survived the battlefield and seeing my friends being blown to bloody pieces around me. I hadn't broken when Harvest hauled me back to their base for interrogation, stuffed me into a prisoner's suit and hung me from the ceiling of a concrete cell.

No way was I going to break now.

I tried to think of the New Vladi mountains. The whisper of snow and wind. My brother's weight leaning against me. The smell of fresh pine and the taste of vodka on my tongue. The logs crackling in our campfire, embers whirling into the sky. I wrapped myself in my memories, held on to them like a lifeline until the monster lurched out of the darkness, claws hooking around my shoulders as it leaned over me and bellowed in my ears to jolt me out of them, louder than a screeching hurricane, louder than anything in the universe.

The juddering of the armour increased threefold. Tightened around me. My suit boiling, burning against my skin as the screeching spiked into my brain like a needle. Animal growls and screams spewed from my throat, spraying my visor with saliva.

I almost didn't notice the scratching running down my palms and over the soles of my feet but then I remembered what Lasky had said about internal wiring. I bucked in the cradle as my suit's inner wires and tendrils fed between my toes, wrapping around my feet and scratching at my soles like raked fingernails. Coiling under my armpits. I snapped my jaw shut as it prodded around my mouth, forcing myself not to scream even as the wires pried my lips open. Curious cables slithered in like playful metal snakes between my teeth, scratching at the roof of my mouth and inching towards the back of my throat. I was exhausted, terrified, shaking, every heaving breath filled with dread for the moment they'd tunnel down my oesophagus and start inflicting permanent damage.

It kept me like that for hours.

It waited until I was on the precipice of passing out before trying something new.

The nightware flipped through fragments of the Reaper War, dragging me through the memories. The pockmarked, scorched battlefields, the Dead Zones where we'd waited in ambush. The towns where we were too late to evac the civilians and found them lying mangled on the streets. The med bays. The rotting corpse pits, stretching through the wastelands, ash raining on their pallid faces. Hellfire thundering down from orbit in the Battle of Lysven. Men in my Battalion screaming as they were vaporized. The stink of ozone, of grasslands burning. The stormtech crackled through me with spitting, furious sparks as the remembered sensations came flooding back, triggering it hard. The whirlpool was dragging me back. My grip weakening.

The videos played on and on and on until it felt like my skull would burst – and then it started up again. And again. Until they slowed, swooping down to focus on a dead Berserker, his bloodied uniform embossed with the Harvest glyph. Except, it wasn't a Harvester. It was Artyom. My brother's pale, lifeless face, during a battle five years ago on a planet millions of klicks away.

The Rubix *knew* me. It was inside my suit; now it knew who I was. Didn't matter how long I held out. If the Rubix knew, *they'd* know very soon.

I had to get out of here.

The armour crushed my chest, my spine, growing tighter and tighter, as if it knew what I was thinking. The cradle vibrated against my back, sending bone-shuddering pain scattering up my body. A cold numbness spreading along the soles of my feet and palms, up my legs and arms. An image of the suit's inner wiring, metal and matte, worming into my flesh like tendrils festered in my skull as my hearing faded. Darkness smearing along the fringes of my HUD, biting off my senses one at a time, ensuring I only saw and heard and felt what it wanted me to.

Sweat clouded my vision as fast I could blink it away. I looked at the red terminal pad connected to the cradle, the peacefully blinking button that would release me. It was a straight shot – a mere metre away. But strapped down like this, a metre might as well be a lightyear.

I still had an iron projectile hidden in the sleeve of my armour. But could I even get close to the right angle from here?

There was nothing more I could lose.

The numbness had reached my armpits like frostburn and was busy inking across my collarbone. I drew a breath around the wires in my mouth. Tried to steady my shaking arm as I aimed with my wrist, barely able to see that red panel. Blinking away as if daring me to miss. I had one shot at this. If I missed, the next few hours would slowly churn my brain into mush.

I reached for the stormtech for the first time in years. Pulled on it to sharpen my focus like it had on the battlefield; let it drench me in calm and clarity. Took a slow, calming breath before I toggled the command to fire.

The missile whistled out of my wrist.

Thudded into the panel.

My restraints popped open and I hurled myself clear of the cradle. Every limb was a numb, dead weight, my hearing gone.

The nightware construct burst from the darkness into my vision, clawing and shrieking with the garbled voices of a hundred dying creatures in my face. It drowned me in blackness, filling my helmet with ruptures of ear-splitting sound. I scrambled in a moment of blind panic, unable to find the case and knocking it away with numb hands when I did. When I finally managed to grab the case, I brought it slamming down on the rotten floorboards. The monster construct was sent smashing backwards, as if kicked with a hammer. Chunks of its thrashing body smeared into stuttering pixels as I smashed the case down, again, again, again. Its mangled face shuddered, warped with black static, its outstretched claws peeling back into strips of writhing circuitry, legs hacked into broken metal stumps. It looked like something was trying to tear and claw its way *out* of it. Gritting my teeth, eyes locked with the monster, I brought the case down with one final, splintering *crack*. The monster's dripping, roaring jaw was blasted into a screaming void of violent dark matter, its body disintegrating chunk by chunk until it was gone.

A sob burst out of me. Pieces of the casing crunched as I sprawled on my back. My senses returned, numbness dissipating like mist, the decrepit hallway peeling away to become the server room once more. My armour slowly resumed normal functionality as the HUD and all standard readouts regrew. The wires stopped writhing against my flesh. I didn't even have the strength to kick the case again.

I was free. And weak. And disoriented. And on the verge of puking in my helmet. And still in the middle of a maze, in the middle of an abandoned floor, surrounded by my captors.

Got to start somewhere.

I dropped a hand to my chest and felt the stormtech snuggling up against my ribs. If it wasn't for the alien DNA I had no doubt that the trauma would have sent me into shock.

For the first time in years, now I felt it slithering through me with concentrated purpose. Swelling my veins and muscles with fury as I thought about the people who had done this to me.

And what do you know? One of them opened the door.

12

Prey

Lasky's small mouth hung open, body tensed as he gaped at the cradle, empty of one very angry, very dangerous captive. But he cottoned on fast. Fast enough that he could have bolted out the room and raised the alarm and recaptured me.

Not fast enough for a Reaper.

I slammed my foot into his kneecap. He toppled like a felled pillar, head thunking off the terminal as he tumbled to the floor. He tried to scramble away but I yanked him back, wrapping my arm around his neck and kicking the door shut. He spluttered, legs thrashing against the metal floor. 'Soundproof, you say?'

Strength charged into my battered limbs as I twisted my legs around his, using my weight to lock him down. The little bastard was stronger than he looked, but against my armour and my training, really, what chance did he have?

I slammed him against a server cabinet, grabbed his wrist and gave a sharp, practised *twist*. 'I told you I'd break it,' I panted. But he was too busy whimpering on the floor to hear. The stormtech spiked and I drove the heel of my armoured foot into his other hand, the bones shattering like breadsticks. He shrieked again as I hauled him up and dumped him into the cradle, restraints that had held me now locked tight around him.

'Who the hell are you people?' I croaked out.

Lasky spat at me, globs of saliva flecking my visor.

'Really?' My voice was still husky and choked up after my torture, scant wires still lodged in my teeth and around my tongue, but Lasky whimpered all the same. All his bravado up in smoke. A coward, like all bullies once the tables are turned. My body told me to kill him, and I knew I would if I stuck around. Instead, I pocketed his keycard and bundled out the door.

I was in a telescopic passageway, tangled with tight jungles of powerlines that plunged into ducts and cableways. I breathed deep, still furiously hot inside my armour despite the cooling-fans whirling away. Voices floated from further down the hall. It was tempting to stay and see what I could learn, but I was alone, cut off and surrounded by people who wanted my head on a spike. There was no telling how badly I was injured. And whoever Lasky's boss was, meeting her was low on my list.

Time I was long gone.

I slipped down the passageway, eyes peeled for an exit, and noticed a room where it looked as if it was snowing as I passed. Razorstorms. Serious, high-end tech. Microscopic, artificial snowflakes swirled around the space, programmed not to float past the constraints of their allocated boundaries. The dark-red light in the room indicated they were deactivated, but the moment that changed the nanoflakes would whirl around, shredding anything and everything in their path. Even deactivated they were a significant deterrent. Someone *really* didn't want people entering that room.

Aware that precious seconds for my escape were burning away, I got my visor to snap a photo on repeat every five seconds. Harmony would make more sense of this than I could.

Chatter floated up from the staircase, abnormally clear. My hearing had sharpened, enough for me to notice it was the *stormtech* doing it. It was enhancing my auditory senses, letting me detect footfalls and the clanging of objects a room or two further away than usual. At the end of the room, embedded in concrete, was the same pattern I'd glimpsed coming in here. Now, I had the opportunity to expect it in greater detail. A blue crosspiece, a little like an inverted letter Y. Didn't look like any glyph I'd seen around Compass. Could have been an offworld design, maybe even outside the Common.

My visor took a snapshot, and that's when everything went to hell.

The quiet was shattered by a skirling siren pounding through the compound and turning the walls an ugly, strobing yellow. Someone must have discovered Lasky. If they recaptured me now, I was dead. The stairs were a concrete blur as I tore down them, clearing floor after floor.

Someone suddenly slammed into me from the side, sending us crashing to the concrete and my head smacking against the wall. Lyndon. He was out of his armour but we both wore the same shocked expression as we picked ourselves up. And then it connected. 'He's over here! He's—'

He choked as I slammed my fist into his sternum. I dove in for another swing when he feinted left, tangled one leg and let the momentum clang me into the railing. My weight warped the metal inwards with a great creaking groan. I tried to right myself, but he kicked me down the stairs, concrete scraping against my armour. I rolled away as he fired his particle blaster with a low, warbling crack, burning a crater-sized hole where my shoulder should have been and spraying flecks of concrete in my face. He swept closer, getting a better aim in the darkness. His mistake. I ducked low, lurching upwards at the last moment to ram my elbow into the crook of his arm and drive my heel into his kneecap. He tottered backwards, the blaster clattering away down the steps. I leaped for it, scooping it up as he came charging.

I squeezed.

A burst of blue energy punched clean through Lyndon's face.

He twitched, still flying towards me, as if his body was figuring out what had happened to it, before slapping down on the concrete next to me. My chest shivered with stormtech, the beginning of its chemical calmness lapping at my senses. Sliding me into the rhythm of combat-readiness. I felt good. Peaceful.

I jerked myself back out of it, resisting the stormtech, the alarms still pulsing like a seizure around me. The fight had cost me time I didn't have.

Someone had heard the shot and now the corridors were starting to swarm with assailants. I was already sprinting away down the hall when I heard screams at my back. The rapid fire of weapons crackled, bullets spraying across the walls behind me, pinging off my armour as I put my head down and ran faster, breath echoing in my skull. The corridors burst with sun-bright flares of light, concrete spraying around me. Every shot felt like being smacked with a hammer, but the hard-sheeted plating of my armour stopped any from punching through—

—until a flash of immense pain, as if someone had stabbed a hot rod into my flesh.

Armour-piercing rounds.

If they'd hit my spine, I'd be done for. But my limbs were still pumping and I was still moving. I burst into the massive ship garage I'd seen on my arrival, the footfall of my pursuers behind me. I whipped around, barely registering the charging figure before he slammed into me with bone-crushing force. Crates shattered and went skidding away as we crashed into the chainship skeleton, the hull buckling around my armour. My assailant hooked my legs out from behind me and tried to pin me in place as someone in an exoskeleton came running to help.

'I got him!' he yelled, fumbling out another one of the soot-black gizmos to paralyse my suit. It whined to life, inches from my face. 'Now, hold him! Hold—'

I wriggled a leg free, gritted my teeth and kicked him in the stomach, sending him windmilling away. I punched my second assailant in the sternum in a wild, blind panic, slamming the gizmo against his head. He didn't have time to scream as it latched onto his skull and blasted him with a healthy dosage of EMP. Barely unconscious, his exoskeleton smoking, I hefted him up and threw his bulk into the incoming path of my pursuers. They yelled as two hundred kilos of metal and meat slammed them to the floor. I tore ahead, feet skidding across the polished decking, heart pounding in my throat.

There was no exit. No convenient doors leading to freedom. I was trapped and had no time to double back. The only other option was an inconspicuous, boxy garage holding an autovehicle. Its bloody chainglass door was locked. The footsteps pounded closer as, not daring to get my hopes up, I fumbled Lasky's keycard out and swiped it.

The garage door chimed open. I plunged inside and into the autovehicle. Hands shaking as I boost-started the engine. The display warmed to life with an array of icons as the windscreen shattered, glass and bullets bursting around me. Someone yelled as I revved the engine and stabbed in an address, overriding every option I could see.

The autovehicle roared forward, punching through the garage door with a great wrenching crack. I hunkered as far down as I could as a salvo of gunfire shattered the rear window and clawed at the sides. Dust and ash swirled through the windows as we went swerving around a turn. Bullets crackling along the bumper, and then tailing off as the autovehicle curved onto the main road. No one followed as we negotiated the cracked roads of the Warren and calmly merged into the traffic on the main streets.

My visor fogged up as I breathed a belly-deep sigh of relief. I heaved myself up, strapped myself into the bucket seat and breathed easier as we slipped deeper into the floor.

Then I remembered that whoever those people were, Artyom was with them.

I spent the rest of the ride in sour silence.

13
Skin & Bone

I don't remember where I parked the autovehicle. I didn't care. Don't even know how long it took me to get home. The stormtech boost had dissolved into my guts, taking my high with it. I barely had the energy to walk and ordered my damaged armour to do the job, hydraulics moving on autopilot.

The bullets in my back ground like bone fragments with every burning step. Impossible to tell how injured I was with adrenaline masking the worst of the pain. But I'd managed to contact Grim and, for once, he hadn't argued and had agreed to come straight over. *It's almost night,* I realised, staring up at the gloaming in the artificial sky as my armour marched me up the stairs. It'd been almost twenty-four hours since I'd first spotted Artyom.

I collapsed out of my suit the moment I got through the door. It was like shedding a layer of stone flesh. I spluttered and gagged as I tugged the wires out from my mouth and painfully dislodged them from my teeth. I gasped, finally able to close my mouth, before unwrapping the wires from my feet and hands. Light-headed with exhaustion, I staggered to the sink and gulped down ice-cold water from the tap, letting it burn down my swollen throat. I drank until I was on the verge of being sick before sprawling out on the floor. My underskin was drenched in so much sweat it was like I'd been swimming. I peeled it off, kicked it away and let the coldness of the floor seep into my back, lowering my temperature, aching limbs spread out as I breathed in fresh air.

'Goodness me. Is everything quite all right?' I peeled one eye open to watch the Rubix's rabbit avatar hop towards me and sit by my side, its ears pricked and whiskers twitching, a note of genuine concern in its voice. I bit back a groan. A Rubix was possibly the last thing I wanted to speak to right now.

'Never better.'

I didn't want to ever move again, but I had injuries to deal with. The armour-piercing bullets had punched into my skin, but they'd not reached bone or nerve. I got the printer to print me up a medskin as I headed for the shower. I examined my wounds as I scrubbed away the layers of grime coating my body. There were neat incisions around my ankles and wrists where the Rubix had cut off my circulation. I was covered in plum-purple contusions, a showcase of lacerations, bullet wounds and sprained muscles. So many crisscrossing aches and pains it was easier to call my body one big bruise. Physical exhaustion crashed down on me like a scattershot blast, the world fading and blurring between blinks. I blinked hard and wiped my face with both hands.

Stormtech is like a muscle. Don't use it and it atrophies. Mine had grown slow and sluggish – weak tendrils of blue wriggling up my left side in slow motion. After its bout of excitement, its reserves were depleted. Nothing left in the tank to heal me.

Finally clean, I was ravenous as I stumbled into the kitchen, found nothing but a box of ultra-sugary cereal. I hadn't eaten in twenty-four hours so I wolfed it down anyway. When I wasn't being kidnapped by Harmony, chased by knife-wielding Shifters, or tortured by psychopaths, I was really going to have to go shopping.

The printer *pinged!* behind me. My medskin was done. I slipped into its warm, skin-hugging embrace. The thick material tightened to my flesh as it vacuum-sealed around me from the neck down. Developed by Sector Prone, Harmony's science and research department, to treat serious injuries, it was a pupil-black, rubbery suit with a hexagonal pattern system, capable of pinpointing and treating all kinds of pains and injuries. The interior was covered with a carpet of gel-coated tendrils, stirring to life like sea anemones on contact with flesh.

Never much liked this part. I shivered as the tendrils tickled my skin, searching me for wounds as it prepped the necessary antibodies, chemicals and healing ointments. Its jellyfish tentacles curled warm and wet around my limbs.

I sprawled out on the bed and did my best to ignore the pinch and prickle of the medskin getting to work. Having been strapped into a single, immobilised position for so long, I felt the searing pleasure of joints popping as I stretched my aching limbs.

My lead-heavy eyes fluttered closed. 'Hey, pesky rabbit?'

'Yes?' the AI asked immediately.

'If anyone I don't like comes through that door, please murder them.'

'Oh, certainly. It would be my pleasure,' the rabbit said, as if I'd asked it for coffee. It hopped away and disappeared. The autocannon slithered out of the ceiling, targeting software switching on. I slowly sank towards unconsciousness. It's amazing how well you sleep when you've got a military-grade, high-velocity autocannon watching your flank.

It felt like a nanosecond later when someone prodded me in the chest. I forced my sticky eyes open to see Grim standing over me.

137

I'd snatched a forty-minute nap. I needed more like forty hours. There was a nasty dryness in my chest and my head was pounding with white-hot stars. I blinked away gauzy webs of sleep as Grim glanced at the oscillating patterns of red and purple flickering across the hexagonal fabric of my medskin.

'Man, they really messed you up.'

'No, really? What gives you that idea?' I coughed and my body gave an involuntary shiver as the tendrils massaged the muscles under my back to smooth out the knots. 'It's a big operation, Grim. This isn't a couple of guys stealing stormtech to shoot up at their academy house parties. Their product isn't killing Reapers by accident. It's an industry. And Artyom's part of it.'

I attempted to sit up, but the medskin had immobilised me. It was like I had a kilo of lead in my limbs. I felt my hands balling into fists. 'I don't know what to do.'

Grim perched on my bedframe. 'Can I talk you out of pursuing this now?'

'Can't see it working.' I winced as the tendrils sniffed along my shoulder blades with a slimy wriggling sensation, easing writhing silica inside my entry wounds. I jolted as the medskin applied antibodies, sterilisers, collagen, fibrinogen and military-grade morphine to numb the pain, the names popping off on my shib. There was a distinct crunch as it started gouging the bullets out. My back arched, creaking at the abrupt agony. I had a sudden memory of when I'd first been turned into a Reaper, having all sorts of uncomfortable apparatus plugged, rammed and inserted into all sorts of places. 'I'm not letting them get away with this,' I managed through gritted teeth.

'You bet they won't.' I don't know when Kowalski had entered my apartment. I only knew that when my body went numb, it wasn't the medskin. Apparently the Rubix had decided I liked her.

She was wearing the same leather jacket over her Harmony underskin, open at the neck. Her look of quiet fury flickered between me and Grim, as if weighing up who was getting dragged through the verbal slaughterhouse first.

'How did you get in here?' Grim's humour and easy posture had vanished. He was up and taking slow steps backwards, hands bunching into fists as Kowalski and the organization she represented came deeper into the room.

Kowalski began undoing her scarf. 'The Rubix alerted me to a medical emergency. Standard protocol.'

'Thanks a lot,' I growled.

'Oh, you're quite welcome,' the rabbit said.

Grim folded his arms. 'You should have let me shut it down.'

'I heard that,' the rabbit sniffed.

Kowalski poured herself a steaming mug of coffee. 'Come on, then, Fukasawa. The full story: out with it.'

'This isn't the best moment.' There was an audible squelching, like squeezing raw mince paste. I sank into a full-body spasm.

'Hey, it's not a great time for me either. That's the job. Talk.'

'It wasn't anything serious,' I rasped. Then stopped as the medskin expelled two silvery objects as if it was spitting out watermelon seeds. They hit the floorboards with a distinct tap, one after the other.

The bloody, armour-piercing bullets gleamed up at us like two little lies.

The room was very, very quiet. I opened my mouth to speak and closed it again.

'So I see.' Anger rippled over her face, before rapidly dissolving into exasperation. 'I'm going to hazard a guess and say you *didn't* forget our conversation, the one where we agreed to work as allies and share information. You just chose to ignore it and risked compromising this whole investigation before it even began.'

The medskin permitted movement now and I rolled to a sitting position, my body still on fire. 'Compromise it how, exactly? This organisation is too smart, too well organised not to know Harmony's looking into them. They've been provoking you by taking out Reapers. You're the ones firing blind in the dark here, with no idea what who you're hitting or what dealing with.'

Kowalski folded her hands. 'Then, please. Enlighten me.'

I did. Horror slowly grew on her and Grim's faces as I described the way I'd been tied down and tortured by an interrogation AI that enjoyed inflicting pain on people.

'Are you sure you're okay?' Kowalski asked finally. 'Do you ... do you need anything?'

'I survived the Reaper War. I'll pull through.'

I knew Kowalski wasn't fooled, but I wasn't prepared to share how badly I'd been rattled. We Reapers learn to wear our armour like a second skin, trusting it, depending on all its functions. Keeping us alive in battle, keeping us in a stimuli-managed environment that helps control our bodies. Being wrapped in our armour is one of the few places we feel safe. When that same space is reconfigured to hurt you with its full, brutal capacity, it turns your place of refuge into a nightmarish torture chamber. Stripping away your trust. I already felt my flesh itching with the unease of being subjected to the interior fabric sandpapering against me, the tendrils clawing hard at my skin as if trying to puncture through.

'You still haven't told me *why* you were there to begin with,' she said. Grim was dealing with my traumatic revelations by helping himself to a generous serving of my cereal and perching on the end of my bedframe, waiting to hear how much I'd reveal.

'It's complicated,' I said.

'Nothing we didn't know from the start.'

'It's a different kind of complicated.'

'Work with me, Vakov. Don't make me find out the hard way later on.' She planted herself next to me on the bed. 'Please.'

The memory of Artyom's relaxed grin as he joined that man for drinks twisted in my guts like a katana blade. That same boy who would walk through the markets with me as a kid, looking for music tracks for us to listen to. Grinning sheepishly one night as he confessed he'd screwed up his first kiss with a girl.

Growing up to betray everything I stood for.

But that was his path. There were other people that needed protecting, other lives at stake.

Kowalski didn't say a word as I spilled my guts. She let the information sink in. Making sure she hadn't missed anything or jumped to any false conclusions. 'You're sure he was delivering our canisters?'

'Without a doubt.' Each word was razorwire on my tongue. The stormtech had climbed up to my throat again, as if my body didn't want me to talk about my brother either. 'It was a regular delivery. Artyom knew exactly what he was doing.'

Kowalski's fingers turned white around her coffee mug until she carefully set it aside. 'So. He's not being blackmailed after all.'

I glanced up at her. 'You knew from the start, didn't you?'

'I suspected. But I didn't want to tip our hand without being sure. I've been wrong before. I wish I was wrong now. I'll have to report all this to Kindosh.'

I felt a disagreeable expression pass over my face. Katherine shook her head. 'I'm sorry, Vakov. But if we get a Sub Zero shockteam to storm that compound, we can end this today.'

'Sub Zero Division?' My skin prickled with unexpected fear. 'I thought those guys were just a myth. Standard SSC gossip.'

'No more than Reapers are,' Kowalski murmured, looking away as if she didn't want to admit that one of the nastiest rumours about Harmony was true. 'Nor are their methods.'

Grim looked perplexed, his curiosity overtaking the fact that he disliked Harmony more than I did.

'They're the worst in Harmony's ranks,' I explained to him. 'Born out of necessity for the Reaper War. They do whatever Harmony needs done, but can't be implicated in. Suicide missions, assassinations, political sabotage in far-flung corners of the galaxy. They'll get the job done.'

Kowalski nodded and turned to Grim. 'You know those rumours about going to underprivileged families, usually in isolated areas of the Common, with offers of training their kids to be Reapers? Kidnapping them if they didn't agree? That was Sub Zero.'

It's rare that Harmony admits its darker truths, let alone this one. But Kowalski had. Even though Kindosh could have her head for it. Had to respect that.

Kowalski's face smoothed over into a tight smile as she patted my shoulder. 'I know you're worried about your brother, Vakov. You did the right thing.'

Except doing the right thing rarely ever feels that way. Not when family's involved.

'If Kindosh gives the go-ahead to storm the Warren there'll be no time to waste.' Kowalski scooped up her scarf and began knotting it around her neck with one foot already out the door. 'If you decide you're up for it, be ready to leave at a moment's notice. I'll be in touch.'

Then she was gone.

'She's right, you know,' Grim said.

'About what?' I asked.

'Going in there alone. Not your finest hour, man.'

'We're all wiser in hindsight, aren't we?'

'Not talking about that.' He pointed towards the blue streaking like comets in slow motion around my belly. 'If it messed with your judgement once, it'll do it again.' His shoulders sagged, hands twisting together. 'I don't want you to go down that path, Vak. I really don't.'

'I won't,' I promised.

'You mean it?'

'I mean it.'

And I did. Because the risk of Bluing Out was the least of my problems. That brief thrill of combat, being in danger, pulling the trigger on Lyndon, all of it stirred up sensations I didn't like. Even now, my body was tense on the bed, cycling through the memories like the departing shreds of a dream, looking for a leftover scrap of adrenaline.

I'd departed the Reaper battlefields a long time ago. But I'd never stopped being a Reaper. The training and trauma done to my body were written in bloody scars, my mind sharpened to an edge that couldn't be blunted. I'd just learned to ignore it, live with it. I didn't hate the stormtech, because it'd become part of me. Like my pounding heartbeat, the throbbing pulse in my fingertips, the drumbeat of my breathing. It was all a part of my biorhythms, the organic clockwork of my body. We don't notice our own bodily status quo after a while, just like smokeheads don't notice that their breathing is constricted or their chest is abnormally tight.

So I had no way of measuring what the stormtech was getting me to do, what microinfluences it was having as it went sniffing under my skin, slithering along my arteries, squirming between my organs, up my spinal column and crawling into my brain.

How much of me had deliberately walked into that building? How much had been at the stormtech's urging? Had I wanted to kill, or had the stormtech simply given me that little extra nudge?

After all this time, was there still any difference between me and the stormtech?

14

Dirt and Dust

My body knows something is wrong.

I don't know when I started to read the signs. The tightness in my gut. The prickle of sweat across the nape of my neck. My slowly elevating blood pressure. I shouldn't be feeling this yet. I haven't had the stormtech long enough. But now, standing here on the valley slope, with the blue alien biotech squirming along the length of my arm, I understand what it means. It's excited. Agitated. Pumping me up for danger. A warm glow stirring my body to life. It feels so good I almost forget what the sensations mean.

Warning me.

I'm about to tell the others, but if I'm feeling it, they must be, too. Got to remember that.

Alert, I follow the rest of my squad — Fireteam Ghost, of Tusk Battalion — down into the sloping valley. My bulky, olive-green armour chafes against my shoulders, heavy in the low gravity. I've been wearing it for about six weeks now. There's padding where padding needs to be, and the flexible, interior material fits well enough. Still haven't got used to the smell. Don't think I ever will. There're nozzles and pipes plugged in all the right places, with tubes taking the necessary waste out and bringing the right amount of liquid-nutrition cubes in.

I carry a standard-issue designated marksman rifle. My rifle specs, ammo count, and the names and vitals of my squad beam in my HUD. The others are all similarly armed and armoured. Wind whips through a bleak wilderness that's scattered with forlorn, twisted trees and dark grass. Stormclouds the colour of bruises churn over the mountain range. Tributaries wind through the sprawling fields and wet landscape. No Harvesters in sight. No enemy infantry. But the anticipation swirls in my guts all the same. We're on the outskirts of a remote town in the highlands of Renchio, the latest in a long line of besieged planets. Intel's scarce, but we've heard reports of SSC squads and Reapers going missing here, along with sightings of rogue Harvester squads, screwing up our comms facilities. We're scouting the area to sort it out, restart the comms systems if need be.

'Don't like this,' Cable grumbles, armour plates grinding as he rolls his massive shoulders. I'm a tall guy, but Cable's got at least a head on me. Sheathed in his bulky armour the colour of a thundercloud, he looks like he was carved out of solid rock. He carries a heavy autocannon, supported by a sling around his shoulder with the power battery strapped to his back. A distant lightning flash reflects in his mirrored visor.

Ratchet, a weaselly runt with a wicked sense of humour and a fetish for collecting Harvest knives, sniffs the air, as if picking up a scent. 'Smells sour, boys. Harvesters about, most likely.'

Drummer, our expert technician, shakes his head as he tweaks the scope of his autorifle. 'I wish you wouldn't do that. Creeps me right out.'

'I've got a gift,' Ratchet says, thumping the chestplate of his scarred armour. It's dark red, not that you can tell with all the mud and grime caked to it. We hop over a small chasm, the rock rumbling under our boots as we land. 'Not my fault it ain't to your liking.'

'Gift?' Drummer snorts. 'You mean freak.'

'That's not very nice,' Cable says.

Ratchet sniggers. 'Hear that, love?' At first, I think he's talking to us, but he's whispering to the Harvest combat knife in his hand. It's a vicious-looking thing, black steel, the serrated edge sharp enough to carve through bone. 'They're calling me names again. That ain't right. My feelings are hurt.'

'God. Now he's talking to the damn thing,' Drummer mutters.

'None of that.' Ratchet twists the blade to catch the light. 'Her name's Fero, and you'll show her proper respect. She's killed for the enemy. Now she kills for us. But above all: she's mine.'

Myra scoffs, tightening her grip on her black-bodied sharp-shooter rifle. 'I guess it is about as close as you're ever going to get to a woman.'

'Always did want someone with an edge.' Ratchet moves to tap the flat of the blade against Myra's shoulder, but she's ready, shoves him backwards just hard enough that he stumbles in the dirt, though it's a playful gesture. He slides back up to us, shaking his head. I'm pretty sure he's not totally sane. 'As I was saying, my sense of smell is a gift.'

'If you want to play this game, ask Fukasawa,' Drummer says. I straighten at hearing my name. Reaper Fireteams are a tightknit bunch and I've not earned my place yet. Drummer's the only one who'll give me the time of day.

'The new guy?' Ratchet jostles next to me, his armour scraping against mine. 'How about it, Fukasawa? Gifted? Or freak?'

It's the first time he's really spoken to me and I'm not sure what to say. 'Not going to give you the satisfaction of answering that,' I say.

Drummer snorts as Ratchet shakes his head. 'Can't understand a word. That New Vladi accent is a real cheese grater on the ears.'

'Enough,' Alcatraz says. He's fireteam leader, so everyone snaps to. 'We're approaching the waypoint. Weapons up, eyes peeled.'

Myra's perched up on a lip of mossy rock, peering down the scope. 'Down there,' she mutters. 'Get ready, boys. It's not pretty.'

My insides sour as we climb down the rocky slope and cross the bridge into the outskirts of the bombed-out town. Rows of bodies have been nailed to giant metal poles. There're thirty, maybe forty of them, their armour dented and damaged. They've been savagely beaten, missing fingers, ears, teeth, and eyes. All Reapers. Some are still in their armour, their legs and feet burnt black where flametorches melted their boots away. Others have been twisted into tortured positions with razorwire and spikes, their crisscrossed arms pinned to their chests, heads propped up.

It's a grotesque mockery of the Reaper salute.

'They left them like this for us,' Drummer says, a hoarseness in his voice. As nausea claws up my throat, I feel the stormtech tighten around me like a secondary suit of inner armour. I sink into it and the sickness seems to fade, my senses sharpening, as if numbing parts of me and diluting others.

Alcatraz steps forward. 'It's the work of the Canine King. See how they've had their helmets ripped off? He takes them as trophies.'

We stiffen. We've all heard the rumours of the insane Harvest warlord, prowling the battlefield like a mad wolf. Posting bounties for famous Reapers and Commanders, hunting down our best squads, baiting Reapers to chase him while setting traps for them. There's a rumour he's building an army of Dog Commandos, a killsquad, the beginnings of his own empire of killers.

Ratchet's trembling with rage beside me. 'Screw him. We cut our people down, now.' He's already pulled the same blade from his harness when Alcatraz puts a hand on his chest, stopping him.

'Those bodies are rigged with smelter-grenades,' Alcatraz says.

'I don't care.'

'I do. You go near one of them, you'll be nothing but smoke and meat. Stand down.'

148

Drummer pulls Ratchet away, still grumbling and glancing back at the bodies. Behind me, Myra's calling in an ordnance disposal unit to deactivate the explosives and retrieve the bodies. If I draw on my stormtech, listening hard, I can hear the dull click of a primed grenade from the nearest pole. The stormtech enhanced that sense to keep me alive.

Just how powerful is this stuff inside me?

Alcatraz steps back, his head tilted up. 'Nothing we can do here except stop it happening again. Move out.'

We tear ourselves from the horrific display. I realise I'm resisting the urge to glance at the forests and hillsides for incoming hostiles. The stormtech's writhing inside my chest, spreading fire through my limbs. Alcatraz falls into lockstep with me. 'Don't let them get to you.' He presses two armoured fingers to his mirrored visor, before pressing them to mine. 'I'm looking out for you. That's what we do for each other out here. I need you focused. You hear me, Reaper?'

I nod, swallow. It doesn't stop the memory of those tortured and butchered Reapers flashing through my mind. But it helps me deal with it, makes me feel more connected to my fireteam as we move through the bombed-out town. Corrugated silos and agricultural domes sag against tumbledown housing, shattered into mountains of rubble by artillery fire and jamming the roads. Gravel and glass crunch underfoot as we pick our way around, the waypoint reconfiguring to match our new path.

'Smell anything yet?' Drummer asks Ratchet. I swap my marksman rifle for a close-range, black-barrelled scattershot as we leap down an escarpment and enter a waterlogged tunnel, our helmet lamps flickering on. Our tech crackles in the darkness. 'Any berserker squads or warlords you'd like to tell us about?'

'Can we talk about something else?' Cable asks.

'I'm with the big guy,' says Myra. 'Shut up, you're doing my head in.'

Ratchet pretends not to have heard. 'Don't much care for your scepticism, Drummer,' he says with a loud sniff as we emerge in an abandoned shipbreaking facility. Collapsed cranes and scaffolds shatter the geometry of space into a nightmare of concrete and metal. 'Actually, there might be something—'

I drop to the ground, pulling Ratchet down with me and yelling for the others to join me before I've fully realised I've moved. The rest of the fireteam's barely down when a salvo of superheated gunfire shreds through the concrete wall, blasting through the metal walkway where we were standing. The bullets thunder-clapping inside my skull, clouds of dust spraying up around us.

My HUD lights up with warning icons as it tracks the bullets, noting the weapon make and model, velocities, trajectories. Our vitals have gone ballistic. The stormtech shudders like an engine inside my chest, every muscle tense, my breathing furious. Two seconds later and I'd have been blown into a shredded mess of twitching meat.

This alien tissue fused to my body saved my life. All our lives.

The fusillade ends. Curses. The click of weapons being reloaded. Alcatraz screams something down the comms and bursts into the fray. I sprint after him, staring down the barrel of my rifle. The world screams with clashing colours and furious lights, but my HUD picks out the Harvesters through the swirling smoke. High-lighting their wartech, displaying weapon specs in gold, analysing the threat. There's two fireteam's worth of them, positioned around the raised walkways. Their painted armour and angular helmets are smeared with Harvest slogans, the notches on their shoulders indicating rank.

I roar into action alongside my fireteam. Throttling the trigger of my marksman rifle, my armour's motion stabilisers neutralise the kickback as I exchange fire with a Harvester in red armour. My shielding shudders with blue ripples as the Harvester's rounds hit home, denting my armour in a dozen places. I throw all my *focus into putting him down as I squeeze off a salvo of super-heated, high-calibre rounds, punching through his armour and through his chest.*

My pulse pounds in my fingers. I'm hyperaware of every detail. Bullets crackling and sparking around me, pinging off armour, shreds of screams, choked curses, the roar of dirt showering in the air. I'm the eye of this hurricane.

No. I am the hurricane. And the stormtech lets me control it.

I twist around, hackles raised, desperate for a new target, when a Harvester blasts his scattershot inches from my head. I smash my elbow into his helmet, then headbutt him, cracking his visor open. His face is splashed with sweat and twisted with fury. I'm slammed sideward into the dirt, my helmet cracking on a stone. My left side aches and I'm vaguely aware a second Harvester blasted me with a scattershot. He's standing above me, the muzzle parked on my visor. I'm sure I'm dead, but the flat crack of Myra's sniper rifle saves me, snapping through the shipyard and pitching the Harvester sideways, his skull smoking. The second Harvester dives for cover, but Myra's faster, the round sparking off a guardrail and slamming into his chest. I snatch up his fallen scattershot, the world thudding like it's got its own heartbeat, multicoloured gunfire grazing past my head.

Ratchet's slammed up against the ground by a Harvester in gunmetal armour, a boot in his face. The Harvester snaps his head around towards me as I dash towards them, my reflection distorted in his visor. Ratchet reaches upwards to shove his blade into the Harvester's gut. It sinks through the shielding and armour, hilt-deep, deeper still as Ratchet smashes the hilt with his fist, stabbing through his spine. I haul Ratchet to his feet, his depleted shields spluttering, our armour scraping together. A grenade rips out five metres away, polarizing my visor and showering clods of dirt over me. A Harvester in bulky blue-black armour feints around us, unleashing three-round bursts. We turn on him together.

151

He ducks around me as I aim down the scattershot, the weapon shuddering in my hands as the convex slug-rounds tear into him. He's slammed back, his hand blasted to a bloody stump, his crumpled chestplate smoking. He tries to go for his handgun, but I level the scattershot upwards and punch a slug through his face, splitting his head apart, his body spinning down the walkways. Another tries to hack me apart, but Ratchet's already skidding around him, shoving the blade into his neck, black blood flowing.

And that's when I see Drummer.

He's sprinting up towards the Harvesters on the raised walkways. More enemies. More monsters who'd string Reapers for us to find. The stormtech roars with anger as I run after Drummer. There's a red-hot flash overhead, and I open my mouth to yell a warning, but Drummer's slammed to the floor, armour clanging, clutching at his abdomen. Thick, red liquid pumping out.

White-hot rage tears through me as I hear the Harvesters above cheering about taking one of us down. I gather myself and leap, ignoring the covered staircase and powering up the ruined walls towards them, mind nothing but fury and rage. A volley of bullets explodes inches from my face, pinging off my armour, carving up the support walls. The world has tunnel-visioned as I throttle the trigger of my marksman rifle. Crack! The bullet explodes out, punching into the first Harvester's chest. I'm leaping across the support beams, lining up the second. Crack! The second Harvester is kicked backwards into the sheer drop below, clanging off the cross-linked pylons. I hear the high-pitched whine of a smelter-grenade being primed. The Harvester's face twisted with fear as she bends back to throw it. Crack! I blast her in the arm, the grenade dropping to the floor and igniting, bright as a sun going supernova, wrapping her and the remaining Harvesters in a roaring explosion. Adrenaline rolls through me, muscles tight against my armour, already sweeping for the next target.

At the edge of my hearing, a wet, choking sound.

Drummer.

I rush back to him, the battle-adrenaline ebbing out of me. He's spluttering on the grating. His eyes twitching and confused when I rip his helmet off. His hands leaving smears of blood as he paws at my chestplate.

'Hold on, man, hold on,' I pant, trying to put pressure on the wound. But there's so much blood. So much damage. Too much for the stormtech to repair. His shaking hands find mine, and we lock fists against his wound.

Wind whistles over the mountain ridgeline. Lightning strikes the distant horizons. I can smell rain.

Between one blink and the next, my friend is gone.

I'm sitting on a munitions crate in the hangar bay when Alcatraz plants himself next to me. I watch the bruised storm clouds churning over the sweeping landscape. We're both still in armour. There's blood caked on my chestplate, in my gloves. Underneath it, I can feel the blue, alien essence twitching through my flesh like seaweed in a never-ending current. Curling around my ribcage. Squeezing my heart.

It saved my life today.

I reach for that feeling, gripping the stormtech hard. Letting it wash over me. Lapping up its sensations, the quiet fury bubbling inside my chest. Feeling the untapped potential inside me for the first time.

Alcatraz sighs. The crackle of gunfire from training VRs echo from the barracks. It seems like an age before he speaks. 'Not going to lie to you, Fukasawa. This is just the start. Tomorrow is going to be hard, and the day after even harder. You're going to feel so angry and exhausted you could die; you'll feel you'd rather eat your own gun than return to duty. You're going to be dropped in some of the worst places in the universe to be shot at, stabbed, ambushed and slammed into the mud. You're going to see more friends die in ways no one was ever meant to see.' A hiss of air as his helmet unseals, he removes it and glances at me with blue strands lashing up his cheeks. 'But the rest of your fireteam will always be there for you. Doesn't matter what those Harvest pigs throw at us, we're going to fight them to the bitter, bloody end. Together. Maybe you'll die on the battlefield tomorrow. Maybe I will. But you'll die in the arms of a friend, of a brother. Come hell or high water, we stick together.' He drops his dog tags into my palm, the Reaper salute engraved in gunmetal. It's a declaration of loyalty, of shared brotherhood. Thunder grumbles in the distance as I turn them over. 'That's a promise, Fukasawa. You're a Reaper now. We're blood brothers. Forever and always, until we're nothing but dirt and dust. We'll do right by you. Will you do right by us?'

I remove my helmet, pull off my own dog tags and drop them in his hand. Alcatraz nods, slings an arm around my neck and pulls me over in a half-hug, half-headlock. 'Until we're dirt and dust,' I say, my throat suddenly tight.

Alcatraz releases me, claps me hard on the shoulder. 'Come on. We're going to bury Drummer. Can't do it without everyone present.'

My armour groans as I stand to go to the funeral of a man I barely knew. A man who died for me, for people he loved, and for people he would never meet. Everyone has congregated outside, around his armoured body. His arms were placed in the Reaper gesture for the last time, his tags given to his closest friends. Reapers nod to me as I pass. My fireteam clapping me on the shoulder for the first time.

They'd die for me.

As I would for them.

For the briefest of moments, I feel at peace.

15

Return of the Storm

Our slipship rumbled as it soared to the top of the pixelsheeting roof, the Hovergardens sprawling beneath us. Towering fruit trees, crop fields, vertical orchards, botanical enterprises and vineyards were smears of red, yellow and orange against the deep, verdant green of the rainforest. Climate-controlled biospheres glistened like giant ovoid eggs laid by some alien creature. Lines of guided tours twisted through Compass' central greenhouse, forking off to the sectors housing alien flora, grown from seedbanks donated by various species. Octodrones swooped through the thick foliage, scooping up bulbous fruits. From this angle, our little ship was the axis and the rest of Compass was the wheel, rotating around us like a planet in orbit.

The microinsulation didn't quite muffle the outside roar and Kowalski had to raise her voice to be heard. 'You've ridden in these before?'

I nodded, readjusting my grip on the webbing straps. I elected not to mention the conditions weren't quite the same. The hard spacedecking floor wasn't spattered with blood and severed limbs. Or littered with twitching bodies, ear-shattering explosions rippling under us as we tore into the churning sky with Anti-Hull Targeting Missiles streaking past and nanogun rounds hammering our armoured hull. No dread icing through our guts as we waited for the one lucky round that'd blast us out of the sky.

So, yeah. Very, very different conditions.

I'll say this about Kindosh: she wasted no time in making a decision. No red tape, no bureaucracy, no argument when I insisted on tagging along. I wasn't exactly in prime condition for the field, but someone needed to guide them through the compound. And if my brother might be in there, I would be, too.

As a First Class Primer, Kowalski was able to work solo in the field, and to commandeer any enlisted servicemen under Harmony's Special Service Command. Today, she led a six-strong squad of Shocktroopers, under the name Team Twilight. Trained for flexibility on the battlefield, Shocktroopers were the backbone of Harmony's infantry, working closely in their tightknit fireteams and outfitted with supersoldier augmentations for various assignments. Like Reapers, their long-term operations in the field had evolved into their own gestures and lingo. They were distinguished by their angular, sturdy armour built to resist heavy damage. I was introduced to two of Kowalski's most trusted men: a short man called Kuen who said too much, and a lanky weapons expert called Vanto who said too little.

Backup was a smattering of gunrunners in light tactical gear with standard-issue service weapons. I saw Kowalski deep in conversation with her SubPrimers – her second-in-command on the field. Armed with handcannons and heavy assault autorifles with high-calibre rounds, they wore armour with a triple slash on their chests and shoulders. They generally led the charge on high-priority assignments and tactical operations. You knew something was going to go down when you saw them in the field. Jasken, the SubPrimer closest to me, stood in his heavy cerulean armour, the metalwork scuffed and blistered and cov-ered with dozens of names. He wore a dour, distant look on his scarred face. More cynical than disinterested. He was scratch-ing the final details of a skullface onto his spherical helmet faceplate, doing a hell of a job at ignoring everyone else. One of the SubPrimers, Arya, rolled her eyes at the display. I caught a glimpse of stormtech curling under her flesh. I wondered but dismissed it. Reapers have a way of standing; their training written into their composure on the field. She didn't have it.

The Sub Zeros were easy to spot, even without their fin-dragged helmets and bulky armour that made them look like monsters wrapped in concentric layers of metal and rock. They all stood a little too straight, chests puffed out, staring straight ahead from behind black triangular visors. Their hands seemed to have fused to their long-range assault rifles and scattershots with underslung micronade launchers. They somehow carved out a space around them, like a shockfield, keeping others at least a metre away. Only the most effective and battle-hardened of soldiers in Harmony's SSC rose to this specialised rank. They operated with their own rules on their own terms. I tried to imagine them stealing children in the night, bundling them away from their homes and parents because Harmony had decided they were prime Reaper candidates.

A different time. A different era. A different set of people making the decisions. But the same blood staining Harmony's hands.

I turned to Kowalski. 'Won't they see us coming?'

'Not in one of these, they won't.' She pointed to a flexiscreen displaying a feed from an exterior starboard cam. The slipship's polished hull had a black, glossy sheen, before it disappeared in a slow wave that rolled from aft to bow. Only the faintest gold outline of the nanoshielding remained. We were totally cloaked. Had to say, it was impressive. 'And this is for you.'

Kowalski offered me a thin-gun. The black gel handle adjusted to my grip as I tilted the hardware over to inspect it. Oil-black, snubbed nose and ultralight. You wouldn't be taking down a mechsuit with this, but at a short to medium range you could still deal out some serious damage. 'Better safe than sorry, right?'

I flexed my aching shoulders against my armour. There'd been no time to repair or clean it, so I was painfully aware of the two holes in the back and the thick coating of my sweat and blood slathering the insides. I'm used to being trapped in my own stink, but I hoped no one else would notice the awful smell. Hadn't the chance to get any more sleep, either. Four triple-shot coffees and my rising adrenaline level was the only thing keeping me conscious.

'That hurt much?' Jasken turned his skullface towards the bullet-holes in my back. News spreads fast among SSC men.

I shook my head and raised the shoulder in question. 'Nope. Tickled a bit is all.'

Jasken chuckled. With his deep, sandpaper voice, it sounded more like a grunt. 'Stupid question, I guess. Still, you want to get that fixed. There's a guy down in the Upper Markets who knows his stuff inside out.' A passkey was exchanged between our shibs. Everyone glanced at the exchange. Seemed Jasken interacting was a rare occurrence. 'A little something from me. Show it to him and he'll sort you out.'

I nodded my thanks as we fast approached the Warren. Ugly up close, and ugly from a distance. The roads were clotted, charcoal veins that bled through the slate-grey grid of cracked tenements, crumbled warehouses and scorched walls. It looked completely detached from the rest of the level, as if Harvest's weaponry had for ever ripped the place into two opposing worlds.

It was a perfect hiding place. And still would be, if I'd not followed Artyom.

My guts twitched as we spiralled into a rapid descent. I could only hope Artyom wasn't caught in the crossfire. I couldn't hold back the assault on my own, so if he really had stuck around, it was his own fault.

If I told myself that often enough, maybe I'd believe it.

Dust swirled as we landed on a grime-smeared rooftop, cluttered with ratnest shacks. The Sub Zeros surged ahead like a shifting mass of black sand, kicking out the doorway and spilling into the darkness. The rest of us followed as they spread out, searching each room. I waited for the crackling echo of gunfire and screams, sour dread knotting my guts as the seconds dragged by.

It took them three minutes to confirm the place was abandoned. They'd all seen the footage I'd taken in the debriefing. Our rats must have fled their sinking ship the moment I'd escaped.

Kowalski looked ready to punch a wall, and even her Shocktroopers were maintaining a healthy distance. She fumbled for her vaper, soaking up the cloud of fumes. 'Couldn't have been more than a few hours,' she puffed. 'You're sure it's the same place?'

I just looked at her. 'I know, I know.' She sighed. 'I had to ask.'

But it was the same place. Same white-washed walls moist with condensation, the same empty hallways, the same powdery smell. The same particle blaster scorch on the wall.

A rangy SubPrimer called Saren leaned towards me. 'How many did you see here?'

'I saw a half a dozen but heard more. Maybe ten, fifteen people?'

'Could have moved,' Saren told Kowalski. 'Taken the canisters, dumped everything in a deprinter, reprinted them up again later. Torched what they didn't need.'

'That's mighty quick work for an entire base,' I said.

'This is nothing,' Saren said. 'Stormdealers practise a fast-track escape if they're ever cornered. They call it burning out. EMPs, false DNA sprayers, chem-bombs that scour every surface with microbes to destroy any evidence. The bastards can clear a lab in under ten minutes.'

'Which means they've got somewhere else to move to,' I said. 'This wasn't their only base.'

One of the Sub Zeros – a man with a cinderblock helmet and T-shaped visor – stepped up alongside me. Like the others, his ID tag was an ominous blur in my shib, *Classified Intel* blinking up when I tried to access it further. He was a ghost. A bloody wraith that existed only to complete Harmony's most sordid tasks across the Common. 'There must be some evidence remaining. One way or another, we'll find it. Even if we have to tear this whole building down.'

I'm no saint, never will be. But something in his quiet, rumbling voice chilled me.

We walked down a hallway slathered in stuttering blue light from a malfunctioning adboard outside the viewport, describing some well-to-do place called Cloudstern. I'd fooled myself into thinking this'd be easy; that the biggest challenge would be protecting my brother while we wrapped the culprits up with a bow. War taught me there's only so many times you get to make that mistake.

My armour cranked and wheezed around me as I hiked up the stairwell, loud enough to grab Saren's attention. The Rubix and the armour-piercing rounds had screwed up the circuitry and servomechanisms big-time, and the HUD was locked in a constant spasm. Among all the elite soldiers outfitted in top-notch gear, I found myself annoyed at being the one stuck wearing damaged armour.

I'd been right, though. They had left something behind.

We found the cradle, sitting like a gaping silver jaw, limb restraints popped open, gill-like grooves flickering with a sickly green. I could so easily still be strapped into it, my brains being slowly turned inside out. I saw the others keeping a careful distance from it, as if it might lunge out and grab them if they got too close.

Not Jasken. He grunted and smashed the fuse box on the side with the butt of his autorifle. The cradle's steady hum spluttered and died out as everyone stared at him. He shrugged, propped a casual knee on the armrest and turned his skullface helmet towards us. 'It ain't going to bite.'

'How long were you held here for?' Kowalski asked.

'I don't know,' I said, my voice hoarse, flesh tingling at the relived memory. 'They were waiting for someone to come and interrogate me. They never said who, but they were determined to know who I was working for.'

As I could have predicted, all the servers, substrates and memory crystals had been stripped clean. Even the broken nightware casing was gone, leaving the memories of my torture and escape behind to stir my body up. With my hearing sharpened, the heavy footsteps of the Sub Zeros before me were marginally louder. But it was just an echo of my full sensory capacities on the battlefield, when my body had fired on all cylinders. Kowalski was two steps ahead, orchestrating the search. Between her instructions I heard a sound I couldn't ignore, like the faintest scratching at the back of my skull.

Kowalski shot a glance at me. 'We should look—'

I broke into a run and tackled her to the floor as the razor-nade we'd been standing on activated. A controlled explosion of slashing nanometal wires writhed like a squirming monster, catching the gunrunner behind us. He screamed as the nano-flaked edges sliced him apart, cutting through armour, skin and bone like cheese wire. A burst of red and he was smeared thick on the walls and floor, his right arm thunking near my foot with a clean-sliced, chalky bone jutting out.

We picked ourselves up as everyone backed away. Only the Sub Zeros seemed unshaken. The glinting wires settled to the ground like lifeless tentacles. 'They knew we'd come,' I said, thick ropes of blood dripping from the ceiling.

Jasken stooped down to poke at the razornade, ignoring everyone's instructions to do the opposite. 'That's darkmarket munitions tech, military-grade. Heavy ordnance. Blade Hunters plant these on their hulls to stop hijackers,' he said, referring to the mercenaries and pirates that roamed the lawless fringes of the Common.

'I'm not going to ask how you know that,' Saren muttered.

'Doesn't matter where the trap came from right now. What matters is there could be more,' Kowalski said. 'Infrared and subsonic detectors on, now. Find the rest of these.' She laid a heavy hand on my shoulder. It was shaking, just slightly, as she offered that half smile of hers. 'Thanks for that.'

'Any time,' I said. Paused. 'Well, maybe not.'

'No,' she agreed. 'Maybe not.'

A few minutes more of searching and we struck diamond. 'That's it,' I said, pointing to a doorway. 'The door guarded by nanoflakes.' Though the dangerous barrier in question was long gone.

'No more mines or razornades in the area,' Saren said, but we were too focused to listen. A grey smudge flickered past the doorframe.

Someone was still inside.

Holes exploded in the doorframe and sizzled past us, the distinct smell of ozone wafting out. We scrambled to hug the walls as whoever was inside unloaded their firepower. When it was empty and we heard the dull click, I charged forward, splintering through the weakened door to find Hausk staring

162

at me down the sights of his particle blaster. I'm a hard guy to miss, and he recognised me in an instant.

We moved at the same time. Him throwing the empty blaster in my face, me lunging for him. He rammed me aside and punched Kuen in the neck, kicked him backwards into two more Shocktroopers. He might have even escaped, only Jasken casually thrust his leg out, killing his momentum and sending him stumbling straight into a Sub Zero's fist. I felt the blow in my bones as Hausk was punched to the ground, his slingshiv clattering away.

'Oops,' said Jasken.

'Bad, bad move,' whispered the Sub Zero as he hauled Hausk to his feet. 'You *really* shouldn't have done that.'

Kowalski stood in front of Hausk while they restrained him with electracuffs. 'You've got one chance to make your life much easier.' I could hear her biting back her rage. 'Talk. Now.'

But he wasn't going to say anything, I could see it in his eyes. The same die-hard look so many Reapers and Harmony and Harvest soldiers wore – that I had worn. Absolute, single-minded dedication to the cause, hard as chainmetal. We weren't going to crack him here.

'Get him out of my sight,' Kowalski said, before checking in on Kuen. Any other Harmony squad leader would have chewed their squad out for being caught off guard and almost letting Hausk slither away, but her approach was different. This squad was her family, I realised.

'Just a second.' I shouldered my way through the armoured men before anyone could object. The stormtech blazed in my chest as I stood in front of Hausk, his smug expression stoking the coals in the pit of my stomach. 'Remember me?'

'I knew we should have killed you,' Hausk said. 'I told them—'

I headbutted him. His nose broke against my helmet, trickling blood as the Harmony men struggled to hold him up. He laughed as they hauled him away.

Kowalski was suddenly at my elbow, arms folded. 'I'd reprimand you,' she said dryly, 'but I don't have the energy and I'd be lying if I said he didn't deserve it.'

I noticed a few approving nods from the Shocktroopers. But as I walked back to the room, the gunrunners didn't stand quite as close to me as before. They'd no doubt formed their own impressions of Reapers over the years, fuelled by rumour and exaggeration. Seeing me in action, no doubt they were also fearful of what else I'd get up to if I was in a sour mood.

'Thought you'd find this interesting.' Saren pointed to a rack of canisters in the corner. All stamped with Harmony's blue and white flag. The stolen stormtech canisters.

Katherine gingerly picked one up in her gloved hands. 'They're empty. So what was he still doing back here?'

'Trying to destroy all the remaining evidence,' Saren said. 'He did a pretty good job, too. Almost everything's torched.'

'We're too late,' I said.

'Maybe not.' Saren had a widescreen palmerlog in his hand. The screen flipped out, showing a swirl of geometric particles. 'Most of the data's been scrambled and shredded,' he said, indicating blocks of data on the screen encased in black crystal. He pointed to another sector, where glowing clusters were haloed in a gentle golden outline. 'But there're plenty of subroutines still salvageable down in the mainframe. We'll get the tech boys onto it.'

'That's it.' I pointed to a glowing symbol. 'That's the glyph that I saw.'

Katherine scanned the symbol and performed a quick cross match through her shib. 'No affiliations with any known factions or syndicates. Not in this galactic region, at least. Maybe some other species uses it. Did you see any aliens here, Vak?'

'No. Only humans.'

'It might not matter. There're plenty of aliens running around and selling all sorts of unknown tech. We'll do a boarder search later.'

Meanwhile, Saren had been doing some more digging through the salvageable parts of the mainframe and projected our findings into the air. Spidery lines sprouted from nothing like silvery roots in fast-forward. 'Looks like they were delivering packages throughout Compass. Along the way they've got stashhouses, mothballed storage units, weapon caches.'

'Three guesses what they were delivering,' I said.

'They'll be long gone by now,' Jasken grumbled from the corner of the room, fidgeting with his rifle.

'A little optimism never killed anyone,' Saren said.

We caught the failsafe denotations rigged up on the canisters and stripped them down before they were tagged and wheeled away. Warbling noises echoed from above as short-range transit craft swooped down to deliver additional Harmony personnel, starting to swarm the hallways. 'We'll raid those locations, see if there's anything we can work with,' Kowalski said. 'Call in any suspected affiliates, known stormdealers, informers, see if they know who these guys are. That includes Artyom Fukasawa.'

'On it,' someone said, deliberately not looking at me. I said nothing. What the hell *could* I have said anyway?' Kowalski dropped her hand on my shoulder again. 'I'm sorry you went through . . . all that for this.'

'I've survived worse,' I said, hoping she wouldn't pry. Images of Reaper battlefields, dead Harvest combatants and stormtech in action writhed at the fringes of my consciousness. Artyom's dead face looming large in my memory. 'If the next few drinks are on you, all's forgiven.'

165

'If we get these guys, it'll be more than a few.' Kowalski cast a smile at me before it smoothed over into a serious expression. 'Sub Zeros will get our prisoner to talk. The mainframe has to hold something we can use. Take a break, Vakov. You've earned it. Let us get take it from here.'

I truly wanted to believe her. But my mistrust of Harmony was deep-rooted for a reason. Stormtech stitches an extra layer of survival resistance into the fibres of your flesh. Whatever you called it – animal instinct, a sixth sense – it was real. I'd survived the Reaper War because I'd learned to trust my gut, not my surroundings. I'd listened to my rising hackles and tensing muscles and acted on them, sometimes escaping a trap non-Reapers claimed didn't exist. And now the stormtech squirming in my gut was a pretty good indicator the search wasn't going to run as smoothly as Harmony thought.

But I was smart enough to shut up about that.

16

Gunpowder Milkshake

The world was a slow-motion blur by the time I crawled into bed. I don't even remember undressing. But I emerged, groggy, twenty-five hours later from the trenches of unconsciousness. I gulped down some water, wrapped myself back in the duvet and dozed for another eight hours before my palmerlog chimed me awake. It was Kowalski, inviting me out for breakfast.

Since I couldn't remember my last proper meal, I agreed.

I was pulling on something decent when I heard the rattle of footsteps outside. Still shrugging into an underskin, I opened the door to see Arya leaning against the opposite wall.

The over-enthusiastic stormtech shivered down my muscles. 'I don't need protection,' I grumbled, wiping my face. I'm not a morning person.

Arya shrugged. 'Kowalski wanted me here, in case they came after you.'

'Got a Rubix for that.'

I invited her in as I made coffee and began lacing up my boots. Arya paused to dismiss the two Strikers hovering at the base of the apartment complex. Their mottled white armour was designed to allow movement and dexterity over protection. Blade-thin and lithe, they were lightning-fast operatives trained for operations that required a stealthy sharp edge.

Arya raised an eyebrow at me as I handed her a steaming mug of coffee. 'I'm not a Reaper, if you were wondering.' I must have been staring. 'Just a skinnie, plain and simple.'

'Sorry,' I said, and meant it. 'How long?'

'Three years. I was offered a tiny shot by some guy at a party. I always thought I'd know better.' She pulled a face. 'But one mistake, one slip-up, and you're paying a life-long debt.'

Wasn't the first time I'd heard that story and it wouldn't be the last. 'Isn't Harmony the last place you'd want to be?' I asked as I sipped my coffee.

'My family said I disgraced them.' Arya was counting down on her fingers. 'I lost my job, and then my friends. I had nowhere to turn. Nothing to do with myself. Not until Kowalski recruited me. She said she needed people who knew first-hand what the stormtech did, who had empathy when dealing with victims of drug trafficking.'

'And that's enough?'

'Of course not. But it helps, and that means something.'

Arya wasn't the first skinnie, or Reaper, I'd met who'd fought to retake some residue of control over their body. I'd spoken to skinnies throughout Compass who'd found a way to cobble together something resembling a life. They were doing better than hundreds of thousands who'd simply surrendered to the stormtech. Whether or not it truly won you over sometimes depended on how determined you were to keep fighting back.

For every exception like Arya there were thousands of desperate skinnies prowling the streets and recycling centres of spaceports. And even for someone like Arya, years of work could all be undone with one bad day, one mood swing. People compare overcoming addiction to climbing a mountain, but that assumes there's a peak to climb towards. Stormtech was more like swimming in an endless, churning sea. You never truly beat it. You just found temporary ways not to drown.

'Harmony paid for all my therapy,' continued Arya.

I smiled. 'How nice of them.'

'I'd heard Reapers are a cynical bunch.'

'You would be too, if you'd seen what I'd seen.'

'I saw enough of Harvest to know Harmony made the right decision,' she said. 'You really think we should have let Harvest bulldoze us? Nuke our planets with cobalt-clad warheads, fill our stations and habitats with toxic gas, butcher entire populations? You saw what they did on Arcadius. Whole cities razed to the ground, water sources poisoned, crop fields burned, families dragged onto the streets and slaughtered. They forced civilians to walk through minefields, then set their hunting dogs on the ones that survived. Made a *sport* of chasing them through the burning forests. That's what would have happened all over the galaxy. We'd be standing in the ashes of billions upon billions. And for what? To say we're the better people?'

'You don't get to tell me what it was like,' I snapped. No one can begin to imagine the experience of being on one of the Dead Zones – the planets that sustained the most damage from Harvest's onslaught. Bodies piled up as far as the eye could see. Refugees scrambling over razorwire to get into the overcrowded camps. Civilians covered in grime and blood, screaming for help, others dead-eyed and clutching at whatever was left of their families. Harmony SSC men collapsing with exhaustion. Reapers on the verge of insanity. 'Don't lecture me about something you can't understand.'

'I didn't mean—'

'And don't tell me there was no choice. I couldn't live with myself doing half the things Harmony people did.' My fingers turned white around the laces of my boots. 'They performed experiments on *children*. With biotech they *knew* was dangerous.'

'They were wrong. We all know that, now. Maybe there was another way. Maybe, at the time, there wasn't.'

'Doesn't give Harmony a free pass.'

Arya nursed her steaming coffee in silence as I stood. 'Do you know about Kindosh? How she came to be where she is today?'

'No. I don't.'

'Do you want to?'

'Not particularly.'

'Maybe you should. It's relevant. She grew up on a station called Petroni, in the Sumikem System. They got rich from mining the local asteroid belt. Until Blade Hunters came along and forced them into quarantine with minimal life-support while they stripped their station bare. Five hundred people and food for fifty. Until Kindosh discovered a secret stash of emergency rations. The way she tells it, she divided up the rations day by day, eating exactly what she needed and no more. All done in secret. If anyone had discovered her stash it would have been stolen and fought over and no one would have eaten. She survived when half the station went mad, killing each other for scraps, until the day they were rescued.'

I was starting to see where this was leading. Arya set her half-finished coffee down. 'Kindosh knows the cost of survival better than most of us ever will, and when she says it's a price worth paying, I believe her. So every time I look at the worlds Harvest killed, the cities they levelled, the people they destroyed, I know where I stand.'

Kowalski's breakfast venue turned out to be a French dessert bar on a Compass high-floor that also happened to do breakfast. The walls and furniture were a lavish baroque, festooned with gold filigree. Vast classical paintings peered down at us while soft Vivaldi carried across the room and echoed up to the swirling, vaulted ceiling. There were so many intricate patterns in the artwork I couldn't stop staring.

Kowalski followed my gaze upwards. 'That's all handcrafted.'

'It's not printed? Not even installed by octodrones?'

She shook her head. 'It's all designed, drawn, and created by hand, exactly as it was back in the seventeenth century. That's why this place is so special.'

We sat at a table overlooking a sun-washed courtyard full of flapping awnings, rose gardens and an ivy-covered trellis. Kowalski had already ordered macaroons and pastries for our entree. I scrolled through hundreds of menu items before settling on French toast with butterscotch and a side helping of fresh fruit and yoghurt. Kowalski had the same.

'It's not much of an apology,' she told me as she poured coffee for the both of us. 'But I honestly thought we'd destroyed all nightware constructs decades ago. I'm so sorry you had to endure that.'

Strapped into the cradle with an insane AI, I'd not expected to ever chew solid food again, so I was grateful for the meal all the same. 'Not too shabby a job, tracking them so quickly,' Katherine continued. 'I just wish we'd seized the base faster. We could have wrapped this up with a bow.'

'We did what we could, all considered,' I said.

'You think?' she asked. She must have seen something on my face. 'Do tell.'

Was I really going to open up to someone from Harmony? I so expected their games and exploits and micromanipulation it was hard to pin down what was genuine. But I thought of the way Kowalski led her men, protected them when they needed it, how they'd instinctively protected her when Hausk had barged out. She commanded respect. Not fear, not blind obedience. Respect. It was the same intangible loyalty that Commander

Sokolav had wielded, that got us through our eternal nightmare. You've got to admire that in a person.

'People need figureheads to give them stability, someone to look up to, to survive the chaos the world throws at them,' I told her. 'It's a messy job, and Harmony needs people with guts to get stormtech off the streets. Otherwise, we're all dead in the water.'

Katherine took a few seconds to weigh my response up. A spray of piano key notes activated in my shib as the soundtrack changed to *Debussy*. 'That's some praise, coming from a Reaper. My men are a stubborn, rock-headed bunch, but I've made do with them. Harmony or not, we all want the same thing.'

'But very different ways of achieving it.'

'People change, Vakov. Harmony got us into this mess when they experimented with stormtech. Now it's our duty to fix it.'

I laughed. 'Compass is a hell of a lot less diplomatic than New Vladi. It's all contracts and bargains there. If we have a problem back home, you either go to the *Babushka* or you go to the Five Courts. Or settle it via combat. Guilty parties fight it out to the death.'

Kowalski cocked her head. 'The *Babushka*? You mean like the *grandmother*?'

'Exactly like the grandmother.'

'And what does this *grandmother* do?'

'She's the one person on New Vladi who can give you permission to break the law if she sees fit. And you do not mess with her.'

'Did you ever go to her?'

A shockwave travelled up through the coils of memory. 'Just once.'

Kowalski nodded but said no more. I liked that about her: she sensed discomfort like a bad wound. Knew exactly when to stop speaking, when to let the moment pass undisturbed. It's a skill more people could use.

I glanced up at her. 'So. What happens next?'

'We're all over it,' said Kowalski. 'We're reaching out to stormdealer syndicate leaders, informers, folks who used to work the streets and know the spaceports and shipping routes these guys use. If any of them know who our new friends are, we'll know, too.'

'You think they'll turn on another stormdealer?'

'The only thing they hate more than each other is us. The question is whether they're *afraid* of each other more than us, or want to get an advantage by turning someone else in. And unfortunately, the top dogs know it. They'll skin anyone who talks, if they're lucky. We're talking about the control of entire asteroid floors here. Plus, we've got a prisoner to interrogate and salvaged intel to trawl through. Forensics are tearing the Warren apart. If they've left anything there, we'll find it.'

'And Artyom?' I asked.

'He's gone dark. His apartment's cleaned out and he hasn't shown up for work. Plenty of lowlevel hideouts he could be biding his time in, places that won't look at new arrivals too closely.'

'You were going to arrest him, weren't you?'

'Before, not knowing if he was wired? No. But now we've found the base, he's wanted big-time.'

I'd known it the moment I'd seen the drug exchange. I leaned forward. 'How about this. If, *if*, I could find him, would convincing him to come in help his case?' I knew the odds were astronomically against it, but what sort of brother would I be if I didn't try?

'Too big a risk for you to go looking for him solo,' Kowalski said. 'If we nab him, I promise you'll be the first person I call. If you can win him over this time, that'd make a world of difference.

By all means, give him a call and see if he gets in touch. Otherwise, we don't need you urgently. I'll call you in a few days — sooner if there's something to be done. Until then, you've earned a breather.'

'One other thing. Grim's been having trouble with his Compass residency card. I wouldn't have found Artyom's route or their base in the Warren without him. I don't want a reward, but I think he should have one.'

'There's good news on that front.' A series of documents flitted into my visual overlay, the pages trimmed with platinum. Kowalski smiled at me as I realised what they entailed. 'It took a while to bring Kindosh around, but I convinced her.'

I grinned at her. 'Grim's going to go bonkers when he sees this. Thank you.'

'We're up one live prisoner, one compound and several servers of intel. It's worth it.'

'So Harmony does have a heart after all.'

Kowalski swept sandy hair back from her face. 'Honest question, off the record.'

'Completely off the record?'

'Completely. Do you think Harmony deserves another chance? To try and rebuild the Common?'

I glanced out the window as I turned the question over. Watching people trickling into streets where tiny eateries and niche shops were nearly hidden under a canopy of silver-flecked ivy. My gaze rose past the tiered balconies and townhouses, all the way up to the parklands and stalwart trees the size of highrises. I turned back to her. 'In all honesty: no. No, I don't. Harvest was a monstrosity that needed to be put down, but Harmony doesn't get much credit from me either. Though the mess both left behind isn't going to mop itself up.'

'You're very honest.'

'I'm very practical.'

'Maybe practical is what we need. Like any drug, stormtech hits the little guy the hardest. The poor, the young. The stupid. Have you heard of the Blue Wave?' I shook my head. 'It's part of an underground music festival. Bluesmoke and grimwire is popular enough, but now there's a concert where the band, the DJ, the audience, everyone has stormtech. They turn the lights off and blast the music, so the only light in the room comes from the stormtech. The audience makes patterns, shapes, Mexican waves. Sometimes, they select half a dozen people and sync the soundtrack to their heartbeat as they dance. You, quite literally, dance to the beat of your own heart. Your body *becomes* an instrument.'

'That's insane.'

'Yeah. The same alien biomass used to win a war, used to get high, used by drug traffickers, and now used for a night out. I don't want to imagine what it might be used for in a decade.'

Breakfast arrived and halted our conversation. I hadn't realised how ravenous I was. I speared a wedge of French toast and smeared it with the butterscotch sauce. I was halfway through the bowl of fruit before Kowalski pulled up the restaurant menu again. 'Working nights does my head in. Nothing a good breakfast cocktail can't fix.'

I looked at her. 'Booze? With breakfast?'

Katherine gave something between a shrug and a nod.

'And here I thought I was the only one who drank this early in the morning,' I said.

'Shall I make it two, then?'

'By all means.'

Soon, I was trying my first breakfast martini. Didn't much like it at first, but by the third I was coming around to the taste. We shared knowing grins with each other, happy to have found a kindred spirit. It was our first chance to talk, really talk, and our conversation leaped from alcohol to technology to recent arrivals of alien species to Common politics, to the new Compass floors under construction and soon to open for business. I found I could talk to Kowalski easily. She always had something vital and interesting to contribute, something that would surprise me. I enjoyed the conversation with her, the time flying by. It was good to focus on something so mundane and simple. We both deserved the distraction.

When we were done, Katherine scooped up the bill and we parted ways, with me promising to take her out some other place when we had time. I was sorry to see her go, watching her walk down the steps just a little bit tipsy, her blonde hair flowing in the breeze behind her.

My mood elevated, I went straight to Grim to tell him about the citizenship card. His eyes were wild and happy at the news, grinning wide like a kid who got a dog for his birthday. '*You* did it,' he breathed out, crushing me in a hug. He was practically shaking with joy. 'You actually did it, you big, mad bastard.'

I peeled out of his embrace. 'Take it easy. Drinks on you, by the way.'

Unfortunately, I made the mistake of letting Grim choose *where* we drank. He dragged me to an underground bar in a subfloor sandwiched between two larger Compass levels. I've sat in some rundown bars in my time, but I've never been to a place that took pride in being so *deliberately* shoddy. Sticky purple, turquoise and red lights glistened around the darkened, smoky space. The booths were too small and the low ceiling too close. Subsurface lighting turned faces sinister. Metallic, pulsing membranes throbbed on the wall in tune to the music. One glance at the customers in their heavy, hooded clothing, cheap bioaugs wired into their bodies, exchanging

176

circuitry-laced cards with hands with pulsing colours at their fingertips, and I knew this was where Grim's hacker friends hung out. Databrokers, system divers, people who knew the digital world inside out. I spotted a scattering of aliens among the mostly human crowd. Had to be one of the many bars that offered food and drink catering to their biology. A collage of tattoos and florescent glyphs adorning cheekbones and necks indicated three, maybe four separate hacker collectives in here. They circled each other like sharks, but left it at that.

Grim was on a rampage. He jabbered non-stop about the eateries he'd take me to, the markets we could shop at. 'Did I end up telling you how big the genome pay-out was?' Grim asked as he downed a geometrical glass brimming with spicy rum.

I sipped mine at a more measured pace, shook my head.

My shib chimed with an incoming transmission of currency. 'That's your half,' Grim said.

The stormtech flared like a lightning bolt down my arm as a figure blinked up in my vision. A grin spread across my face. 'That's insane.'

'I know! We don't ever have to work again.'

'You? Retire? You'd be bored in a week. At least you can move out of that dump you're living in.'

'Yeah, about that.' Grim fixed me with his best toothy grin as I poured two more shots. A glass should never be empty, as far as I'm concerned. In the background a fight between a human and an alien belonging to a species I didn't recognise had broken out, barely earning a glance from surrounding customers. Probably standard in here. 'Property's tight at the moment.'

'Grim...'

'Come on, man. We've lived together before!'

'Spending three miserable weeks in a shabby flophouse in a

glorified mining dockyard two systems away from civilisation is not *living*, Grim.'

'It's the experience that counts.'

I swear he dredged these conversations up *just* to test me. 'Grim, you're my best mate, but we're not living together. End of discussion.'

'Can't blame me for trying.' Grim thunked his glass down and allowed me to pour more rum. 'So what d'you think of the place?'

I glanced over my shoulder to see a man with a pulsing tattoo make a connection between a wall socket and the open port embedded in his skull, interfacing directly with substrate. Grim had told me you could tweak the modules and get a little extra kick when you dived in and out. 'It's . . . unique.'

'Pretty cool, right? Just don't ask the bartender to surprise you.'

'Why not?'

'Just . . . trust me.' The booze was hitting him faster than I'd expected. 'I pick up most of my gigs here. It's neutral territory. Hacker collectives, smugglers and brokers are always at war for fresh intel, always trying to sell each other out. But there's no stealing from or breaking into other people's neuralware allowed in here.'

'What kind of data gets exchanged?' I asked.

'Everything,' Grim slurred.

'Could you be a bit more specific?'

He shrugged. 'Everything. Bank details, trade routes, dead-drops, navigation firmware, darkmarket narcotics buyers and sellers. Everything. These guys know stuff before it happens. They can even target select organisations if you pay them enough.'

'Well, that's comforting.'

'Not all of them are like that. Some just like to mess with

people. Send them on scavenger hunts all over Compass, making puzzles, planting clues in mainframes, that sort of thing.' Grim pointed to a Torven with blood-red tubes snaking down his spine. 'A few months back, Kashyk got all the octodrones in Limefields to play a twenty-hour game of tag. Before that, he rerouted a bar in the Upper Markets, nullified all the payments. Free booze for a whole week!'

I drained my glass. Worlds within worlds within worlds. It didn't matter how well you thought you knew Compass, there was undoubtedly another five hidden layers, buried beneath the asteroid's surface.

I didn't have high hopes for Harmony tracking Artyom down, even as I sent him an urgent transmission asking him to pull his head out and get in contact immediately. Didn't have much else to do but sit around and wait. Relaxing, really relaxing for a length of time, isn't something I do too well anymore. My body and muscles always want to move, sniffing out anything that gets my blood up and muscles pumping. The stormtech's always looking for a way to strain the human body, pushing me over the edge one inch at a time.

But now, I had the time to try and relax.

After another twelve hours asleep, I spent two quiet days in my apartment ordering takeaways, soaking in the jet-shower, sipping gin and working through Grim's filmlogs. I enjoyed most of them, but would never give Grim the satisfaction of admitting it.

I checked my shib's comms regularly. Nothing from Artyom. No surprises there.

Knowing it was hopeless, I sent another message before heading out to explore Compass and get some shopping done. The Rubix can monitor my supplies and put in an automatic order, but I'm a hands-on type of guy. Not everything can be printed, especially not food if you want something that tastes better than blended leftovers. Besides, if you're going to go shopping *anywhere* in the Common, Compass is the place to do it. Grim, shopping entrepreneur that he thinks he is, told me that if it exists, it can be bought here. And if it doesn't exist, it can *still* be bought.

First order of the day was getting my shoulder-length hair shorn back to a crew cut. Afterwards, I trooped to the upper echelons of Compass, home to a luxurious health centre. A swimming pool, an assortment of saunas and spas, timbered steam rooms and fitness equipment greeted me. Tension from my little experiment in the cradle was still playing out in my muscles and I needed to unwind. It wasn't quite as good as the Russian *banyas* back on New Vladi, but there's something special about doing laps in a pool with a kilometre-long viewport that offers a sweeping view of an asteroid field against the backdrop of distant stars, under and above the water. The sauna was less successful. The compressed heat and tight space was uncomfortably close to being tortured inside my armour, and my stormtech lashed in response. I was getting a definite sense of being stared at. People avoiding sitting next to me, like I was going to attack them.

They didn't realise that if you treat someone a particular way for long enough, they'll become exactly that.

I ended up relaxing by myself in a private spherical spa, the transparent glass turning into a shifting canvas of space. Ambient sound effects rendered from a surveillance drone speeding along a planet ravaged by ion storms played to me as I was gently whisked through simulated space. I floated past swirling nebulae and dwarf stars gently pulsing with solar flares and drifted across the quiet, cratered surface of a moon. I passed a massive gas-giant, its brown surface swirling with turbulent storms. Brown, black, blue and white, coiled together like a marble painting in motion, a breathtakingly peaceful piece of cosmic art. Hot water dripped down my back, the gas-giant's belt of dust-rings rippling as I was sped through them. I let my hand drift through a sweeping asteroid field, breathing in the calming scent of petrichor as we swooped down to a green forest planet wreathed with white mist. Whatever shreds of peace I had in this place, I was going to enjoy them while they lasted.

Several galaxies later, I headed back to the eternal chaos of the Upper Markets. As I threaded my way through the cluttered and packed hallways, I passed an alien cultural centre. I casually inventoried the products in the display windows. Books, language groups, translation software for various alien dialects, support groups for aliens who wanted to assimilate better into the Common.

A thousand shops tempted me, but I wasn't here to browse. Thanks to my good friends in the Warren, my armour was in desperate need of repair. Already, I was starting to feel uncomfortable without it. By the time we'd left the Warren, it had been two steps away from scrap metal, the suit's inner surface pushing uncomfortably against my hamstrings, tendrils squirming furiously like sandpaper against in my armpits. It would be just the thing for faulty wiring to catch fire and roast me alive for real.

I ordered the suit to march behind me as I picked my way to the outermost sectors of the Upper Markets, towards the armoury Jasken had spoken about. One sniff of the suit's reeking insides and I'd decided my stomach wasn't strong enough to wear it again without a serious chemical clean.

The suit's hydraulics wheezed and complained as I found and entered the shop, the sign *Gunpowder Milkshake* lit up above the lintel. I stood in the middle of a three-storey armoury.

Black and gold timbers with geometric engravings rose up around me. The smell of woodsmoke and burnt copper scented the air. Armoured suits of varying colours and designs gleamed on dark podiums in a showroom, crafted and custom-built for humans and aliens alike. I heard a scrabbling noise and glanced up to see a giant metal spider picking its way over the highly stacked shelves. It was a mechsuit, its many-jointed limbs replacing and re-ordering a dozen items on the shelves simultaneously. I waited until the insectoid head swivelled around to peer at me with aquamarine photoreceptors. The mechsuit climbed down the shelving with a slow, oiled grace, reached the bottom and peeled apart to reveal the owner.

'Fox, at your service.' Fox wore a stonewashed T-shirt and sloppy grey beanie that couldn't have been more of a contrast to the filigree furniture around me. A toothpick jutted from his cracked lips. 'Come now, what's the order of the day?'

I pointed to the two holes in the back of my suit. 'What can you do with these?'

Fox barely paid me heed as he ducked and swerved around the suit with the casual grace of a dancer, fingerless gloves skittering over his datapad. 'Heavy damage, this.' He glanced at an icon on his datapad. 'Oh, look at you, you little bugger. Nasty bit of foreign malware in the deep-layer substrate. Been putting your metal right through the ringer. You aware of that?'

'Intensely aware.'

'All bad news here. Your metal's a write-off. Total miracle you were still using it.' He gave it another professional look-over and twirled the toothpick around in his mouth. 'Half the circuits have gone to the dogs. A deal on the parts is the best we can do today, I'm afraid.'

I'd grown attached to the armour, but I found I was thankful I didn't have to go to the trouble of cleaning the thing. Just as well I was stinking rich right now.

'An upgrade sounds good,' I said, resting my hand on its shoulder one last time. I found the passkey Jasken had sent to me and forwarded it to Fox. 'Would this do anything for me?'

His expression rippled as Fox inspected the passkey. 'This is an Iron Prism. Pyroxene Class. Pyroxene, I say!' Respect and a touch of disbelief in his voice. 'How'd you get your mitts on *this*? Which deepspace smuggler gang you been hauling for, eh?'

I returned his stare, deadpan. You've got to go along with these things, sometimes.

Fox slapped the side of his head, straightened his beanie. 'Oh, where are my manners! That's all miscellaneous. A customer carrying a Pyroxene deserves . . . something little extra.'

I was starting to understand why Jasken had been so familiar with the darkmarket tech in the Warren.

'We'll have to nip 'round back. Allow me to call my esteemed partner. Badger!' Fox called out. No response. Fox hit the cabinet, wood rattling. 'Oi! *Badger!*'

There was a soft thud from the backroom, like someone hitting their head on shelving. A Torven appeared next to me, the mask of a vidgame simulation dangling in his hands, the blue curl of stormtech squirming up his chest. 'How many times have I bloody told you?' the alien yelled, coating my face with a fine mist of saliva. 'Don't shout when I'm wired in. Scared me half to death! I almost—'

'Badger,' Fox stressed with great strained patience, 'our customer here is Pyroxene Class. Pyroxene. Class.'

Badger blinked rapidly, coal-dark eyes going big as moons as I wiped my face clean. 'Then . . . then we should take him out the back!'

'Right.' Fox clapped his hands together. 'Now we're all caught up, let's do some business.'

Badger reached down and punched a button under the desk.

The display windows of the armoury turned glassy, a lattice-work of reinforced bars slamming across to restrict entry. 'Can't be too cautious,' Fox explained. 'Bad neighbourhood and all.'

Fox deactivated the razorstorm guarding the back of the shop and ushered me down a creaking stairwell into a niche showroom. 'Exclusive products are reserved for exclusive customers, you see. Things the common person ain't geared up to appreciate. For a Reaper of Pyroxene Class such as yourself, this should hit the spot.'

The suit he pointed out was a rich dark blue, the metalwork glistening and glimmering like cords of wet, twisting rope. Violent silver stripes swiped up the sides, lights winking around the forearms, chest, shoulders, and back.

I grinned as Badger rattled off the extra benefits. 'The inside is layered with a nanocomposite sensory system. It's got a protective reactive metal crystal and a hydrostatic gel layer that will pump you with antibodies and biofoam to seal wounds. The inner material regulates temperature, changes density and thickness when it needs to. The exterior is a multilayer electro-active polymer shell, shielded against energy, radiation, kinetics, and static. It won't stop a concentrated full-on spray, but it's impervious to small-arms fire and protects well against most ballistic attacks. It's EVA-approved, if you've got business out in space.'

I gave the outer titanium alloy shell a few raps and allowed my hand to slide down the cool, reassuring metal. 'What's the score on armour-piercing rounds?'

'Won't stop them completely, but there'll be better protection than your last. Remember: it's the sustainability that's important here. The suit's got top-of-the-line anti-malware programming, and the helmet has a rear-cam. Useful in the shabbier neighbourhoods.' Badger touched a button, got the armour's chestplate to slide open. The Torven pointed to the carpet of bio-organic tendrils oozing out of the interior surface. 'The interface is top of the range; you can expect instant responses on a biomechanical level. You'll get readouts across the whole electromagnetic spectrum: biochemical, acoustic and pheromonal, everything. It monitors dopamine, adrenaline, blood-glucose. This beauty bonds with you and adapts to your body, making you more intimate with the hardware on a full neural and physical integration for sharper reflexes.' He pointed again to the tendrils. 'These are our selling point for Reapers. This suit is more sensitive, more precise; the stimuli is more powerful, completely adaptable to your physiology. Whatever sensations you're experiencing, whatever stress levels your body is riding out, the suit will equalise and match up with you. You could almost say this suit *becomes* a part of you when you wear it.'

I was dully aware that I was grinning. 'Where'd you get this stuff?'

'Not something we can disclose,' Badger sniffed, rubbing the freshly made wound on his head.

'The free market is a wonderful thing,' Fox agreed, readjusting his beanie, 'and needs protecting. Now. This armour ain't quite sentient, but it's equipped with a smart processing-core, same as an AI, wired so that protecting you is its one and only goal. In a way, these suits *like* being worn.'

I stared at him. 'You're kidding.'

'I ain't. Welcome to the future, mate.'

I couldn't not take it. I mean, I don't think I could have physically walked away. And after Fox took my measurements and made some alterations, the armour fit me to the millimetre. After the interior padding around my limbs was adjusted for flexibility, I slid into it for the first time. I itched as the tendrils squirmed across my body like sentient liquid, dripping down my flesh, finding the notches in my spine. Connecting to me on a biomechanical level and jumpstarting the bonding process. The cobalt spinal ridges tightened against my body, running from the nape of my neck down my spine and along the curve of my tailbone. Badger attached the shelled armoured plating over my kneecaps. I raised my arms and allowed him to do the same to my elbows. I felt a familiar blistering sensation, like a bucket of electric, icy water being poured down my back, the electrostatic interface hooking in. Locking to my pheromones and reading my biometrics. A vibration rolled up the suit, shuddering down on a musculoskeletal level. The hydraulics began pumping, my body heat equalising and my flesh merging into the hardware. I unclenched my fist, armoured fingers clacking together. Lost in the composite layers of hardware and sensation, I wasn't sure where my flesh began and the suit ended.

There was a much bigger suit in the corner, so bulky you'd have to climb *into* it as opposing to strapping it on. 'I'm guessing you won't tell me where that came from either,' I said, rolling my shoulders and feeling the suit's inner tendrils scramble along my back.

'Those heavyweights there are reserved for Iron Class customers.' Fox placed a hand on his puffed-up chest. 'I'd sell it to you, truly. But the code's got to be respected, a chain of command to be followed. It's the way of things.'

'The way of things,' Badger echoed sagely.

I nodded along, as if I knew what they meant.

'Now.' Fox clapped his hands together. 'Weapons.'

A tall, antique wardrobe peeled apart in a flurry of golden and black cubes to expose a series of a gleaming racks. Microgrenades, razornades, neurotoxins, shardpistols, handcannons, EMP pistols, carbines, autorifles, marksman rifles, scattershots, railguns, fancy slingshivs and all manner of sharpshooters. There were even smatter-turrets, missile launchers, and nanoguns used in space warfare. Military-grade hardware, all sheathed in gel-padding and plastic casings.

A lot of weapons manufacturers had gone out of business after the Reaper War. Not on a large scale, of course. People always want better ways to kill each other. But the sudden drop in demand meant a lot of wholesalers selling cheap to buyers who saw an opportunity in places like Compass.

'You want to raise some pulses? This one will set you right.' Fox handed me a silver scattershot with a polished wooden stock. Good balance, solid textured grips.

'It's all untraceable,' said Badger, stormtech flashing down his arms. Standing next to me, the alien carried the same over-ripe, sickly-sweet musk I did. Guess the stormtech altered alien pheromones as well as human. Wasn't too sure what to think about that. 'The scattershot's equipped with a magnetic system, allowing you to retrieve the slugs after you've fired them.'

'Anything else?'

'Yeah,' Fox piped in. 'If the rest of the gun doesn't work, you can always hit 'em with it.'

But it was the heavy handcannon that drew my attention. Matte-black with bursts of red streaks down the ribbed barrel, like crimson rain bleeding across metal. Lights winked on, thrumming to life in my hand as I hefted it and stared down the holographic sights, getting an idea of its weight and balance. You've got to feel just right with your handcannons.

'Ah. That's the R-32 Titan,' Fox piped in. 'A semiautomatic death machine, my friend. Multicalibre printer, adjustable sights and spread, jet propulsion energy charges. It's packing four ammo types: standard, armour-piercing, EMP, and explosive rounds for the times you're in a bit of a tiff.'

Had to be an offworld manufacturer. These things were suitbusters, equipped for zero-gee combat. You fired this thing at someone, there wasn't going to be much left to bury.

So, obviously, I was taking it. Along with the scattershot, an autorifle with textured grips, nonlethal neurotoxins and a shard-pistol with crystals dipped in cyanobacteria that autoprinted near instantly, along with thirty quickmatter magazines.

'Send them to my apartment,' I told Fox as he punched in the necessary permissions for my printer to sketch up the weapons. I imagined the AI rabbit's wide-eyed bafflement as my new arsenal spilled out of the printer.

I attached the Titan handcannon to the magnetic holster on my thigh and pocketed a few of the neurotoxin needles before parting ways with the two darkmarket sellers, and was back into the bedlam of the Upper Markets, wrapped in cutting-edge armour. The armour was far bulkier than my previous iteration had been, but manoeuvring in it felt effortless. I had the hydraulics along my spine to thank for that. Fox hadn't been lying about the faster response from the interface either: it felt like an extension of myself rather than something I was wearing. I flexed my shoulders and the armour seemed to flex with me, muscles and servos in unison. Oh, this was going to be fun.

In the corner, Aras' shop had been sealed up, already leased out to some space-manufactory. Seemed like the Bulkava had wised up and taken the window of opportunity I'd given him. He'd be four or five space sectors away if he had any sense.

Knots of shoppers drifted by, two squabbling Torven knocking into me and slamming the thoughts out of my head. Over in the corner were some hunched figures, built like tanks. They were Rhivik, reptilian bipeds with scaly, rock-like skin that appeared to be covered in barnacles. An aggressive, combat-driven species, they were the latest species to arrive on Compass with the intent of establishing a home on the asteroid. The aliens were renowned for naturally growing their own rocky armour plating by way of thick scales, and were capable of shedding it at will. They'd sold the plates as trinkets to traders, creating a market for other species to graft them into their own flesh. They were in the middle of a deal, handing over boxes of their own biology to a vendor specializing in tattoos, skingrafts and body piercings. They'd soon carve out their own niche in the body-modification industries. As if there weren't enough ways to meld alien DNA into human flesh already. One glanced at me with slitted crocodile eyes that blinked upwards, bits of meat wedged in between his tombstone teeth. Their business concluded, the aliens rumbled away into the crowds.

A few floors down from the Upper Markets was a winding racetrack that ran along the outer edges of the asteroid, used for fitness laps and obstacle courses. It was well past midnight, but nothing really closed on Compass. Plenty of chances to test the capacity of my new suit out, see if it was everything Fox chalked it up to be. I was halfway down the escalators when my palmerlog rang with a call. No number, no ID. I connected it to my HUD. 'Hello?'

'Vakov!' Artyom practically spat my name out, like it was poison. 'Was that bloody you down there?'

'Nice to hear from you, too.'

'You sodding, maggot-brained moron. You stupid insufferable little prick. I told you to stay the hell away. You could have ruined *everything*!'

I hadn't had the easiest of weeks, even before I'd been kidnapped, held at gunpoint, strapped down and locked in my own suit and then tortured by a psychopathic AI for almost thirty hours. Even before I'd held out to protect *him*. The knives were out. 'You mean: I've made stealing stormtech from Harmony and selling it to drug traffickers *inconvenient* for you?' I said. 'And you're calling *me* a moron?'

189

'What part of *sod off* did you not understand?'

'You're part of the plan, aren't you? You're actually trying to sabotage Harmony by poisoning stormtech.' I attempted a mirthless smile. 'Did someone kick you in the head?'

'Shut up, Vak! Just shut your ugly pig mouth. I don't need your advice, and I sure as hell don't need you in my life. We had to relocate because of you.'

'Oh, so it's *my* fault now?'

'You could have been *killed*, breaking in like that! No one survives the cradle.'

The rage had started to slip from his eyes. He was afraid. Afraid for me. I felt the metal pendant resting against my chest and for a moment saw the boy who had given it to me by the edge of a mountain. Remembered the scars he carried. What the world had done to him. What we'd done to each other.

'They're making plans for you, Vak. They want to staple you to a wall with metal spikes and vivisect you; melt your eyes in your skull and slowly cut pieces off you. When they get bored keeping you alive, they'll let dogs eat you from the feet upwards. They'll film it and send it to Harmony as a warning. *That's* what they're capable of.'

'Then why are you with them, Artyom?'

He slowly shook his head. 'You can't possibly understand.'

'Try me.'

'I can't. Jae will take you out if she suspects you're an ongoing threat. Forcing the whole set-up to relocate put you right on her radar.'

'Jae?' Both Hideko and Lasky had mentioned a *she*. 'Who's Jae?'

Artyom froze as he realised he'd said too much. 'Walk away, Vak. They don't know about us, not yet. I'm trying to keep it that way, but I can't do it for ever. They don't know we're brothers.' The last sentence came out choked and thick. He blinked hard and looked away.

'You know I can't walk away,' I said quietly. I wished I could hug him. That we could go back, before all this mess, and try again. 'You'll always be my little brother. Doesn't matter what you do or say. And I'll never give up on you, Artyom. I can't.' I leaned forward and spoke past the hardness in my throat. 'Even if it hurts, even if you hate me, I will never pretend you don't matter. I'll never stop trying to make things right. Because that's what being your brother means.'

Tears glistened in the corner of his eyes, matching mine. There was a quiet moment between us. He squeezed his eyes, hard. But his face morphed back into anger and the moment vanished into smoke. 'So that's it, then.' His voice was dark and knotted, his words forming a wall between us as he smeared the tears away. 'It's all just a way for you to feel better. Make up for abandoning me to Dad?'

'Don't,' I forced out through gritted teeth. 'You have no right.'

'Stop playing the hypocrite,' Artyom yelled. 'I have every right, I—'

'Shut up and listen to me, you ungrateful little bastard. I tried to protect you. I took beatings for you until I was blind and coughing up blood. Don't you dare pretend I didn't try.'

'It did nothing in the end, didn't it? You couldn't stop Dad killing Mum, right in front of us. Couldn't save Kasia. So now you're trying to save me from myself.' He choked back the surge of emotions like a physical thing and scoffed. 'What, you thought doing what you did to that boy would bring our sister back? Make everything better?'

My hands clenched. It wasn't right for us to be here, digging into each other's wounds. 'Shut up the hell up, Artyom. Just *shut up*.'

'I expected you to be sent home in a box. It ate at me, Vakov. Every day for years.'

'Shut up!'

'But you didn't care. Our promise to protect each other didn't matter. You just wanted out. You chose that war over *me*. You chose *yourself*.' His voice went hoarse, eyes galvanising into cold steel. 'I'm glad—'

'Don't,' I growled, my hands twitching by my sides. 'Don't you dare.'

He went for the heart. 'I'm glad Kasia's dead. If she saw you now, she'd probably just kill herself. Better yet, since the war didn't finish the job, why don't *you* kill yourself?'

He disconnected on me as I punched a wall, hard. Concrete sprayed. Fury rose in my throat, so hot and barbed I was choking, spluttering on it. I punched the wall again, again, again, until my armoured knuckles were smashing against rebar.

I let out a furious growl between my clenched teeth as I stood there, panting. Then in my rear-cam I saw a familiar figure shouldering through the crowds with purpose. Even dressed in a heavy hood, I recognised Hairless and his pale features. He must have spotted me coming out of the armoury and followed me down here.

Only one way he could have homed in on me so easily. Artyom had called to see if I'd back off. When I wouldn't, he'd made the decision to take me out of the game. Had my own brother lured me into a trap?

My muscles tightened, the rage swelling back into my throat. Rage at being used by my pig of a father. Rage at Harmony using me as a lab rat in the Reaper War. Rage at Kindosh using me like a pawn while my friends, my bloodbrothers, were hunted down and murdered on the streets like rabid dogs.

Rage that my brother was helping them do it.

I was done.

Screw them all.

My mouth tightened, saliva swelling in my gums. The stormtech clawing hard and wet against my ribcage. My left hand tightening around the textured grip of my handcannon.

Harmony wanted answers? Fine.

I'd get them.

17

The Lone Wolf

If you can, choose your battleground. And if you can, fight in small, controlled spaces. Never out in the open. Never where your flank's unguarded. Never give your enemy a clean target. You only get one chance at a first encounter on the battlefield, so pick your terrain wisely. Which is why I waited until I spotted a dark, disused alleyway before setting my trap. I hid in the doorframe of the back entrance to a stormtech simulation lab, where folks who wanted to try the real thing could be discouraged by discovering what having the stuff kicking around in your system was really like.

I shoved the handcannon under Hairless' chin as he turned the corner, a glow from a lightwell giving him an unhealthy, pallid look. 'If you wanted something,' I said, 'you should have asked.'

Hairless did a good impression of a man choking on his surprise as the stormtech slid up my arm, the urge to shoot coming with it. One squeeze. One squeeze and the antipersonnel shells would punch through blood and bone and turn his head to a dripping smear on the walls. After the hurt Artyom had dealt to me, my body was eager to pass the pain along. I readjusted my grip and fought the sensations back. 'Now, you're going to take me to whoever's been getting you to follow me around.'

His mouth opened with terror. 'I— I can't!'

'You can,' I said patiently, nudging the muzzle against his throat and adding an edge of venom to my voice. 'Either I let this handcannon finish our conversation, or you take me on a little trip to your boss.'

Didn't take him long to decide.

I frisked him and confiscated a thin-gun and a slingshiv — probably the same one he'd used to slice me open last time, as well as an ID card. Avin Simmons turned out to be his name. I nudged the handcannon upwards to strip off his coat, and Simmons reared backwards and spat out a vile yellow liquid. I ducked sideways, the stream missing me by inches, spattering against the wall. The metalwork hissed, melted inwards. He had *acid glands*. The irony. He drew his head to go for round two, when I slammed the full weight of my armour into him, crushing him against the wall, his claws breaking off as they were scraped across the brickwork. I hauled him over to the railing and forced him half over, letting him stare down the barrel of a hard floor with eight storeys of the Upper Markets between them. 'If I drop you, do you explode into acid when you hit the bottom? Or do you just melt through the floor? Got to say, I'm curious.' He struggled feebly in my grip, which was probably the worst thing he *could* do. 'Maybe you should have been outfitted with wings, instead.'

'Get shot,' Simmons growled, the ends of his splintered fingers bleeding.

I could have questioned him right here. It would have been the Harmony way. But I was sick of running with whatever scraps others had seen fit to feed me. You've got to do things your own way. In my case, that means grabbing the bull by the horns. 'Let's try again. You'll walk slowly ahead of me. If you try anything, if you warn anyone, or try that spitting trick again . . .' I shoved him a little further, as if I was really going to let him fall.

He frantically nodded.

For the first time since all this started, I was in charge.

My hand felt fused to the handcannon grip by the time we spiralled up to a high-floor called Ruskin. Townhouses, local hotels, small concert halls and multicultural bistros stood along the wide cobblestone streets. Shavings of dawn light were prickling over the artificial horizon, a smattering of people visible through the glass of dimly lit coffeehouses. Everything had the soft, gunmetal sheen of recent rain. Beyond the buildings, you could just see a rolling grassland, dotted with life-sized pieces of bio-organic artwork and sculptures carved from condensed cosmic dust. This was the sort of place that fostered creativity, community living. Even the air was tuned to simulate a fresh spring morning, scented with lime and saffron.

So what the hell were we doing here?

I stuck the handcannon into the small of Simmons' back. 'If you're screwing around with me . . .'

'It's around the next corner,' he said, almost begrudgingly.

It was. And it smacked the words out of my mouth. I started laughing. 'You've got to be kidding me.'

It was the Tipei Corporation facility. The heart of the Jackal's operation. Was this just his revenge? Nothing to do with the stormtech? No, he wouldn't be that sloppy. If it was personal, he'd be doing the hunting himself. Me and Grim had stolen his tech. He wouldn't send a goon to stalk me over Compass. Something stank.

Just as well I was in the mood for answers today.

The facility was a bizarre fusion of chainglass, solid steel and dark wood, the edges deliberately slanted so the entire building appeared to be tilting to the side. The back was one of those buildings built into the asteroid's rockface. Perfect if they didn't want someone sniffing out a back door. I weighed up patching Kowalski into my discovery. I wanted her input, wanted her to know I was making progress. But she could just as easily tell me to stand down and turn Simmons in. Get a search warrant approved. Launch a proper investigation. There was no evidence of anything dodgy going on in this place, only the word of a would-be assassin. I was still riding out the fog of rage I'd felt at Artyom's behaviour and I wasn't in the mood to bail out now.

I dragged Simmons up a side stairwell to a employee-entrance, where a scanner pad surfaced out of the wall. Once Simmons had keyed in the code and the door cracked open I sank a neurotoxin needle deep into his neck, letting him fold to the grillwork floor. It wouldn't kill him, but he'd wake up with a hell of a headache.

I stole inside.

I stared down the barrel of my handcannon into a carpeted hallway with clinical white walls. I walked across, almost silent in my armour. The peace unsettled me. Stairwells crisscrossed above and below me, forking into separate branches of the building. I descended the nearest one. I was about halfway down when the stormtech kicked furiously against my torso. I pressed a hand to my chest. What was wrong? My heartrate was steady, my adrenaline levels weren't up, but it was reacting to something. I scanned the area again. Nothing to see. Yet, the stormtech continued strumming along my nervous system. Something in the facility had to be triggering it.

I heard a pair of voices approaching. I stooped down, peering through the staircase. A figure walked by, deep in conversation with a blue-haired woman in a utilitarian grey suit. I snatched a glimpse of the man. Grey eyes, hard face like ocean-weathered rocks. A familiar accent as he spoke.

No. It couldn't be Sokolav.

Kindosh had said he'd been MIA for two years and counting. And what would my former instructor possibly be doing here, anyway? Even if he was alive, he'd been too smart, too loyal to Harmony to consider working for them like Artyom. Hadn't he?

Nothing I could do about it now.

I filed it away for later, waited until they passed before continuing down the stairs, sweeping past corridors with the stormtech maintaining its frantic beat inside me. I followed its intensity until it jolted in my chest on the second last door. I slid inside and found a long line of stormtech canisters, each marked with Harmony's symbol, locked in place. Above them were racks of little stormtech flasks, blue swirling inside like trapped smoke. Just waiting to be opened and inhaled. I had to tear my eyes away before I made a decision I couldn't undo.

The canisters were just the start. A long smear of workstations were cluttered with flexiscreens, printers, databanks and stacks of servers, all tethered together with a web of snaking cables. My HUD detonated with detections of synthsilver, bluesmoke, grimwire and even cloudhead, chemical compositions rising out of the stained desks and glassware. The stormtech continued tying frantic knots inside my chest. Arytom said their operations had moved, but this couldn't be their new base. Too small and too conspicuous. They wouldn't be stupid enough to plant the heart of their operations in the dead centre of Harmony's busiest highfloors. Had to assume this was a third-party operation, maybe a glorified storage base.

There was one person who'd tell me for sure.

Grim answered my call on the fourth ring. He rubbed blood-shot eyes, the glow of a paused filmlog showering across his pale face. 'Vak. What the hell? It's only—'

'Grim. Shut up and look at this.' I accessed the nearest flexi-screen, sending the terminal ID over to Grim. 'Quickly.'

Still grumbling, Grim cracked his knuckles and did his Deep Dive. Using the data I'd provided to scour the databanks for backdoors and previous passkeys on the mainframes. In his skeleton underskin and white eyes, he looked like a demented techghost in some lost nightmare.

The screen blinked. He'd broken in. A galaxy of data erupted around me. Literally. A universe of stars, comets, planets, moons, supergiants, swirling blackholes, each size and shape indicating their data size and type. A carmine datasphere, patterned like a gas-giant, ghosted straight through the sights of my handcannon before peeling open to expose a network of data. 'Oh, these boys have been busy,' muttered Grim as multicoloured papers, transcripts, blueprints, video and sound files scrawled around us in mid-air. 'These are our guys, Vak. There's five substrates worth of academic papers and intel here. Most of it has been classified.'

'Classified?'

'Classified by Harmony, anti-narcotics institutions, militia groups, and scientists. Not banned, just highly sensitive data.' A twisting comet, ringed with spiralling intel, froze in front of me. 'Vak, this is thirty years' worth of—'

'—research,' I finished, figuring it out as he did. 'Their research and experiments on the stormtech. They're looking for ways to strengthen and bolster its potency.' My hand dropped to my weapon. 'And how to poison it.'

'Yeah.' Grim's voice was low and quiet.

Compass was ripe with stormdealer syndicates, cartels, and networks that operated across the criminal underbelly of the asteroid. Doing business, selling their products in clubs and street corners, in spaceports and dockside bars, in skyscrapers and business districts. Some so powerful they fronted businesses that dominated the economy of entire neighbourhoods, sometimes entire floors. It was a business, and like any other business, they had three particular interests: money, power, influence.

If this whirling galaxy of data was telling me anything, it was that these guys operated on an entirely different level. One with an agenda: a deep-seated grudge against Harmony. Stormdealers tended to take the view that customers going on a killing spree, dying on the streets and attracting the attention of galaxy-wide government forces with a zero-drug policy were bad for business. Not this group. This was about something other than getting rich. Something they needed a darkmarket pharmaceutical company up their sleeve for.

The door jerked open and a gaunt-faced man in system technician gear gaped at me. I had him in my handcannon sights already, his mouth gaping wider once he saw it. 'Not a word. Stand facing the wall, hands behind your head.' I used the voice-masking feature in my armour, turning my voice into a menacing rasp. It made him move faster than he'd probably ever moved in his life. I gritted my teeth. I'd been seen, and now had a hostage to deal with.

'Hmm.' Grim's voice broke back into my commslink. 'Looks like we've got ourselves a name.'

'A name?' Artyom had mentioned a *Jae*.

'Yeah. Some egghead called Viklun Ryken. Worked at a deep-space dockyard called Quyn, in the Tungyian System, owned by the Rhivik. Used to be a betting house for illegal chainship races through asteroid fields.' A neutron star swung out of its orbit, ripping open in a blur of glowing prisms. It materialised into an elongated space station, equipped with a sprawling dockyard. Beyond, chainships were on their way to the asteroid field, framed by a small cluster of stars. 'Harmony had a few things to say about that, of course. The Rhivik caused a hell of a fuss, bitched about humans to other species for a while, but the place got retrofitted into Quyn Research Station, studying nearby cosmic events.'

'Sounds too clean to me.'

'Oh. Now, that's *interesting*.'

'What is it, Grim?'

'I did a little searching on public search engines. This Ryken guy isn't just a xenobiologist. He's one of the few people studying the Shenoi.'

And maybe the very guy telling our stormdealer friends how to poison the stormtech.

I went about looping a set of plastic cables around my hostage's wrists, tying him to a workstation while Grim did what he did best: find data he shouldn't. He relayed his findings to me as fast as he found them. They had shops fronting their business scattered over Compass. Dead-drops for picking up canisters. Shipping routes. Distribution channels that flowed through at least four spaceports, ten floors and twelve business chains. A hit-list of rival stormdealers. Two stormdealer syndicates interested in handling their product. An offworld spacecraft manufacturer building chainships honeycombed with compartments to smuggle canisters off Compass, with a conceptual schematic of a chainship attached to the transmission. And at the very bottom of the transmission was the same symbol I'd seen in the Warren. An inverted Y, the edges squared off.

And three words: House of Suns.

'That's it,' I breathed.

Grim glanced up. 'What's it?'

'House of Suns,' I said quietly. 'That's their name. And their symbol. That's who we're after.'

Quyn Research Station was winked away, and a cluster of ice-giants grew around me as Grim plugged the names into his network. 'That's impossible.'

'What?'

'Vak, there're no search results for these freaks. Absolutely zero. That's *never* happened before.'

The stormtech trickled down my spine like molten lead as the pieces finally snapped into place. The House of Suns couldn't be based exclusively on Compass. Compass was a minor part of their ecosystem of operations. This could have come from anywhere in the Common. I thought back to the Warren. The substrates, the cradle, the darkmarket razornade. Now, offworld research stations, spacecraft manufacturers, stormdealer syndicates. They were heavy-hitting, professional, and brutally efficient. You didn't look beyond Compass unless you had to. Shuttling goods across galactic regions of deepspace is insanely expensive and borderline suicidal – at least without a heavily armed effort – when smugglers and Blade Hunters are swarming along the moons and waystations, looking for easy pickings.

So this was bigger than Compass. Bigger than us.

Artyom had known how dangerous and far-reaching this was. He'd been so furious *because* he understood the magnitude of this operation. My guts felt like they were melting inside me as I realised how little I knew my brother.

We weren't going to find anything more here. More importantly, I knew where we had to go next. I was telling Grim when I heard the approaching footsteps, disconnected him, and snapped away from the flexiscreen. Poised in a crouched position as the door dilated open and I found myself staring at a guard. He had a shock of dishevelled hair, a local militia insignia stamped on the shoulder of his tactical gear.

My handcannon cracked twice, punching into the guard's chest as he fired his thin-gun from the hip, mistaking the technician for an attacker and blasting him in the head. The two bodies hit the ground one after the other, the echo of the gunshot crackling down the halls.

18

Bulletstorm

There's a unique kind of silence after the echo of a gunshot dies down. Pure. Complete. As if every living thing is scared of drawing any attention to itself. It gets the survival mechanism kicking in like no other sound does. So I knew I wasn't mistaken when I picked up the clatter of heavy footsteps heading my way. If *that* wasn't enough, the stormtech sparked like electricity in my chest, welcoming the incoming attack. Eight, ten, fifteen assailants. All coming to carve me up.

I was screwed. No way could I battle my way through that many men.

Or maybe I could.

The flasks of stormtech glistened at me from the shelves. Before I knew it, I was holding one. My hand was twitching. My mouth webbed with sticky saliva, sweat prickling across the nape of my neck. I couldn't. I couldn't take a dose like this, not after spending so long wrenching every possible drop of it out of me. Not after the rehab centres had pounded and strained me to the breaking point to be almost clean of it. I couldn't predict what I'd do. It could be tainted. Even if it wasn't, the knockback might fry my brains, melt my organs into my guts.

A gruff, muffled voice echoed from a few storeys above. 'He's downstairs. Direct shots only, can't risk hitting—'

The words went out of earshot, but I'd heard enough. My new armour was top-market quality, but even it wouldn't repel sustained fire for long.

I looked back at the stormtech.

It was like standing on the edge of a roaring cliff, the wind hard at my back, peering into a thrashing ocean below. This dosage could kill me in minutes. Or it could save me.

Not worth the risk. Slowly, almost painfully, I put it down.

There was only one other thing to try.

I spread my arms. Blocked out the world around me and focused inward. Focused on the depths of my body. I felt the stormtech surging up my arms, up my legs and chest like oil. I invited it to rush unobstructed through my veins, strumming my nerves and circling my heart. I gritted my teeth as I dredged up everything that had happened: my brother, my Reaper brothers dying, the war. I fed the stormtech my fear, frustration and white-hot, abject *rage*. I let the stormtech burn through me like wildfire.

I didn't realise I'd closed my eyes.

When I opened them again, everything *glowed*.

The world had taken on the crisp, shiny edge of raw data. Everything sharper, more precise. I could hear every step of the oncoming men, smell the acid in their sweat. See the microscopic films of dust coating the workstations. My chest heaved and I felt my body crackle and tighten with purpose. The air flowing into my lungs tasted like alcohol fumes. My muscles were tingling, my mouth stretched in a splitting grin as I felt every fibre of my body coalesce under my control. My legs poised in a fighter's stance. My powerful hands squeezed into trembling fists. Ready to fight.

This was what I remembered. *This* was what I'd been.

I'd never realised how much I'd missed it. How *good* it felt.

Scraping of boots overhead. Two people. Maybe three. Coming down the stairs.

I pressed my back to the wall as the door slid open. Breathing and footsteps echoed from the corridor. My muscles tensed. Had to wait for them to advance, to come to me. My heart was thumping so hard in my chest I thought they would hear it.

A shadow fell across the doorway, and with two steps the figure stepped clear. I shot him in the head, the handcannon echoing loud and flat. He smashed into a workstation, the second figure yelling as I charged out through the doorway. Her shot burst above me and the stormtech leaped along my breastbone in excitement. I ducked and shot her twice in the chest, throwing her backwards as, beyond her, I heard the high-pitched whine of weapons priming. I took my chance and dived across the hall into a fully furnished conference area, hoping to split them up instead of fighting them all head-on. There was a yell as one of them saw me, then a crackle of communication, and suddenly footsteps were heading towards me from all sides, pinning me dead in the centre of their sights.

The room erupted into chaos.

Sun-bright muzzle flashes around me, gunfire ripping out from high-calibre rifles and rattling my teeth. Chairs and tables turning into gnarled chunks, pillars smashing apart, workstations blasted across the room and glass showering around me. I hunkered down, aware of men to my left slowly closing in on me. The handcannon jerked in my hands as I nailed the first shooter, sending him crashing through a glass wall. I missed the second, shattering a wooden pillar apart in a flurry of splinters. Return fire hammered around me, rattling off my shoulder, but the armour soaked up the damage, spreading the force of the impact over my body. The room was wreathed in smoke and crisscrossed with volleys of gunfire. I leaned forward, squeezing off a round that punched through a man's helmet visor. Motion stabilisers in the armour giving me perfect, clean shots as I drove two handcannon rounds into another shooter's chest, sending them crashing backwards over a desk.

A high-calibre round whined past, inches from my helmet, and crunched into a guard's kneecap behind me. He rolled screaming on the floor as I darted to a concrete pillar for cover, a salvo of blaster bolts streaming down from above. My pulse pounded in my fingers as walls exploded inwards, showering splinters of metal and plaster around the room in angry bursts, stray projectiles ricocheting off me and the guards' armour alike.

'We want him alive!' someone screamed. Not that anyone in the room seemed to be listening as the room plunged into darkness. A siren screeched around us, the noise catapulting me back to the war for a moment, the ghostly outlines of my fireteam around me between blinks. The air felt denser, gravity higher. Poisonous yellow lighting turned the hallways into a shuttered nightmare. Barely able to hear or think. All rational fear squashed to a pulp by the stormtech grinding against my ribs.

I was slammed hard against the wall, knocking me back to Compass. Felt like I'd been hit in the chest with a sledgehammer. I saw the scattershot shooter the moment he squeezed off another round square into my midriff. I choked on my own breath, panting in my cover, splattering the inside of my visor with saliva. There was a warm prickle as the hydrostatic gel inside my armour tightened for protection, a stinging sensation as biofoam oozed into my wounds.

A table beside me erupted into smoking splinters, the scattershot shooter charging. But now I knew where he was. I sprang forward, the armour giving me inhuman speed. My armoured bulk smashed into his, sending him staggering off-balance.

I jammed the handcannon under his chin and fired, black blood splattering out.

Search beams slashed across the darkened room, hunting me. I hugged the floor and gripped my weapon as I had in the Reaper War. Close, tight, familiar. The handcannon crackled as I aimed down the sights towards incoming guards, throttling the trigger, blasting through a kneecap, the guard's legs thrashing as he smashed to the floor. Heart in my throat, I fired up through the walkways, shedding sparks and chunks of metal. Someone collapsed, legs mangled, screaming until a stray bullet from a comrade shattered his face apart.

A warning beamed up on my HUD: out of ammo. The handcannon hummed in my hands, autoprinting bullets. I couldn't afford to wait and reached to grab a scattershot dropped by one of the guards when a furious spear of pain shivered down my shoulder, a high-calibre round hitting home. I scrambled forward, scooped up the chunky scattershot, grips readjusting to my hand-size as I blasted away with ear-splitting echoes. Chunks of plaster ripping and spraying from the wall as I tracked the shooter with my sights, nailing him on the fifth shot and sending him spluttering against the wall.

I heaved in a series of gulping breaths as sirens continued to scream overhead. My eardrums were throbbing. Plaster rained down on the dead and injured among the wrecked room. Handcannon recharge at twenty-three percent. Had to get out of here.

I burst out of the room, spraying blind fire into the stairwell. Yells sounded as the stairwell collapsed in a screech of tortured metal. I leaped clear with a heavy thud, running for the second stairwell, cocooned in a world of adrenaline and the throttling joy spiking through my body. Had to retrace my steps to find the exit before they trapped me in here.

I reached the second landing, a grenade going off, violent

shockwaves spreading out as a salvo of gunfire hammered into my chest. I was slammed flat on my back, ears rippling with white noise, throbbing with so much pain that for a moment I thought I'd been killed. My armour went rock-hard around me, pumping me with drugs. The world blurring into monochrome. Blinking hard, trying to focus, gunfire growing from a muted rumble into a thundering echo as my hearing slammed back to me. A three-round burst tore a chunk out of the wall by my head. I crouched and fired blind bursts into the smoke, my muzzle flash giving me away. Gunfire returned, clattering against my shoulder. Teeth clenched hard enough to crack, the handcannon coughed as I aimed down the holographic sights and fired. There was a wet splatter and the guard collapsed, twitching on the ground before going still.

Mangled yells tore through the constant shriek of the siren. My body clenched, soaking up the dread and excitement of this war-torn nightmare. Given the chance, the stormtech would make me hack and blast my way through every last man, make me do anything to survive and to sustain this rush of adrenaline. That's what made it so invaluable: it wouldn't let me stop until I was dead, or they were.

But I needed to be smarter than that.

The exit loomed above: a neon-white rectangle shrouded in the smoky darkness. My palms were sweaty and my throat was tight with hunger. Body curved like a predator as my prey came galloping into my outstretched claws.

Had to remember my training. Years of battling these desires, dodging the pitfalls. Remember my Reaper brothers, telling me not to cave, to be stronger than that. For Alcatraz, Cable, Ratchet, Myra, all the others in that bloody nightmare. The people that had fought beside me. Pushing away my body's desires. Lifting me back up to the light.

Think of my brother. I couldn't give in now. I never had before. And if I stayed, I'd be lost.

Something rumbled in my throat, my body battling itself for control. I tore myself away with bone-wrenching force, tendrils of desire still squirming inside me as I ran through the exit, bullets chasing me into blinding white light.

19

The Locked Brain

The world blinked and stuttered around me in electric waves.
My body was as taut as a chainmetal cable, my heart jackhammering against my chest. My vision tilted, my legs wob-
bling as I stumbled into the shadow of a droid docking pod.
Safe. I'd had enough sense to smash the access panel before I'd
dived out of the facility, locking them inside. I'd been madly
sprinting for at least an hour, my body still geared up after the
fight. No one would find me here.

I drew back my helmet and raked deep, shuddering breaths,
aware of my body and the sticky, fluid warmth flushing through
it. Every sensation heightened to the hilt: the shuddering of my
heart, the sweet-sour scent of my sweat, the blood rushing to
my muscles. Blue mist swarmed at the edges of my vision and
there was a sickly-sweet taste tickling the back of my throat.
If I didn't get a grip on myself the stormtech would swallow
me and I'd be lost to it again.

I had to go through the steps to comedown. I let the armour's
inner tendrils and abrasive surfaces press up against my body,
itching, tickling, grounding me with stimuli to loosen the
stormtech's grip while I inhaled deeply. It had started to rain
and I tilted my face upwards, letting the cool drizzle of water
trickle down my cheeks. I ran through a set of stretches and

cast my mind to the calming landscapes of my childhood home, exactly as I'd been trained. The peaceful tops of snowy, razor-backed mountains stretching over the horizon. A cold breeze whistling through the windswept tundra, through beaches of black sand and soaring cliffs. Taking myself elsewhere, beyond the suffocating cage of my body.

I breathed out, hard. I'd passed the worst of it. I blinked, able to think straight again.

Had to get out of this place.

The blood and smoke coating my armour was a dead give away. They hadn't seen me outside of my suit yet. I assessed it, and decided I'd done enough to loosen the stormtech's grip. I released myself from the suit's protective embrace and stepped out into open air. I shivered at the cold and suppressed the urge to slide back into the armour's warm insides. Instead, I smeared the blood off its chest and sent it home with my weapons. Now, I was able to get a good look at myself through the underskin. Before, the stormtech had been faintly visible on my body. Now I was livid with it. Thick blue strands inched along my ribs and spine like curious fingers. It spun vicious patterns along my chest and stomach, globules dripping down my legs.

Stormtech doesn't just enhance your body, it submerges you in it. Fills your entire conscious being. It's literally like being cocooned in power. But it can also drown you. I was through the worst of it, but still dangerously within range. Had to be somewhere public, keep following my training, where I could feel human again. Even though my flesh crawled as I stepped onto the people-packed promenade. I felt every glance, every smell and gush of air, every brush against my skin.

I found myself stumbling back towards the sweeping park-land I'd noted earlier. It was distant and public enough that they wouldn't look for me here. I rubbed my eyes and blinked at my surroundings. I'd gone further than I realised. A line of coffeehouses and bakeries rose upwards to form small glass cube-shaped structures tilting sideways at precarious angles. Creatures that looked like jellyfish floated in the air, dust motes falling from their tentacles. They'd been brought from some local planet to add to the rich biodiversity here. Loose knots of people were scattered around me on benches, enjoying a day out.

I sprawled out on the long, damp grass like a star. Chest rising and falling, my breathing starting to slow. Feeling the stormtech rumble through me in long echoes before gradually seeping and fading away again, as it had always done. You can't go instantly high and stay there, it doesn't work that way. It takes time, consistent use and aggressive feeding to crank the stormtech up to maximum output levels, just as it takes time to dial it back down. Always being surrounded by combat during the Reaper War meant I was kept on what we called Cloud Infinite. It hypersensitised you and dulled your empathy, your humanity. The most terrifying Reapers were always the least human. Organic killing machines wrapped in flesh. By that stage, they had to be kept drugged up to their eyeballs with mood-controlling meds before being unleashed on the enemy like hunting dogs.

Was I headed that way before this was over? If I managed to save Artyom, would he even recognise me? Would I?

I wasn't back at Reaper levels. But I'd torn through the mental and physical suppression that held the stormtech at bay, wedging myself back open to it. Stormtech was like any other drug: the harder and longer you used it, the stronger it became, the more difficult to quell its urges. After the whole Tipei payroll had tried to blast me into pieces, the stormtech was wrapped all that much tighter around my body, all that much harder to resist it again. I felt it scrape against my bones, claw up my bloodstream. I closed my eyes and concentrated on the tickle of grass against my neck, the cool wind against my sweat. Thick, slow drops of rainwater pattered across my torso. Slowly, slowly I felt my senses rolling back down, my sight, smell and hearing growing duller, like I was gently descending from high altitude on a low-gravity world. The raging aggression churning in the pit of my stomach like flickering flames slowly being doused. I breathed deep. If I could control this, I maybe had a chance.

With the fog wrapped around my mind rapidly evaporating, I pasted my shredded thoughts back together. I wasn't dealing with some drug syndicate, it was clear they were studying and modifying stormtech. But for what? Altering it for increased sales was one thing. Flooding the market with a substance they knew was toxic was another. These deaths had to be significant to them. Running with the assumption that they were deliberately undermining Harmony's rule by showing Reapers and skinnies to be loose cannons, they were hell-bent on keeping people away from rehab and keeping them dosed high on stormtech. If this wasn't for money, then what was it for? Political gain? It'd explain why they were trying to pin the deaths on Harmony. But there were plenty of ways to go about doing that without sending Reapers on a kamikaze rampage. Or the very great risk that came with getting on Harmony's radar. Had to be someone with a personal grudge. Didn't much help narrow down my suspects at all. The Common and the greater galaxy at large were scattered with multispecies militia groups, insurrectionists, and cabals who hated Harmony's guts as much as they hated Harvest's. I thought again of the symbol I'd seen. Of the scale of what I'd uncovered. This was an organisation with roots deep in the asteroid's underworld infrastructure.

And Sokolav. Not only was my old Commander not dead, as Harmony thought, he was working with these people. The man who'd noticed me struggling when I first arrived at the Harmony Training Station, a dozen light years from my home in a world I didn't understand, and guided me through the Reaper Programme he'd helped design. Who put his reassuring hand on my shoulder as they pumped me with chemicals and locked me in restraints before shooting the stormtech into my body, swearing he'd never leave my side for a second. Who stood in the early dawn light with the wind in his hair and a devilish fire in his eyes and told his entire Battalion he was proud of us, prouder than he'd ever been of anyone in his life, and would do whatever it took to get us through the war. He was the father I never had.

Now he was with the people killing my family, the Reapers he'd built. Destroying his entire legacy and everything he ever stood for. And I still had no idea why.

My fists tightened. Why I did have to be involved in this? Why did Artyom have to be?

I glanced out at the rolling grasslands, hearing the susurrus of trees in the wind. I watched a family over by the undercover playground: two boys laughing and wrestling cheerfully with each other for a ball, and their mother sitting on a picnic mat. I watched them for a little, an unbidden smile on my face.

I stood, turning to go when a seismic *craaaack!* shattered the soundscape, a high-pitched whine rupturing through my head. The windows of storefronts and autovehicles exploded, a blizzard of glass raining down on the crowds. I saw people's mouths moving. Everything a muffled, high-pitched whine. Figures stumbling by me, bleeding from their ears, bleeding from the glass. Dust and fire were gouting out of a medium-sized building across the lake. At first it looked like the building was wrapped in a heat haze, until I realised it was toppling forward. Cables snapping, concrete crumbling, glass splintering. I saw black shapes spilling from the broken windows, thudding into the pavement.

People. They were *people*.

Screams and sirens punched through the white noise in muffled blasts, but I was already racing through the wet grass, the crowds running with me, heading for the safety of the concourse as the building's foundation made one last tortured groan and crashed into the lake. The shockwave shuddered up my legs and up my spine, throwing huge dark waves up from the lake like towering monstrosities of water, showering over the grassland in great splattering heaves. Lake water surged towards and through the crowd, up to my knees and already flooding coffeehouses. Panicked people sloshed past me, emergency and medical drones streaming the other way to the collapse site. Black smoke rings slowly corkscrewed into the sky.

The two boys and their mother were nowhere to be seen.

Terrorist attack. That's what the constant trickle of newsfeeds popping up in my shib said. Terrorist attack by a skinnie, high on stormtech, who'd threatened to blow up the bank unless they gave him half a million Commoners. They'd complied and he'd pulled the plug anyway. Killing thousands and toppling the building. The whole Ruskin floor was slowly being sectioned off, the floor's spaceport closing, rerouting hundreds of ships.

I didn't have to look at the details to know he was an addict, poisoned by darkmarket stormtech. Nor did I have to wait long for the headlines blaming Harmony, demanding an answer for this, demanding retribution against anyone with stormtech. The newsfeeds clogged with angry retorts as the report spread like a virus across the asteroid and then the entire system. Politicians, security personnel, bureaucrats and media spokespeople from various space stations and boards of operation chipping in.

Whoever the House of Suns were, whatever they wanted, they were weaponising terrorism and public outrage against Harmony. This was a victory for them. I had a feeling it'd be the first of many.

I'd found myself a tiny alcove in a packed-out restaurant, hunched over a bowl of cheese and onion pierogi and a shot of vodka. With the stormtech threading through me like crazy, I was ravenous. Too hungry to trawl all the way down to the Upper Markets, I made a beeline for the first level that caught my attention. It was fashioned after an Eastern European city, complete with onion-domed buildings garlanded with flowers and engraved with stern wooden carvings. I'd followed signs in Polish, Russian and Ukrainian pointing me towards a quiet place to eat.

I watched the lunch crowd, made up of more aliens than humans, and took my first bite of pierogi. It tasted much better, more pronounced, than I'd expected. The onions were spicier. The cheese creamer. The meat juicer. I hunched deeper into my seat. Were the conversations in here louder? My nostrils twitched. The smells more potent?

The realisation hit me hard as a slug round. The stormtech was still sharpening my senses, letting me hear the hushed conversation about chainship schematics two Torven were having in the back of the restaurant, letting me see the individual feathers on birds wheeling around the domes outside. Every clatter of utensils, every hiss of steam, every breath. I felt it all. I clenched my fist and felt the stormtech instantly swirl under my skin. This was how I'd felt when I came home from the war. The heightened effects of the stormtech slowly dissolving, while still desperately searching for something to hang onto, a way to keep itself active.

As long as I let it dissolve and didn't give it anything it could work with, I'd be fine.

I'd be fine.

I leaned into my wooden seat, gazing through the flexi-screen porthole that showed chainships, frigates and cargoships ducking in and out of various glowing dockyards honeycombed in the lower regions of the asteroid. I watched the stream of ships, unable to help wondering if any had New Vladivostok on their course schedule. I hadn't been home in years now. Couldn't say I sorely missed it, but there's a sense of comfort in the familiar, in a space that's shaped and nurtured you. Kuraishiguro, New Vladi's largest settlement, was big enough to get lost in, but small enough that you could learn every street, roadway and mountain pass.

It was ironic I'd been drawn here. Kasia and I had always wanted to escape Kuraishiguro. Take Artyom and our mother and escape our father for good. But we knew he'd hunt us down and kill us if we did. He'd said as much, usually while delivering one of his thrashings. *Just try it, Vakov. I'll find you. See if I don't.* He had connections with every criminal enterprise he'd worked for. People he'd use to find us, the same people who protected him whenever we reported his violence. But we were planning to risk it anyway. Only then Kasia had been taken from us. I'd held Artyom tight against my chest as he sobbed and sobbed for hours, while I held back my own tears because I was the oldest now, and I had to be stable and strong for him. More than ever. Our mother couldn't protect us – she was too afraid of my father to do anything but jump to obey when he barked at her. She never had the guts Kasia did. Never raised us like our sister had.

I'd thought bringing justice to our sister's killer would bring us some sort of peace. It only made me angry. Angry with the people who allowed it to happen. Angry with the people who'd sighed and shaken their heads and muttered appropriate things and forgotten about her the next day. Angry with the whole planet. I don't know how many nights I spent on the streets, full of too much booze and too little sense, sniffing out a fight. Didn't know what to do with myself, except get into trouble.

When I was about sixteen, one of the few hotel highrises on the planet hosted a soiree for businessmen and entrepreneurs. On New Vladi, that meant organised crime families. Me and Artyom had explored all the underground bars and seedy vidgame dens, and we wanted a bigger adventure. So we'd walked into the marbled lobby, pretending to be related to one of the smaller families. Somehow, we got access to the opulent penthouse bar, where hundreds of the most dangerous and violent people on the planet had gathered to talk business. Swirling, intricate tattoos of animals and bones indicated their ranks. They didn't suspect a thing as we mingled among them, enjoying free food and drink that'd have cost us half a year's wages. I still remember sipping a silver-dusted vodka sour, leaning against the balustrade and taking in the sprawling view. Overlooking the dark wilderness of the silent forests and brooding black mountains on one side, the concrete cityscape on the other. Lonely highways winding through mountain passes like black veins through to hinterlands populated with dormant volcanoes and glaciers. Neon signs ten storeys tall plastered across brutalist buildings, blinking through the fog. I'd never seen my city like that before. Never realised how *small* it was. How isolated. Or how many stars there were in the sky, glinting like neon dust. I'd glanced up to see the green concentric lights of a chainship lifting off from its shuttle pad and sailing into the dark skies, disappearing into the infinite ocean of stars and galaxies. I wondered where else I could go. What places in the universe that offered escape from the poverty and violence I'd known all my life.

As the night had worn on, the arriving guests became more and more notorious. We'd glance at each other across the lounge, both wondering if we should slip out now or risk staying longer. Giddy with the rush of adrenaline and expensive vodka, we'd kept pushing it. Ordering crazier and crazier drinks from the bar, trying the most expensive dishes while we could get away with it. It was only around 2am, when the older members had begun to bleed out of the venue, that people noticed us. Including men with irezumi tattoos.

I saw them approaching before Artyom did. They'd made a mistake in waiting for the superior families to leave. We made our escape down a side stairwell, our footsteps echoing as we raced through the hotel corridors. My head foggy with booze, I'd pushed us into the sauna, dark and abandoned at this hour, and we'd leaped fully clothed into the plunge pool. Treading water in the darkness, shocked sober by the cold as we listened for their footsteps. This was New Vladi. Neither of us harboured any illusions about what would happen to us if we were caught, underage or not.

We submerged, flattening ourselves against the side of the pool when someone barged in. My heartbeat had thundered in my ears as we held each other down under the water, locking gazes as the flashlight arced around the room, each of us trying to stop the other from moving, from giving us away.

An eternity later, the light had vanished. We surfaced in the same moment, both of us desperate for air, both of us still trying to be quiet. We must have stayed in the water for an hour before the coast was clear. We'd dried off on the hotel towels before slipping out of the highrise and onto the predawn streets. Leaning against each other, hungover and high with the thrill of danger, trickles of faint light yawning down to the streets around us. We couldn't quite believe we'd got away with it. We'd stumbled to the shabby train terminal and collapsed into hard plastic seats. 'How many shots did you have?' I asked Artyom.

'Eight,' he mumbled. Blinked. 'No, nine.'

I shook him playfully by the shoulder. 'Liar.'

'Ten! Who cares, we didn't pay for it.' Artyom shook water out of his hair and grinned up at me. 'Same again next week?'

But I'd been looking up at the brightening sky. Searching for the chainship I'd seen, while knowing it wouldn't be there, knowing I'd never see it again. I remembered the little moment of quiet peace I'd experienced, seeing it gently soar away to be swallowed up by the stars, imagining for a moment that I was escaping on it. And I remembered too, the harsh reality that came crashing down when the moment passed and I was still a sixteen-year-old boy stuck on a backwater planet. It made me realise how truly confined I was on New Vladi and that I'd never find that peace here.

It wasn't until Harvest declared war and Harmony put out the call for combatants that I'd found my chance to be free.

All these years later, here we were.

We don't choose the cards we're dealt. We can only choose how we play them. No matter what the universe throws at you, you've got to keep swimming. Doesn't matter how bruised and broken and bloody you'll be by the end. We're all orchestrations of carbon. Blood and bone and dreams and madness and love and hate swirling inside us all. And with it, the capacity to destroy or save ourselves and everyone around us. You just have hope you won't destroy, because, in the end, hope's all we have. Hope that you won't self-destruct. Hope you'll do right by the people you love. Hope that you'll be a better man tomorrow than you were today. You lose sight of hope, and you've already lost.

20

The Book of the Dead

The Compass Academy building was a mad hybrid of animal and architecture. Merging squid, elk, wolf, bat, its flesh was made out of sheer cliffs of bright steel, columns of black marble and glass. The wings were forged of hollowed obsidian, the thrashing tentacles from an alloy threaded with grinding machinery, the howling jaws a dense polymer, the antlers a sparkling cobalt. It was twenty kilometres in diameter, carved with angles and wacky, geometric complexities. Everything was disorderly, nothing symmetrical. You couldn't tell where one animal's biology began to fuse and bleed into the next. They sported bizarre fungal growths and jutting body-modifications. A series of black spires burst out of the creature's shoulders and back at random intervals, extending from its spine like spikes and turning the whole building into a gothic superstructure for the space-age. It was as if they were *trying* to look monstrous but had fallen just short of succeeding.

If you didn't know its backstory, you'd assume it was the creation of insane architects, who'd fought each other over every metre of space. The truth was, this sector of the inner asteroid had been particularly rich in minerals. Instead of gutting it, the architects had hollowed the rocks out, carving the exterior into this bizarre mesh of creatures and honeycombing the interior with walls, gaskets, supports, electricity, all the usual plumbing, turning it into the asteroid's biggest and most prestigious place of study.

If you ask me, it was an outrageous and bizarre expense. But no one was asking me.

Determined to stick out like a bloodied thumb, Grim was dressed in an underskin that gave him the appearance of being made of charcoal and perpetually moving black ink, as if he was a hand-drawn figure in some grotesque artbook. Drones designed to look like flying gargoyles swooped overhead. We'd hiked up steps carved into the wolf's claws and into an elevator climbing its hind leg. In the southwest quadrant, the xenomuseum had been built inside one of one extended squid tentacles. Dedicated to showcasing the diversity of known civilisations, cultures and history of intelligent life across the Common, it was designed to allow humans and aliens alike to learn about their own and other species. Could be our next port of call if this didn't work out.

We crossed the gently lit atrium, past departments dedicated to astrophysics, dark-matter energy, megastructures and xeno-biology. Groups of students, technicians and teachers walked past, deep in conversation. The modern gothic aesthetic didn't let up as we entered the huge, catherdral-like space of the Academy library. Sweeping shelves stretched all the way up to the arched ceiling, packed with stained glass windows and intricate machinery like dark grey clockwork that appeared to be dripping with slime-coloured wax. Rows and rows and rows of books, folders, dossiers, articles covered the shelves, each shelf attached with a robotic appendage, gears and cogs whirling and sending them tunnelling away through silver chutes that crisscrossed over the architecture. They catalogued these soaring skyscrapers of data: an ecosystem of information.

And I'd thought this would be easy.

'So, Vak.' Grim still hadn't woken up yet and the sight of this hadn't helped his mood. 'Did you want to search alphabetically, or by genre?'

'Not helping,' I said.

'Hey, this was your idea.'

'Welcome.' The Rubix's voice carried clear across the marbled floor. I'm not sure what the librarian stereotype is, but it appeared to be a gaunt-faced woman with long grey hair and flowing robes, her glare demanding complete silence. 'Do you have a booking?'

From the way she said it, it was clear she didn't expect us to have one, though she showed no surprise when I handed over my reservation details. She took us past quiet alcoves, giant terrariums filled with miniature environments, and various mechanisms wheeling on little gyroscopes, before we reached our study room. A leather sofa, computer system with archive access, an elliptical desk flanked by wooden chairs. I'd handle the physical side of our search while Grim dug up his digital underworld. 'Find me everything to do with Viklun Ryken,' I told Grim.

Trawling through the archives was like looking for a white rabbit in a snowstorm. A very, very small white rabbit. But Grim's never one to let me down and we shortly had an answer.

'Look at this,' I said as relevant dataspheres materialised around us in an orrery of multicoloured globes. When I touched one, it splintered outwards like snowflakes in a blizzard, before coalescing into scrolling sheets of paper. Digital ink swirled into words like black ivy in fast-forward. 'Ryken isn't just studying the Shenoi: he's an expert on them. Wrote several books about them.'

'That's one hell of a subject to devote your life to,' Grim said, fully roused from his torpor.

'It gets better.' The digital pages hissed and crackled as I turned them. 'He's researched which systems and planets the Shenoi might have occupied, and whether they were a space-faring species, their civilisation and culture, if they were phys-ical or energy beings, their artefacts.'

'There are Shenoi artefacts? I thought all traces of them vanished.'

'He says they left artefacts behind. They could be Shenoi, or they could belong to some other alien species that jumped the rail or were wiped out by some disaster.' I scanned the next page, doing my best to ignore the stormtech grating along my ribs. 'One of his most controversial theories is that the stormtech is their blood.'

'Folks back on Earth used to drink the blood of their enemies.' Grim sniffed and scratched his chest with a dripping black claw. 'Sound like decent folks.'

'He argues that taking the stormtech is pretty much the same thing. Not exactly the most positive of analogies.'

'The bloke spent his life writing about dead aliens. How much fun do you think he'd be at a party?' Grim sniffed and flicked a sheet of data to me. 'Interesting ... all of his books were given the seal of approval by the Shenoi Collective.'

'The Shenoi Collective?'

'Seems to be a slice of academia who specifically investigate, analyse and theorise about the Shenoi.'

'So it's not just Ryken who's doing in-depth research, there's a whole curriculum based on it?'

'Yeah. These guys are borderline obsessive, by the looks of it. They've systematically added his work to their official archives, and those loons rarely seem to accept third-party submissions.'

I looked warily at the digital mountain of articles, books and transcripts Ryken had written, feeling crushed. I don't have much patience for reading, even less when I'm not sure what I'm looking for. No way was I going to probe through all this while the House of Suns were still on the prowl. The stormtech likes mental stimuli and activity as much as physical, and I was itching to find something. I knew pieces were missing, I just couldn't see what shape they took or where they went.

Maybe Viklun Ryken himself could give me the answers. We plunged back into the Tungyian System, Quyn Research Station expanding to fill the room. I watched the visualisation package as three corvettes broke out of warpspace, their hulls distorted with a dark haze, before making a beeline for the space station. At an optimal distance, they aligned in battle-formation, gimballed multicannons rotating forward. They unleashed a simultaneous bombardment of Antimatter Missiles, blasting the dockyard into debris. A timestamp showed it had happened three years ago. Grim watched with me, in silence. 'Ryken was on it at the time,' I said quietly.

'That doesn't sound like a coincidence.'

Of course it wasn't. Quyn Research Station had been mentioned in my assailants' databanks. Didn't take a genius to stumble to the conclusion they'd been the cause of its destruction.

Just when you're making progress, the universe bends over backwards to kick you in the urethra.

I leaned back in my chair. 'So, let's say the House of Suns killed him. They went to the trouble of arming themselves with military-grade weapons used in space warfare and flying into regions of deepspace swarming with Blade Hunters, smuggler crews, hostile species, and god knows what else. They knew there'd be questions, evidence tracing back to them, and they risked killing him anyway.'

'They were afraid of him.'

'Or they were afraid of what he'd discovered. Something in his work as xenobiologist.'

Grim slumped back in his seat, feet propped up on the table, gesturing to the vast array of data. 'Hate to break it you, but even if the answer *is* here, we're not going to find it. We might not even recognise it if we did.'

That much I could agree with. 'I think someone else might be able to help us,' I said. I thought of the symbol I'd seen in their hideout. It was a long shot, but there was a chance. 'Stay here, dig into anything that could be useful. Ryken's key areas of study, his pet projects.'

Grim pulled a face that said there were other things he'd rather be doing. He held up a tome. 'Vak, the covers of this book are too far apart.'

'You better get started, then.'

He made another face, indicating I owed him big-time for this. 'And where are you off to, Mister Reaper? The bar?'

I grinned. 'I'm going to class.'

21

Who Goes There

The Shenoi Collective was part of the Academy's xenobiology faculty. I'd assumed they'd be right next door. In a sense, they were. Only, their doors were two hours and four kilometres of study halls, auditoriums, laboratories and access tunnels apart. I was in a sour mood by the time I hiked up a hairpin stairwell racked with cable conduits and instrument paneling along the upper cervical of the building's spine and stood at the entrance of the Shenoi Collective.

Based on what I'd heard — that they considered the study of these long-dead aliens to be of prime significance to an almost religious degree — I expected to stride into a darkened hallway filled with symbols and sinister towering statues, rites playing from the speakers. Instead, I found myself in a long, sunlit room dotted with plants and antique wingchairs. Paintings of spacecraft and ominous-looking landscapes, presumably a Shenoi homeworld, were rendered in thick, oily brushstrokes. As if reminded of its ancestral origins, my stormtech was already reacting to them, flaring up in broad blue strokes. I locked it down, hard as I could.

'Can I help you?' At first I'd thought it was a Rubix sitting behind the reception desk, but it was a lissom young woman, fixing me with an all-too-human glare as if I'd disturbed her meditation.

'I'd like to speak with the teacher in charge, please.'

An arching of a perfect eyebrow. 'You mean the Head Professor?'

'Yes.' I gave her a sour smile. 'Please.'

'I'm afraid I take meetings by appointment only, son.' I turned as a hale, middle-aged man seemingly appeared from thin air behind me. He had wine-dark eyes, shrub-thick eyebrows and unruly dark hair, shot with grey. The tan trousers, ruffled shirt and tweed jacket fit him to a tee.

I remembered just in time to offer my forearm rather than my hand for him to shake. 'Vakov Fukasawa. And I'm afraid I must insist.'

'Michael Luciano.' His grip was stronger than expected. He glanced at the stormtech swirling around my wrists, but didn't offer a comment. Did he see a lot of Reapers and skinnies in here? 'It's exam season and I don't have time today. You're welcome to visit the library and lecturelog hall if you—'

'I wanted to ask you about this.' I showed him the mysterious symbol I'd sketched on my palmerlog. His face turned ashen, mouth slowly hinging open.

'Where did you find this?' he asked. I said nothing, hands held behind my back, waiting for what I knew would happen. And it did. Luciano turned to his receptionist. 'Cancel all midmorning appointments.'

She didn't look too happy about it, but obliged.

He led me into an obscenely narrow hallway that smelled of oiled wood. Light easing through the louvred shutters painted rows of golden slices on the floor. Modest posters about the Collective's teachings, appointment bookings, and history lined the walls. Students sitting in alcoves glanced up at us from their quiet studies as we brushed past. It reminded me of the school libraries I'd hung out in to avoid going home as long as possible. I felt underdressed in my one-piece underskin, but Luciano struck me as the sort of person who'd say if it bothered him.

'Where are you from, son?' Luciano asked. 'Palakin? Borr? New Vladivostok?'

'What gave me away?' I asked.

He grinned. 'The features.'

'You've been there?'

'Once. The people are lovely. The weather? Not so much.'

Surprising. New Vladi's on the outer edges of the galaxy and just outside of the Common's territory. Most people in the Common don't pay attention to worlds outside of it, let alone find reasons to head over there.

If Luciano's office was anything to go by, the man thrived on disorder. Drawers hanging open like extruded tongues, terrariums scattered around like abandoned afterthoughts, dusty books squeezed tight as molars along the bookshelves, reams of papers piled on his heavy wooden desk threatening to spill to the floor. Looked like the guy had hardcopied every message and datasheet he'd ever received in his life. Between the gaps in the heavy drapery, stained-glass windows peered out to the pinnacle of a black spire.

'Coffee?' Luciano asked as I eased into a highbacked leather seat, indicating the fancy-looking machine. 'A good cup of gold's my speciality.'

'Maybe later,' I suggested.

'You might need it soon.' Luciano rubbed his face as he eased into the seat opposite me. 'I'd hoped never to see that mark again.'

'It's not just a mark,' I said softly. 'The House of Suns are a cult.'

It was only an educated guess, but I got some grim satisfaction

229

from Luciano's grave nod of confirmation. 'Cult ain't the half of it. They're psychopaths.'

I settled deeper into my seat.

'What do you know about our Collective, son?' Luciano asked.

'Not much,' I admitted. 'You study the Shenoi, almost obsessively. Think they're of high value to the greater galaxy.'

'Close enough. Though you can study the Shenoi without assigning them a special significance. Hell, we keep a closer eye on those students who start to move towards faith rather than science. Everyone likes developing their own ideas and theories. You can't expect someone to dedicate their life to something and not be passionate about it. There're big enough gaps in what we know about so many species for wild theories to fill them. But when someone starts elevating a dead species to a cult-like status and spreading their own theories as dogma, we do try to suppress it. We usually manage to squash the crazier ones before they go too far. Emphasis on usually.'

'It's always the one percent that kills you,' I offered.

'Heh. Very good. We've become more alert to it since a group formed within the Collective. Our "status quo" wasn't good enough for them. We were too old-fashioned. Boring old men held back by tradition, all the usual crap about wasting our time with books and research, when we should be out in deepspace, conducting interstellar expeditions for burial sites and ruins among the stars. Like there's not enough people doing that already.' Luciano sniffed. 'The universe is full of people concerning themselves with what others do, if only to tell them they're wrong for not doing it their way. But these guys got louder and louder and eventually broke away as an offshoot from the Collective, forming their own crazy little echo chamber. And then that got bigger and bigger.' He pointed to the symbol on my palmerlog. 'They became the House of Suns.

They believe the Shenoi are still hiding out there in some far-flung region of the galaxy. That we haven't received all their power yet because we're undeserving and unworthy. They're obsessed with finding the damn creatures and earning their approval. Siphoning their power. And they'll do anything: extortion, sabotage, or murder.'

There was the small hiss of drones jetting past the window. I shifted in my seat.

'You know what?' I said carefully, 'I think I'll take that coffee after all.'

Luciano got up to prepare them. I found I liked him. A man of his calibre could be doing anything in life and he'd funnelled his energy and intelligence into education and study. You've got to appreciate such clear sincerity.

It seemed I'd found the House of Suns. I knew who was behind the deaths, but that was only half of it. I was in the dark as to why they were killing Reapers and skinnies and setting Harmony up for the fall. I'd have known if these people were on Harmony's radar.

'So this band of enthusiasts are on a scavenger hunt for an alien civilisation that's been extinct for millions of years?' I asked as Luciano returned with two small porcelain cups of steaming coffee. No milk, no sugar. Just straight, the way I liked it.

The professor tapped the side of his head. 'You're forgetting: these sons of bitches don't think straight. One of our core theories is that knowledge of the Shenoi strengthens us in a way that other alien species don't. Their existence as a sentient organism that's also a drug – a drug that has the same effect on a human's body and an alien's – opens up entirely new areas of study in the fields of biology, physiology. The House of Suns took that further: they theorise that greater knowledge of the Shenoi is fundamental to your existence in every way.

They're quite intransigent in that regard. Anyone who questions their vaunted word, or dares to hinder them in their pursuit, is an enemy. So, yeah, they're out there, sniffing out alien scraps in an interstellar treasure hunt.'

That explained why they were collecting stormtech, but not why they were poisoning it. I downed my coffee and let the silky bitterness melt down into my stomach. 'I've had a few run-ins with these people. Most of them don't have stormtech. If they're already that obsessed with the aliens, why haven't they shot themselves up?'

'Some are naturally resistant to stormtech. Others leave their obsession at a distance. The one thing we agree on is that stormtech is lethal and makes you unpredictable, prone to urges. You can't risk that around your fellow cultists. You can be obsessed with chainships while still knowing taking one for a spin through an asteroid field like those lunatic racers is a bad idea.'

'Do you think they killed Viklun Ryken?'

'You've done your homework, son. Ryken was a stubborn old bastard. His works are in our archive, but he kept the best findings for himself, to publish when he was ready. They got wind of it. I can't imagine they asked nicely. If he found something they wanted, or they didn't like what he stumbled upon, they'd have killed him.'

The warble of a speeding chainship rattled through the windows as I turned this statement over. There've been plenty of fanatics, cults and crazies floating around, before and after the Reaper War, some more dangerous than others. But these people were spreading corrupted stormtech around for some more immediate reason than finding their beloved aliens.

'Why didn't you come forward about this?' I had to ask.

'To who? Harmony?' He flapped his hand, made a *pfft* sound. 'You think they're going to listen to me, ranting about aliens and super-secret cults? I've been dismissed before, and it doesn't get any more fun the older you get. Besides, Harmony's hardly the most approachable of organisations.'

I thought of Kowalski, the authority and respect she commanded over her men, how she'd looked after me because she saw me as a human being. Not another disposable tool of Harmony. She'd listened to me when I'd told her about Artyom, and she'd put her career in my hands in an effort to clear stormtech off the streets and make a difference in the world. If I trusted this man, then I knew she would. She'd make this work.

'Now, if you'd be so kind, tell me where you saw their mark,' said Luciano. By the time I finished telling him, his face had turned white as the reams of papers around him. 'They're back on Compass?'

'Everything you said matches up,' I said. 'They're the ones Harmony's after.'

Luciano chewed his lip. 'I was wrong. We have to alert Harmony to this and make sure they don't leave Compass and hurt anyone else.' He looked straight at me. 'You did well coming to see me, son. I'll go to Harmony, tell them everything I know. The universe is better off without them, believe me.' He raised his coffee mug in salute. 'I'll go after this.'

I settled into my seat, at ease for the first time in weeks. If Luciano knew these people and who was leading them, we'd solved half the problem. It wouldn't clear up Artyom's involvement, or give us a motive, but you've got to take one step at a time.

Kowalski would love to hear the news. I reached for my palmerlog to tell her. I frowned and my body tensed two seconds before the reality of the situation caught up with me. Opposite me, Luciano jerked hard, his coffee cup thunking to the carpet in a spreading black stain. He was frothing at the mouth as he collapsed. I rushed to roll him over but only got halfway when a laser sight on my chest froze me in place.

'Neurotoxin,' someone whispered. 'Just like you used on my man. Only, I use the deadly stuff.' The Jackal stepped into the room, eyes trained on me like restraining bolts. He gestured at me with his handgun. The silver-bodied weapon glinted dully in the light. 'Hands behind your head. Now.'

The palmerlog was active in my hand, but if he saw me flick the switch to call Kowalski he'd put a shell through my face. Without taking my eyes off him, I pressed the closest button on the scroll-down menu. No way of knowing if I got it right. I dropped the device, fists clenching.

Luciano was clawing his throat with gnarled fingers, gasping. His feet twitching violently.

The Jackal tilted his handgun. 'Go for it. Help him out. Maybe you can do something.'

I knew an invitation to get myself shot when I heard one. I stayed put and glared at the Jackal. He'd been a part of the Suns this whole time. Tipei, his biolabs and darkmarket connections, all channelling their resources into the one cult. No wonder they'd been able to take root so deeply in Compass.

The Jackal smiled, as if knowing I'd figured it out. He gently tilted Luciano's head, ensuring he didn't choke on his own tongue while the neurotoxin ran its full, brutal course. 'Remember what I said in the alleyway?' He leaned over to press the handgun against my forehead. The cold touch of death against my warm flesh. His face twisting with an arrogant streak a kilometre long. 'I don't need augs to hunt a man down.'

I was starting to wonder how many holes I'd have punched in my chest before I tore the Jackal's throat open. I looked over his shoulder and saw the receptionist in the doorway. Of course she was one of them, right here in the Shenoi Collective. She must have seen the symbol and known to call the Jackal.

Next I saw Simmons step into the room, a perverse hatred burning in his eyes. The stormtech screamed at me to charge them. I made my fists tighter and forced myself still as Luciano continued to splutter and twitch, glaring at the killers who had invaded his sacred place of study, unable to raise a finger to stop them.

'Miss me?' Now Lasky walked in, his grin wide. The little bastard grabbed me and locked an arm around my neck with his handgun pressed against one eye, his chin resting on my shoulder. You never appreciate how big handguns are until one's jammed square in your face. 'We're going to have fun, you and I.'

Simmons rifled through Luciano's books, ripping the pages in full view of the dying man. The Jackal stopped him with a hand. 'No, no. That's not the way we do it. He loved his papers so much? He can choke on them.' The Jackal bundled the shredded sheets into a tight roll, thick as a rifle's muzzle. His eyes locked with mine. 'I'm not one for metaphors, you see.'

Then, his gaze still fixed on me; he shoved the roll of papers deep into Luciano's frothing mouth. I shook with fury, the handgun against my eye keeping me parked where I was. The Jackal gave a faint smile and drove the papers deeper and deeper. Luciano squirmed feebly under him. His eyes twitched to the side and met mine, filled with a furious determination that I put these people down as we'd agreed we would. I bit back my rage and nodded, once.

Something cold and wet punched into my neck. I felt myself lurching forward, like it was happening to someone else, before I was jerked backwards, smothered by the darkness collapsing around me.

22

Ashes

There's nothing like seeing a planet slaughtered.

I knew the war-sims and visualisation packages they showed us in training weren't telling half the story. Turns out, they weren't telling any of it.

The stink of grasslands burning. Highrises collapsing like they're made of paper, the concrete smashing down the length of a city. Screaming civilians. The ear-splitting sirens. Blaster cannons streaking gunfire down from fighter-ships in a blazing hailstorm, scarring the sky with lacerations of fire.

It's so bizarre, so outlandish it's almost unreal. Like you've been dumped in someone else's fragmented nightmare and told to fight your own way out.

Harvest turned its bloodthirsty sights on Renchio, so Renchio has become the frontline of the Reaper War. I'm sent with Fireteam Ghost to rally points across the planet, co-ordinating with my Battalion or any other Companies that make up the grizzled constellation of Harmony SSC infantry. We see destruction and terror wherever we go. Roads filled with fleeing civilians like clotted arteries. Dockyards for interstellar ships smashed to blackened ruins. We walk through the smoking shell of a once-opulent coastal city where pylons jut through the rubble like broken fingers. What looks like black snow swirls around us. I stretch out my hand to let it melt in my palm.

Ash. It's raining ash.

But the killzones are the worst. The towns and cities Harvesters seized for a tactical advantage. They sealed them off, marched inside and killed every man, woman and child. Any civilians they didn't kill, they enslaved or used as target practice, or for whatever other sick game passed the time. There are so many bodies on the streets you can barely see the pavement. Sometimes, we find survivors. Kids, usually, pushed into some small crevice when their parents heard the door crashing in. Cable's the best with them. He gets his helmet off, kneels down to their level and speaks to them in their language, lets them grieve. But they've all got this dead-eyed gaze, staring at the blackened, ashen wreckage of what used to be their home. Sometimes it's an accusatory stare, levelled at us. Asking why we didn't do something. Why we didn't stop this.

'Nothing makes you feel worse than failing a child,' Alcatraz says as evac airships lift off from various strongpoints, down into the bodies and destruction.

I'm barely listening. There's another mutilated Reaper nailed to a pole in the centre of an ash-caked courtyard. Only, this one's arm is jutting outwards, pointing east.

Directions.

The skull and lightning bolts on his chest indicate he's part of the Space Battalion: Reapers who've been in orbital combat and boarded enemy spacecraft. His name is Paz Viska. I've never spoken to him, but I know he's been missing for weeks. I get the feeling I'm about to find out why.

We go east to another tortured Reaper. And another. And another. Each one with an arm strung up and nailed to the post to point in the same direction. Until we reach a bombed-out garrison holding a rusted cage dangling from the ceiling. Inside are

Reapers, so mangled they're barely recognisable. And with it is a video transmission; a Harvester with a scrambled voice explaining that since we've been scavenging their weapons and tech to learn their strategies, so in turn they're going to take the one thing we have that they don't.

Stormtech.

There's video footage of them vivisecting Reapers and subjecting them to horrific experiments. Learning how it alters and strengthens our biology for the battlefield. Testing how much strain our bodies can take. How the stormtech responds to torture. How Reapers respond to unimaginable pain and horror. Showing us how they're going to keep capturing Reapers and pulling them apart for their little studies, including us.

Ratchet stumbles sideways and just gets his helmet off before he pukes all around his boots. I'm doing likewise, heaving next to him.

'What they were doing to him,' Ratchet half-growls, half sobs.

'I know, man,' I say.

'We're in a nightmare,' Cable says from behind us.

It's more than that. This is horror beyond everything else. This is the squirming, evil rot hiding beneath the skin of civilisation, devouring and consuming everything good and right that's ever happened in the universe.

Ratchet turns to me. 'Don't ever let that happen to me,' he pants, his bloodshot eyes darting back and forth.

I squeeze his shoulder. 'I'll kill them all before I let them touch you. I swear.'

'No matter what,' Ratchet says.

'No matter what.' Cable helps me to my feet while Myra and Alcatraz help Ratchet.

'Even if you have to put a bullet in my brain, you don't let them take me,' Ratchet says, putting his helmet back on.

Alcatraz gets right up in Ratchet's face, their visors knocking together. 'Don't you ever say that again.'

'I'll die before I end up like that,' Ratchet snarls back.

'We start thinking like that, we're already dead. They've already won.' He taps his commslink. 'Why do you think they sent this transmission to every Reaper and Harmony outpost on the planet? They want us to give up. They want us so scared we forget to rely on each other. We don't let this trip us up. We use it. We turn it against them.' He looks at each of us in turn. 'You hear me?'

That's the thing about war. It's a hurricane of chaos. It's volatile. With every operation, we don't know what horrors we're going to find or who's going to make it out alive again.

In this hellscape of horrors, this overwhelming darkness, there's only one thing anchoring you to sanity. The men and women standing by your side, facing it with you. More than that, we're each other's hope of surviving. Harvest knows that. So they try to go for the heart.

One by one, we nod an affirmative to Alcatraz's question, giving the Reaper gesture with a sincerity that didn't previously exist, and we start to free the murdered Reapers.

When we're not in the field, we're training for it in the state-of-the-art gravity gymnasium and the training VR, pushing our stormtech-fused bodies as hard as we can. First we weight-train in gravity chambers, then with hand-to-hand combat, and finally the worst part: pushing our metabolisms and stamina with a test of endurance, submerging ourselves in pools of icy water. Everyone else does the required ninety seconds, but Ratchet bets he can beat me by a full minute. I'm stupid enough to take him up on it. Six minutes later, I drag myself shivering from the tank while the rest of the fireteam laughs. Ratchet grins at me through the glass and lasts eight and a half minutes, just to prove he can.

His pale body is almost purple with cold when he finally climbs out, grinning. 'What's the matter, Fukasawa? Can't handle a bit of chill?'

'How the hell can you do that?' I manage through still-chattering teeth.

'He was raised by wolves,' Myra calls.

When Ratchet turns his back on me, I shove him into the tank. He splutters and thrashes while the rest of the fireteam laughs.

'He's going to get you back for that,' Alcatraz says.

'He can try,' I say.

Alcatraz shakes his head. 'Oh, he will.'

I turn to see Ratchet launching himself out of the pool. He slams me to the ground and starts punching with frozen fists. My fireteam cheers as I try to wrestle him into a lock. He punches me in the armpit, reaches around to grab a fistful of my hair. My scalp burns as he jerks my head back, digging his knee into the base of my spine, his fingertips scrabbling and clawing at my eyes, going for the kill.

I've got no reservations about doing the same. Teeth gritted, I slam the back of my head into his nose. He gasps as I drive my elbow into his stomach, right below his ribs. His grip weakens and I tear free, flip myself over, chopping a strike at his throat to daze him as I wrap my arms around his body, crushing his arms to his sides while he thrashes and tries to bite me. It's like trying to hold down a psychotic goat. Finally, I pin him under me. 'Truce?' I ask into his ear.

Ratchet growls and thrashes. I repeat the question and he gives a begrudging nod. I'm expecting him to be furious. Instead, he's got this ear-splitting grin on his grime-smeared face. 'You won the battle. But I'll win the war.'

Soon, we're all able to last eight minutes in the freezing water. Then ten. Then fifteen. Our endurance, strength and agility slowly improves with training. During one session, I notice people watching us from the observation port. They're without name tags, their rankings a blurred smudge in my shib. I've heard rumours of Intelligence Officers hanging around, but I dismissed it. No non-combatant comes to a planet under siege unless they've got a death wish. But when they watch us train, I can't help but feel they're taking notes.

The gymnasium's large enough to accommodate entire squads of Reapers, including members of the Drop Shock Battalion. These heavyweights specialise in getting dropped from orbit in coffin-sized pods and landing behind enemy lines. They're tough as chainmetal and can't stop talking about the killer that is gravity, but friendly enough. We're chatting away, until a squad of non-Reaper SSC soldiers enter the room. The new arrivals keep a wide berth, giving us dirty looks. A Shocktrooper looks at me and spits on the floor. Ratchet bares his teeth and gives off a low growl until they back off.

'I didn't ask you to do that,' I say, sitting on a padded work-bench, the armpits of my suit dark with sweat.

'Nah, you didn't,' Ratchet agrees. 'But you needed me to.'

'What's with them, anyhow?' I ask.

'Maybe it's pheromonal,' Ratchet says. 'The stormtech changed the way we smell, yeah? Well, I reckon something about it freaks them out, down in the brain stem.'

Myra snorts at that. 'Hardly. They're just jealous.'

'He didn't look very jealous to me,' I say.

'Reapers are the frontline elite. We're stronger, smarter and faster. More adaptable. More responsive. Even our armour's calibrated for Reaper response-times. They'd break their own necks if they tried to wear our gear. In the field, we make them look like bright-eyed trainees.'

'We're all on the same side,' Cable mutters.

Myra squats down in front of him. 'Cable, I love you, but you're beyond naive if you're swallowing that. You've seen the crap the Common's been saying about Reapers? What they've been calling us?

The only difference is that these guys have seen us in action.' She nods towards the SSC men gathered in their tightknit circles. Staring at Reapers in gravity chambers cranked to three times what their unaugmented bodies can handle. 'They want to be us. They can't. So instead, they hate us.'

'They aren't the only ones,' Alcatraz says. 'You hear Harmony's set up a tightbeam relay for interstellar communications? They want us to talk to a bunch of trauma counsellors.'

I stare at him. 'You don't think that's a good idea?'

Alcatraz snorts. 'Don't tell me you were thinking of signing up.'

'It wouldn't be such a bad idea to learn how to cope a little better.'

He spits at his feet. 'What would you say to them that we can't say to each other?'

He's got a point.

'What would you say?' he prods.

I think about it for a moment.

'I'd tell them how I can't wait to get back into the field,' I say. My fireteam listens in silence. 'That I wake up sweating and itching at night, counting down the hours to our next mission. That I'm agitated when I'm not in my armour. That the sound of incoming fire doesn't scare me like it did. That I know none of this is normal, but something deep inside is telling this is good news. And that freaks me the hell out.'

It's not until the words are out that I realise how much I needed to say them.

'I feel it too,' Alcatraz says. 'I heard sub-orbital cannons raining down from the VR training rooms and half-hoped it was Harvesters. Had my rifle out and everything. Got halfway down the stairs before I realised.'

'I spend hours in the gravity gym, working out until I can sleep,' Cable admits.

'That doesn't sound normal,' I say.

'There's not much normal about alien DNA,' Myra mutters.

Alcatraz nods. 'That's why we talk. We communicate. Hell, if we don't trust each other in here, how can we trust each other out there?' He nods towards the SSC troupers. 'If we don't, we're just like them. And if I was out in the field with those guys, I'd be more worried about them than the Harvesters.'

I'm in the middle of my armour diagnostics check-up when Commander Sokolav comes to see me.

I know Harvesters are dialling up the pressure, homing in on our outposts, raiding supply ships, blockading civilian evac routes and shooting down observation drones. Trouble's brewing. The Commanders and Primers feel it, too, so do all the Reapers in Tusk Battalion. We're on Prime Standby Alert. If there's an emergency we've got to be out the door in seconds with our fireteams and straight into a dropship for rapid deployment. I haven't been out of my armour for nearly two months. During a PSA I can't leave it at all.

I stand in a spotlight on a metal podium while eggheads and armour technicians fuss around me. Lifting my arms, rotating my shoulders, replacing a kneecap. Tightening a plate here, readjusting a seal on my helmet there. The armour straps clamp down hard over my shoulders, my chestplate tightening. The latches locking me in place loosen and I step off the podium with a hiss. The technicians stand to attention as Sokolav approaches, but he makes an at-ease signal. I follow him across the scuffed and scarred armoury.

He claps me on the shoulder. 'You keeping well, son?' he asks in Japanese. He's long insisted we disperse with the formalities.

I switch easily to the language. 'Well enough, given the circumstances.'

Sokolav snorts. 'You never did do small talk, did you?'

The walkway wraps around our home base. Him a slender

figure in his dark blue Commander uniform with his mop of grey hair and eyes that look like they're chiselled from salt-weathered rock. Me clad head to toe in bulky armour. He's the only other person from New Vladivostok I've met in the army. The only person from my past. He feeds himself a burner, lights it. Drugs are banned for all Harmony SSC servicemen, but who's going to tell the man who built Reapers what to do?

I glance around at the secondary home base we've established as we've ventured further across the planet. Vast swathes of dark green rainforest cover the landscape, sprawling across jagged terrain of squat mountain peaks and deep valleys. Above us, the cloudy sky's that same bruised colour. The unpleasantly muggy air heaves with shockwaves as interplanetary dropships and troop-transports lift off the landing pads. Below us, armoured Reapers and SSC men carry munitions and supply crates between the assembly of prefab barracks, armouries and hangars that make up our home base.

And looming over it all are these immense, overlapping domed shields. A smoky cyan with a hexagonal pattern, stretching dozens of kilometres across. Without them, the never-ending barrage of Harvest artillery fire and sub-orbital railguns would have smashed us into powder. Through the warbling shields, and through a clear patch in the clouds, there're squadrons of Harvest combat-ships circling us like vultures. Harmony gunships and countermeasure drones soar up through the shields to meet them. Red and blue streaks of plasma fire and flashing nanogun rounds burst through the clouds like metal thunder.

We walk past overflowing civilian shelters. Most of them missed the narrow evacuation window when Harvest dreadnoughts swarmed the Renchio skies. The ones that weren't killed in the initial onslaught lost everything. We provided shelter, food. Now they're trapped here hoping we'll win, otherwise they'll be at the mercy of Harvest.

244

'It's good to see you still alive and kicking,' Sokolav tells me.

'They haven't found a way to axe me yet.'

'Damn right they haven't. As your Commander, I forbid you to go down without one hell of a fight.' He grimaces as he tugs at his sweat-stained collar. 'I miss the cold. A man's not meant to work in these conditions. The heat melts the brain, turns your muscles soft.'

'Is that a fact?' I ask.

'It is if I say it is.' He leans towards me, that playful glint in his eye. 'Maybe we should ask for a couple days leave, steal a chainship and shoot back to New Vladi. What do you say?'

'Since when did you need permission to do anything?'

'I don't call all the shots around here, much to my astonishment. It all has to go up the chain.'

'Better you than me.'

Sokolav takes a long drag of his burner. 'Could be we need a change in management around here.'

'You've got my vote.'

'Wasn't thinking of anything so democratic, but I'll count on you all the same. You've never let me down, Vak.'

We lapse back into a comfortable silence.

'We're going to win this war.' Sokolav squints up at the sub-orbital dogfight high above us. I imagine the deafening roar of the artillery fire from my shell-cannons. The adrenaline soaring in my gut as I spin into a barrel roll. Detonations rippling around me. Boomboom. Boomboom. Boomboomboom. My hands tighten into fists.

'Because of the stormtech?' I ask.

'Because of you Reapers,' Sokolav says. 'Because of Harmony. Because we're brave enough to use the stormtech to do what needs to be done.' He raps his knuckles on my chest. 'I've seen you in action, son. I know what you're capable of. Which is how I know you can do what I'm going to ask.'

245

'What do you need?'

'Two things. I want the Canine King dead. I don't care how you do it. I won't have any more Reapers end up in his skinning labs. I won't have him decorating the landscape with our men.'

'Understood,' I say. I roll my burning shoulders, armour plates grinding, watching the dogfight continue. 'And the second?'

'That if you've got something to say to me, you say it.'

'About?'

'Anything. Your fireteam. Your body. Your headspace.' Sokolav puffs out a stream of smoke. 'Remember. The stormtech demands respect, Vakov. Fight it, and it'll fight you. Draw close to it, and it'll draw close to you.'

I nod. As if we hadn't heard this half a hundred times already.

'I'm your Commander, Vakov. Hell, I'm the one who brought you here.'

'I chose to come.'

'Doesn't mean I'm not responsible for you. You know you can talk to me, like you always have. If you need a listening ear, mine's available.'

Alcatraz's words come back to me. To Harmony, we're nothing. A bunch of freak experiments, fighting their war for them. I'd tell my Commander how I'm feeling, like I used to do when I first enlisted. Talk to him about Drummer's death. The urges fighting through my system. But something holds me back. He's my Commander, he oversaw my mutation into a Reaper, but there're subjects I simply can't talk to him about.

Not like I can talk to my fireteam.

How could he possibly understand? What does he know about what the stormtech wants?

'I will,' I say.

Sokolav smiles. He grinds the stub of his burner into the dirt and claps me on the shoulder.

A ground-to-orbit railgun turret rotates upwards. A section of *the shielding dilates open as the railgun barks an earth-shattering crack that I feel rattling in my molars. The muzzle flash is so bright my visor polarises. The missile streaks through the clouds and into a Harvest fighter with an electric-blue flash, lighting up the sky. The fighter streaks to earth like an asteroid, smearing a smoke trail across the sky before smashing down in the mountains. Flames go mushrooming up at the crash-site. The shielding irises closed, shrugging off the damage of return fire, a deluge of furious green plasma. Harvest fighter-ships roar away in defeat.*

23

Deadlocked

Floating. Spinning. Echoes rattling off metal. Light knifing down as I stirred back to consciousness. Muffled yells, cheers, screams.

I wasn't strapped to a cradle this time. I peeled my eyes open to see I was locked inside a gravfix, floating in a tube-shaped statis of artificial gravity that throbbed around me with a droning hum. My arms were held out to the sides, legs dangling uselessly below me.

Not the worst way I've woken up, but it was pretty high on the list.

I was somehow bobbing, as if being swayed by an invisible ocean current, but held tightly in place. Sweat had frozen on my chest and shoulders, held by the gravfix as if already dry and crusted. I wrestled my head downwards to see the stormtech raging across my body like an oil spill. Blue ribboning from my neck down to the soles of my feet. The bare concrete cell I was in should have been cloaked in shadows, but the blooming stormtech painted it with shifting blue. Watching it play over my body, I felt like a robot, manipulated by it the whole time.

'Well, you've been busy.' Lasky wore his usual unpleasant grin. Perched on a stool, the Jackal looked at me like a hawk spotting a rat in a field. Smoke streamed from the burner glowing between his gloved fingers. 'What shall we do with you?'

What would they do? Lock me back inside my suit with a Rubix until my brain turned to mush? Vivisect me and feed me to dogs like Artyom had said they'd planned? A hundred grisly images surfaced and I used my training to kick them back down and plaster a layer of calm over myself. The stormtech wasn't helping, trying to break through my senses with an edge of panic. 'Is he dead?' I croaked.

Lasky looked puzzled until he realised I meant Luciano. 'Yes, of course. He betrayed the House. He had to pay for that.'

It's one thing to face an enemy soldier down the barrel of a rifle. It's another thing entirely to be in the clutches of a murderous cult with a grotesque sense of self-righteousness. 'And I thought the Shenoi Collective was crazy,' I grunted, trying to ignore the feeling of ice growing down my spine. 'You guys are a bundle of insane.'

Lasky smiled, his eye twitching furiously. He raised his arm, broken wrist held in a gelcast. 'Just give me an excuse.'

'You let him provoke you that easily?' The Jackal snorted out a jetstream of blue smoke. 'Retard.'

Lasky turned his glare away from me to train it on the Jackal. 'Don't call me a—'

'A retard.' The Jackal stood and slowly thrust his face into Lasky. Holding his gaze until Lasky dropped it, seeming to shrink under the Jackal's cold, silent menace. The Jackal cocked his head. 'Go on. Say it. "I'm a retard."'

Lasky said nothing. The Jackal slapped him hard across the face. Lasky stumbled back, mouth gaping open in shock and the Jackal slapped him again, harder. 'Say it,' the Jackal repeated, almost whispering.

Lasky wilted under the Jackal's gaze like flowers under a

flametorch. I began to see who really was in charge around here. 'I'm a retard,' he croaked out.

'That's right,' the Jackal said. 'A stupid, snivelling, pig-headed retard who left a Reaper alone with the nightware briefcase. What next, were you going to hold the exit open for him? He should have stomped on your fat, worthless head and done all us all a favour. Now, watch. *This* is how you treat a prisoner.'

Lasky cowed for the moment, the Jackal reached into the gravfix. Almost casually, he pressed a dirty thumb into my right eyeball. Trapped by the gravfix I could only scream as he pushed harder and harder. The nail cut in deep, as capillaries popped and the tissue stretched. I thrashed and kicked furiously against the stubborn gravity, the stormtech whipped into a panicked fury along my spine. He took the burner from between his teeth and pressed it inches from my left eye as he spoke. 'You've cost me a lot of money. That, I could let go,' he said over my agonised screams. He dug deeper and electric pain shivered through my nerves, the lit end of the burner crackling so close I could feel my eyelashes scorching. 'But you went after me. You made a fool of me. No one ever, ever makes a fool of me. So I intend to make quite an example of you.'

He stabbed down harder, punctuating the last words before releasing me and withdrawing the bluesmoke. I gasped. I could barely see. No way to tell how much damage had been done. Waves of agony crashed over me, so hard I wanted to puke. I went limp, trying to get my breathing and body under control. Had to gather my strength.

Lasky and Hideko's malice had been random, thoughtless. The Jackal used cruelty like a surgical blade. Prodding the bruises and broken bones, going for the weak points to hit hardest. His eyes inspected me and I was reminded again of an intelligent animal that hunted for sport – but there was something deeper inside them. Like everything he did was for a reason only he could understand.

The Jackal's palmerlog rang. His gaze still pinned on me, he answered. His brow creased as he listened. 'It's for you,' the Jackal snapped.

The palmerlog crackled into loudspeaker mode. 'For someone who's new to Compass,' the speaker said, 'you've done an incredible amount of damage.'

The voice was young. Female. Calm and mirror-smooth, chamfered of emotion. I guessed I was finally speaking to whoever was in charge. What had Artyom called her? 'Flattery doesn't work with me,' I responded, 'but I'll take the compliment anyway.'

'You could have walked away,' she sighed, as if I'd asked for any of this. 'This was never any of your business.'

I tipped my head back to laugh. 'Walk away while skinnies and Reapers drop dead like flies around me? While your men stalk me around Compass? *You* involved *me*.'

'Believe that, if it makes you feel any better.' I could almost hear the shrug in her voice. Jae? Was that what he had called her? I had to risk it.

'I'll tell you what, Jae, let's meet up and talk. You can tell me all about your little cult. We'll even have coffee, if you promise not to spike my drink.'

I didn't even need a reaction from her. The wide-eyed look on Lasky's face was enough. The Jackal gave a silent, mirthless scoff. I could hear that I'd made her reassess me and felt a moment of triumph.

'Very clever, Vakov. Very clever. You know, that blubbering Bulkava was right. You really do look like your brother.'

The smile melted back from my face. 'Wait—' But she was gone. The door crunched open and Hideko and Simmons filed in. They exchanged nods with Lasky and the Jackal, loosely

251

steepling their fingers before bringing the tips to their own foreheads, muttering something inaudible. Had to be their cult's greeting.

Hideko looked at Lasky's fresh bruises. 'What's going on here?' she asked the Jackal.

'Nothing,' he said calmly. He glanced blankly at Lasky, daring him to respond. Lasky didn't rise to the bait and looked away. That slap wasn't a fit of rage. It was to remind Lasky, without saying it aloud, who really had control around here, who was really watching, daring you to speak out about him. Using manipulation and fear to control which people saw him the way he wanted to be seen, until he had power over them.

Guess how I knew what it was like to live with someone like that.

Hideko frowned, but turned and tapped something on the control panel. The gravfix abruptly shut out. I fell to the concrete floor, hard. Before I could react, my head was slammed into the ground and my arms twisted behind me, shackles snapped tight around my wrists. Hideko hauled me to my feet by my hair with an arm locked around my neck. A secondary door, disturbingly fleshy, opened like a ribcage spread open for surgey. I was pushed through and into dim, throat-like corridors stinking of mould and unwashed bodies. I heard screaming in the distance, an echo of what I was feeling. Jae picked Aras up after Grim and I questioned him. I had no doubt her men had twisted everything possible out of the little alien, and then killed him.

What would Jae do to Artyom? Did she know about Grim and Kowalski as well? Were they already dead? I had to get out of here. Contact Harmony. Somehow. Now I knew who they were, they weren't about to let me go.

The smarting pain in my eye returned. The walls seemed to be sliding together, crushing me between them. Nausea rushed over me in a sickening wave and only fear kept me from puking. The Jackal must have almost taken my eye out. I blinked hard, my bare feet scraping concrete as I was marched into smoky darkness. 'I bet you're thinking about how to escape.' The Jackal's voice sounded hollow and thick in the murky tunnel. 'Even now, you're probably testing those cuffs. Gauging how long it'll take you to break out of them. Lining up which one of us is the weakest, which ones you should take out first before making a break for it. You're thinking of ripping out my throat with your teeth at this very moment. Am I on the right track?'

I didn't have anything to say that wouldn't get my head smashed against the wall.

'Of course you are. I know how you Reapers think. I've seen it before. No shame in it. It's in your nature. In your blood.' I could swear there was a shred of admiration in the Jackal's voice. 'You don't blame a wolf for hunting its prey down, ripping the screaming creature into little pieces while it's still alive, and feasting. That's what you Reapers are. Hunters. Predators.' He clapped me hard between my shoulder blades and my muscles tightened with instinctive fury as I imagined breaking every bone in his body. But I'd given him the reaction he wanted. At that moment I hated my body for caving into him so easily, showing what he wanted to see. 'Don't worry. We're going to give you the chance to do exactly what you're made for, Reaper.'

I heard a staccato cheer echo through the stone. The stormtech sparked down my arms, my hairs standing up like bristles, realisation and dread taking root in my gut.

The Jackal noticed. 'Yes. You're a creature of the battlefields. You've got a living weapon inside you, after all. Such a waste of your talents to leave them behind, running away and forgetting who you are. Just as well you've got us to dump you exactly where you belong.' He clapped me hard on the back again. The little bastard enjoyed playing with his food. 'Don't worry, we'll be fair. You want your freedom? To earn it, you'll have to do what you do best. You'll have it fight for it.'

We were in the Pits.

Another fleshy door cracked open to reveal a filthy overlook concealed by one-way chainglass, splattered with flecks of blood. People had tried to kill each other in the *waiting room*. I was suddenly shoved to my knees, Lasky wrapping his arms around me from behind to lock me in place, Hideko holding my jaw upwards. I growled and bucked against the net of arms. I'd been without armour and the reassuring brush of its bristles and tendrils for hours now, the dread heightening my body's irritation. I felt horribly exposed, hating the feeling of being touched, violated, by these people.

I saw what the Jackal was holding and a glacier shattered inside my chest, pouring a fury of frozen water through my body.

He loomed over me like an enemy warship in orbit. 'You've probably forgotten what's it's like to fight tooth and claw for your life. All that rehab, suppressors; they *tamed* you. Well, we're going to fix that, right here and now.'

He was holding a hypodermic glowing with swirling stormtech. I could smell it: sweet and syrupy and cloying. My mouth watered for it, even as a wildfire of fear spread through me. An animal growl tore out of my throat as I struggled furiously against their hold on me. My muscles flexing, legs quivering, my body kicked into hypergear, unable to think about anything except getting away from the stormtech.

I froze solid once the Jackal poised the hypodermic over my eye.

'Let me explain something to you, Reaper.' In my vision, the thin needle was a pylon of glistening steel, as if already protruding out of my eye-socket. 'This stormtech is going in you, one way or another. It can go in your chest. Or it can go into your eyes. Totally up to you. Me, I'd be happy to make a little experiment of it. I mean, have you ever seen what happens when you shoot stormtech into a Reaper's eyes? Keep struggling like you are, and we'll send you to fight blind.' The sharp, nanometal edge of the hypo seemed to gleam. The stormtech jerked hard in me, and I barely managed to ground myself in place. One muscle twitch could be all the excuse he needed. 'Or we send you down there with a fighting chance of making it out alive. Your choice, Reaper. Your choice. What's it going to be?'

My eye was still on fire from the Jackal's thumb. I imagined the unspeakable agony of the metal rod stabbing down into both my eyes, stormtech flooding down into my brain like acid. Whatever damage it did, my own body would ensure it wasn't enough to kill me. I'd survive long enough to feel every second.

Had to play along.

I allowed myself to ease into the flowing channel of my body's urges, fighting back the instinct to struggle. I nodded towards the hypodermic. 'Say it.' The Jackal's eyes dissected me. Watching everything. 'Go on. Say you want it.'

'I want it,' I growled between gritted teeth.

'Louder,' the Jackal said.

'I want it!' I choked out.

'Louder!' the Jackal roared in my face.

'I want it!' I roared back.

'Yeah, you do.' A stabbing motion and a blinding pain. I looked down to see him jerking it out of my chest. 'People bet a lot on these fights,' the Jackal said as my shackles were removed and I was hauled up and thrown onto the platform. Panting so hard it felt like I had a breach in my lungs, clawing and sucking all the oxygen away. My head bent down, I watched tidal waves of furious blue charging up my breastbone. Couldn't move, couldn't think. The world twisted in nightmare kaleidoscopes, faces smeared along the colours. His voice stretched, rushed towards me like a head-on collision. 'The fights get boring pretty quickly. But seeing a Reaper high on stormtech fight? Well, we've all got money on you. My bet is four rounds at least. Try to stay alive that long.'

The platform jerked as it lowered me into sweltering darkness, then tilted, rolling me onto the gritty sand of the arena. Between matted strands of my hair, I watched someone being cleared away, leaving a gory furrow in the dirt. I gulped for air, the world swaying around me as I stood on shaky legs. How much had he shot into me? I'd cracked myself open to the stormtech so recently that there was nothing to hold back this fresh surge. I felt it roil through me, hardening like cement around my bones. Already building my body back up.

I blinked up at the audience high above me. A mix of aliens and humans, locals and travellers, casual onlookers and arena veterans, all waving their digi-cards high in the air as one bloodthirsty crowd. When they saw me and the bands of stormtech, they roared their approval. They'd be frantically upping their bets, pounding their shibs and ordering their Rubixs to calculate the odds. Trying to predict how long I'd last.

I had only one way out of here alive.

I couldn't fight the stormtech.

I embraced it. Closed my eyes and felt the heat from the high-intensity floodlamps sear my skin. Drank in the enhanced noise, the smell of blood, the cheers. Pulled the fresh, livid stormtech closer to me, fed it all my fear and worry. Soaked up its strength, just as I had when our troop-transport swooped closer to the muddy frontlines of the battlefield.

When I opened my eyes again, I was ready.

24

Blood Hounds

A sea of white noise. Two hundred, three hundred pairs of eyes staring down at down at me, drones equipped with cams jostling for the best angle. They didn't care where I was from or why I was there. They just wanted to see me in action. I rolled my burning shoulders, the stormtech ripping up my throat and preparing me to fight for my life.

I was spotlit in the middle of a ruin. The arena was designed to resemble the bombed-out remnants of some dockyard or hangar bay. A hellscape of chairs, crates, platforms, terminals, workstations, and smashed objects were lodged in the walls and floor at haphazard angles, thin paper barricades walled up around me. Concrete and metallic chunks that had been smashed and strewn across the sandy floor were, on closer inspection, only some flexible, semi-hard material. These lunatics had turned this place into the re-enactment of a *warzone*.

My attention moved to my opponent. A huge man with a cinderblock head who was bulging with knotted muscles. His grin withered at the sight of my stormtech but was instantly restored as he lunged forward, punching me square in the gut. I flailed backwards, the world tilting, as he followed up with a devastating blow, just under my ribcage. At the damage, my body seemed to jumpstart into action. Cranking through me like internal machinery turning fully operational. The stormtech coalesced throughout my body, tightening hard against me and flooding to where I'd been struck, the pain being stamped out as the blue curled there in frantic knots. My muscles burned and teeth gritted. I stooped low, my head down as I grabbed his waist, butting him square in the solar plexus, the breath punching out of his lungs. The crowd roared their approval. I couldn't afford to take too much damage – I had no idea what the consequences to my body would be. Had to finish this fast.

Cinderblock grunted, hurling a wooden chair at me. I ducked, and it exploded into splinters on the opposite wall. He used the distraction to lunge, his rock-like fist pounding furiously into my ribs. My skull throbbed as I soaked up the pain, runnels of sweat pouring down my body. I waited for my opening, grabbing him and smashing my fists into his ribs. Every blow was a feedback loop to my stormtech, increasing my strength. Blue pooled into my right arm, charging strength into those muscles. I delivered two more brutal strikes to his lungs, pain shivering up my arms, his body rippling with tension. I reared back, smashing him across the jaw, following up with an elbow into his throat. Panting hard, I swooped in – but he caught my arm mid-strike. I tensed. He'd noticed the stormtech flowing into the parts of my body I was using to attack. And he'd realised he could use them to predict my movements.

Oh, hell.

A flash of a grin on Cinderblock's face. He drove my arm up, driving his knuckles into my armpit, once, twice, three times. Pain poured through me in relentless waves. He locked me in a furious, sweating frenzy. Our legs tangled, faces inches apart, his breath blasting in my face. I headbutted him, his nose popping against my forehead, him stamping down hard on my toes. I locked my legs around his, sent us tumbling forward and tearing through a thin sheet of panelling with a great shredding sound and smashing onto a table, the flimsy object shattering under our tangled weight. I twisted away first, kicking to my feet, heart hammering, our chests heaving as we faced each other.

Never assume your enemy's stupid, Alcatraz always told the fireteam. Observe them, get every advantage you can.

I feinted forward, the stormtech charging into my right arm as I raised it. He easily parried the blow. Only, I'd tricked him into staring at my stormtech. I chopped at his throat with my left hand, following up by clubbing him across the face. The stormtech now driving into my left arm, I instead thrust my right shoulder into his bulk, sending him smashing backwards into the faux-concrete, chunks of metallic foam spraying. I stuck my leg out to trip him and finish the job, but I'd overreached. Off-balance, he charged me, flipping me over his shoulder and slamming me to the floor so hard I expected to hear my spine snapping like a twig.

Head stabbing with pain, he wrapped his bulky body over mine, his weight pressing me down in a lock as his fists hammered into my sides. I thrashed for all I was worth, kicking up waves of bloody sand. Nothing. I was locked down. He rolled me onto my back, knees pinning my arms as he choked the life out of me. I gurgled, spraying his face with saliva as darkness faded in around the edges of my vision, my struggles becoming weaker and weaker. The stormtech twitching like crazy inside me, plunging into my arms to give me the strength to fight back. He was waiting for that, clamping down so hard around me I felt something inside me give a soft crunch. If it weren't for the stormtech, I'd have already been killed. But my body couldn't, wouldn't, let me die.

My fumbling hand gripped a broken-off chair leg, nails peeking out at the end. I brought it clubbing down across his toes with everything I had. He howled and released me.

I tore away, staggering to my feet. Body throbbing, skin dripping with sweat, mind on fire. I scooped the broken remains of the chair up as he ripped the wooden leg out of his foot and came charging. My body was striated with throbbing blue as I brought the heavy object smashing across his head like a hammer. It shattered, showering splinters across the arena with an ear-shattering crack. He was slammed sideways, head thunking off the wall, crashing onto the gritty sand. Unmoving.

I stepped away, my breath burning in my throat as blue strands swirled faster and faster around my ribcage, looping around my thighs. I hadn't seen it this furious in years. I looked at Cinderblock's mangled head, dripping blood and twisted at an odd angle. My muscles seized, my hands opening and closing, still ready to fight. High above me, customers exchanged winnings.

In an awful moment of clarity, I wondered what Kasia would think about this. Or Artyom. What would Kowalski say if she could see me now? I looked at my bloody hands and I hated them, hated the stain on my skin. But another part of me basked in being centre stage, in being the battle machine Harmony had made me.

I prodded my side tentatively. Had I broken a rib? Torn a muscle? The pain had dulled to an ache. The muscle already hardening, like a katana blade being folded over. Whatever it was, the stormtech was already repairing me as I fought. I stretched, feeling the power roll through muscles reforged by stormtech, smelling the toxic sweetness of my sweat.

My next opponent entered the arena. Tattooed face. Black hair, black eyes burning like a furnace. We circled each other, weighing each other up like panthers. My bare feet crunched on glass and wooden splinters, but I didn't dare glance down. His lithe fists clenched and unclenched, knuckles festooned with swirling tattoos. His body was taut and lean. Made for quick, brutal strikes that would slowly chip away at me if I gave him the opportunity.

Someone above began spraying us with a firehose, turning the pit to gritty mud. Tattoo-Face was distracted, wiping water out of his eyes. I chopped a strike at his neck, stabbed a kick at his kneecap. I tried for a third blow, but gripped empty air. Lightning-fast, he went low and rammed his fist into my sternum before clubbing me in the side of my head. Blackness swarmed. I tried to feint, but he must have been watching the previous fight, seen the stormtech's movements. He grabbed me by the scuff of my neck and drove his knee between my legs. The blinding pain dodged the guard of stormtech and I was drowning in agony so deep I thought he'd killed me. I choked on my own breath as I staggered, back scraping against the hard wall.

A glint. Someone had thrown down a slingshiv, buried hilt-deep in the bloody sand. Tattoo-Face was too close and too fast, scooping it up and slashing twice across my forearm, tearing open a flap of flesh the size of my thumb. A mist of blood sprayed three metres away to spatter on the wall. His arm blurring as he swiped at my forehead, nicking bone, the stormtech desperately trying to plug the pain. Blood sheeted into my eyes. The cut in my arm was slowly healing, stormtech welding flesh together again. Not fast enough.

We circled each other again through the wreckage. Our bodies heaving and bloodied. He routinely lunged forward with a vicious little strike, hacking and slicing me away piece by piece. I kept my arms up in an attacking stance. Sweat and blood dripped into my eyes, blinding me, but if I wiped it away that would be the opening he needed to bury the slingshiv in my throat. My opponent's eyes dissected me. He spun the weapon, the bloody metal clicking and clacking. A shard of glass speared into the flesh of my foot and I tensed, my stride momentarily broken. Tattoo-Face lunged on rangy legs, performed a hacking slash across my elbow. Metal gouged into me, dangerously close to a vein, jarring off a bone. He slashed me across the cheek, then feinted and chopped downwards, trying to cut my hand off, grazing my fingers and hacking a table in half. Splinters sprayed in my face. I skidded backwards, putting distance between us as we resumed circling.

The stormtech spiralled through me, repairing damage, but it couldn't hold back the pain that was throbbing harder and harder through my body. My savaged and sliced knuckles ached to the marrow. My heels scraped the sand. Sweat smeared my vision. Jeers poured down from above, trying to throw me. My heart pounded in my throat, limbs aching as I held them in striking positions. My body seemed to be on the verge of shutting down, jumpstarted at the last second by stormtech. The end was closing in. Tattoo-Face's circles tightened. He was already timing the strike. The stormtech thrummed faster inside me in response, pooling into my right arm, prompting me to attack. He flipped the slingshiv around, the dripping blade pointing downwards. Our ragged breathing was heavy and echoing in the enclosed space. Our unblinking gazes held. He dared me to make a move first. A rusty nail bit into my heel. I stamped down on the rising pain, didn't break my stride.

The stormtech could use my body. But it couldn't choose my strategy. Let Tattoo-Face work with this. Unmoving, not tearing my gaze away, I let the stormtech flood through me again, building up as one, solid mass. My breath hooked in my throat. My body was shaking from my multitude of stinging wounds, sweat and blood dripping down my hamstrings. Tattoo-Face circled in, trying to gauge the stormtech's reaction, where I'd strike. But I wasn't readying my body in a singular fighting position. Wasn't telling it how I wanted to enter combat. It gave away nothing.

This confused him. Between one blink and the next, he flickered his gaze away, skimming over my body.

It was long enough.

He lunged, fast. I was faster. The slingshiv grazed over my stomach, slashing into empty air. In one fluid motion I broke his wrist, tore the slingshiv away and used his own momentum to pin him against the panelling. Me and the stormtech were one unified being as I punched the slingshiv up through his eye and into his skull.

He was dead before he hit the ground, and I dropped kneeling to the sand with him. Screams and gasps were muted as they echoed above me. My whole universe, my entire sensory being, was my body. Sweat was beading on my arms, only now the sweat was bright blue, staining the grit covering me. There was a sucking, liquid roar in the centre of my chest like a black hole. Demanding more kills, asking to be fed.

And I'd feed it. Saliva dripped from my jaws as my muscles rippled and tightened. Heaving, sweating, I swayed to my feet. Dug my heels into the sand and waited for my next opponent.

A figure staggered forward into the arena, coming into the light.

The world deflated and I felt myself stepping backwards. No. No, no. It couldn't be.

It was Grim.

25

On the Edge

Not Grim. Anyone but him. Anyone in the whole of Compass but my best friend

I tried to put distance between us. My mind knew I should have been looking at my friend. But my body, my primal instinct, said this was another enemy. A Harvester wearing camo-armour, hiding in the treetops, an armour-piercing sharp-shooter rifle cradled in his hands. The House of Suns must have kidnapped him and brought him here. Their revenge was me tearing my own friend apart while people cheered me on.

The speakers crackled to life above us. 'Bets in quickly, folks. How fast will our prize beast tear this little man limb from limb? He won't be able to stop himself!'

He won't be able to stop himself. Kasia had used those words about our father; we knew he would kill us all. I clenched my bloody fists together. Had I become him and never realised?

My back hit the wall as the chanting above swelled to a crescendo, getting my blood up. Grim staggered towards me. 'Vak, you're hurt.'

'Grim,' I choked out, waving him away. I didn't recognise my own voice. 'Don't. Don't come near me.'

'Vak, I—'

'Don't!' I shouted. 'It's not safe!'

Grim seemed to notice the bodies piled up around him for the first time. To realise where we were. He took a cautious step back. The sly playfulness drained away, leaving a cornered animal. My hands tightened on the railing. I'd been so stupid to lean into the euphoria and energy, to let the whirlpool drag me back down. But now it was up, I had no way of clamping it down. Blue sweat slithered down my ribs and oxygen burned in my lungs. I knew my reserves were draining fast, but my body told me it was a lie and I had to keep fighting. It's how we won the Reaper war: we were very hard to kill, and we didn't stop until we were dead.

Because we didn't know when to stop killing.

My eyes locked on to the Harvest clan tattoos on Grim's bare arms. The same pattern I'd seen so many times, on the Berserker killsquads who ambushed and attacked us. On the Harvesters who massacred civilians and laughed as they died. On dead Harvesters in mass graves. I felt my jaw locking, and was halfway to Grim before I realised I was moving. One step, two steps, four. He didn't cower, didn't run from me. I gave him a violent shove. 'Get away from me!' I croaked, tears blurring my vision.

But he didn't. He just stood, back against the wall, watching me approach. His loyalty, our friendship, anchoring him in place. He was too good a friend to leave me. He thought too much of me to believe I would do it. It was like fighting against a wave of molasses, to stop the stormtech for the sake of my friend, this little scruffy guy who'd befriended a Reaper. But I couldn't hurt him. I was better than that. He'd follow me to the edge of the universe, as I would for him, because we were best friends. I tore away from him without throwing a punch, screaming out the stormtech and sinking to my knees, panting like a battered dog.

'One of you ain't walking out of here alive,' crackled the announcer. The stormtech tugged and strained against the insides of my flesh, as if trying to rip itself from my skin to attack Grim. It wouldn't let me die. If it had to overpower me to kill him to survive, it would.

Me or him.

Then I heard it coming for us. The crowds screeching in protest as it ran through them. A metallic scrape, and then a shape plummeted over the banisters and thudded into the pit.

I couldn't have called Kowalski without being shot. But I had been able to use my palmerlog to summon my armour.

I slid inside. Its powerful limbs, the whirring interior, clamped around my body and sealed tight, lending me strength and clarity, helping me push back the stormtech. Servomechanisms clicked. My HUD flickered on, all systems functional. I leaped into the air, hydraulics giving me that extra distance. The stormtech wanted me to keep fighting, to keep the blood pumping so I'd stay alive.

But it didn't care *who* I fought.

I'd caught a of glimpse of Simmons from the area. Now I snagged a chain off the banister and flicked it as I fell, looping it around his neck. He was yanked forward, my weight choking him. He gurgled as I hit the floor, trying to pry the crushing chains away from his throat. My body clenched and my armpits strained as I pulled down harder, harder still on the chains, choking the life out of him.

'You did this to yourself,' I rasped as blue circled up my chest. He'd put me in the arena to kill my best friend. Now, he squawked and thrashed wildly as his face turned red. 'Got nothing to say?'

He flipped backwards over the banister, smashing through a platform and hitting the floor with a dull *crack*, his neck broken and larynx crushed to a pulp.

I turned to Grim, peering at me through the strands of his wild hair. 'Let's get out of here,' I croaked. He gave a nod as people began yelling, figuring out that the fight wasn't what they'd paid to see.

'Don't let them escape!' That sounded like Lasky. *Put that rabid Reaper down!*'

My armour allowed me to spring upwards, running along the arena's infrastructure, punching through the jutting beams that prevented arena combatants who had second thoughts from following up on them, and climbing over to freedom. Grim grabbed onto the chain, my body's newfound strength allowing me to haul him upwards to safety with me. I drew my hand-cannon as we turned into chaos. People trying to claim their bets at the now-shuttered stations, others fighting over cards and stacks of Commoner winnings, people surging to escape. My trigger-finger itched. They'd been delighted to bet how fast I could break someone's neck or have my own broken. To see me go crazier and crazier as the stormtech took over.

I could have mowed them all down like they were Harvest soldiers.

But I wouldn't. That wasn't me. It never would be. Instead, I fired three flat, echoing blasts into the ceiling that got the message out pretty clearly. They scattered. I made my way purposefully through the crowd towards the exit, taking Grim with me. I looked, but there was no one from the House of Suns to be seen.

There was a squad of armoured soldiers between us and the door. I'd aimed at the leader before I recognised them, a Harmony chainship landing outside, armed men and women spilling down the disembarkation ramp.

It was Kowalski.

I lowered the handcannon. 'Right on time,' I said.

*

All the smart folks from the House of Suns had slipped away. Well, not Simmons. But something told me he wouldn't have been very forthcoming in Harmony's interrogation room anyway.

We didn't say much on the way back to my apartment. Grim told me they'd snatched him coming out of the Academy library. His answers were brief, his thin shoulders hunched over. He seemed to be looking away from me. Like he was afraid I'd hit him.

I'm not my father, I told myself. *I'm not my father. I'm not that monster.*

Autonomy. It's a classic human issue that's been repeated ad nauseum by stormtech: how much are you to blame for your actions when you have non-human biotech manipulating every element of your behaviour? I'd seen it during the war, convicted Reapers blaming stormtech for their war crimes, including the torture of Harvesters. Denying all responsibility. Saying the drugs had morphed them into bloodthirsty, rabid dogs. It wasn't until I'd been in the battlefields and mud pits and then the barracks afterwards that I fully understood how the stormtech ravages your thoughts, twists your body into something you're scared to live in. I'd never known where my instincts and emotions ended, and where the borders of stormtech's manipulation began.

I'd heard similar excuses before. Like when I was twelve and sprawled out on the floor, my body striped with belt lashes, warm piss trickling down my leg, my father standing over me. *You provoked me. You brought this on yourself. It wasn't me. It was never me.*

I never imagined I'd one day be making these same excuses to a friend. Was the stormtech really turning men into monsters? Or was it just nurturing the evil rooted deep inside us all? Would the stormtech have killed Grim to survive, or would I?

268

When we got home, I got in the shower and set about cleaning out the fistfuls of sand caked under my armpits and thighs that had been grinding the whole walk home. The water turned muddy around my feet, layers of grit and grime and blood washing away. The stormtech was livid now. The bands thicker, the colour brighter, the movements faster. I traced a ripple of them down my bruised ribs with scarred fingers. It was hot to the touch. I felt it knocking and jarring against my bones, hungry for more.

What had I been opened up to?

I shut the shower off and rested my head on the fogged-up glass. Breathed in the steam. I had this under control. I had this under control. I hadn't killed Grim. I hadn't ploughed into the audience.

I so easily could have.

I heard footsteps as Kowalski arrived and guessed I'd better face the music.

'Are you okay?' she asked. 'Are you hurt?' She placed her hand on my shoulder. 'Do you need autosurgery?'

'I'll live,' I said.

'Just as well.' Katherine leaned against the wall and crossed her arms. Weirdly, I felt guilty for rebuffing her question of concern. 'You'd better explain.'

I did. And by the time I was done she looked ready to throttle me. Probably would have if Grim hadn't been there.

'When you agreed to work with Harmony,' she said slowly, each word carefully measured, 'what part of our agreement did you not understand?'

'I never agreed to work as a team,' I said.

'You really don't understand, do you?'

'I didn't have a choice—' I started before she cut me off.

'No. You could have contacted me at any time. Before you

269

stormed their hideout, before you started your book hunt. Before you went to the Collective and got yourself get captured. I trusted you, Vakov.' In a flash, I saw the disappointment beneath her fury. Disappointment not just in what had happened, but in *me*. 'I trusted you enough to give you the space you insisted you needed, and you threw it in my face. After you promised we'd investigate this *together*.' She poked me hard in the chest and began pacing around me, making no attempt to hold back her anger. 'Your heroic stunts might have worked in the Reaper War, but they don't work here.'

'Because Harmony's been making such great progress,' I said. 'You don't even know what's been going on. These aren't petty stormdealers looking to make an extra buck. This is a *cult*, Kowalski. Crazy zealots determined to find the Shenoi, murdering Reapers to burn your credibility into the ground.'

'But you still *disobeyed* us. There's a chain of command, Vakov. I'd think a Reaper would get that. We follow procedure to get things done.' She blinked heavily and I saw her exhaustion in her eyes. This was the last conversation she wanted to have. 'And procedure sure as hell doesn't land you in an arena about to kill your best friend.'

I knew she had a point. But my body was still livid from the fight and I wasn't in any frame of mind to back down. 'You wanted answers. You got them. We know Sokolav's alive, and we know who we're dealing with. Or would you rather not know, and let them continue playing you?'

'Discretion, Vakov. Discretion. They know we're onto them now. It's not a matter of dragging them out onto the streets; we have to build a case in order to tear them out by the roots. Do you know how we found you? Remember Hausk? That fellow we captured at the Suns' compound, down in the Warren, told us they operate in the Pits. The moment our backs were turned, he slit his wrists on the edge of his chair.' She looked me straight in the eye. 'We work together, or we're going to lose.'

'What makes you think Vakov wants your help?' Grim had been silent this entire debate. Now he was by my side, his fingers clenching into a tight fist. 'He cares about saving his brother. He's had enough help from the likes of you.'

'Since when are we the enemy here?' Kowalski actually recoiled, as if she couldn't believe he was speaking. 'He agreed to help on our terms, not the other way around.'

'You *put* that stuff into him, knowing what it'd do. You bastards screwed up the rest of his life. And you think he should play by your rules?'

'We haven't arrested you for multiple hacking infringements,' Kowalski told him, her voice creeping into a low and dangerous tone, 'or for the smuggling ring. We gave you citizenship here. You want to keep it?'

'You think I care about that?' Grim snorted. 'Vakov doesn't owe you people *anything*. Least of all his brother.'

'Of course.' Kowalski clapped her hands around the nape of her neck. 'This isn't just about Vakov, or you. It's about us, isn't it?'

I was confused, right up until I saw her looking at Grim's Harvest tribal tattoo and the dots connected. The tendons on Grim's neck stood stark like bridge cords.

Oh.

There aren't many taboos left when it comes to cultural prejudice, not even on colonies late to join the Common. But trying to paint Harvest immigrants as Harvester supporters – the same Harvesters who had tried to wipe out a good chunk of the human race – rarely ends well. I'd seen people get killed for it, even when it was meant as a joke. Only Kowalski wasn't joking about Grim.

271

Grim raked in a breath and whispered something to himself in his own tongue. His shoulders shook not with rage, but pain. The anger in Kowalski's eyes guttered out as she realised what she'd done.

'I'm so sorry. Please, I—' She shook her head. 'Forget I said that. That was so terribly cruel.'

Grim gave a dark chuckle, masking the sob beneath it. I'd always known he kept a sensitive side buried beneath his jokes and infuriating cheer. Watching Katherine scrape it all back to expose the naked bedrock of his pain with such ease hurt. He was trying so hard not to look at me, but it was only making it worse. He swallowed, spread his arms. 'Going to send your Sub Zero buddies to raid my place at midnight? Drug me, stick me on the next lungship out of here? Nothing stopped your folks from doing that before. Why not now?'

Katherine couldn't meet his eye, but after a few seconds Grim backed away, wiping his face. I realised it was a strain for him just to share space with someone from Harmony. Kowalski couldn't have been finding it easy, either. And here I was, caught in the middle.

'You didn't deserve that, Grim. Neither of you do.' There was an ache in Katherine's eyes, like she was barely holding herself together. 'They want us divided, working against each other. We can't let that happen. Which is why you can't go off alone like this, Vakov.' Her eyes met mine, pleading. *Help me help you.* 'You can't fight for this and pretend you're working alone. You have to trust us to get this done together. Otherwise more Reapers die, the stormtech keeps flowing on the market, and this cult gets stronger. *Do you understand that?*'

I did. I dredged up an image of water flooding a cracked riverbed, cool wind filling up an airless room, as I'd been taught to do when the stormtech grew too strong. Kowalski was fighting to make Compass a better place for everyone, because this

272

was her home, because she had family here, because it was the right thing to do.

She didn't just need my help to do it. She *wanted* it. And in that thought came the guilt at betraying the trust she'd given me. Not Harmony. Her.

I wanted to regain that trust. I nodded. Katherine gave the tightest of smiles. 'I've spoken with Kindosh already. Harmony is pouring resources into this. We're launching undercover operations to hunt the House of Suns down. There're SSC patrols and checkpoints at five Compass spaceports. We're sending out a galaxy-wide transmission across the Common to all outposts, habitats and installations, in case they try and make a break for it.'

I nodded again, not trusting myself to speak.

'It's going to take a while to build a case against them. While we do, lie low for a bit, and I *mean* it this time.' She threw one more apologetic look at Grim and left, leaving me wondering how the hell any of this happened.

Easy.

One step at a time.

273

26

Confessions and Gin

I'm a restless guy. Maybe it's my size, maybe it's the stormtech, maybe it's my body chemistry, but I can't sit around for long. When I'm worked up, I've got to get out of the house. Once Kowalski left, my apartment walls were pressing in on me like a prison cell and I had to find a bar someplace.

'There're some wicked bars around here,' Grim told me. 'You'd never find them on your own. Come on, there's a very special place I know.'

Grim's Very Special Place was on one of the top floors, near the edge of the asteroid. The whole thing was shaped like a giant egg or cylinder, running at least four or five kilometres tall. A conglomerate of bars, lounges and exclusive establishments had been built into the outer edges of the structure, looping around and around, each with its own specifically styled atmosphere and audience. The central bulk of the structure between the bars had been hollowed out, so it looked like you were staring down into a small canyon in the middle of space, with venues chiselled into the surface. Tubes at least five metres thick were grappled to the sides of the bulk, allowing various aquatic creatures to swim along the structure's length in a winding loop. The bars and eateries narrowed as they reached the pinnacle, becoming more and more exclusive, before seeming to grow outside of the asteroid rock itself: offering a naked view into space. I craned my neck to stare at the endless floors honeycombed into the raw asteroid rock, drinking in the mind-boggling view as Grim dragged me up the various stairwells branching through the floors.

The first bar was drenched in gentle white light. Widescreen windows ran the full length of the room, superimposed with ever-changing views of space. Navigational charts, lungship parts, paintings and sketches of spacecraft and various celestial bodies decorated the area. A nearby terminal boasted that it had served patrons of nine different species, from fifty-seven solar systems. It was the bar closest to a nearby spacedock, with furniture and glassware designed to accommodate clientele still wearing their heavy suits.

Sure enough, the place was packed with folk in exoskeletons, spacesuits, EVA suits for spacecraft repairs, thick armour with temperature-regulating tubing for extended journeys where crews wore their gear for months at a time. Glyphs and jargon indicated crews and syndicates who travelled together across the far regions of deepspace, operating independently. There was an entire network of them out there among the moonbases and habitats and stations, where the law was more fluid. I recognised one from Darkstar: a ragtag, multispecies, interstellar crew that explored the greater galaxy, performing odd jobs no one else wanted to touch. Last I'd heard, most of those jobs weren't legal, but I'm in no position to judge.

We made our way to the very back. An armoured Torven slid out of the booth, leaving it free for me to slide into the seat the alien had just occupied. It was the only available space. Perfect. I needed room, but I also needed to be around people tonight. Needed the atmosphere to swallow me up and drown out the past few days.

I sprawled across the wooden table that showed years of alcoholic spills, and watched the blue-white planet slowly turn beneath us as Grim went to get drinks. I was no stranger to places like this. On New Vladi, I'd go with Artyom and our friends to similar little bars sandwiched between buildings and in basements. Niches in the city. We'd sit there, letting the conversation and music wash over us as we drank. As if the bars could hold off the darkness outside. But the flexiscreen was always on, and we couldn't ignore the reports of Harvest carving their way across deepspace, more and more worlds going dark.

I sat up and wiped my nose. Glanced up at the dark canvas of space through the domed viewport. There were promontories of ochre and crimson powder, billowing backdrops of green and violet, like pastel oil colours smeared across light years. Through them, a myriad of pulsing stars glistened. It was an overwhelming abundance of richness, a galactic tapestry. I felt light-headed, as if the world could tilt sideways and I'd fall into the infinite ocean of stars swirling above me. I shook my head, grounded myself in my body and focused on the bar around me. Glasses of vodka, liqueurs and whiskeys sliding across bar-tops made from obsidian, the chink of bottles knocking together. Limes and olives dropping into planetary-themed cocktails. People cracked crude jokes, made advances, boasted about surviving combat encounters with hostile aliens in deepspace. Glyphs shone on armoured knuckles and nebula patterns swirled down chestplates. I drank it all in, savouring the press of people while deciphering the wide-ranging accents and dialects that stemmed from all over the Common.

They really weren't kidding when they said that Compass was the capital of space, and just being here made me want to get out there and explore the universe. Apparently, an ocean planet called Kholan had built an entire metropolis deep under the sea. I'd go there and further: as far away from cults and drug markets and war as I possibly could. Though a glance at the tangle of blue in my arms reminded me it was pretty hard to escape something fused to your blood cells on a molecular level. But that didn't mean I couldn't ignore it for one night.

'Here we go.' The table jolted as Grim returned with two towering glasses brimming with a bubbly sunset-coloured liquid. 'Get that in you.'

'What is it?'

'Dunno. Bartender said it's an offworld brew. A real hit on space stations, apparently.'

'So you don't know what it is?'

'Only one way to find out.'

I drank. It had a strong, fruity flavour and a spicy aftertaste that crackled down my throat and buzzed vibrantly in the back of my skull. We grinned at each other and ordered the next round, and another after that, the stormtech burning off the alcohol.

The next beer was a reddish, copper colour and had to be drunk from the bottle or it'd go sour. Two more of those and we were both starting to crave a nibble or two. We picked another lounge at random: a seaside-style bar decorated with carpets stained with crustacean ink, terrariums filled with sea shells and sand, dangling windchimes and white timber floor-ing deliberately ridged and roughed to appear as if belonging to some beach villa resort. We moved past a soiree of party-goers to an alcove in the corner of the room, where a table was already filled with complimentary offerings of soft bread, oils and balsamic sauces, chunky salt and pepper. I'd eaten half of it by the time Grim returned with a food called pizza I'd never had before, and more beer. Black in colour, tasted like liquorice and roasted nuts.

'Isn't this food a bit ... cheesy?' I told Grim as I chewed through the pizza.

'Don't look a free horse in the mouth, Vak.'

'What?'

'Never mind. Just eat.'

I did. When we'd finished, I discovered we were dining in one of Compass' most prestigious gin bars. I meant to put that to the test, ordering two gin and tonics, mixed with Cointreau and Curaçao, blue as my own stormtech. As with every time I went drinking with Grim, it didn't end at one round, and we were quickly onto our third. Grim swore he'd keep pace with me to the tenth, not counting the beer we'd had in the previous bar. He was tipsy by the fifth. By the eighth, he was passed out, stone-cold drunk, snoring loud enough to turn heads. I smirked, knowing I'd have to get him home.

I spooned the blueberries out of my gyroscopic glass, my thoughts turning back to the House of Suns. This was more than some sort of alien obsession. And they were hoarding stormtech for something more than to poison it to kill Reapers and skinnies. They were stockpiling the stuff, studying it. So why kill scientists? What did they not want the rest of us to find out? By killing Reapers off in public, they obviously wanted to send a bloody message. But if anything, turning people away from stormtech seemed counter-intuitive to their zealot manifesto.

And how involved was Artyom?

The flexiscreens above me began replaying the terrorist attack from a few days ago. They had more intel now, about where the terrorist had sourced the bombs, how he'd gained access into the building, and as the piece unfolded I noticed people were staring at us. At me. Not directly, of course, just side glances and quick looks. Wasn't like I wasn't used to it. But there were more of them now. And where before there'd been curiosity, now there was a quiet anger. Fear. Trepidation. As if I'd snap off the leash at the slightest provocation.

I felt my fingers tighten around the glass, suddenly feeling vulnerable without my armour.

I glanced up to see Kowalski. 'You got my message,' I said. I'd invited her when we'd left the second bar. I'd only half expected her to join us. Not sure why I did it. Maybe I'd enjoyed our little chat in the French restaurant more than I'd realised.

But I knew I was glad she was here.

She stood awkwardly in front of the table. Her hair was wet from a recent shower, her trademark scarf around her neck. 'You still got room for one more?'

'I don't know,' I said, leaning back in my seat. Grim stirred and gave a loud snort but didn't wake up. 'That alpha-male quip cut me deep. Fragile masculinity and all.'

Katherine rolled her eyes. There was a vacant chair, but I moved sideways so she could sit next to me in the booth. She did. 'Reapers don't hold grudges,' I said, 'not worth it. Except for when we do.'

'Yeah.' The cloudy residue of her vaper clung to her clothes with a vague peppery smell. 'Well, I'm no stranger to that department.'

'What's your poison?' I asked, gesturing at the menus bobbing in the air, held out by drones designed as various aquatic creatures. Katherine placed her order with the drone built like a stingray. Vodka, triple-filtered through porous asteroid rocks. I guess you'd need something strong if you worked under Kindosh's belt.

'Today's been a kick in the gut for everyone,' she said as her drink came. She plonked the entire bottle on the table between us, poured herself a decent measure and knocked it back. Poured herself another. 'Kindosh knew you didn't like us and locked you into a deal you couldn't refuse. It's hard to stay angry with you when you do exactly what she expected.'

'So I'm off the hook?'

'Nice try, Vak. But Harmony understands you had your reasons.'

She twirled the glass in her hands. 'Remember Andrezj? That nephew of mine who dabbled in stormtech?' She didn't look up, as if she didn't have the willpower to raise her head. 'That was him today. The one who brought down that building.'

My throat went tight. Her behaviour in my apartment now made sense. 'I'm afraid to call my sister.' Her gaze was still fixed down, searching for answers in the clear liquid. 'I keep trying to come up with things to say. Playing them in my head over and over and over. None of them end well. He won't be the last, Vakov. Not by a long shot. And it scares me. It scares me that so many people are going to die before we stop this.'

'There's not much that hurts more than losing family,' I said.

Only now did Katherine look at me. 'Is that what happened to your sister?'

I opened my mouth, closed it again. I've very rarely let people see me, really see me. It's not that I care what they might think; it's that some things should be private. Especially from Harmony. Us Reapers spend so long wrapped in our armour, in our fireteams, in the sensations of our bodies, that the concept of opening up to anyone outside of our comfort zone is an alien one. It's why so many folks with stormtech suffer from depression and suicidal tendencies: we've been biochemically altered to feed on our own hyper-stimulated mentalities, to block support and logic off from third parties. Most therapists give up on us out of frustration.

But sometimes, against all logic and reason, you take a leap of faith. If I couldn't trust Katherine with this, how could I trust her with my life?

More than that: I wanted to trust her. Wanted her to trust me.

I let the words spill out of me. 'Rent isn't cheap on New Vladi. My sister was planning to leave home and take me and Artyom with her. My father was . . . difficult to live with. We wanted out. Kasia knew a few guys who were in gangs, controlling the local drug trade. Spacefaring traders had just brought grimwire and synthsilver to New Vladi. Most of it was seized by the local forces, but not all of it. They issued a public warning to stay away from the stuff. And guess what happens when you tell people they can't have something?'

'You've sold them for life,' Katherine confirmed.

'It spread through the main city, reaching across to towns and remote settlements. Shipping it became a high demand, rewarding business. All Kasia needed was a few deliveries and she'd be set. There was this one guy called Joon. Joon Szymanski.' We looked down simultaneously as the stormtech burned an enraged blue up my arms, twisting in furious knots. I worked some saliva into my throat. 'My sister did about half a dozen shipments for him. But there'd been raids and people were on high alert. When Kasia told him she wanted out, he had a choice: let her go and trust her silence. Or silence her for good.'

Katherine looked at me for a long moment. Not saying a word, she poured me a glass of vodka and slid it towards me. I wished more than ever that I could get drunk.

'It took us a week to find her body. He'd have come for us, too, but Kasia was smart enough to use a false identity. We overheard Szymanski boasting about killing her to his mates when he thought no one was listening. Everyone knew he did it.

'On New Vladi we don't bury our dead. We leave their bodies on the mountain for the animals. Only one family member

281

is allowed to take them up. I was the one who did. But she deserved better than to have her body torn apart by animals.' My words were thick and raw, catching in my throat. 'I dug her grave out of the frozen dirt with my own hands, right on top of the mountain where we'd go sometimes to sit and watch the view. There's no sight like it, Katherine. Not in the entire Common. Fields and snowcapped mountains and vast, empty tundra as far as you can see, no sound but the wind in your ears. It was our one place of peace. And she's buried there for ever, right in our spot. I'm the only one who knows where it is.'

'How old were you?' Katherine asked quietly.

'It was my thirteenth birthday. The day Kasia promised we'd be free to live a new life together.'

Katherine set her glass down very carefully. 'Vak . . . I don't even know what to say. Some folks wouldn't have come back from that.'

I managed to plaster on a tight smile. 'We're a different breed on New Vladi. Everything's tough there. If you want justice for a crime, no matter how big or small, you go to the Five Courts. If they cannot reach an acceptable settlement, you fight to the death. I've seen people butchered over land disputes and reach a settlement agreement for war crimes.' Even thirteen-year-old me knew I'd never have enough evidence against Szymanski: with his family name and privileges he would always walk. 'Or, you go to the one person on New Vladi who has authority above all others: the *Babushka*.'

'I remember you telling me. *Babushka* means grandmother, right?'

'By title only.' I'd heard of folks unhappy with her authority who'd tried to take her out. They tried once. Only once. 'She decides whether to remain neutral, mete out justice herself, or allow you to take it into your own hands with no consequences.'

'And that *works*?' she asked, as if I'd told her we used death by stoning as a capital punishment.

'It's worked for hundreds of years, ever since the first settlements,' I said. 'We've got about half a dozen crime families running the show on New Vladi. They only have one thing in common: they all respect the *Babushka*.'

'What did she do for you?'

'She allowed me to decide Joon Szymanski's fate, and helped me deliver it.' The stormtech was cycling through me now, stirring up the old wounds like a storm dredges up the ocean floor. I let it. I needed to say this, needed someone to hear it. 'She gave me a toxin to mix with his synthsilver. It made his body dependent on the drug. It also meant that, over time, synthsilver would become deadly to his system. If he didn't use it, his system would slow down, his organs would fail and his motor functions gradually decline.' I swallowed, my throat parched but unable to raise my glass to drink. 'So he had a choice. Use it and poison himself slowly. Or don't use it and suffer as his bodily functions shut down one by one.' I stared into the vodka, shimmering like mercury in my glass. 'I don't know what he decided or how long he lived. But I never saw or heard from him again.'

Katherine said nothing. Not intruding, not questioning, just letting me speak.

'Everyone told me to forget it, always forget,' I said. I felt myself drifting down the backstreets of my mind, dark places I swore I'd close. 'To leave Kasia behind. Get some sort of closure out of moving on. But she made me who I am. She's *part* of who I am. It's not such a terrible thing, grief. It means you carry a bit of them with you. Forgetting her would be forgetting that. Forgetting how I got here, who I am. I can't do that to my sister. I can't imagine anything worse than drifting off, unremembered and forgotten. She deserves better than that. Even if no one else remembers her, I will.'

Katherine reached out to me, holding my hand, allowing my fingers to fold into her's. She wore a sad, tight smile on her face. 'Thank you,' she said quietly. 'I'm glad you told me.'

'So am I,' I said, and realised how much I meant it. How glad I was that Katherine knew this about me. 'So am I.'

27
The Kaiji

Everyone tries at least once to out-drink a Reaper. And everyone learns that it's impossible and never to do it again. Everyone except Grim. No matter how many times he drank with me, he never learned his lesson. He was roaring drunk as he sagged between me and Katherine, his breath smelling like a gin-distillery and moaning that he felt like death. Katherine wasn't looking so great, either.

We were in some kind of small parkland. Miniature greenhouses growing tropical fruits and vegetables were scattered around us. Rinds glistened behind chainglass walls, streaked with condensation. Globes of white light were strung above the trees as we stumbled down the pathway. But the scenery was lost on the other two. I grinned at both of them, not so much as tipsy. 'I could go for a few more rounds. What do you guys say?' I raised my voice. 'Vodka? My treat?'

'Oh, please god no,' Grim said, clutching at his head.

'Maybe some gin? A couple of shots will do you right.'

'I'm going to puke my guts out,' Grim groaned.

But come the morning, I knew he wouldn't regret it. We'd both needed this. What had happened in that arena hung over us, even if Grim was a good enough friend not to say so.

Getting smashed in public together wouldn't fix everything, but it helped. As had talking to Katherine.

Katherine's palmerlog rang. 'Please don't let that be work,' she muttered as we set Grim down on a well-worn park bench. He rolled over, falling to the soggy grass and somehow managing to grab onto a bergamot tree. He lay there like a dead fish, still groaning, paying no heed to the flustered octodrones harvesting the tree, wondering what he was doing to their property.

'Wait. Say that again.' Katherine's mouth was set in a grim line as whoever was on the other end of the palmerlog spoke. 'You're serious. No, he's with me. Yes, I'll tell him.'

'What's happened?' I asked tentatively.

'It's the Kaiji,' she said, not taking her eyes off me. 'They want to meet with you. Alone.'

They gave me the choice of saying no, of course. But it was the sort of choice you know is really no choice at all.

I hadn't seen Saren since the raid on the compound down in the Warrens, not until he invited me for lunch at a lavish hotel buffet for a pre-meeting briefing. Turns out, he wasn't only a Harmony SubPrimer but was on Harmony's Alien Affairs Committee. 'We're still in peace negotiations,' he told me as we sat. Jasken stood guard in plain clothes, angled away from the other customers. 'Anything you do could jeopardise our task, so you have to play their game.'

'Oh, good. No pressure,' I said.

'They're ... different.'

'In what way?'

'In *every* way. They haven't assimilated into human society like the Bulkava or Torven. They're a heavily militarised, regimental species. Rank, hierarchy, order, are of the highest priority with these guys. They don't like to waste their time, and they don't tolerate fools. Their homeplanet is a hellscape, ravaged by brutal metal storms and a thin ozone layer. Until they escaped their system, both space and resources were incredibly scarce. They've been a spacefaring species for at least several millennia, with a presence on over a dozen planets and three star systems. Nevertheless, specificity and frugality has been ingrained into them.'

I leaned back in our alcove. The buffet area around us was minimalist grey and white, though the food spread was set out like a photoshoot. Thick wads of prosciutto, rolls of bacon and spiced salami, membrane-thin. Fried tomato, slices of melon and bowls of glistening berries. Omelettes and hash-browns and lacquered duck and dripping pork. White yoghurt and honeycomb swirl and sottocenere cheese with winks of nutmeg. Thick, chunky sourdough and raisin bread and cake, light as a breath. Carafes brimming with freshly squeezed juice. It all looked fantastic, but I settled on spiced egg with red onion and shallots with a side of steaming black coffee.

Compass never sleeps, so despite the predawn hour, the buffet was quickly filling with people. Most of them were pilots, Navigator crews, Shipmasters, all getting their last proper meal before reboarding their spacecraft. To say shipboard food is terrible is like saying engine solvent doesn't mix well with vodka.

'Why meet with me, and not anybody else?' I asked.

'My guess is because you're a Reaper. Maybe they think a soldier represents their interests better. Their Shipmasters, Commanders, Naval Officers are big leagues in their hierarchy, so maybe they assume we operate on a similar wavelength. They've got a specialised military intelligence called Elite Tactical Force. If they're around, they mean business.' Saren began carving his way through a cheese platter. 'As part of the peace negotiations, Kindosh has been providing them regular status updates of your investigation into the Reaper deaths. They'll probably want to talk to you in person.'

I extended an arm, livid with churning clouds of stormtech. 'You think this has got something to do with it?'

'Definitely. They'll probably ask you to see it. Do what they ask, but within reason. Don't agree to anything. They'll hold you to it.'

Maybe I was out of my depth. 'It's that serious?'

'From what we understand, they're top political players. Could eat the Borgias for breakfast.'

'I don't know who that is,' I said evenly.

Saren looked as if to explain, but evidently decided it was too much trouble. 'They're powerful creatures with massive armadas. They've got superior-class dreadnoughts, battlecruisers and frigates at their command, packing high-class artillery weapons and defence systems. As far as political, technological and military might goes, they're the most powerful alien species in the galaxy. We need to stay friendly with them. If we went to war we'd probably lose.'

'They're that powerful?'

'They're that powerful. They're still upset that Harmony used stormtech in the first place, so their being here at all means they're ready to take action. We need that action to be in our favour. Just so you know who you're meeting with: Ambassadors and politicians all carry a *van* in the middle of their names. Military and Naval personnel have *dan*. Presumably, you'll be meeting with three of them.'

'Three to one?' I asked.

'Their politicians usually work and travel in threes.' Saren drained his third coffee that morning. 'Oh, and whatever you do, don't touch their horns. The males find it incredibly emasculating and offensive.'

'Wasn't *planning* on doing that.'

'You'd be surprised what people try to get up to with aliens. They're not intelligent animals who learned to talk, like pro-human groups like to pretend they are. Most aliens have history and culture stretching back three times further than humans do. That goes double for the Kaiji. If you're condescending, they'll react badly. Understand?'

'Be polite, be diplomatic, don't say anything stupid.'

'That's the gist of it.'

I waved Jasken over. It wasn't like I was going to get shot in here. 'Food's going to go to waste,' I said, gesturing at the spread.

'Thanks, kid.' Jasken planted himself down and swiped a hunk of meat before Saren could protest. 'Barely eaten all day. Shoddy shift rotation.'

Saren elected not to comment on that. 'I owe you for the armour,' I told Jasken. 'It wasn't cheap, but it was worth it.'

Jasken shrugged. 'Your money's not going to be worth much if you kick the bucket tomorrow. Live it up now, I say.'

'That's such a moronic philosophy to hold onto,' Saren sighed. He and Jasken seemed to disagree about everything except how much they hated the House of Suns.

'It's true!' Jasken protested through a mouthful.

'But it doesn't make it wise!'

Jasken shook his head. 'You Navigators. Always about the long game, waiting and waiting for something to pay off. Not everything's light years away, you know.'

'You trained to work on spacecrafts?' I asked Saren.

Saren nodded. 'It's in the family, so it was expected of me. Trained for astral navigation and onboard management on chainships, lungships, even deepspace dreadnoughts. Wanted to be a Commander one day. Compass might be our home, but there's a whole other universe out there that needs discovering.

289

Not everyone's got the aptitude for spending years in a ship surrounded by vacuum or surviving warpspace, but I do.'

'Why'd you stop?' I asked.

'Things didn't work out. But I landed with second best. I can't say I'm sorry it ended up this way.'

Two more rounds of coffee and a pastry each and we wrapped up the briefing. I returned home to give my armour a good scrubbing before strapping into it and heading to Spacedock 409D, as instructed. I went early to make an impression. Three hours later, I was still sitting in the brightly lit arrivals hall, watching the never-ending stream of ships docking. Of course the military-minded aliens with the mega-sized space fleets were late. A good reminder as to which species was waiting on who around here.

By now, whatever cohesive thoughts I'd cobbled together had quickly fallen apart. Meeting up with the mysterious creatures from the verge of the Common will do that to you. I knew people who'd hack off their right arm to get a few minutes alone with the Kaiji. It was more likely they'd hack off both my arms and beat me to death with them by the time the day was done.

They weren't there one minute and the next they were. Three of them, just as Saren predicted. A little taller than me, wearing elaborate, ceremonial suits with high collars, long sleeves and heavy hooded cowls. No helmets or any kind of space-appropriate gear. They were slender and elegant, ash-skinned with large eyes and a crown of horns atop their heads. Two of them had soot-black eyes, while the other's eyes were cerulean, matching the sash over his shoulder. Their noses wrinkled, as if already smelling the stormtech in me.

The tallest spoke first. A sharp, multi-layered voice with a strange depth to it. 'You are Vakov Fukasawa?' He'd completely butchered my name, but I'm used to that. It's not exactly John Smith.

I nodded, but they showed no reaction. Then I remembered Saren's words. 'Yes. I am.'

And they whirled away, robes dragging on the floor, apparently expecting me to follow. Well, this was going to be interesting. His words about their social niceties seemed to be proving true, too. I caught up and noticed they were wearing armour under their ceremonial clothes. High-tech and curved close to the body. Designed to go undetected.

I followed them to their docked transport – a black pod in the shape of a balloon. It looked like a short-range transit craft, but it's hard to tell with alien tech and I had no idea where they planned to take me. My knowledge of the entire species ended at the fact that they were pissed at Harmony for using stormtech. And once away from Harmony's jurisdiction, they could do whatever they wanted with me.

But if I wanted answers, I had to trust them.

I entered their pod.

'You must be Fukasawa,' a voice like thunder said.

A single Kaiji stood at the far end of the craft. He was taller than me, just over two metres by my reckoning. He was broad-shouldered and barrel-chested, clad in a heavy tower of gold and black armour. His chestplate glistened with sun-bright intensity, a line of sweeping lights stencilled from the shoulders down to the angular gauntlets. His eyes were piercing and intelligent as they flicked over me: one black, the other a dirty gold that matched his armour. Two large horns jutted from either side of his skull, like the horns of a bull or a yak. He pressed a fist to his armoured chest. 'Thanks for showing up.'

I'd been so accustomed to the idea of Kaiji being slender and lanky that I had to mask my surprise. Seemed there was as much diversity within their own species as there was within humans. 'Happy to be here,' I told him as I strapped myself into a full-body seat that clearly wasn't built for human bone structure, while one of them tapped a few buttons on the controls and had us jetting away. The one with blue eyes introduced himself as Ambassador Nsurev van Jorren before glancing at the bigger Kaiji. 'May I introduce Space Marshall Xanrimaeyr dan Juvens. He is in charge of military tactics and Elite Tactical Force regiments in this sector.'

I sure as hell hadn't expected to be meeting with one of the top dogs, especially not informally. Still, Harmony had been clear: they would get whatever they wanted. 'Good to meet you, Space Marshall,' I said vigilantly.

The big alien made an indignant snorting sound and waved a hand. 'Juvens is quite fine here,' he grumbled out. 'Formalities give me a headache.'

I allowed myself a grin. Perhaps this visit wouldn't be so bad after all.

The other two made no efforts to introduce themselves, but Harmony wouldn't have allowed them on Compass without clearance, which had been passed onto me. Their names appeared over their heads on my HUD: Maadichi van Szev and Petrych van Chwekli. I kept my knowledge to myself. Never knew where it could come in handy.

Nothing more was said as the transit craft jetted out into space. The Kaiji seemed very good at not looking at me, but I knew they were. They had a spicy, gunpowder sort of smell to them. It wasn't quite unpleasant. Juvens fidgeted next to me in his seat as if he were unused to remaining idle.

The small spacecraft was monochromatic. The walls were skinned with a concave geometrical pattern and scattered with little gleaming strips of light. What few devices I could see were angular and weirdly gothic. Szev stretched out a bony hand near the wall and a panel of intricate knobs surfaced like smooth stones in ink-coloured water. Nothing like the bright and complicated design of Torven technology.

I glanced out the viewport as we approached the Kaiji dreadnought. It was shaped like an elongated bullet that slowly curved upwards to form a bulky, sharpened point, scintillating like a sword's edge in the sun. The hull was purple-black with armoured plates slotting over each other, coated with a hexagonal matte-black surface that twitched, as if alive. A vibrant blue pulsed between them, like thousands of heaving gills. It looked like it had been created with the brush strokes of an oil painting. I suddenly had the impression of stumbling across a mythological monster in the depths of an ocean trench, biochemically modified to withstand the crushing pressure of its atmosphere.

But I know a warship when I see one. Between the scattering of docks and hangars was an arsenal of railguns, plasma cannons, nanoguns, heat-seeking launchers, devastating smatter-shells, and anti-ship weaponry that fired high-velocity tungsten rods. They bristled out from the hull like hostile creatures peeking out between beds of coral. The pod slowed to a standstill as stabilising thrusters balanced us in the void of space, leaving us within the dreadnought's vicinity. I felt its full mass; dozens of cubic tonnes of this massive alien warship pressing down on my shoulders. 'We're not entering the ship?' I asked.

'No.' I'm hardly an expert on alien emotions but Szev seemed to adopt an expression of dour amusement. The pod lights dimmed, as if going into power-conversation mode. 'We would not allow a human onboard our ship without quarantine.'

No. But by being in the proximity of their dreadnought and seeing their full might of ship-shattering military hardware on display, they'd made it clear we were in their territory, their world, playing by their rules. I'd played this game with people above my rank before. I could play it with these aliens now.

'Then why are we out here?' I asked, feeling uncomfortable in the rigid mould of the chair and the awkward five-point harness. I noticed the wide straps had locked tight in place, securing me into my seat. Hopefully so I couldn't tamper with the controls or see anything they didn't want me to see, rather than because they planned to take me out.

Juvens inclined his head, jutting horns gleaming in the light. 'We can't risk anyone overhearing us. Not with what we're about to discuss,' he said. His English was light years ahead of the Ambassador's, his tone casual and confident, as if he were a native speaker. He had to have spent time at alien cultural centres to learn the language.

'We have been observing you,' Szev declared, 'since Harmony asked you to help prevent the spread of the Shenoi DNA on Compass.'

I caught myself nodding and said, 'Yes. We call it stormtech. I understand you've asked Harmony to stop it spreading.'

'Stormtech.' I wasn't sure if the Ambassador was amused by the phrase or not. 'Using *stormtech* may have won a war, but it was still unwise. Your people did not listen then. Perhaps they will now.'

'Why did you object to the use of stormtech from the very start?' I'd lived too long with this mystery to keep my curiosity bottled up any longer. 'How could you possibly know what it would do?'

The Kaiji all seemed to weigh up their response, but Juvens was the first to speak. 'Show us,' he said.

I wasn't overwhelmed with enthusiasm at the idea, but I'd known it was coming. I allowed the armour plates on my arm to peel back, revealing the swirl of blue under my flesh. The Ambassadors inhaled sharply, as if the stormtech would leap out and bite them. All except Juvens, who was watching in fascination as it curled between my bones. The stormtech had been itchy ever since the arena fight, and seeing it made me want to scratch furiously.

Juvens unstrapped from his seat and strode to the viewport, hands behind his back. Different species or not, I recognised the ease with which he wore his armour. Like me, he was more comfortable in his suit than his own skin. 'I don't mince my words, and I don't think you do either, Fukasawa. Honesty's in short supply around here, and that's no way for our two species to form an alliance. So I'll say it directly.' Juvens glanced over his shoulder at me. 'Stormtech is a piece of the Shenoi themselves, living on inside other organisms.'

I raised my arm. 'You mean, this isn't just DNA scraps . . . it's active, living pieces of the Shenoi?'

'Yes.'

It wasn't a dawning realisation. More like a complete re-imagining of my situation, hitting me with the force of truth. I had a long-dead alien race trickling through my bloodstream and nervous system, swimming around my organs, coursing through the hands and feet that killed and hurt people at their command. And it was grafted inside every Reaper, every skinnie, everyone who'd ever dabbled in stormtech.

All diseased. All tainted.

Was this why it seemed to have a mind of its own? I balled my hand into a fist, watching the stormtech – the Shenoi – accelerate to the crook of my elbow at the sudden flexing of sinew. 'You knew the aliens lived on all this time.' My voice was husky, raw. 'You knew the stormtech wasn't just leftovers. And you didn't tell us?'

'We informed some senior Harmony dignitaries about our suspicion,' said Chwekli, hands folded together. 'Either they did not believe us, or they decided not to share that information. But humanity was warned.'

I had a pretty strong suspicion it was the latter, because dismissing inconvenient information was exactly what Harmony would have done. They hadn't needed another complication, especially not one that'd have made willing men and women stop and think twice about becoming Reapers. Rage built in my chest as Juvens laid his seven-fingered hand on my wrist. I could read the other three Kaiji's disapproval as easily as Cyrillic script. They hadn't wanted the Space Marshall to come. They'd wanted to keep this discussion political, under their control. He knew it, and that's exactly why he'd come.

'Harmony continued the Shenoi's existence, spread them around,' said Szev with an undercurrent of steel. 'The Shenoi were an all-powerful, all-consuming, savage race with no regard for life or mutual existence.'

'That's putting it lightly,' Juvens grumbled. 'They refused to engage in negotiations or consider a truce. Too many species and galactic councils have tried over the millennia. The Shenoi are a parasite, by nature and by culture, infecting living tissue and taking life-forms as their vessels, slowly seizing control until they've eaten cites, planets, solar systems.' His armoured fingers traced the swirling strands of stormtech, his voice adopting a dark, thunderous tone. 'They've destroyed fourteen civilisations this way. Maybe more. And with the stormtech plague humanity's dealing with, they could make it fifteen.'

I leaned back. No wonder the stormtech was able to heal us and regrow biomass, it was their own DNA. *Our* DNA. I was sharing my body with a power-hungry, parasitic alien species whose life goal was to consume me. Little wonder stormtech sent our aggression rocketing sky-high. They needed us to be the strongest organisms walking around. Top of the galactic food chain.

Of course, this changed nothing. It'd make little difference to the stormdealers selling their goods in back alleys and underground workshops, and even less to folks hooked on it. No matter how deadly it was, as long as there were people willing to buy and people willing to sell, the drug market would exist.

'Why are you telling me this now?' I asked. 'Why not someone else from Harmony?'

Juvens snorted. 'We tried, once. It didn't work out so well. You're a soldier. You've seen what the stormtech does in the war, and what it's still doing to your asteroid. You can make a practical difference the others can't.'

I was starting to see what Saren meant about the Kaiji respecting military hierarchy. In giving us another chance to make this right, they were going to someone they believed wouldn't ignore them again.

'What happened to the Shenoi?' It wasn't as important, but I had to know.

'We destroyed the bastards,' Juvens boomed with undeniable pride. 'We took the full force of our fleets and armadas and met them on the battlefield before they reached our homeworld. It was a bloody, brutal war. It cost us almost all our munitions, resources, everything. Took centuries to rebuild. But we halted their rampage across space.' The Space Marshall made an exasperated, snorting sigh. 'We were naive enough to think that was the end of it. Then we found that even fragments of stormtech scattered across the galaxy have done plenty of damage on their own.'

'There're tens of millions of people infected with stormtech,' I said. 'If they're kicking around inside us all, shouldn't they have taken over already?'

'If that were true,' Juvens said evenly. 'You'd already be dead. Remember, stormtech is like any other virus or parasitic organism. The more accelerated and late-stage the disease is, the higher the impact on your body. If you combat it, the virus dies down. Fukasawa, if the Shenoi had fully possessed your body, you'd know, because you'd be busy trying to tear me limb from limb.'

'Trying?' I asked.

Juvens nodded towards a slim, black-bodied handgun that emerged out of his thigh-armour. The alien gave a grim smile as he tapped my chestplate with an armoured finger. 'I don't miss.'

My rehab had weakened the stormtech, allowed the organism to die down. Now I had given it a sudden boost, I was in a hell of a lot more trouble than I'd originally thought. 'It can't . . . hear me, can it?' It was stupid question, but I had to ask.

'Fortunately for all of us, no. Without contact with a Shenoi mind, the organism's about as smart as a slab of fungus.'

'But the risk is still present,' interjected Szev, as if we didn't all already know this. 'It'll still influence your behaviour. In that sense, it controls you, and always will.'

Little wonder they'd been so desperate to get stormtech off the market. I wondered if they had their own people addicted to this drug back on their homeworld like other species. 'How much stormtech is swimming around in the universe?' I asked them.

They all glanced at each other again. Szev burst into rapid-fire conversation that I couldn't understand a word of, and suddenly all four were wrapped up in a fierce debate. Juvens gave that exasperated snorting sound and thumped the side of the pod with his armoured fist. The others were instantly silenced.

'Enough of this drivel,' he said, speaking to them but glancing at me. 'He has the right to know.'

'No.' Szev's voice was cold enough to freeze water. 'The human has no right. You have no right. Your generation has no idea what our ancestors went through, you—'

'Don't you dare say that to me. Not now, not ever.' Juvens spoke with thunderous rage, his eyes hard as granite. He lowered his head, thrusting his horns towards them. Regardless of species, I know what a threatening gesture of dominance looks like. 'I have every right. I understand the sacrifice our people made. I've stood on the ruins of planets ravished by the Shenoi. I've seen the civilisations and species they turned to ash, knowing that could have been us. Could *still* be us. I've spent my entire life training for a war to make sure that never happens. Now that it might happen, now we're facing them again, do you really think I'm going to allow snivelling *politicians* to get in my way?' His mismatched eyes ricocheted between the three Ambassadors, daring them to argue, daring them to give him an excuse to tear them apart. But they took the hint and shut right up.

I swallowed a face-splitting smirk. Until I ran through what Juvens had said.

'What do you mean, an upcoming war?' I asked.

Szev and Chwekli's eyes were narrowed into dark slits, but they were too proud to speak up again in defiance. Juvens' chest swelled and deflated as he snorted out a gust of air. 'We suspect the Shenoi are still out there,' he said. 'We believe they are planning a return.'

28

Ruins of the Future

I wanted to laugh. I almost did. I actually felt my insides shaking. Instead I managed, 'What?'

'Our long-range scanners have detected navigational trajectories and bio-signals matching the Shenoi's, approaching Compass.'

'You said you destroyed them,' I said.

'Every species has attempted to destroy viruses and hostile organisms. Winning one skirmish doesn't mean you've won the war,' Juvens said crisply. 'The Shenoi are largely energy based, operating on a hivemind. They could easily have stored parts of themselves within stormtech, deep inside a planet somewhere. They're not flesh and bone like us. They have to construct bodies out of living tissue infected with stormtech. If they had enough, they could rebuild themselves.'

'And just when I thought we didn't have *enough* problems.' As I spoke, I noticed the stormtech throbbing in my arm. As if the evil little parasite *knew* I was talking about it.

I understood why they had come to me about this. If this information went public, the damage would be unimaginable. Skinnies being killed in the streets. The conflicts between stormdealers exploding over into outright warfare.

'There have been humans,' said Szev, 'interacting with stormtech for more than recreational use.'

'The House of Suns,' I said. The image was coming together, focusing slowly. 'You're after the House of Suns.'

Another shared glance between the aliens. 'What do you know of them?'

I gathered up my scattershot thoughts. 'They're psychopaths, obsessed with the Shenoi. They've been spending a fortune on researching stormtech. I think they've been working themselves into the stormtech drug industry, spreading it through Compass. It's not about beliefs or values or even money. It's a pseudoscience cult. I don't know what they're planning, but they've been undermining Harmony and stirring public outrage to get it.'

I suddenly saw it from the Kaiji's perspective. Through the millennia, they'd watched stormtech slowly but surely gnaw its way through over a dozen other species. They were seeing the same happen to us humans, now with the looming threat of the Shenoi, speeding across the galaxy to make a return, likely hell-bent on revenge.

'There's no way to put it delicately. You'll never be free of stormtech entirely,' Juvens told me, armour creaking as he leaned forward. 'No species that's made contact with it ever will. But you can contain the explosion, stop it spreading further, treat those afflicted. And you do that by putting the House of Suns down. If you don't, humanity's going to tear itself apart from the inside.'

'We cannot finalise peace negotiations, only to pair ourselves with a society on the verge of collapse,' Szev added. 'It would be like boarding an infected ship. You understand first-hand the extent of the stormtech's damage, yes?'

'We can help you if you do this,' Juvens said. 'I wish we could anyway, but there are ... complications. Bureaucratic

301

complications.' The alien's mismatched eyes flickered back to the Ambassadors before glancing back to me. Like me, he was a soldier. A hands-on guy that saw a problem to fix and wanted to get it done. 'We have an armada ready, prepared to join forces with yours. Get rid of these Suns bastards, and we can move forward.'

'The Shenoi threaten both our species,' Chwekli said. 'A mutual threat. Should they consume you, the threat to us will multiply.'

I raked in a hard breath, as if I could somehow shrug off my new knowledge of stormtech, as if hearing that the Shenoi were still alive and kicking in the far corners of the galaxy and gunning for the human race was no big deal. In the span of a brief few hours, I'd gone from drinking the night away to playing politics with alien galactic affairs. I had a feeling I'd just locked Harmony into a human-Kaiji alliance that Kindosh would kill me for making, if Kowalski didn't get there first.

Juvens removed a torus-shaped device from a slot in his armour and pressed it into my palm. I flicked my shib on and an encryption key blurred into my system. The device shuddered and died in my hand and I set it aside. 'In the meantime, if you ever need us desperately, you know how to call.' The Space Marshall had a wicked gleam in his eyes, as if he wasn't supposed to do what he just did and couldn't have cared less for it. 'I'm not going to assume I can understand what your people are dealing with. But I've seen what stormtech does to human bodies. Anyone who has, and keeps selling it for profit, is a monster. The exact sort of people the Shenoi love. So when you find these Suns—' his teeth clenched together, jaw tightening '—do me a favour and deal with them... brutally.'

I locked gazes with the big alien, my own jaw tightening. 'I wouldn't have it any other way.'

Juvens watched me for a moment. 'You know what every

species has in common, Fukasawa? We all can get very, very angry.' A grim smirk began to spread across his face. 'And that's good. Because angry gets ugly work done.'

The Kaiji swiftly dropped me back to Compass. I made a beeline for my apartment, where Grim and Kowalski were waiting impatiently. I told them everything. They took it better than I'd imagined.

'All right,' Kowalski said slowly, running a hand through her hair. 'You know I have to tell Kindosh. If she doesn't know already – there's probably surveillance equipment in here.'

'There was.' Back in his neon skeleton underskin, Grim poked his head out of the kitchen – a grinning red skull – and glanced at us. 'Until I disabled it.'

'Of course,' I said. 'But this changes nothing. We have to take down the House of Suns, exactly as planned, and quickly.'

'I guess we're unofficially officially in bed with the Kaiji,' Katherine muttered as Grim emerged from the kitchen with three mugs of tempered glass, containing coffee. We both took one. 'I'm surprised they didn't ask for a seat on the Harmony Command Board in return.'

'If the Kaiji are right, more than a dozen civilisations have been killed because of stormtech. No other spacefaring species we know of has had prior combat experience with the Shenoi, let alone achieved a victory. They could be demanding servitude or worship or whatever it is aliens want. Instead, they're offering us help. We'd be stupid to turn them down.'

Kowalski fixed me with a sceptical look. 'You saw the size of their armada, the level of their tech and materiel. You don't raise your civilisation to that stage by having the interests of other species at heart. We don't know what they got up to in the greater galactic community. We get dozens of alien species every standard year requesting to join the Common or seeking refuge, trade agreements, alliances, whatever. First rule of interspecies diplomacy: if an offer sounds too good to be true, then it probably is.'

'We know they've got demands. They made that clear the moment they asked to join the Common. Doesn't mean they won't have an offer of their own on the table.'

'There's a difference between genuine concern and profes-sional manipulation.'

'You think that's what's going on here?'

'I think we'd be naive not to consider it.'

I thought of Juvens, and how the big, sly Space Marshall had been willing to share private information and risk the wrath of his Ambassadors, just to give us a leg up. If they were giving us a chance, we had to return the favour. 'You're the ones who wanted a peace alliance with these guys,' I said. 'Here's your shot.'

Kowalski nodded reluctantly. I could hear the air rising from her lungs, steaming out of her mouth. My skin rippled with goosebumps, my arm hairs all standing up. My senses had been heightened since the fight in the arena. The metallic stink of the spaceport, the spicy scent of the Kaiji, the smoky stench waft-ing from nearby ventilation shafts were all bouncing around in my skull. The world swayed in sticky and surreal motion, everything hyper-elevated, like fragments of a dream. It was all the stormtech.

If I stopped feeding it entirely, I could start Shredding again. I hated the idea of it. The process would cripple me for weeks, maybe months, as my body wrung the alien DNA out of me. The stormtech would put up one hell of a fight with every agonizing day. Harmony's suppressors were off the table, and I wasn't about to risk darkmarket meds.

Whatever my body was doing to me, I was stuck with it.

Would Artyom still be doing this if he knew he was pouring

gasoline on the fire? Had my brother looked me dead in the eye, knowing what was *really* in those stormtech canisters and swirling around in my bloodstream? I felt the cold metal of the pendant against my collarbone and for a moment I wanted to tear the cord away completely. Cut him out as he had me. But I couldn't give up on him. If only for Kasia's sake.

Kowalski's voice floated up from somewhere distant, as if on the other end of a crackly comms line. 'Vakov?'

I snapped up. 'What?'

'Remember those stormdealer trafficking routes we picked up in the Warren? Well, they got results. Took a hell of a paper trail, tracking them across shell companies, orbital refineries, space-factories, dockyards, distribution channels in and out of Compass, but we got them. Most of them were operating out of a dockyard front, concealing stormtech supplies in shuttlecraft and carrier-pods going to half a hundred spacedocks. We did a raid last night, nabbed half a dozen stormdealers with direct connections to Reaper deaths. These guys aren't working alone. It's one tiny cog in an entire syndicate of stormdealers, running like clockwork. Suppliers, distributors, factories, everything.'

'But you found a source.'

'We did better than that. The dockyard manifesto led us straight to several House of Suns suppliers.'

'They're not cultists, though.'

'No. They're third parties, operating on Compass and across several systems worth of outposts and stations. But they're just as responsible for the Reaper deaths. Caught them in the act and hauled the whole lot in for questioning.'

'What about those biolaces? The suicide triggers?'

'Sector Prone's been working on an override key. It neutralises the hardware, but they're constantly supplying updates to get around us. We had two suppliers die on us, both killed remotely. When the rest survived, they sent a squadron of gunships armed with heat-seeking missiles after us. Fortunately, we've got better combat pilots then they do, and blasted them away. We've got the other four suppliers, nice and secure in lockup. If asking nicely doesn't work, we'll apply pressure until someone cracks. There're thousands of other stormdealers out there. We can only guess how many of them are shipping the Suns' product. But it's a start.'

'What about the stormtech canisters? You tried tracing those back?' Grim asked.

'Dead ends, false leads,' said Katherine, taking a long swallow of coffee. 'Informers who come forward with intel in exchange for a fresh start go missing or end up shot to death on the street the next day. Space-factories and warehouses full of canisters and drug labs one day, cleared out and scrubbed clean the next. We even found a chainship, retrofitted into a moveable storage unit. By the time we found out, it didn't exist anymore. Turned to scrap in a darkmarket shipbreaking yard, the debris jettisoned out into space. They're ahead of us every step of the way. Almost makes you think they've turned someone within Harmony.'

'How likely do you think that is?' I asked.

'Kindosh has her suspicions.' She stabbed a button on her palmerlog. Oddly shaped dataspheres containing charts appeared in my apartment, rippling at her touch like the surface of water. 'We know there's been a steep growth of stormtech on the market. More are infected every day, and hardly a fraction of them come to us for rehab or substitutes. They're too proud, too guilty, or think they'll kick it on their own. Meanwhile, stormdealers have been getting more organised.'

'Because of the Suns?'

'In some cases, definitely. Drug trafficking's rarely a solo operation. It's too high-risk for that. They're not hustling it on street corners like the idiots who sell grimwire do. They've

306

started operating behind firewalls, and on darkmarket servers. Others sell within exclusive circles. And then there're the stormdealers who work themselves into neighbourhoods. Get friendly with the locals. Maybe set up a front, work themselves into the social infrastructure. Deal stormtech out the back, giving out free samples of bluesmoke and synthsilver, selling cheap to the locals. Letting people know they're a legitimate seller. Build their workforce; get people on their side, spread the word. Before you know it, they've occupied the entire neighbourhood, then the whole floor. They use children as foot soldiers and mules. Start buying out businesses to occupy their territory. Anyone who objects, anyone who tries to rat them out, gets silenced. Often by their own neighbours.' A grainy edge came into her voice. 'We're seeing it most in the toughest areas. Working classes. People looking to get ahead after life's kicked them into the gutter. The stormdealers know they're easy targets.'

She hid it well. But I know what barely supressed guilt sounds like when I hear it. The oblate dataspheres scattered and vanished like burst soap bubbles. 'It's still a work in progress. Give me a day or two and I'll have something we can link to the suppliers. We'll go from there, see what the connection is to the House of Suns. If Kindosh tries to chew me out for this whole business with the Kaiji, I'm sending her your way, deal?'

'Deal.'

'You look after yourself, Vak. You too, Grim.'

Grim nodded but remained passive even after she'd left. He'd barely spoken a word about the whole arena incident. He knew we had bigger things to deal with. It's so easy to see the big picture that you lose sight of the smaller things that make it up. I know that better than most people.

'How you holding up?' I asked him. He shrugged but didn't look at me. Outside, the pixelsheeting swirled with darkened cloudbanks, the sprinklers activating. The windows pattered with rain. 'Did the Suns hurt you?'

Grim pulled his knees up to his chest. 'No. They just grabbed me off the street and tossed me into a carrier-pod. They wanted to, but they didn't. They said you'd do that for them.'

'Did you believe them?'

Grim shook his head, but I could see a part of him had believed it. I placed a hand on his shoulder. 'You're like my brother, Grim. I'd never hurt you, no matter what they did to me.'

'I know, Vak. I know. But being taken like that, having you look at me the way you did, scared me, Vak. I haven't been that scared since I left Harvest, you know?' He stared out the rain-streaked windows, as if expecting to see something lurking there.

'Do you want to move in here?' I asked.

Grim glanced over at me. 'Seriously?'

'I don't want you going back home, Grim. Not anymore. You hang here, at least until we sort this out. If they try anything again, they'll have to go through me first.'

I expected him to break out into a zany, toothy grin. Start cheering at how he'd finally wormed his way into my apartment, even if it meant getting kidnapped. Instead, he sniffed and thumped me on the back, muttering his gratitude. He was more shaken than I'd realised. I was going to have to watch him. I returned the gesture, pushing out vivid images of me stumbling towards my friend, teeth bared, hands reflexing with the urge to rip him apart.

That would never happen. That would *never* happen.

Grim insisted on celebrating the occasion the way he always does: with drinks. I wasn't about to complain.

He whirled me away to yet another bar that did space-themed

cocktails while actual footage of space played around you in a broad spectacle. The bar, designed to look like the revolving endcap beneath a giant space station, was outfitted with large dome shielding, displaying an elliptical galaxy full of etiolated young stars known as the Asamotah Cluster. The screen zoomed in to show the ever-changing surface of a small hydrogen-helium gas-giant. The debris from shattered moons had given it an extensive ring system, like a soot-black belt. We watched as fast-forward footage showed the heat of a nearby star slowly blasting the gas-giant's atmosphere away. By the fifth round, I called it a night on the drinks, not in the mood to carry Grim home after last night's incident. It was a wonder he could even stand after how much he'd drunk.

Kowalski was right about the stormtech blooming, as we found out on the return trip. There were more skinnies wheezing in the alleyways, coughing as they shielded themselves from leaking pipes. Scratching furiously at scabs and wounds as they rifled through the trash for a hit. Twitching under bundles of rags. There was a woman with sunken eyes wrestling with a protesting sweeperbot, trying to claw the bags back in hopes there'd be a sliver of stormtech left. I turned to witness a man on his knees near our apartment, vomiting up a gush of blue, retching like an animal. His sweet, sticky stench got my stomach muscles tightening.

Shrugging it off, I followed Grim back to my apartment. He'd brought along a collection of cult films. I wanted to think about anything but stormtech, and Kowalski had not called us with her follow-up intel, so I agreed to a marathon. We sprawled on my couch, printing up an endless supply of snacks from Compass' weirdest and wildest establishments as Grim's films got bloodier, crazier and more abstract.

After the fifth feature and second bowl of seaweed-flavoured chips, the Rubix's rabbit avatar hopped onto the coffee table and eyed the screen with a wide yawn. 'Oh, films. How very droll. Really, is there nothing else you can do?'

'Toss off, bunny. I'm educating Mr Fukasawa here,' Grim said. 'Have you seen the trash they play in New Vladi?'

I nodded at the screen, where a young woman in a bloody dress was spewing curses and violently strumming a guitar equipped with chainsaws, the incoming crowds of dull-eyed, brain-dead adults being blasted backwards with shockwaves of righteous sound. 'Yeah, and this is the height of culture.'

'*My* culture.' He slapped my arm and grinned. 'It's a rite of passage.'

I endured it, more for Grim's benefit than mine. I wasn't sure what time it was when we were done, but I printed out a mattress for Grim, the sweeperbot gobbling up the crumbs, and then crashed down into my own bed. I stank, but couldn't bring myself to move.

Tendrils of stormtech were squirming hard along my sides, digging into my armpits. I ran my hands down my body, trying to dislodge it, but it didn't work this time. I tossed again, feeling the bodies of the men I'd killed in the arena floating over me. I replayed myself. Kicking, punching, clawing. Stormtech or not, that had been me. And I was ready to wave it away as an excuse.

Was I already becoming my father?

The thought was so dirty I was going to need a shower right now. I rolled off the bed to shower and change when I heard a strange, muffled scratching coming from the door. A faint yellow light flitted through the cracks. The soft blip of a security bypass programme. The Jackal hadn't received the satisfaction he'd wanted from the arena fight. I'd beaten him, publicly, and cost him money. Not only was I still alive and kicking, I hadn't killed Grim in front of a crowd. He was sending people along to remedy that right now.

The door crashed open, a shadowy figure rushing forward. The flashing stormtech was like a beacon on my chest. I threw myself sideways as he fired his scattershot. The muzzle flash flared up in the darkness, the shot blasting a mouthful of concrete and wood from the wall behind me. A shell went clattering to the floor, surprisingly loud. My assailant whirled around, firing another shell towards the AI's rabbit figure. The projection stuttered from the shot, as it turned its black, furred face towards him. 'Oh dear. I fear you have made a very grave mistake,' the rabbit informed the intruder in a huffy tone. He aimed his scattershot upwards as the turret slid out of the wall and levelled towards the shooter. 'Mine's bigger,' the rabbit said, an evil gleam in its black eyes as the autocannon ripped to life. I hugged the floor, hands clamped around my ears, the thunderous roar bursting in my skull. The high-calibre rounds punched through the intruder's chest like nails being hammered into wood, the kitchen exploding in a shower of glass and plaster. Pipes burst and sprayed water into the room.

A second figure charged into the scene, out of range of the autocannon's sensors. I stole forward and hurled my mattress at him. He punched a smoking hole through the fabric with his scattershot, missing me. Heart jackhammering away, I kicked the coffee table into his shins. He yelped, smashing down onto the wood, the broken glass cutting into his cheeks. He growled, firing blindly and gouging a hole in the ceiling. Debris rained down as I clawed for my handcannon on the end table. Not fast enough. The world crunched as he slammed the butt of his weapon into my face. I grabbed a wooden stool, brought it smashing down on the hand holding the weapon, and then his kneecap, splinters scattering with a loud crack. He dropped the weapon but had the strength to stab a kick straight into my stomach, right below my ribcage. He turned, frantically searching for his discarded scattershot. Head ringing, blood in my mouth, I crawled over the broken glass and snatched up my handcannon, rolling on my back. There was the dull whine of a scattershot priming as my assailant turned towards me. I squeezed down, the recoil vibrating in my hands. The round punched through his neck just as he tilted it upwards and went spitting out the top of his skull. His head whipped backwards with a splitting *crack*, taking the full force of the blow. He sagged to his knees, almost comically, before falling face-down on the glass.

A sound from behind. I swung around, aiming down my handcannon sights, finger tight on the trigger. It was Grim. He was lying on the floor and his face was speckled with blood. I blinked. His expression was somewhere between confusion and fear – the same wary look he'd worn in the arena. I reached down to help him up, but he'd climbed to his feet himself. He'd been hiding behind the door ever since the autocannon went ballistic. 'How'd they get in?' he croaked.

I picked up a membrane-thin pad, filaments squirming in the translucent gel like trapped nerves. 'Overrode the security system.'

'How'd they find us?' Grim was slowly stepping away from the bodies and their spreading blood. The room was a shattered mess behind us, rapidly filling with wastewater from the burst kitchen pipework.

'Well,' I said, pointing to the bodies, 'you can ask, but I don't think we'll get much of an answer.'

I'd expected a weary chuckle. But I got no response. Grim was instead muttering what sounded like *oh dear oh god oh no* under his breath. I suppose I'd be panicking too if the stormtech hadn't rewired me to cope with shellshock.

'We have to clear out,' I told Grim. 'Find somewhere else to stay.'

'I think I know a safehouse,' Grim said. 'It's not comfortable, though.'

'We'll make do.' I bent down to rifle through the belongings of the would-be killers. They carried a palmerlog each. I flicked one on and opened a recent transmission and the House of Suns symbol projected in the air, brightening the room. If this had been from the Jackal, he'd have come along to pull the trigger himself. Jae, or someone high-ranking within the Suns, must have decided to put the two of us down.

We were getting quite popular.

I sent a transmission to Kowalski, warning her in case she'd be getting any unpleasant visitors tonight, before pocketing the devices. The rabbit avatar was sitting atop the mangled, bullet-ridden man it had killed, whiskers twitching in triumph. Between then and the conversation I'd had with Grim, it had found the time to spatter its fur with fake-looking blood.

'If anyone except Kowalski comes in, feel free to take care of them,' I told it.

'That would please me very much,' said the rabbit. Its ears twitched. 'May I ask when you will return?'

I was about to respond when I realised we'd never be coming back. We were hunted men, now. It wouldn't be over until the Suns were defeated, or the two of us ended up like the corpses piled at my feet.

29

Hideout

We took only the bare necessities with us. We slithered out the window, navigating through the rain-drenched back alleys and taking three separate autocabs before arriving at Starkland's Travel Depot. Couldn't risk being tailed by anyone the Suns had stationed outside. We bought two tickets to a lowlevel called Saharatown and sat in a private cubicle as our chainrail plummeted down through the asteroid. I was back in armour, while Grim had printed himself a closefitting spacesuit with a helmet that obscured his face.

Getting to Grim's secure location involved walking through a Middle-Eastern style bazaar, where the stalls were crammed together like seeds in a pomegranate and the Rubixs had been programmed to appear as djinn: swirling, muscled, mythical creatures that hefted curved swords that crackled with lightning and threatened passers-by not to steal anything. We took a set of narrow alleyways packed with foodbooths selling baklava and kebabs, the rich smell of meat following us as we looped around to the outermost edge of the level and into a warren of storage units.

It was like a giant filing cabinet, stretching hundreds of metres across and down, cocooned in creaking walkways and disappearing into the mesh of the asteroid superstructure.

Half of them winked red, indicating they were in use. Others were empty or being used as temporary dens. Faces wrapped in cowls and protective optics poked out as we clanked along the walkways. Toxins leaked out of swollen pipes strung along the streets like mechanical intestines. Grim approached a Torven sitting in one of the vacated units, wearing heavy hooded clothing and watching something in her shib. I'd since learned to discern between alien genders, and the slimmer shoulders and sharper face told me this one was female. The display vanished as she noticed Grim.

'Oh, it's you again.' I hadn't heard many Torven speak, but this one sounded like her daily diet was nothing but whisky and bluesmokes. 'What is it this time?' She leaned towards me and took a long sniff. 'Ah. With a blue friend, too.'

I raised an eyebrow behind my visor. 'How can you tell?' I asked.

'You smell bad, even for a human.' She sniffed again, wrinkled her small nostrils. 'Overripe. Soiled. You smell worse than a Rhivik's underskin.'

Grim elbowed his way into the conversation. 'Nice to see you too, Mugalesh. You been enjoying those films I gave you?'

Mugalesh's curved mouth twitched into what I thought was a smile. I noticed she wore a nasty-looking handgun holstered at her hip. 'They're all right for human entertainment. What do you want?'

'Me and my blue friend need to stay hidden for a while,' said Grim.

Mugalesh's sulphur-coloured eyes narrowed to slits. 'Is it going to bring me grief?'

Grim offered a nervous laugh. 'Me bring trouble? No, no, no. Nothing like that. No trouble at all.'

The alien snorted. 'Like the *incident* with the octodrones was no trouble?'

'That wasn't my fault!' Grim protested.

'And the shipment of rat poisons?'

Grim's face went red as he winced. 'That . . . was a misunderstanding.'

'Oh, I'm sure. And the chainship job? They're still after us for that.'

Grim winced again, harder this time. 'Yeah . . . that wasn't my finest hour.'

Mugalesh spat on the ground. 'You, Grim, are an impenetrable wall of problems. A tower of trouble. A skyscraper of setbacks. I'm not stupid enough to have it come crashing down on my head.'

Grim dropped a Commoner currency card into the alien's calloused palm. 'Does this help things?'

Mugalesh glared up at Grim, weighing up the decision before pocketing the card and rocking to her feet with a roll of her eyes. 'This way, this way.' She led us through the winding maze of stairwells and balconies squeezing between the towers. Colourful clothes and streamers snapped in the dry breeze. Each storage unit was filled with little knots of people, staring intently at flexiscreens or tabletop vidgames. In one of them, aliens wearing layers of hooded clothing so thick I couldn't tell *what* species they were, had crammed a dozen printers into a shelled-out office space, forming a lucrative printing farm, glancing up at us with thick, wrap-around optics as we passed. They were packaging freshly printed goods, I guessed for sale in the Upper Markets. Mugalesh turned her glare on them, and suddenly they all doubled their speed.

We arrived in a storage compartment in the heart of the level. Mugalesh slapped the access card into Grim's hand. 'Steal so much as a nanofibre cable and I'll rip your kidneys out and use them as footrests,' she told Grim. 'Understood?'

'You're a darling,' he said as she scowled, tugging her hood over her head and disappearing into the streets.

'How do you know her?'

'Smuggled some stuff for her a few times. She's all bark and no bite. Unless she doesn't like you.'

'How do you know if she doesn't like you?

'You get bitten.'

Grim had described the place as a room, but it was closer to a storage unit, the sort you found at the bottom of cargo-haulers. It was packed to the ceiling with boxes and magnetically locked crates. A hundred lights twinkled at us from databanks and computers. At least there was a decent printer in the corner. Cramped, but good enough.

I sent a secure transmission to Kowalski with our co-ordinates. By the time I slipped out of my suit and unpacked my gear, she had arrived. 'Did you find anything?' I asked her. She dodged the ropes of filaments, flailing like octopus tentacles seeking out a socket, to stand next to me.

'One step ahead of you. We traced their suits and weapons. Your assassins aren't from the Suns. They're not even on Compass. They're Blade Hunters, those offworld mercenaries who serve whoever's paying them the most. In this case, the House of Suns.'

'So they slipped through customs?'

'Must have. Contract killers, most likely.'

'I'm guessing the House of Suns isn't going to come calling for them?'

'Wouldn't it make life easier if they did?' Kowalski settled into a cream leather chair that had certainly been stolen from some penthouse apartment from the highest Compass levels. 'The House of Suns don't know where either of you two are, and we should keep it that way. If they're sending deepspace mercenaries out in the dead of night to silence you instead of

317

doing the deed themselves, they're trying to play it safe. More importantly, they're scared. They saw what you could do in that arena, Vak. They thought they had you on a leash.'

'And I chewed through it.' I grinned.

'Unfortunately, it also means they've limited any way of tracing them back. The only leads we have are the stormtech supply-lines. We're chiselling away at those, but it'll definitely be a route directly to the Suns. Grim, maybe there's some back-tracing you can do from here, but otherwise you two should lay low. You're in the wind. Make the House of Suns sweat, maybe tip their hand in trying to find you.'

'You think the Suns know about the meeting with the Kaiji?' I asked.

'I doubt it. The aliens would never expose themselves like that.'

'Kind of hard to miss the Kaiji, floating out there with their dreadnought,' I said.

'That's nothing of consequence. There's probably spacecraft from five different species docked in spaceports around the asteroid this very moment, with five more requesting clearance. A third of all intragalactic trade on Compass is done with non-Commoner species. Even within Harmony, our talks with the Kaiji are restricted to the Intelligence Officers and the Command Board.'

'Doesn't mean they don't suspect what we're doing. If they're as well-researched as we're led to believe they are, they could know about the Kaiji's involvement in the war against the stormtech. And if they know, they'll want to kill this alliance before it bears fruit.'

Katherine nodded and settled deeper into her seat. 'I've been thinking about what the Kaiji said to you. Even if the Shenoi aren't coming back, even if we put the House of Suns down, the stormtech will always be here. How do you weed something like that out of society?'

'I don't know,' I admitted, 'but we have to try. We had days on the battlefields where we thought we would surely lose. But we strapped on our armour, got into our fireteams and fought anyway. Sokolav made sure we never had any doubts what would happen if we lost.'

'And you think Sokolav's involved like Artyom is,' Katherine said.

'I don't know why. But if he's doing something, he's committed to it.'

'I've never met the man. But if a former Commander is in their labs, he knows what they are and what they're getting up to. He knows he's associating with people directly opposed to Harmony.' Katherine rubbed her eyes with her knuckles. 'Your old instructor went missing so he could join them. It's the only way this fits.'

I've learned to know when I'm hearing the truth: because it always hurts. This was no accident: Sokolav had to have known exactly what the House of Suns were up to, which meant that Artyom did, too.

I got Grim to go off on a food errand while Kowalski and I talked.

'I'm really glad you told me everything about the Kaiji,' she said.

I looked up. 'Why?'

'Because you didn't have to. You could have sold the information to us, bargained for a better deal for your brother. But you offered it freely to me first. Maybe you wouldn't have, at one point. I know you meant what you said being a team. I need to see more of that. Can you manage that for me?'

The Harmony way wasn't how I did things, or how I *wanted* to do things. But I had to trust someone, and I trusted Kowalski's

319

judgement. Same as before, I saw she sincerely *wanted* me to trust her, for us to build that relationship together. And I wanted to help her do it. 'I can do that,' I said.

Kowalski was off the clock today, and without an immediate link to a supplier there wasn't much we could do. We started talking again. Our conversation drifted through half a dozen subjects before we came around to the city of my birth. Like most people who knew about New Vladi, she'd never visited but was fascinated by it. I told her about its high mountain ranges, the sloping forests with biodiversity and constellations of ecotones unseen on any other planet. The wild, beautiful tundra stretching under the sky, where the only sound was the howling wind. The ragged coastline composed of beaches of black sand where millennia of ocean spray had shaped rocks into sculptures of lumbering monsters and towering giants.

'Now it's your turn,' I told her.

'For what?'

'Tell me something about you.' I folded my legs under me. 'You've never told me what you folks get up to. You Harmony folk try to be squeaky clean. Surely you've got skeletons in the closet.'

Katherine looked as if to deny it at first, but changed her mind. 'Gambling,' she admitted, a sly smile spreading across her face. 'And not just your average CreditParlors. This stuff was high-stakes, played with games that came from the corners of the Common. Half of them aren't even legal anymore.'

You wouldn't find anyone with stormtech gambling – it's hard to maintain a poker face when your body literally glows when you've picked up a winning hand. 'And how did that happen?'

'There's a small ski resort on the top floors of Compass,' she said. 'All my friends were going. This was when it was just opening up and the waiting list was hundreds long. You could get the express entry, but only for the right price. Then there were all the snowboards, the snowskins with thermal stitching, all the equipment. A small fortune.

'Not many ways to get hundreds of Commoners when you're still a teenager studying at the Academy. So I taught myself gambling. The games to start out with, the safest bets, the fastest earnings, and the most popular ones. The loopholes, the exploits, everything. There's no such thing as a fair game, Vak. There's always a back door, always a crack you can slip through. And while everyone else was out drinking and having boyfriends, I was sitting on the itchy carpet on the floor of my cramped little bedroom, finding a way in.'

'And did you?'

Katherine's eyes shone with mischief and memory. 'You should have seen their faces when they called the scoreboard with me in top place. A week later and I was tearing down the slopes with the edgiest snowboard the store had. There's nothing like feeling the snow shredding beneath your feet as you cut down a mountain, feeling the wind in your hair. I fell over a hundred times, had bruises all over my legs for ages. But it was the best week of my life.

'But I never went back there. Whenever I see a gambling house, I think about it. And every year, I make plans to get the old board out and give the snow another shot, but it never works out.' She looked up, offered me a little smile. 'I've never told anyone that story before.'

'I'm glad you told me,' I said, returning the smile. 'I'm glad I got to know you better.'

Katherine looked at me for a moment before reaching out and placing her hand on my arm. My knee-jerk instinct was to move away, not let anyone touch me. But I fought it back despite the stormtech, liking the feel of her, liking that Katherine with her piercing grey eyes and wicked little smile and sandy hair tumbling down her shoulder, was sitting so close to me. 'You know, when this is all over, maybe I'll grab a snowboard and get back on the slopes again for a whole week, just like before. Maybe I'll even take you with me.'

'That'd be nice,' I said, and meant it. And for a minute, I almost forgot about the stormtech. 'That'd be really nice.'

30
Ghosts and Glass

The thrusters beneath my armoured feet erupt as I launch upwards, punching through the high mountain rainforests. I cover forty, fifty, sixty metres like a human rocket before gravity yanks me back down. Dust billows up as I land on a jutting ledge of rock, my armour's absorbers soaking up the impact, thrusting me back up over the swaying treetops and into the sky. There's the rhythmic metallic echo of my fireteam doing the same behind me. We go skimming like stones across the top of the forest.

It's in all the timing. Too fast, you'll smash your skull and splatter your brains over the rocks. Too slow, the railguns and pulse-rifles Harvesters are fond of scattering around the planet will smack us out of the sky. Good incentive to learn and learn fast.

I listen to my body. Temperature. Pulse. Heartbeat. The ever-present stormtech circulating through me, slithering from my armpits to the soles of my feet. I'm starting to learn it's always speaking to me. It's just a matter of tuning in to the right wavelength. I burn and streak through the muggy air. Accelerating to optimal speed, pumping my body up to lend me that extra edge that lets me glance sideways off the slope and go shooting through a narrow cleft in the treetops, narrowly avoiding a jutting chunk of cliff face. Leaves and branches are left smouldering under my boots as I burst back out into the open sky. It's like I'm on autopilot. Trees, foliage, rivers, terrain whipping past my visor. The ground rushing up and down so fast it's like it's heaving beneath me. I grin wildly. I could do this for ever.

Our HUD waypoint blinks on. I touch down, my fireteam land- ing around me in a series of successive shudders on the stone shelf. There're millions of vibrating metal bubbles itching beneath my skin, each one releasing a tiny burst of adrenaline. Even shelled in armour, with their faces hidden behind visors, I know my team- mates are running on the same wavelength.

The rainforest around us is alive. The hissing of water. The hoots and growls of distant creatures. The wet-hot stink of the air, dripping with damp moss and bark. The susurrus of trees tall as highrises with a nervous system of branches, and leaves as big as houses. The world feeds into me like the soundwaves that appear on my HUD in radio chatter, only plugged straight into my brain, threaded into the dermis of my body. Everything's got a polished, crystalline sheen.

This isn't just another sector of the forest. Blanket-surveillance tech has intercepted commslink transmissions between the Canine King and the Dog Commandos taking control of the area. Not content with sticking bounties on our heads, he's been marking Reapers with White Skulls for live capture. We're rendezvousing with Russo, a reconnaissance team deep behind enemy lines, tasked with pinpointing their exact location. Getting there involves cross- ing a dozen klicks of thick mountain forest.

Alcatraz kneels down and peers through the foliage. 'Under- growth is dense, and the fog's screwing with our visibility,' he says as we unstrap our weapons. 'Sonar and thermal overlays on. We use the 8-way formation. Everyone copy?'

Five affirmative icons chime in my HUD. We devised the 8-way formation together, splitting up in two parties and scouting the area in a wide loop, meeting again in the middle and then scouting again.

We cover a wide range, while any enemies we encounter get hammered in our crossfire. I walk with Ratchet and Alcatraz, their breathing heavy in my ears. Even with the armour's interior cooling, in this sweltering heat there're rivers of sweat dripping down my back and chest. I'm caked up to my knees in mud and sticky wet leaves. Our boots squelch through the bloated soil.

'I hate the forest,' Ratchet grumbles.

'You hate everything,' I say.

'That ain't true.'

'Fine. Name one thing you don't hate.'

'I'll give you two: stabbing Harvesters with their own knives and a good juicy steak.'

'It's slightly worrying that both your passions involve sticking sharp objects into meat.'

'A man's got to have his hobbies.' He reaches into his armpit, where there's a gap in the armour to allow for flexibility and scratches it with the hilt of his combat blade. 'You know what? Steak tonight, boys.'

'And onions,' I add.

'I could murder a side of bacon and hash-browns,' Cable says.

'I miss eggs,' Alcatraz adds.

'Stop making me hungry,' Myra grumbles.

'You're always hungry,' Ratchet snorts. 'You eat even more than Cable.'

'Don't make me sit on you,' Cable grumbles in that low, deep voice of his. Which shuts Ratchet up for all of thirty seconds. Squawking birds with bulging eyes and leathery wings swoop past like brushstrokes of colour. Ratchet tracks one with his rifle. 'Steak's good. Chicken's even better.'

I grin and let the comfortable banter wash over me. I've only known these people for two years, but it feels longer. It's a hell of a messed up family, but they fit.

*

We reach the windswept cliffs. The unrelenting forest yawns below us, interrupted with outcrops, jutting trees and webs of foliage. The jagged mountain landscape is a smudge of dark greens and earthy browns. There're whole swathes of empty patches, like bullet wounds several kilometres wide in the forest. Myra scans the horizon for snipers while Alcatraz picks at abandoned Harvest tech and discarded helmets. Cable gives a pent-up sigh next to me and kneels down on one leg to review the scenery.

'Hell of a sight,' I say.

'The forest used to be twice the size.' Cable brushes his hand along patches of pale purple flowers. Digs his fingers into the rich soil. He turns his visor up to the muddy sky, perpetually churning with dark storm clouds. 'Funiculars up and down the mountains, ferries on the river. It was dangerous and wild, but it was ours, and it was beautiful.'

I turn to him. 'This is your homeplanet?'

'It was, a long time ago.'

'It must hurt like hell, seeing it torn up like this.'

'This is not my home anymore. The Harvesters took it. I have another home, now.' Slowly, he climbs to his feet, lays a heavy hand on my shoulder. 'With all of you. Home isn't where you're born, Vakov. It's where you feel calm and peace, even in a storm.'

Alcatraz reaches our access point first. We unhook our harnesses, reinforced to support our armour's weight, and slowly abseil down. My harness groans around me, metal buckles scraping against my back and shoulders. The thin abseiling cable creaks. There're so many blind spots in this area. A patrol unit could walk by and see us dangling here like idiots.

The deeper we go, the harder I can feel my biorhythms spiking. The stormtech is telling me there's no immediate danger, but it's incoming. I swallow. It's looking forward to the danger.

I could push the sensations aside. Just because my body's

speaking doesn't mean I need to listen. I think of Drummer, shot to the ground, bleeding out because his body didn't warn him. Reapers, tortured and skinned and stuffed into cages. Clear signs of what happens if you don't take note of the warnings.

I pull the stormtech around me. With every day, reaching for it gets a little easier. Depending on it feels a little more natural. We haven't slept for over twenty-eight hours and yet we're all operating at prime performance. The tension begins to ease. I'm aware of each movement and groan of my fireteam, can hear the quiet whirr of their armour and the rapid thudding of their hearts.

I feel so alive.

We abseil down to a ledge that leads into a yawning, mossy cave. We detach and walk through into the splintered remains of a Harvest warship, smashed from orbit in battle, years ago. The rainforest is taking its time eating it up. The dark grey hull's plastered with Harvest propaganda posters. A fist festooned with Harvest tattoos is squeezing an armoured figure with a grotesque face, blue gore bursting from his crushed chest. Quiescent terminals flicker in the semi-darkness. The rotten, metallic stink of blood hangs heavy in the air, getting my own blood up. We clatter down a telescopic tunnel towards the hangar bay. Platforms that once held ships and interplanetary spacecraft slump like broken ribcages.

My heart leaps into my throat before I see the shapes dangling from the scaffolding, swaying in the sour wind. Reapers. Nailed to thick, tapered posts and strung up with razorwire. My visor picks out their IFF tags. They're the remains of Russo.

No. Not remains. They're still alive.

I'm hugging cover on instinct as the world shatters into horror. Railgun missiles scream above our heads and slam into the roof of the tunnel, bringing it down in a scream of concrete and metal. A burst of red plasma fire chews through the rusted metalwork of a barricade. Ratchet's helmet slams into mine as he scoots up next to me, cradling his weapon.

We walked face-first into the Harvesters' trap. The recon team was the bait. Russo's squad leader twitches, spasming as a sniper round slams through the back of his skull and explodes through his open mouth. Another screams as a fist-sized hole punches through her abdomen. There're still four of them dangling in their sights, struggling and hyperventilating.

'Hold,' Alcatraz snaps, knowing what we're feeling because he's feeling it, too. We've all seen what Harvesters do to Reapers, pulling us apart to learn how we work, and then turning it against us. My mouth's salivating with hunger, body clenched with rage. I'm moments from charging headfirst into the bullet storm to tear the Harvesters limb from limb. An ear-splitting crack echoes through the spaceport, blood spattering. Another Reaper screams. I'm growling now, but I stand my ground. I cast a long look at my fireteam, huddled down here with me. Got to stick by them, form a tactical approach together.

I swing upwards, carbine crackling in my hands, muzzle flashing as I lock onto a target and return fire. But they've got the high ground on the walkways above us and our shots ping off the scaffolding, earning laughter. I get a glimpse of black armour, an insectoid helmet. Berserker killsquads. Specifically trained to kill Reapers. A slash on their shoulders for every Reaper they've slaughtered.

Russo did what they set out to do. We've found our Dog Commandos.

A slug the size of a fist cleaves through the barrier and slams into the ground between me and Ratchet. He jerks back, fists clenched around his service pistol. I see him glance towards the dangling Reapers, see the reflection in his visor as one has his foot blown off, screams rattling like shrapnel in my skull. I see the stormtech firing rage and heat into his body.

'Don't!' I roar, even as Ratchet tears out of cover and sprints towards the walkways. It's suicide to follow him, and it's exactly what the Berserkers want. But I won't let him die like Drummer died. I run after him, spraying covering fire, the others charging in beside me, refusing to let me down.

Gunfire blazes down. I see every glinting round as it comes punching towards me. My armour crackles with disrupted shielding as the rounds hammer home. My body takes the pain the armour doesn't neutralise. Muscles pumping like pistons. My feet echoing on the hard decking. There's a pause, Harvesters exhaling hard. The clack of their weapons priming. The combat zone seems to unfold like a map in my skull. Enemies, weapons, vantage points, blind spots, popping up like glowing tactical outlines in a schematic. We slide into our 8-formation again by instinct. Flanking wide on the lower levels. Gunfire tears up the decking around me as I hammer out three-round bursts.

I slide behind a concrete wall for cover, a Harvester launching a salvo of rounds into it with devastating force. The urge to throw myself into the line of fire spears into my head like a blade. I'm so surprised I almost don't back away as the concrete wall bursts inwards in smouldering chunks. I charge out through the choking dust, up the walkway and slam my armoured shoulder into the Harvester. He's sent tottering backwards, gun going off. I hose him in the chest and he's sent flipping backwards and crunching to the decking below.

Beneath me, my fireteam's carving their own way up through the screaming chaos. Rounds streaming past. Sparks spitting in glinting orange arcs. Harvester bodies spinning, smashing to the floor. A micronade explosion rips a chainship from its berth. Adrenaline throbs in my veins as it comes smashing down towards us, hooked metal whipping past, spraying engine fluid on my visor.

My hackles prickle and I lunge sideways as a sharpshooter round grazes my helmet and punches a smoking hole the size of my head in the hull. I slide into cover, breath burning. The stormtech telling me where to look for the sharpshooter.

I focus.

The clack of his sniper rifle as he loads another round in the chamber. Watery sunlight glinting off the metallic stock as he takes aim.

There.

He peeks out and I let rip, pumping high-velocity rounds through him, his arm jerking sideways, rifle going off and shooting another Harvester through the head. The sniper screams as I leap up to the final walkway, their covering fire gone. Two remain, so busy blasting away pieces of the Reapers they captured that they're slow to turn their rifles towards me. I charge, throttling the trigger of my carbine, thunderclaps exploding in my skull. The first shooter whips backwards, his skull smoking. The second tries to keep up the assault, but I cut him down to the walkway, dark blood spreading and dripping over the edge.

A last noise behind me. Weapons up, primed. Finger stroking the trigger.

But it's just my fireteam.

I lower my weapon. Electricity streaming down my throbbing body, every fingertip on fire, my eyes darting around for enemies that aren't there.

We'd taken them all out, and I didn't even realise it.

Or that all four kidnapped Reapers are dead.

The lone Harvest survivor's been stripped of his weapons and tech. The red engravings across his shoulder tell me everything I need to know. Even if I didn't know how to read Harvest ranking, the sneer on his face, the way he holds himself, would have told me he's the veteran of the lot. When he stares up at us, he'll see two-metre tall men and women wrapped in bulky armour and helmets, our bodies crawling with alien biotechnology that morphs us into living weapons. And he doesn't even blink.

Alcatraz returns from their supply crates and dumps a dog tag on the bloodied deck between us. It's the snarling face of a vicious dog. The metalwork's some sort of nanotech, the dog's jaws tearing into dripping blue flesh on an endless loop.

Alcatraz steps forward and dangles the snarling dog tag in front of the Harvester's face. 'Where's the Canine King?' I know they're running translation software similar to ours, so even if the gesture isn't clear there's no misunderstanding.

The Harvester laughs. 'He's planning to play with you blue freaks.' The words jump across my HUD in neon-red text as he speaks. 'He cuts Reapers open, likes to watch how the blue pumps through your arteries. Takes it slow enough you last the whole day. And when you're broken, he staples the ones he likes to the front of his ship, gives them a little tour of the planet while it burns.'

I can feel slow fury shooting into every joint and every limb, so hard I can feel my veins prickling. I want to hurt him and keep hurting him until he's spluttering on the concrete in front of me. I flinch. I've never felt like this before. There's a thick, overripe smell in the air. Something intoxicatingly sweet. It's coming from me. It's coming from my fireteam. We're all struggling to hold ourselves in check.

He's still talking. 'You ever seen a Reaper cut open while they're still screaming? I have.'

Ratchet slams his blade into a crate so hard the metal breaks inwards. 'Let's gut him.' His voice is strangled and thick. 'Give me thirty seconds and a pair of pliers and I'll have your answer.'

'No,' Alcatraz barks. Myra moves behind them to start rifling through their munitions for salvageable intel.

Ratchet's almost spitting. 'Fine. Fifteen seconds and a hot screwdriver. I'll make it quick.'

'I said no.'

'They'd do it to us,' Ratchet snarls back. He gestures towards the dead Reapers, strung up and swaying in the muggy wind. Kept alive as long as possible, but drugged enough so they couldn't escape.

'I say we send the Dog King and his pack of bitches a message. You screw with Reapers, we screw you back.'

Alcatraz starts to speak, but closes his mouth again.

'I know you five,' the Harvester continues. Every word oozing out of his twisted, smiling mouth sets my nervous system on fire. How many civilians and children have men like him killed? 'The Canine King's been watching you. Put bounties on your heads. It's just a matter of time before you're screaming in his—'

The words die as Cable's armoured fist crunches into his jaw.

He's slammed backwards, his head thunking off the guardrail. Cable picks him up like he's a sack of dirt, starts smashing his head against the metal wall with a wet crack. Cable slams him again and again and again, harder every time. The Harvester's struggling grows weaker, his legs starting to shake.

My instinct is to reach for Cable, to pull him off. But the urge is swallowed by the electric fury the stormtech's been feeding into my body, arming me with the reflexes needed to survive this nightmare. Reapers, hunted down like animals. Towns and cities vaporized into blackened shells. Harvesters gunning Harmony personnel down and watching them howl in the mud.

The stormtech holds me back.

The stormtech makes me watch.

The Commando's feet stop twitching. Cable lets him go. The body slides down the wall, leaving a long streak of blood, his skull smashed apart. Cable clenches his hands, his body hunched, his muscles tightening inside his armour, his eyes darting in search of new enemies before swinging around to us. He blinks hard, then glances down at the man he just killed.

No. Not killed. Murdered.

I know I shouldn't be glad. But I am.

I let the stormtech's wet warmth crawl up through my body like thousands of sticky ropes. I feel my body heat declining. My breathing regulating now the last of the threat has gone.

We're alive. And staying alive is the only thing that matters.

Myra mutters something.

I shake my head. Listen again. 'They had the data with them the whole time,' she says, holding up a passkey she's removed from their commslink device. 'Not precise co-ordinates, but close.'

'Move out,' Alcatraz snaps, his breathing shallow. The sticky wind rushes through the hangar bay. Rusted walkways creak. The sky rumbling as rain comes hurtling through holes in the roof and spatters on my armour. I roll my shoulders and scoop up my weapon. But as we pick our way back through the rainforest, it crosses my mind that we didn't need to kill that Harvester. And how much we had wanted to do it anyway.

31

Head in the Clouds

I'm not good in small places.

The memory of being trapped in my armour with the night-ware wasn't helping much. And someone of my size and height doesn't work too well when you can stretch your hands out and feel both walls. And I was sharing this space with someone who was no less hyper than me. Worse, with the never-ending whine of hardware, substrates, powerlines, and memory crystals, the room was an airtight sauna. There was a constant stripe of sweat down my back and soaking into my underskin collar. I could practically feel the walls pressing in on me, the agitation barrelling along my synapses. Still, it wasn't safe to leave, given the likelihood the Suns were still determined to feed me my own balls on a silver platter.

I wished Katherine would call, even just for the chance for us to talk. But the lines remained silent. It made me realise how she'd felt when I'd gone out on my solo hunting expedition, leaving her to rely on me occasionally forwarding a few scraps of intel. Now, perhaps for the first time, I understood how much of a limb she'd gone out on to trust me. And how she'd swung around to give me a second chance, even after I'd betrayed her.

I wouldn't repeat that mistake.

Kowalski had made good on asking Grim to trace the

supplier-chains. All acquired intel, manifestos, datastacks and substrates were made accessible to him. I don't think I've ever seen someone so excited to work. He'd wasted no time setting up his technest, adding even *more* clutter to the room. Grim was seated in the centre of a wrap-around terminal, membrane-thin display panes swirling around him like interstellar bodies in orbit. Data feeds streamed in rivers of neon blue, complex graphics and icons churning over the display facets. Grim's eyes were that creepy milk-white, arm hairs stiffening, body jerking as he trawled through search parameters, codewords, logs across a dozen spaceports. I swear I could hear the firehose pressure of data flooding through the stream of ribbed cables.

'Why is this taking so long?' I asked on the third or fourth day. I was flat on my back, lying in my armour. The inner tendrils and gritty abrasives were set to massage-mode, the vibrations shuddering up and down my body.

'Lot of variables, Vak,' Grim called out. 'You know how difficult it is to do a Deep Dive across space? With a tightbeam commsline?'

'No, Grim. I don't.'

'And allowing for infra-species spelling, mistranslations, broken waybills, faulty substrates? Or maybe I could sit around, and you can be the one translating alien space-jargon and their systems of record-keeping.'

I swallowed a retort, blackened my visor and interior lights and submerged into my thoughts. You don't get much time alone as a Reaper. Any moments during travel, holing up at wayward outposts, or waiting to be relieved were the best you got. I used the moment to think. House of Suns had to have a base; a centralised core of operations. The Warren and Tipei Corporation had just been temporary outposts. If they were stationed elsewhere and shipping to the asteroid, that presented another problem: there was no way they could be sneaking stormtech through the spaceports. Compass had insane security, handled by firms I'd heard of even when I was on New Vladi. Armed with thermal detectors, pheromone-sniffers, and scanners that went down into skin-flakes and dust motes. Unless they had someone high on the ladder who was being bribed to turn a blind eye, which I found very unlikely, they had to be manufacturing their product on the asteroid.

For an insane moment, I wondered if Artyom would help me out, if I asked. In the next moment I wondered if he was still alive. Jae had known we were brothers, and it hadn't been Artyom who'd informed her of that inconvenience. But in our brief conversation, she'd struck me as the pragmatic type. A businesswoman. If Artyom was as much of an asset as he appeared to be, they wouldn't have axed him.

But I also felt sure if they had, that I'd have known. Somehow, I'd feel it. He'd almost died when we were kids. I'd had to go into the mountains for three nights, as everyone did when they came of age, to live in the wilderness of New Vladi's mountain ranges. Didn't matter if there was a blizzard, or wild animals stalking about. When you came of age, you went. It was to remind us of Siberia, our ancestral land.

Frostbite had nearly gnawed my fingers off, but I'd done it. I was climbing back down the tree-studded slopes when I saw someone stumbling towards the frozen lake near our home. At first I thought it was a drunk, struggling home after a hard night. Something told me to take another look.

That's when I saw Artyom holding the knife.

By the time I'd caught up with him, he'd cut his wrist open and was trying to start on the other. I wrestled the dripping blade away, one hand clamped over the wound as the other rummaged for the bandages in my emergency pack. His blood dripped warm between my fingers as I fought to get him patched up. I'd only been away for three days, but the fresh bruises on his tear-stained face told me the whole story. He'd been trying to end the nightmare first, to at least have that tiny measure of control over his life. The cut wasn't deep enough to do significant damage, but bad enough.

'You can't ever do this, Artyom,' I'd told him gently. 'What about me?' I knelt in front of him. My hands on his shoulders. 'What about Kasia? What would she say if you went away for ever?'

'I'm s-s-sorry,' he'd said through chattering teeth. 'Please don't love me less for this.'

'Never,' I told him fiercely. 'Never.' I held him close as the wind howled over the mountains, the first flakes of snowfall swirling down from the skies. I did what little I could to make it the best week of Artyom's life. But his favourite was always listening to music in the afternoons, before our father came back and we had the house to ourselves. We'd sit with our backs to the peeling walls. The gunmetal sky bruised with clouds, the windows streaking with little drops of rain while the sound of instruments filled the room. He'd close his eyes and tuck his knees to his chest. Nodding along with the rhythm, lost in the little moment of peace I'd given him. I sat beside him, knowing it couldn't last. I remember my heart warming and cracking at the same time. Just wishing there was more I could do for him, but knowing the only thing I could afford was staying beside him, being the best brother I could be.

And I promised myself I'd always be around to do exactly that.

Grim came up with a result on the fifth day and Kowalski wasted no time coming over to discuss it. 'Remember that compound in the Warren where the Suns were hiding out?' she asked me.

'Not likely to forget it,' I said evenly.

Kowalski winced. 'Yeah. Sorry. Anyway. The compound

belonged to Crimson Star Industries. They customised graphic designs on chainships and spacecraft, made them look tattooed. They went bankrupt in the Reaper War and stormtech suppliers have been using them as a front ever since, shuttling shipments of stormtech between docks. Grim traced the manifesto logs to a Remote War Arsenal Unit they'd occupied.'

I nodded. RWAUs had sprung up all over the Common post-Reaper War. Since warpdrives, people tend to forget how terribly vast and empty space is. Even if your spacecraft's packing high-burn engines and the usual fancy tech, getting anywhere of note takes a hell of a long time. In the event of another war, or an invasion of a less than friendly alien species, Harmony had safety deposits scattered across the Common in asteroids and stations, stockpiled with warships, weaponry, battlecruisers, suits, munitions, and factories, for back-up use until the bigger guns arrived.

A diagrammatic projection of this galactic region grew around us. Customized to Grim's aesthetic tastes, the perpetually-moving image was an exaggerated explosion of colour, with the stars exaggerated spheres of light and various local stations and installations little glowing cubes. An overlay showed the course schedules of all recent spacecraft skimming around this part of the galaxy. Their course trajectories were shown in long, arcing circles and ellipses and zigzags, braided like thick cables and colour-coded by class, size and which species or syndicate owned them. One strand highlighted in neon-blue as the ship swerved around to one of these RWAUs before shooting back off to Compass, symbolized as an ever-rotating ball of soot-black spikes.

'It should have ended there. Only, they screwed up, and didn't scrub the substrates deep enough. We traced it back to one of the stormdealers on Compass, got a few of our men undercover to buy some stock. Every time, we got an identical

338

match with the stormtech produced by Tipei Corporation.' Kowalski broke into a wide smile. 'We got him.'

'Where?'

'Cloudstern, of all places. One of the wealthiest levels in the whole of Compass.'

Grim shook his head. 'Folks up there are bleeding Commoners. Bleeding, I tell you. And they *still* try to get a discount on packaged goods. Greedy bastards.'

I stopped Grim before he could confess to any other crimes in front of a Harmony operative. 'They're wealthy, then?'

'They can afford top product.' A datasphere burst apart on-screen, the shrapnel resolving into statistics that detailed the stormtech's potency, reaction time, longevity. 'This stuff is so pure it's almost crystallised. The comedown would be horrendous. We've identified a cabal of high profile stormdealers called the Animal Kingdom. They each get their own slice of Compass to operate in. We're targeting one of their most successful stormdealers: the Ratking.'

'Why haven't you arrested him already?' I asked.

'Kindosh wants it done quietly. If we send the Sub Zeros storming in, he'll run. Maybe put a bullet in his own head rather than be interrogated.'

'He's not wired up with a bioaug?'

'If he is, he won't have anyone else holding the trigger. The guys high up tend to decide their own fates.'

'What about the people that work for him? Mules, informers, blademen, dockhands he bribes?'

'They'll never breathe a word. These guys *own* neighbourhoods. The ones who aren't loyalists are light years more afraid of them than us. No, we go for the top dog. Which is why we need to play it safe.' Kowalski levelled a serious gaze at me. 'These are some of the most brutal stormdealers on the asteroid. They've got zero tolerance for selling or any infringement on their territory. They've marched into rival stormdealer hideouts and massacred anyone inside, strung up their leaders and hung their dead bodies from their ships. No one's going to talk. Getting this guy could be the start of bringing it all down. Can I trust you to bring this home?'

I gave no indication of the throb of stormtech deep in my belly. 'You can.'

'I mean it, Vak. This guy is our last lead. If we lose him, we may be finished.'

Cloudstern was one of those places that everyone knows about, but few have visited. Prestigious, expensive and premium, always seen and ever-present in adboards as the go-to destination for parties, shopping and exclusive clubs for the wealthy, elite and famous. If you didn't already have the means, it was unlikely you'd ever live there. Located in the upper echelons of the asteroid, it was economically quartered in a sector spanning two dozen floors. It wasn't reachable via any accessways or cross-transit routes, only by a specialised chainrail. The slim, bullet-shaped tube was outfitted to travel the entire length of the superstructure in under forty minutes, with relatively easy access between its vast floors.

But convenience never comes cheap. Security at the Travel Depot was heightened after the recent bombing and every third traveller was being submitted to a full dermal scan. Kowalski had given me credentials that permitted me to bypass the security, but not the queue. It was nearly an hour before I boarded the white-walled and spacious compartment, squeezing into a bucket seat next to a Rhivik. I was without armour, only dressed in my usual underskin. The alien's thick scales jutted and jabbed into my right shoulder. I turned to say something when his nostrils flared, as if displeased to be sitting next to someone with stormtech. I wasn't too keen on his earthy, sour

340

smell either, so we'd both have to suck it up. I strapped into my safety harness, waiting for departure.

'Don't take the hardskins personally,' a grey-skinned, black-suited Torven sitting to my left muttered, low enough for only me to hear. 'They're a slow bunch.'

I turned towards him. 'Hardskin?'

The Torven slyly nodded towards the oblivious Rhivik, indicating his scales. 'It's what we call them. Hard in the skin, hard in the head.'

I was about to respond when the chainrail lighting dimmed and engines stirred to life beneath my feet. The walls and flooring turned opaque, pulsing with a honeycomb pattern as our transport got clearance and we shot along the maglev like a bullet in a chamber. I was pushed back into my seat by the force of acceleration, clamping my hands around my shoulder straps as we tunnelled through the veins of the asteroid superstructure.

We were hardly a minute into the journey before a newsfeed flickered on above me. A stormtech-related incident, of course. A woman who thought her roommate had taken her stash had stolen into his room when he was asleep. She'd stabbed him seventeen times with a serrated blade before she'd been wrestled off him, still screaming and howling.

She was only twenty. Now a murderer. Blue strands flared on her neck as she stared at the camera through ropes of matted, blood-streaked hair in paralysed disbelief. Like some mechanism in her brain had malfunctioned and refused to acknowledge what she'd done. In a way, she was correct. Her mind insisted it wasn't her, that she didn't have the capacity for coldblooded murder. But her stormtech-infused body told a different story. She didn't know who she was anymore, what else she would do. The two contradictions could tear her apart.

The newslog flickered off as the chainrail slowed to a more leisurely pace to showcase the diversity of floors for newcomers and tourists. The exterior had been an indescribable blur, but now I got a glance at the levels as we looped in a slow ascent. We coasted through a tropical floor made entirely of rivers, waterways and small oceans, and home to a wide-spectrum of alien aquatic species. I could smell the briny stink of the ocean. Dark waves curled and swelled through a mass of dark, jutting rocks, spray leaping five metres high before crashing to a shingled shore. A creature with pale grey skin and a long bulbous snout surfaced, its gills glowing an eerie pale pink. It didn't seem to have eyes, but I got the sense it was watching. Several more of its kin joined, swimming along the chainrail with cautious curiosity before diving back into the depths.

The next floor resembled a forest planet. Slabs of land masses gave way to a scattering of archipelagos, peninsulas, islands and promontories, the water a muddy green. The land was thick with dark green rainforests and towering spears of mountains wreathed in hoary mist. The trees seemed to be hundreds of metres tall, sutured with walkways, swaying bridges and huts. The onboard Rubix played a pre-recorded message, informing us that this was a recreation of the Torven homeworld, Kereov. The scattered nature of the planet's land mass had required the species to innovate: building boats, pulleys, bridges, walkways, modes of transport, discovering easier modes of accessing resources, trading with neighbouring species. It had significantly increased their survival rate, making the Torven value innovation and business above all else, forming the backbone of their culture. This leading to the eventual flourishing of cities and industry across the planet. In the span of a few short centuries, they had achieved space flight, established colonies in neighbouring systems and eventually made contact with humans. Even today, the onboard Rubix finished as we coasted away from the floor, Torven ships and architecture drew heavily from the nature of their homeworld. The Rhivik sitting next to me made a deep scoffing sound that didn't go unnoticed by the Torven sitting on the other side. I'd heard the two species weren't on friendly terms, but with them cooking insults up for each other, I was starting to see exactly what that entailed.

The chainrail coasted to a polished industrial conurbation of the asteroid. Vast echoing spaces yawned out for dozens of klicks in all directions, used as construction berths for spacecraft. Glinting gantries, beams, cranes and powerlines crisscrossed the manufactory, powerful machinery scattered across the shipyard and crawling with suited mechanics of multiple species. Soot-black tubes several dozen metres wide curled through the length of the hangar like a nervous system, the overhead vanilla-grey light glinting gently off its surface.

A silvery skeletal frame of a Diver-Class Corvette hung suspended by a complication of taut silvery filaments. Interlocking clockwork mechanisms ran up and down the length of the asteroid, imbedded in the rock, indicating kilometres of dense, squirming machinery, meshed into the dermis of the asteroid like intestines. The machinery extended out, growing what looked like massive claws, reassembling to fit some sort of size dimensions. Kilometres away, from a different area of the asteroid, components of the corvette were sent tunnelling down the tubes and sprouting out the other end. Mechanics used the claws to scoop up the ship parts, the apparatus whirling down to lock them to the skeletal hull. Other mechanics in grav-harnesses scrambled over the half-assembled ship in a flurry of drilling, securing, wiring, calibrating. A robotic appendage was inscribing the name *Grey Area* on the starboard hull. The entire thing was one giant complex mechanism, part organic, part mechanical, with the impression of more gigantic open hangars and manufactories nestled out of sight.

The onboard Rubix chimed in again to tell us that this was an exclusive Shipyard, producing up to seventy thousand fully equipped ships of every class, model and purpose, bespoke for orders across the galaxy. I glanced at a side readout displaying the prices in disbelief. Grim was right, this part of the asteroid really was reserved for rich bastards.

We shot out of the shipyard manufactory and continued spiralling upwards, little worlds of wonder slamming past. The higher we went, the more pristine, the more ridiculously extravagant, and less populated the floors became. Until we finally docked at Cloudstern's Travel Depot. I unstrapped from my seat and navigated past the spaceport terminal, standing on the outside boulevard.

It was like Compass knew it had one chance to make an impression on newcomers and pulled out all the stops to make it happen. Giant white latticework loomed over me, stretching for kilometres along the roof of the asteroid like an umbrella made entirely of coral. Slices of brilliant blue artificial sky appeared between the gaps. Experimental-looking chainships glided gently in lazy arcs through the sky. The streets had no roads. No traffic. Just public squares and boulevards, every surface polished and glistening with lights. Hotels, attractions and great glass structures rose up in complex designs: honeycombs and swirling patterns and wood cocoons, painted all manner of greys, whites, deep blues, rich reds. Colourful artworks had been strung up between the buildings. Small hissing rivers filled with gleaming fish rushed along the boulevard. Bars, cinemas, tourist attractions, state-of-the-art restaurants, exclusive clubs designed for space-lagged travellers, tourists, and the wealthy. Everything felt slick, made for quick access and slotted perfectly together, like plating on armour. It was the sort of place that banished the derelict slums and greasy spaceports into distant, dreamlike memories. The buildings were so deliberately extravagant and lavish you couldn't help but marvel.

My target owned Venue 291A, deep in the floor. Although we didn't have an image, the collective description from the three Harmony operatives had been assembled into a computer-generated impression. The name *Ramsey Montenegro* floated above a thin man with a faintly avian face, dark hair sculpted into a permanent wave that never crashed, sideburns razored into sharp, jagged edges.

I closed the image down as I eased my way through the crowded boulevard. With the stormtech twitching up a glowing hurricane through my underskin, I felt every third pair of eyes darting my way. As if reminding me I didn't belong here. I walked past a series of spacious first-class lounges and cheery outdoor restaurants, past people queuing to board an inter-planetary cruiser-liner, before entering a shopping centre with a design that echoed back to some art-deco aesthetic, updated for the space-era. The walls were a polished brown wood that shifted like water when I approached. The parquet flooring was covered with a velvety red carpet, perforated with asteroid fragments the size of a child. They were carved into conical and cubical shapes, pyrite and sphalerite gleaming under their rocky flesh, gently glowing readouts detailing their mineral compositions and which star systems they'd been harvested from. Marbled columns veined with gold swept upwards to higher floors, where customers in fancy coffeehouses and clas-sical bars sat on balconies overlooking shoppers zigzagging between boutique outfitters and designer shops, spending someone else's yearly wage on a single purchase. There were no price tags on anything, of course. I guess if you had to ask, you couldn't afford it.

The place looked fancy. But like anything pristine, had a dark history. The floor had been hit by a protest against Harvest refugees a few years back. Researching the event detailed images of the bloodstained floors, the walls pockmarked with bullet-holes, as well as listing the armouries selling the weapons that had fired them. A few years later, this is what we had.

I ticked off the shop numbers I passed, banks, medclinics offering limb extensions and biomechanical surgery, retailers selling all variety of spacecrafts. Head offices for interstellar companies. One look at how deep the drug-trade industry went on Compass and you were kidding yourself if you thought stormdealers didn't have links to the highest echelons of legitimate businesses. Companies that held Compass together economically by trading billions of Commoners through their infrastructure every day, using their connections to reroute and distribute stormtech through the asteroid, fronting the proceeds through their many sub-channels.

How the hell do you dig something like that out?

Once, I could have sworn there wasn't a hope in hell of causing so much as a dent in the drug-trafficking business. But seeing Kowalski at work, making headway with all her fury had altered my opinion. She was genuine. She cared. And that's not something you can fabricate, you'd see through it like a thermal scanner. I found I believed, if anyone could make a difference, if there was anyone determined enough to hold back the spread of stormtech, it was her. She'd only needed to look at her own family to see how much damage it could do. Which meant she knew how much damage it could do to me.

I glanced down at my own stormtech, inching up my ribs like dozens of little hands, using my bones as ladders. Living with stormtech isn't hard because of what it does to you. It's because of what it makes *you* do to the people you care about. The look on Grim's face in the Pits, in the apartment when I clutched the scattershot trigger, burned behind my eyelids. Thinking about what situation my body would throw me into next scared me more than I wanted to admit. I'd never liked subscribing to the theory that stormtech nurtures aggression. That those animalistic tendencies are buried inside each of us and the drug allows them to grow. It would mean most humans are natural born sociopathic killers, only held in check by social conventions. But the more I enjoyed the sensation of power flooding through my muscles and brain, I wondered. No matter how many people spoke out against stormtech, no matter how many rehab centres popped up, no matter how many tortured, damaged bodies dropped dead, people still flocked towards it. If the countless civilisations had walked the same self-destructive path, perhaps our own was inevitable.

That didn't matter. But I was going to keep fighting this, keep looking for ways to cope with what was inside me. To keep trying to do better.

Because at the end of the day, that's really all you can ask of someone.

I told myself all this, so I knew exactly what I was going to do with our stormdealer.

32

The Ratking

Venue 291A was one of those shops that *reeks* of money. Small readout touchscreens. Walls and floors polished to a headache-inducing sheen. A few display cabinets, holding indeterminate pieces of tech so small and innocuous you knew they had to be something special and obscenely expensive.

When it wasn't dealing alien drugs for a sadistic cult, the shop appeared to be selling neural-laces. A bleeding edge, experimental tech allowing users to share sensory experiences, like smell, sound, and even sight over long distances. Want to smell what's cooking in a restaurant on the other end of Compass, or watch a crew at work on an incoming chainship? Get it sent straight into your brain, as if you're really there. The stormtech swelled in my abdomen as I crossed the floor, responding to my nerves. I locked it down. It helped, but not much. I could still feel thick tendrils squirming against my inner ribs.

'Can I help you?'

I didn't have to feed Montenegro's face into the algorithm to know this was the Ratking, I recognised him just fine. He adopted a pleasant, neutral smile. He was impeccably dressed in some kind of dark, high-collared shirt, embroidered with geometrical patterns. A full spectrum-implant in his skull pulsed

348

cyan like the blinking of a distant star. Not a quickpatch job like the ones down in Changhao. This was authentic neuralware.

'I'm after something special today,' I said, matching his smile.

A subsurface device beamed a holodisplay between us, blinking with icons and datastreams. Montenegro enhanced a neural-lace that looked like an explosion of black ink, frozen moments after discharging. 'Latest shipment came in from off-world. Feeds straight into a drone's matrix terminal, delivering a full-spectrum of sensory feeds. The long-range edition lets you hook into astro-exploration drones performing deep-sea excavations across the Common. There's enough radiation on these planets to wither your DNA in hours. With these, you can *smell* the ozone, hear the—'

'Not after any of that,' I interrupted. Without breaking eye contact, I said, 'I'm after a G17 Module with Systems-Wide Range and full haptic support.'

Montenegro didn't bat an eye, but his pleasant veneer dissolved into cautious suspicion. Stormdealers and buyers aren't stupid enough to just *say* what they're buying and selling. They've got codes, key-phrases rotating on a weekly basis, used so customer and buyer recognised each other. Grim had found this week's phrase on the database.

'Never seen you around here before,' he told me. 'Need some verification.'

'Of course.' My shib chimed as I flicked over the virtual passkey stamped with Animal Kingdom's passcode that told Montenegro I was a verified purchaser who had history with his stormdealer syndicate. It had taken Grim less than three hours to create a very good duplicate and rack up a solid history of purchases. He'd quite enjoyed turning me into the drug-addled psychopath.

Montenegro's eyes glazed as he took his sweet time inspecting the passkey, routinely levelling a stare my way. I feigned irritation and folded my arms. Only I knew he was already reaching out to his fellow stormdealers, authenticating the passkey. I also knew Grim would be waiting on the other end, like a grinning panther in the long grass of the virtual landscape. He'd intercept the transmission, feeding Montenegro falsified intel to confirm my identity and answer any queries Montenegro had. They'd better be good enough, because now I'd entered negotiations, if Montenegro got suspicious, I wouldn't leave this floor alive.

The virtual panes dissolved and swept away like ash in the wind. The Ratking's eyes flicked up at me, an undercurrent of steel in his expression. 'We're good. How much colour did you want?'

'It worked,' Grim breathed down the other end of my commslink.

He never used the phrase stormtech. Smart. 'Three phials,' I said. I scratched at my chest, a flare of blue spiralling up along my ribcage. Montenegro nodded and stabbed a button under the counter, a partition of the white tiled wall swinging backwards without any visible mechanisms. I locked my nerves down as I followed him into the room. Taking my suit would have attracted too much attention. But without it, the stormtech was amplifying my every twitch of body-language with big neon signs. If I was used to buying from stormdealers, dealing with one more wouldn't raise any issues. Had to lock it down, hard.

The Ratking didn't *have* a room. He *was* the room. The walls were laced with a fibre-optic system underneath some sort of pliable material, glistening like rubbery obsidian. It was breathing, moving up and down like a torso. A steady pulse pounding out of the speakers. The room was wired to his *heartbeat*, his breathing. Spindly dark fibres thick as my fingers jutted from the walls like crystalline hairs. They quivered with excitement and tension as the Ratking approached, before swerving around to me. Don't know *how* I knew, but they were inspecting me with suspicion. It was like getting sniffed at by a pack of dangerous, rabid animals. Unsettling didn't even begin to cover it.

I heard Grim whistle down the commslink. 'He's running a full-body skinroom. They grew the walls from his skin cells, laced every circuit of this place to his DNA, his biometrics. It's a darkmarket, military-grade defence system. Vak, you're literally standing *inside* him.' He snorted so hard he almost choked. 'This guy's got some really messed up issues.'

I really love when a world of complication just gets dumped on your head without warning. Makes life that much more interesting.

I swallowed a grimace and made a note not to touch anything that resembled anything remotely organic. Hunks of black machinery were growing in the corners of the room, twitching like the foetus of a biomechanical monster that hadn't yet hatched. The room was still developing. Flexiscreens with dark gold trimmings extended out of the ceiling on spindly supports. A mainframe, dripping with cables. A geometric glass desk, littered with fibre-optic wire. No idea if they too were infused with his biometrics, but always better to be sure.

I made to follow the Ratking into the adjoining annex, but he wasn't having it. 'You can wait here.' He gestured at a pale pink armchair, expecting me to sit. I didn't. 'I don't show my stash to customers.'

I smiled thinly. 'Might be I want to check the quality of your stock.' If the Ratking was smart, his stashroom would be in lockdown, wired with a self-destructive sequence that would trigger if anything went wrong. All our data and leads would go up in smoke. Capturing him wasn't enough; we needed his wares as well. Once he retrieved the drugs I'd asked for, I'd never see it open again.

The Ratking didn't bat an eye. 'That wasn't on the manifest.'

'It is now,' I said.

We stared at each other before he nodded begrudgingly. He scanned his biometrics to unlock the stashroom door before ushering me in. The room was cluttered with workstations, piled high with burners, tubes, cartons and chemicals. The Ratking made his own supply, it seemed. 'We're overstocked on synthsilver,' the Ratking was saying. 'I'll give you a discount if you buy in bulk. Just don't shoot up here. Some guy tried that, nearly OD'd in my shop.'

But I wasn't listening. I could already smell the sickly-sweet stench of stormtech, the canisters concealed under the floor somewhere. The metallic, almost blood-like smell of synthsilver, the lemony-tang of grimwire, the musky, herbal stink of bluesmoke. Had to be millions worth of Commoners stored up in here.

I untangled myself from the arousing senses and noticed the room. The wall-fibres were erect and quivering, like their hackles were raised. The pulse pounding of the speakers was slowly escalating to a volume I felt vibrating in my bones. He'd become suspicious.

And that's when I heard the *clickclickclick* of internal machinery churning.

I snatched up the workstation and held it to my chest as a mass of supercharged fibres came spitting out like hot spears. They thudded through the workstation, the hot, squirming tips inches from my face. Teeth gritted, I hurled the workstation towards the Ratking, the edge smashing into his kneecap, shattering the bone with a sharp crack. He screamed and tumbled to the floor, then groaned, crawling forward on his elbows. My body throbbed with warning as I dragged him back, his hand outstretched. He'd almost activated the self-destruct sequence that would have shredded all evidence in the room.

Almost.

I pressed my fingers hard into his throat, letting him know what would happen if his skinroom tried to play any more tricks on me. One-handed, I jammed Grim's membrane-thin override passkey into the computer system. The fibres on the wall growled like dogs, but didn't fire. The pulse continued pounding, echoing furiously through the room until I could barely think. 'Deactivated the self-defence mechanisms,' Grim told me. 'You don't have to worry about dangerous hairs any-more.'

'Good to know.' Keeping the Ratking in view, I locked the office and shop doors before returning. The walls began heaving back and forth, in synchronisation with his chest. 'I'm not an expert,' I told him, making no effort to be gentle as I dumped him into his armchair, 'but killing your customers can't be good for business.'

'You back-stabbing dog,' Montenegro spat at me. 'We had an agreement. We own this floor, every damn metre of it. You're going to cop hell for this.'

He thought I was from a rival stormdealer gang. Didn't realise I was Harmony. I could swing that to our advantage.

'Shut up. You don't talk unless you've got something useful to tell me.' I jabbed a thumb at the flexiscreen, and the mainframe tethered to it by a string of ribbed cables.

Montenegro scowled, no doubt imagining all the gory ways he'd hack me apart, but held his silence. I couldn't resist messing with him. 'Shipping routes, perhaps? Crimson Star Industries? Stashhouses you've been using on chainships?'

More scowling.

'Come, come, now,' I said, leaning close, 'don't tell me *every-thing*. I can't possibly take it all in.'

Montenegro spat at me, the thick glob of saliva landing straight in my eye. The stormtech rolled down into my clenching fist. With effort, I unclenched it and tore myself away before I did something I'd regret. 'You move and you're dead,' I told him, as much for his own sake as mine. I smeared the saliva away. If he made any sudden movements or came at me my body would react defensively, and I didn't trust I could control my own strength.

Or maybe I *didn't* want to hold back? Montenegro here was one of the top dogs. Wasn't like anyone owed him any sympathy. Keeping one eye on him, I called Kowalski. 'Got our prize pig here, awaiting your knife and fork.'

'Good work, Vak.' I could hear the relief in her voice. But it was a different kind of relief, too. 'Is he secure?'

I glanced down at his shattered knee. 'He'll have to break a leg to get out of here.'

If looks could kill, his glower would have skewered me. Kowalski took me at my word. 'We'll be there soon.' I disconnected from her and waited for Grim to continue trawling through the local files before anyone got too curious and realised the Ratking was compromised.

My hope didn't last long.

'We may have a problem,' Grim told me.

I winced. It's never a good thing when Grim says that. 'What?'

'The databanks are biometrically locked to our stormdealer, requiring a direct neural transmission to open.'

'Are you telling me this wanker loves his body so much he's encoded the system to his brain?'

'Yeah. Before you lose your temper and go smashing his skull open for it, it still wouldn't work. He needs be alive. You kill him, his wetware implant starts to cannibalise itself. I can't do a thing remotely.'

I cursed under my breath. Just when I thought we were making headway.

'You leave now, I'll give you my stash for free,' Montenegro offered.

'I thought I told you to shut it,' I growled.

'No one has to know. Let's work something out.' Montenegro made as if to lever himself upwards, forgetting his injury and collapsing to the ground in pain.

I grabbed two fistfuls of his shirt and shoved him back into his seat. 'You open your mouth again without being asked, I'll go for your second knee. And don't try to play me. Every phial is counted. If so much as one is misplaced, people are going to know *you* screwed them over. You're just stalling.' A smile spread over my face. 'There's something in the room you don't want me to find.'

It took me less than a minute of rifling through the cabinets to dig them out.

Plastic explosives. Alcoholic fluid. Reactive powder used in mineral mining. A glass jar of nanonites —metallic balls you could resize to be microscopic, or large as a marble. Medclinics printed them up, filled them with medjel, osteopathics and antibiotics and shot them into patients to target specific areas of the body. Something told me the House of Suns weren't investing in medical technology.

This was the sort of gear you used when you wanted to blow something up. Like a building. Fill the nanonites with an explosive mixture, eject them into the pipes and cable ducts of a building and detonate remotely.

I shook the nanonite jar. 'You were helping prepare for the next terrorist attack, weren't you?'

Montenegro said nothing. I asked again. No response. If the Suns were collaborating with stormdealer syndicates, throwing us off their scent, they'd be doing the same with anything related to terrorism, which would be an even higher risk.

'What's the attack site?' I asked. Montenegro's scoff vanished as I clenched my hand around his shattered kneecap. He jerked back, his eyes watering in confusion and shock. Pain was unfamiliar to him in his little world of espressos and temperature-regulated offices. He'd never fought tooth and claw for scraps in the back alleys of Changhao. Didn't care about the rundown families and child foot soldiers living in stormdealer-controlled neighbourhoods. Barely even heard of the Warren where skinnies with broken bodies shivered and twitched in the freezing darkness. None of the pain and addiction he spread ever touched him. It was totally alien.

It seemed prudent to relieve him of his ignorance.

I squeezed harder. The background pulse throbbed louder and louder, shuddering up through my skeleton so hard I half-expected to hear my joints popping loose. My chest was heaving, my skin plastered with sticky sweat. 'I'm not hearing an answer,' I growled.

'Vak,' Grim warned over my commslink.

'What?' I asked. My breathing heavy, slurred.

'Ease up, man. I don't like this.'

'He knows something,' I told Grim, my hand still clamped around the Ratking's knee. 'If we don't dig it out of him, thousands more are going to die.'

Grim had nothing to say to that. The Ratking mistook my hesitation for indecision, defiance building up in his expression. I gritted my teeth, squeezing hard enough to hear the broken bones grind and crunch together. I didn't even realise I'd done it. 'I don't know!' Montenegro screamed.

I drew my face close to his. He recoiled but couldn't squirm away. 'I think someone like the Ratking leaves nothing to chance. I think you prepare everything down to the finest detail.' I stabbed his implant with a finger. 'How about you tell me before I open you up and take a look?'

'I don't know!' Montenegro's eyes rolled to the implant. 'They wire instructions over to me. I only get the time and location a few hours before they're ready to go. The message is biometrically encoded to me. Disappears shortly afterwards. I'd tell you if I knew, I swear.'

Was the data actually locked into him? I removed my hand from his shattered knee. 'And you have no idea when the next attack is coming?' I asked. I had no logical reason to hit him. But the stormtech wanted me to, dearly. And keep hitting until I heard things crack and go soft.

If he was wondering why a stormdealer gave a toss about terrorist attacks, he didn't say so. Better to have him confused. 'No. I sit tight until I get the order.'

If this was true, we were screwed. I growled again. Every time we took a step, they were three ahead. Every thread, every investigation, every lead left us further behind. They were manipulating us like a Harvest war tactician. While Reapers continued going insane and Bluing Out and the drug-trafficking market continued to build it's empire on the broken, addicted bodies of Compass citizens.

Unless I did something.

I spun Montenegro's chair around and held up a primed razornade between us. 'You're going to start talking. If I decide you're lying, you and your revolting skinroom here end up as sausage meat. Understand?'

'You're crazy,' he spluttered, eyes big as moons.

'Worse,' I said. 'I'm a Reaper.'

'You'd never do it.'

I glanced at the beeping device clenched in my hand. Would I? 'How often did you get a stormtech delivery from the House of Suns?' I asked.

'I'm the main distributor on this floor,' he said, his voice slurred and rushed. 'I took deliveries as often as I could.'

'Did you have a quota?'

'What?'

'I know the way you people work. What was your daily sales quota?'

'Twenty-five sales a day.'

Twenty-five. Twenty-five people, every day, with stormtech fusing with their organs, their skin, their brains. Twenty-five people who could wind up become Blued-Up killers, crippled in mind and body. And Montenegro here was one of hundreds, maybe thousands of stormdealers.

'How many doses were altered to kill?' I forced the words out through my growing horror.

'How did you know about that?' He spluttered. I thrust the razornade in his face. 'No, not all. Only a very few, for specific people.'

'They told you who,' I managed. A quick nod. 'Open your databanks for me. Now.'

'They'll kill me,' Montenegro whispered. 'You have no idea what these people can do.'

I dropped my hand against his shattered kneecap. 'Let's compare, see who's got the darker imagination.'

The guilt welled inside me and I just as quickly shoved it back down. I thought about the families, couples, brothers, who'd been torn apart by this evil. I thought about the girl who'd stabbed her roommate to death for another quick fix. If I looked at the nearest newsfeed, no doubt I'd hear about a skinnie Bluing Out in their sleep, a parent who'd traded their children's livelihood for one more hit, some Academy student who'd dropped out rather than get help. Reapers who'd survived an interstellar war going insane on the streets, murdering the very people they'd fought to protect, before dying and being labelled as kamikaze freaks.

I thought about Joon Szymanski as he squeezed the breath from my dear sister's body.

This ended here. I was about to crack down on the Ratking when something tugged on my veins like wires. Somehow, without knowing how, I knew it was coming from a bottom drawer in his desk. Inside were several stormtech phials, most of them broken.

Except one. It was still full of stormtech.

It was in my palm before I knew what I was doing, stormtech rushing to my jaws and sticky saliva flooding my gums. The blue poison coiled and twisted inside. The stormtech in my body matched it, the two clawing at each other in unison. It was like I already had it inside me. Suddenly all corners of the room were kilometres away and it was just me and the rhythmic pounding of my body. My skin was the outer reaches of my perception, holding my senses in. My palm heavy with the phial's weight. I could try some. Just a little. Just the whole thing. It would be fine. I *needed* this. Needed it more than anything. I'd *earned* it.

I could kill Montenegro. No one had to know. I imagined the blue purity melting down my stomach, seeping its cool, soothing goodness into every parched crack.

And I reached for my razornade.

33

Haunted Heads

Heavy footfalls, fast approaching. My hand slithered back as Kowalski appeared in the doorway. I blinked. Squinting hard. My vision sharpening like a lens to focus on Kowalski's flushed face.

'I see you found our friend here,' she said, piling into the room. 'Oh, is *this* the accident you mentioned? What did you do, big guy? Sit on him?'

No answer.

'What do you have there, Vak?' Her voice was suddenly artificially calm. Like she was trying to soothe a dangerous animal that's clawed out of its cage. I couldn't reply. 'I think I should take that.' Her hand stretched out, palm upwards. A limb made out of bone, blood and meaty muscle. I could hear her joints clicking. 'Give it to me, Vak. Give it to me now.'

I swallowed. She wasn't an enemy. She was a friend. A good friend.

Before I could think, I dropped it into her palm and stepped back, breathing hard.

'Thank you,' she said.

I realised my hands were shaking. I meshed them together behind my back, my knuckles grinding together, willing my body to de-escalate.

Kowalski levelled an unreadable expression my way. Then something seemed to snap behind her, tugging her into motion as she wheeled on Montenegro and thrust the phial under his nose. 'How long have you been dealing?'

Defiance started to build up in his eyes. But one glance at me and my razornade was enough to snuff it out. 'More than a Compass year,' he muttered.

'And how many?' Katherine's voice had taken on a dangerous tone.

'Twenty-five a day,' I answered for him, and found my voice was raw, as if I'd been screaming. 'Minimum quota.'

'Minimum,' Kowalski repeated. Heat seemed to lash off her skin. 'Twenty-five minimum.' She withdrew a palmerlog and flashed it in Montenegro's face. 'Did you sell to this person?'

'You think I keep track of everyone I sell to?'

Kowalski's mouth became a grim line as she drew her thin-gun and stuck it against the knee that wasn't shattered. 'If you've got any brains, you better rack them fast. Did you sell to him?'

Montenegro squinted at the image for a long while before glancing up at Katherine. 'Yeah. I sold to him.'

Kowalski nodded and cracked the butt of the thin-gun into his nose. Montenegro jerked back with a sharp cry and the palmerlog went clattering to the floor. On it was a young boy. Maybe sixteen or so with a mop of sandy hair and sharp features, grinning in a sun-washed room. Katherine's nephew. The boy who'd committed the terrorist attack that toppled the building.

'He was just a kid!' Katherine's fist slammed into Montenegro's jaw again, again, again. She dragged him out of his seat, his shirt ripping, and slammed him against the wall, their faces inches apart. She slapped him so hard his head snapped sideways. 'You killed a *kid*!' she spluttered, her blows becoming weaker and weaker. '*You killed an innocent kid*. How could you? How could you? How could—'

I wrestled her away. 'Let go of me!' she roared, trying to batter me away as Montenegro slid groaning to the floor. 'I'm going to kill him! I'm going to tear his throat out. What sort of world does this? He was just a happy, innocent kid!'

'Katherine, *don't*.' I glanced down at the picture of her nephew, this bright-eyed young man with his whole life ahead of him, cut down by this evil. 'Don't do this to yourself,' I whispered through a tight throat. 'He deserves it. But if you kill him, he'll win. They'll *all* win.'

I felt her shiver with rage. 'He was seventeen,' she snarled at the whimpering stormdealer at her feet. 'He never hurt anyone, never hurt a soul.' The venom and rage deflated out of her voice with every word, like whatever strength she'd bottled up had bled dry. Her head rested against my chest, her eyes squeezed shut. I wrapped my arms tight around her. The two of us just holding each other for a long moment. Then we stood apart. 'And here I was meant to keep *you* out of trouble,' she half-sniffed, half-chuckled.

Montenegro's face was swelling with bruises, one eye shut and already crusted with blood. 'I'm going to lose my job for this,' she muttered, low enough that our prisoner couldn't hear.

'Tell Kindosh it was me,' I said.

Katherine shook her head. 'No way. This is on me.'

'You can't afford suspension,' I said. 'Kindosh hates me anyway. Not like she can fire me.'

Katherine smiled thinly and reached to pat my shoulder. The Ratking was starting to rouse himself, and I wasn't in the mood to let him jerk me around any longer.

I squatted down on my haunches next to him. 'I think you know there's only one way out of here for you. We get what we want, and you get to keep breathing.'

362

Montenegro's face moulded into a rictus of ironclad resolve. I froze. I knew that look all too well. 'You're right about the first part,' he said, his swollen eye darting between me and Kowalski. He'd figured out who we really were, and knew there was no coming back from it. 'But you two maggots aren't getting a damn thing from me.'

'Don't!' I yelled. But it was already done. Montenegro's body jerked forward, head snapping backwards, limbs twitching as if suddenly electrocuted. His implant stuttered with lights, his eyes going glassy. His face twisted into a fierce snarl, saliva and blood trickling out of his mouth.

He'd activated the suicide trigger.

'Grim!' I yelled, unable to tear my eyes away from the horrific sight. Around us, the walls and floors spasmed like a dying animal, the fibres in the walls palpitating. The pulse boomed at such a high-pitch I could feel the soundwaves ticking up the back of my skull, trying to crack it open like a walnut. Kowalski was yelling for backup that would arrive centuries too late.

'He's triggered an alert,' Grim said. Montenegro slumped lifelessly in his chair, his legs giving out their last muscle spasms. 'The Suns know we're onto them. They're probably shredding the databanks now. Tether him to it! It's our only chance.'

But I was already snatching up the fibre-optic cable I'd spotted in the mainframe earlier. I jammed it into the dead man's implant, the socket plugging in with a sucking noise. Violent streams of data twitched over the flexiscreens. Superimposed over them was a perverted approximation of rat's face, nightmarish and cartoon-like in appearance. The matted fur half ripped back from its skull and dripping with glossy black wax, black eyes twitching back and forth, black jaws peeling back in a mocking laugh. Violent bursts of electricity crackled between its teeth. The skinroom's secondary defence mechanism, the one

Grim hadn't disabled, was booting to life. Bars rattled down across each door, caging us in the room.

We were trapped inside the body of a dying man.

'I'm salvaging what I can, but they're eating it up fast,' Grim said.

'Go faster!' I yelled. The optic cable writhed like a dying python, trying to rip itself free from Montenegro's skull. Kowalski and I held onto the thrashing cable, shoving it deeper into its socket. The ribbed edge slicing into my fingers. Blood welled against the wire. The rat's face curdled into a vicious, hungry snarl. The squirming fibres in the walls screeching as they stretched out towards us. There was a vicious tearing as the black walls swelled. As if there were hundreds of screaming, crawling monstrosities and machines trapped here, thrashing to break free and tear us apart. I caught a glimpse of a robotic claw, tipped with skin-shredding pincers, hauling itself out. The cable thrashed harder in our hands. We gritted our teeth, shoulder to shoulder, our bloodied fingers turning white. Montenegro's body twitched around us with nightmarish spasms, arms and legs slamming against metal.

'Got it!' Grim yelled.

'Now!' I yelled. We let go of the cable simultaneously, throwing ourselves backwards and collapsing on top of each other. The cable thrashed back like a whip with a sharp *crack*, embedding itself in the mainframe, machinery shattering. The walls' twitches slowed, the screams rapidly distorting and garbling, the rat's snarling face being clawed away in vicious tearing strokes, as if someone were furiously scratching out a person's face on a painting, before disappearing and the room dying down for good. Montenegro's body slumped lifelessly with it.

The tension flooded from my body in one great, heaving rush. I managed to clap Kowalski on the back, unable to say anything coherent. She reached to touch my hand before helping me to my feet, breathing hard and meeting my eyes. I wanted to get the hell out of this room and never come back, but we couldn't risk leaving until backup arrived.

I was almost afraid to ask Grim what he'd salvaged. Instead of telling me, he showed me. Sales figures, distribution channels, waybills routing all over Compass. The image of a chainship, sitting in a dry berth in an unidentifiable dock. The type you saw everyday around Compass.

Except I'd seen exactly that image in the stormtech factory and wasn't about to dismiss it as a coincidence. Were they using chainships like this to transfer stormtech on and off the asteroid? If so, they were operating offworld, but within shipping range of Compass. Probably somewhere in the system.

The image had a sender. Jae Myouk-soon.

Jae.

The person who'd called me up in the Pits. The one in charge of this entire operation.

'Anything on future terrorist attacks?' I asked Grim.

'The system's totally clean,' Grim said. 'Nothing that even *hints* at it. They don't even reference any attacks that already occurred.'

'But we know there's going to be another attack,' Kowalski said.

'You don't think it'll be the Harmony base, do you?' I asked.

'Not even they could punch through that level of security. I'll get our departments to do a check anyway. But these attacks have been about public sabotage. Driving fear into the population and undermining Harmony. Attacking us would do the opposite. We'd become martyrs.'

Further discussion was halted by the arrival of Harmony SSC squads, spearheaded by Saren's fireteam. I went to the corridor to meet them, the knots in my stomach unravelling as I stood in clean, lush hallways. That nightmare room with all its squirming technology had messed around in my head. Made me feel like I was never going to leave.

The SSC servicemen didn't waste any time removing Montenegro's corpse while others peeled apart the room's internal organic machinery for answers they wouldn't find in time. Gunrunners cordoned off the area. Salvaging footage captured by cams or drones. By now a crowd of shoppers were starting to congregate, rubbernecking with morbid curiosity at the shop's front. Fasincated by the terrible, terrible things people do to each other.

I'd set my palmerlog to alert me of stormtech-related news, and now it was lighting up like fireworks. More deaths as a result of stormdealer warfare. Crimelords attacking each other in their ships, on the streets. One of the victims was a kid, no more than fourteen. He'd been used as a foot soldier for a multispecies stormtech syndicate, shuttling stormtech between spaceports. He'd ended up in a spaceport his syndicate wasn't allowed to operate in. Wasn't there five minutes before someone shot him in the head and dumped his body in a shipping crate. Journalists and newsfeeds across the asteroid were already dissecting his corpse like carrion to back up their agendas and political stances, ignoring the tragedy, the horror of the casual violence. His body wasn't even cold yet. A kid had died, just to teach his bosses a lesson.

And his bosses? Animal Kingdom.

His parents would be watching all of this. Wondering why we were up here instead of protecting innocents. Wondering what the hell it mattered that we'd stopped one stormdealer, when we couldn't stop the rest of them.

My teeth were clenched. Everything we'd just achieved here felt empty and as useless as a breached airlock. One step forward, three steps back. How the hell do you fight an entire drug industry? How could we fight the Suns like this? Hell, they could be watching now. Through a cam-feed, a drone, anything. Gathering up intel to weaponise our own plans against us.

I stomped out of the room, distinctly aware that Katherine was watching me go.

34

Night Hunters

Kowalski had told me to hold off until she and Grim had broken through the data as they would need my help to trawl through it. I had a few hours to kill in the meantime and decided to attempt the local bathhouse, abandoned at the late hour. I sat sweating in the spherical clay sauna. Water dripped from me and splashed to the wooden floorboards. Somewhere, quiet ambient music was playing. I sipped from a bottle of gin beside me. You weren't meant to bring alcohol in here, but I've never paid much attention to the rules when it comes to alcohol consumption. The stormtech seemed to enjoy the heat, and was spasming in furious bursts through my body. Tonight, it had also decided to wedge itself in my left armpit, writhing there with a furious tickling sensation. I've long learned you can't dislodge the stuff from going where it wants to go: I rode the feeling out until it grew bored and decided to explore elsewhere.

I polished off the remainder of the bottle and got up to shower when I felt something slimy and slick wedged in my throat. I wriggled my jaw, tried to budge it with my tongue. I balled up a mouthful of saliva and spat it out. No dice, it was stuck fast. My chest heaved as I gagged on it, feeling my throat moisten and clench with the effort, until a slimy ball landed on my tongue. I spat it straight out. It looked like a piece of thick, rubbery phlegm, the size of my thumb. Except it was glowing blue. And seemed to be *squirming*. I slowly spat again and saw my saliva was flecked with the same glowing mucus. I looked in the mirror. Chunks of phlegm were wedged between my teeth, swimming along my tongue.

This wasn't totally abnormal – my saliva and phlegm had been blue before. But that was years ago, before rehab had smoothed it out. Even with the Jackal forcibly injecting me, it was happening again too quickly. I didn't want to dwell on it and began the process of scrubbing out my mouth, spitting and heaving all the mucus I could. No matter how much I spat, my body kept churning out a never-ending supply. And maybe it was my imagination, but it seemed to be grower thicker, congealing to my tongue.

Feeling solidly grossed out by my own body, I finished showering and slipped into a fresh underskin. I caught three different traveltubes to throw off any pursuers before heading over to our rendezvous point. The room we'd booked was skimming the outer edge of the asteroid in one of those half-completed floors still in the process of being assembled. The floor-to-ceiling viewport showed a ruffled dark green ocean, heaving with curves and swells. The water rippled as ships from a dozen species and a dozen classes shot out over the ocean in bright blue streams, steering up towards the circular spacecraft tubes jutting from the ceiling.

Katherine was standing on the balcony. 'You're here early,' she said without turning around. She was out of her work clothes, wearing a loose red shirt and woolly scarf.

I joined her at the rails, dangling my arms over the sides, our shoulders touching. 'Just wanted to check in on you.'

She tilted her gaze up to follow the flight path of a yellow Torven ship until it melted lazily into the horizon. 'I don't even know anymore. It's just all so numb.' She was a dark outline against the darkening sky. Her hair was being blown around her face by the salty ocean breeze. 'You know what I hate? People say the right things. They act the way they should. But when they look at me, they're waiting for me to explode. They look at me like I'm a bomb about to go off, and they keep their distance. It just gets everything crashing back down again, and again, and again. And then I go and do what I did to that stormdealer and I wonder if they've got the right of it. Maybe I am a ticking bomb.' She blinked hard and turned towards me. 'I thought confronting him would make me feel better. Give me some sort of closure. And it did, in a way. But it tears a different hole inside you. And you wonder why you didn't fix it sooner. Why you didn't do things differently. And then you run out of ways to hate them and just start hating yourself. My nephew's gone. So is the man that killed him. He tore our lives apart, and yet it's me who's been left behind to pick up the pieces and deal with the consequences. It took him a minute to do damage that'll last a lifetime.' She gave a mirthless snort. 'And that's what's so unfair.'

'I get it,' I told her. 'Doing what I did to that boy who killed Kasia helped. But it made me angry. Angry with the whole world, the injustice of it all.'

'How it seems like no one cares,' Katherine muttered.

'Yeah. All of that. But it was nothing compared to how angry I was with myself. And at the end of the day, that's the hardest part. Fighting the urge to never forgive yourself.'

Katherine eyed me through strands of her wind-whipped hair. 'How'd you win it?'

'I didn't. I just learned to stop fighting. I learned that's the way things are, and that I'm going to have to find a way to live with it.' I met her eyes. 'And I learned to find people like me and talk about it. Help them along the way.'

A quiet moment passed between us. Eventually, a sad smile tugged at Kowalski's lips. 'I'd like that.'

I matched her smile, pleased she'd agreed to the idea. The wind howled around us. The slow trickle of ships like a glowing ribbons streaming out of the tubes. 'It took me for ever to learn the worst thing you can do is try and forget about them. You do that, you rob yourself of everything they ever gave you. You bottle it up, something inside you will break.' I felt a faint rip in my chest, like old stitching tearing loose. 'The people that matter to us aren't always meant to be in our lives for ever. But the things they did to make you a better person can be. Nothing's ever going to fill the hole they left behind, but keeping them in mind makes it a little easier.'

Kowalski nodded, her gaze fixed on the endless curve of rippling waves along the false horizon like a long-lost dream. She withdrew and brushed the hair out of her face to offer me a watery smile. 'Thanks, Vak. Really. This helped. More than I thought it would.'

Everyone grieves in different ways. We all have different shaped holes left in our lives when people we love are gone. But when grief hits hard, it's not about dimensions or angles. Grief numbs. Turns everything so cold you don't know *what* to feel. I could connect with that, even though I couldn't articulate how it feels. Some days, I woke up realising friends I'd known in the Reaper War were dead. Gone for a decade, buried in some mudhole on a distant war-torn planet I'd never see again, and the pain hit me all over again. Because trauma never goes away. Loss never goes away. Not really. But trying to do your best to face up to it, finding comfort in each other, maybe we could survive it.

We continued our conversation until Grim arrived an hour later, and promptly got to work. We sat in a semi-circle around a wide flexiscreen. The virtual space around us was so cluttered with papers, spreadsheets and comparisons I had to fight the urge to swat them away. 'I'm guessing you have nothing about their base, right?' I asked.

'Nothing. No trace, no log, nothing.' Grim rotated the orrery of pages around. 'But there might still be a clue to its location.'

I expanded the image of the chainship until the small spacecraft filled the room. 'This has to be on Compass,' I said. 'Look at the design of the hangar and the flag in the background. I think their base is offworld and they're using this dock to access Compass.'

'The only person who could tell us either way is dead,' Katherine told us. I'd drawn my chair close to hers, our legs touching as we inspected the data together. I saw a slight smile pull across her lips as I brushed my arm against hers. 'I can't say I'm mourning his passing.'

'Wait, wait, wait.' Grim leaned forward. 'There's a "J" at the bottom.'

'A signature. Jae Myouk-soon,' I said.

'We searched the archives for her,' Katherine told me. 'Got no results.'

'Either she's no got no record, or someone inside Harmony is protecting her.'

'The more this goes on, the more I'm starting to think you're right.'

Grim raised a finger, his Harvest tattoos gleaming in the light. 'Okay. Backtrack. How do you know that name?'

'It came up in the files. Why? You've heard of her?'

Grim eased his body into a bean-bag big enough to swallow him up. 'Yeah. Myouk-soon was one of the most feared espionage agents for hire on Harvest. Contract killer, you know? She rooted out traitors and threats to Harvest, led the crackdown on Harvest immigrants and war refugees. Made sure that no one could desert or feed information to Harmony. Even before the war, she made her living rooting out security threats.' My friend's hands were white, clasped tightly together. 'They called her The Killer Chemist. She was the only reason I didn't defect sooner. I was too afraid she'd catch me.'

'What did she do?' I asked.

'If she suspected someone of selling state secrets, or those who had links to threats to Harvest? She'd inject them with genetic viruses, customised to her victim. One made you tear your own eyes out. Another made breathing feel like having glass shards poured down your throat. It'd take her just a few chemicals to drive you insane, or make you kill yourself. The worse the crime, the more imaginative the punishment. She was *seventeen* when she started. Seventeen.'

I remembered our brief conversation. *That blubbering Bulkava was right, you really do look like your brother.* What had she done to that poor alien because he'd helped us? Had she punished Artyom too, for not revealing our connection? 'If she's a biochemist,' I said, stamping the thoughts away, 'she could easily be manufacturing the stormtech, poisoned and clean.'

Grim nodded. Despite the warm room, I felt a chill clamping around my blood and bones like rust, and only partly because of Jae. My body temperature had been spiking into either extremity over the past few days. With the stormtech beaming through my body, there was no secret as to why. I quietly wished I could hide in the dark, tight, isolating embrace of my armour.

'Whether it's her or not,' Katherine was saying from a million miles away, 'we've already prioritised stopping the next attack. We've got a strike team looking into it, but maybe we can find something here.'

I got Grim doing an initial quick search in the hopes there was something surface level he could find in a matter of minutes. As he did, Katherine turned to me. 'You okay, Vak?'

She felt along my shoulder and the back of my neck. 'You're burning up.'

'I'm fine,' I lied. But her touching me had broken through the webs of stormtech cocooning around my body and mind. Just a little, but enough.

'No, no you're not. You need to look after yourself.'

Ropes of blue saliva drooling from my mouth. Glowing flecks in the phlegm. 'I told you, I'm fine.'

Katherine locked sights with me as she slowly stood. 'Vak, you level with me, or I'll do this on my own. I can't work with you if you can't give me a straight answer. Do you understand?'

I rolled my shoulders and exhaled, huskily. 'It feels like my organs are getting chewed up,' I told her. 'But it doesn't hurt. It's almost the opposite.' I clamped a hand against my ribs and watched the stormtech flare up like forks of lightning through sky-obscuring clouds. 'It's solidifying inside me. Working deeper and deeper until I can't tell the difference between it and my body anymore. I'm fighting it with everything I've got, Katherine. But it's not enough. It's never enough.'

Katherine sat back down again next to me. 'Okay. That's how we do things, Vakov. We talk about it. It's the only way this can work.'

'I don't know what it'll do to you.' I had to fishhook each word from my gut. 'This stuff... it's a time bomb. I don't want it to hurt you.'

Katherine's expression changed. 'Don't give me that. Don't play the victim card so you can push me away. If you don't think we can make this work between us, fine. I'll walk. But don't tell me I'm not strong enough to see this through with you. It doesn't work that way. Understand?'

I formed a dozen responses, all of them catching in my throat. Our breathing seemed to be the only sound in this place. Then, sliding my hand in her's, I managed to say, 'I don't want you to go.

I just . . . I don't want you to see me that way.' Blue throbbed along my knuckles and I knew she could feel it, too, pulsing and pushing against her skin. 'I care about you, Katherine. I do. And I don't want you to see what happens to me if the stormtech wins.'

'We won't let it win,' she said. 'We'll fight it together, Vakov. I promise. I don't care how long we have to look, we'll find a way.'

I could only nod, my throat raw and filled with things I didn't know how to say, the words all tangled up in this mess.

Grim broke away from his search and enhanced a datasheet for me to see. 'Vak, look at this endnote. "Target young adult males, those in high-stress roles, Reapers, and if possible, aliens. The more of those scum we pick off Compass the better".'

'They're trying to spread it to aliens?' I asked. 'The House of Suns hate aliens?'

'You think it's as simple as that?' Katherine asked.

'"Picking the scum off Compass" doesn't strike me as terribly peaceful.'

'They're one of those pro-human groups, then. There's been an uptick in them, lately.'

'Yeah, but they *are* an alien-worshipping cult,' Grim butted in. 'Hating other aliens doesn't make sense.'

Kowalski cracked a weak smile. 'They're extremists, Grim. Let's hazard a guess and say they're not operating on sense.'

'In all their science texts and data-readings they've only mentioned Shenoi,' I said. 'No other aliens. And if the Shenoi were at war with other species, as the Kaiji said they were, it's not far-fetched to imagine the House of Suns disliking the idea of aliens running businesses and occupying entire Compass floors, either. Especially not with the Rhivik talking about joining, too.'

375

'There've been a few stormtech alien causalities,' Kowalski said slowly.

Grim toggled some unseen mechanism. All the gathered datasheets whirled apart, then reassembled themselves into a three-dee visualisation of Compass. The schematic was spliced down the middle like a brain, showcasing the vast, intricate network of floors, levels, compartments, interior mechanisms and architecture, spread across hundreds of kilometres. 'Oh man. And we've got this monster to search through,' he said, rubbing his eyes with his knuckles. He craned his head towards me. 'Out of all the people in the Common, why'd I have to make friends with you?'

Grim had tagged high-priority intel we'd already salvaged. Allowing for multiple dialects and interspecies spelling, we cross-matched it with hits matching the House of Suns' frequency across Compass. It was a hell of a mess, trawling through dockyard waybills, spaceport manifestos, shipping routes. Anything that the Suns could be using to disguise themselves. The comment about hating aliens prompted us to check rare interactions between rival species that got the Alien Embassy raising red flags. Maybe some new spacefaring species had been labelled as a potential threat, and the Suns could pin them with their next terrorist attack. It'd be just like them to use a third party as a scapegoat. But trawling through the endless transmissions and trade-requests made by various alien species got us nothing.

'The House of Suns is spreading fatal stormtech to seed fear and turn people against Harmony,' I said. 'They just attacked a bank on one of the wealthiest floors on Compass. They'll escalate, not dial back from that.'

'Maybe it's not size they're after,' Kowalski countered. 'Could be significance. Something in a peculiarly crowded area.'

Hours later, we were still nowhere. The dusty-red colour of

the artificial skies were slowly bleeding away into darkness. My arse was numb from squatting, my eyes sore from staring at the flexiscreen. I needed a drink, badly. I kept scanning each dossier, each particle, each file, running through the parameters in hopes something would click. Nothing. Only vague traces and patterns that trailed off into dead ends. Kowalski's sporadic yawns had become continuous, until she rose to go, planning to be back in the morning. She patted my shoulder as she left. The room was silent except for the humming of the mainframes and computational substrates hidden behind the mirror-smooth walls. The distant tubes continued to wink like the eye of some mischievous neon creature, scattering colours across the frothing water. I was vaguely aware my spine was aching, but I was still focused, enough that it took Grim a few tries to snag my attention.

'Listen, Vak.' Grim was scratching at his pits. 'We've been hacking away at this for hours. Hours. It's not happening tonight.'

I glanced at the digital timer in my shib. Dawn was fast approaching. 'That doesn't matter,' I said. 'We have to keep trying.'

'Yeah. I get that. But our options are limited right now, you know?' Grim stooped down next to me, close enough for me to see the ache for sleep in his red-rimmed eyes. 'We're looking for an attack that could take place anywhere. In an asteroid. It could be outside our door, or down in Changhao, down in Starklands, up in the Greenlakes suburb, anywhere in between. We're not going to find it. Not tonight.'

Images flashed through my head like a flexiscreen burn-in. Katherine's body, shaking against mine. Us standing on the windy balcony, finding solidarity in sharing our grief. 'No. Dozens, maybe hundreds will die if the Suns launch their attack.' I was aware my voice was rising, louder than I realised.

And why was my face so flushed? 'Those pricks don't care who dies. Don't you care about them?'

'Hey, hey! Of course I care!' Grim frowned, leaned forward so close our bodies were almost touching. 'Mate, you all right?' He stretched out a hand. 'Your neck . . . you're so blue.'

I slapped his hand away. 'Don't,' I rasped. 'Don't touch me.'

Grim took a breath. 'Vak, I hear you leaving in the middle of the night. Going out for hours, coming back restless and reeking of booze and sweat. Sometimes you don't come back until dawn. I don't want to get on your case about it, you know? But it's hard not to. When was the last time you had a full night's sleep?'

I felt my neck and tried not to react to the slithering mass under the skin. 'No. We need to keep working, we need to find this—'

'Not gonna happen, Vak. Not tonight. Let it go. Just for a minute, okay?'

My knuckles turned white at my sides. 'Don't,' I heaved out. Sweat slithered down my armpits. 'Don't treat me like I'm going to explode. Not you.'

'I'm not! I'm—'

'Stop, Grim. Just stop.'

'Or what?' Grim was on his feet. 'You going to hurt me? Like you almost did in the arena? Or in the apartment? I saw it in you. You wanted to. So go ahead.' Grim spread his arms. His eyes, usually mischievous and sly, were glistening and wide with fear. 'Take a swing.'

I backed away, the scene crashing down on me. It was like retreating from a mountain ledge, roaring with wind. The world tilted, swam with black spots. No, blue spots. They swarmed my vision until I was drowning in them. My friend stood still, eyes fixed on me.

I was going to destroy him.

I was going to destroy everyone around me.

The twitching virus in my body wasn't just altering me, it was eating me away. I was poison. Had Artyom seen it? Had he left New Vladi not because of what our father was, but because of what I'd become?

'I'm sorry,' I told Grim. The words unlocked something that had been unconsciously building up in me, and all my rage evaporated at once. My arms dropped to my sides. 'This stuff, it isn't me. It's doing things to my head. But that's no excuse. I'm going to fix this, Grim. I swear it. If it's the last thing I do. I'm not going to lose you.'

Grim's shoulders drooped. I hated the way I tore him down and exposed this sensitive core he tried so hard to armour up. With all his jokes and mischief, I often forgot how vulnerable he was. He was more adrift than I was, his home, family and everything he knew destroyed.

'I'm sorry. That wasn't fair of me either,' he sniffed.

I shook my head. 'You've got every right to be angry with me.'

'Maybe.' A watery grin climbed across my friend's face. 'Sometimes it's hard not to be. But someone's gotta say it, right?'

I attempted a smile. 'Right.'

The workspace had two mattresses tucked away in a sub-surface compartment and we took one each. Flat on my back, I watched the curving ribbon of departing ships framed by the V made by my feet as I tried to think. The House of Suns wouldn't launch an attack on a facility that had no immediate value to their cause. They were deliberate and precise. So what did they most want to gain from their next attack?

Sell to as many aliens as possible.

I remember being on campaign, stalking through an evacuated city with the rest of my fireteam. Can't remember the name of the planet, or how long we spent there. I do remember how our armoured buggy bounced as it rode over the potholes and cracked asphalt, my back aching for weeks afterwards. Reconnaissance teams had sighted Harvesters around the city museum, intel suggesting it was a munitions base for Anti-Hull ordnance. We'd scoured the entire museum and found nothing. Nothing except destruction.

Harvesters had been there, all right. They'd meticulously gathered up every piece of artwork in the gallery and destroyed it. Paintings, sculptures, artefacts, memorials, transcripts. Spacesuits, hull-pieces, machinery models, orbital data, spaceflight records, terraforming intel. Anything pertaining to the establishment of the colony, its position within the greater Common universe, or the people who'd settled it: dragged into the vestibule and torched.

They didn't steal a single thing.

Just destroyed it.

'Bastards, aren't they?' Myra had said, her voice echoing among the shredded ruins of half-burnt tapestries. The stink of smoke was ripe in the air, the tiles stained soot-black. 'If they can't have it, no one can.'

'That's not it,' Alcatraz countered. His armour plates grinding as he gathered ash up in his gloved hand and watched it bleed through his fingers like black snow. 'It's about erasure from history. Wiping out everything about the people that discovered, established, and built this colony. It's not enough to take this planet. They want to clean the slate.'

'That's crazy,' Cable muttered.

'That's how Harvest wins. Not by taking their enemy's planet. By pretending they never existed on it at all.' Alcatraz gestured towards the forlorn museum. 'Culture is the heart of any society. So they go for the heart.'

Now, years later, on the other side of the galaxy, I was facing a very different enemy. Yet it was one with the same tenacity.

The same ruthless determination burning in their eyes, going for the heart.

This whole bloody time, it was staring at us, point-blank in the face. I don't know *how* we didn't see it.

I bolted up, startling Grim, powering up the flexiscreen. My heart thudded in my chest as I crawled past the streams of data towards the place I suspected was their true target. I matched their data with the Suns' traffic circulating the location, eager to see how much time and activity our cultists had spent in this location. If I was right, we'd have our next target.

I was.

The traffic was higher than any other venue on Compass by a mile. The Suns had been obsessed with this place. Wasn't a stretch of the imagination to understand why.

I didn't waste any time contacting Kowalski. 'Seriously?' Kowalski slurred, her eyes bleary, 'You boys couldn't let me have five hours sleep?'

'I know what their next target is,' I said.

In the cam's reflection I could see the blue thrumming across my stomach with excitement. Kowalski fought back a yawn. 'Where?'

'That file, telling the stormdealer to sell to as many aliens as possible,' I said. 'They hate other species. Hell, it's probably in their teachings. In a way they're continuing the Shenoi's war against them. So they're going to attack the place most precious to them, the symbol of integration: the xenomuseum.'

35
Denial

I don't think Kowalski believed me. Not at first. 'And you're sure about this?' she asked. Grim planted himself beside me, only half conscious.

I shot over the traffic data to Kowalski. 'Something tells me they're not looking into the xenomuseum to donate funding,' I said. 'If they really hate the aliens as much as they say, an archive to their achievements, history and culture will be their next target.'

Kowalski assessed the evidence I'd provided, slowly joining the dots as I had. She pulled on a stretch top. 'All right, Vakov. We're out in five.'

I'd have been lying if I said I felt comfortable around the Sub Zeros at the best of times. But gathered in this confined office space together, standing abreast like we were in a line-up, I couldn't help but shift on the balls of my feet, gloved fingers twisting and turning behind my back. I was glad my mirrored visor concealed my face. I had to keep reminding myself that these beasts in their rock-like armour were on my side.

Which meant I was on theirs.

Kowalski had called Hillyn Joreth, the xenomuseum's director, to arrange a meeting. I shouldn't have been surprised to see a Torven running a museum of alien artefacts, but I was. The alien's skin was the colour of earthy red clay, his slender face gaunt and cynical in a way that bizarrely reminded me of Kindosh. He wore a dark, high-collared suit that was constantly rippling and snapping in an unseen breeze. What might have been blue ancestral tattoos crawled up his wrist in thin curlicues. He was sitting across from Kowalski and Saren behind a featureless black desk, hands folded in an eerily human-like manner while the rest of us stood around them like a crescent wall of armour. What were presumably Torven artefacts were piled up in great sweeping shelves around him. Joreth's secretaries and guards were all pretending not to listen as they catalogued submissions and inspected the archives.

'And what did you say your evidence was again?' Joreth had a way of making everything you said sound suspicious and ridiculous, just by quoting it. He leaned back in his highbacked chair, seemingly built for alien bone structure and ergonomics.

Katherine leaned forward. 'One of our research analysts found a pattern of chatter indicating your museum was the next most likely target of a terrorist attack.' I raised an eyebrow behind my visor. Research analyst, really? Grim, hooked on the other end of the commslink despite my protests, sniggered loudly.

'Given the scale of the threat, we have to take this seriously.'

'And why would anyone want to blow up a museum of artefacts?' Joreth demanded, with an air of presumptuous amusement only people in power can wield. 'We survive purely on our very generous donations from the community. The Cultural Centre books out a month in advance, the simulation in three. Visitors of all species make long journeys to Compass just to see it.'

'The threat is genuine and tagged as high-priority.'

Joreth narrowed his eyes. 'And you're sure of this?'

'We wouldn't be here if we weren't.'

'Very well. What do you propose to do?'

'We'd sweep this part of the Academy building. Scan for explosives, biohazards, chemical agents, signs of tampering or hostile devices. Install surveillance, armed personnel.'

'For how long?'

'Until you are no longer under threat,' Saren butted in without bothering to hide his frustration. 'Two attacks within less than a month is more than we need.'

'The search you suggest could take days, weeks. Months, even. Your evidence is insubstantial.' Joreth looked at each of them in turn with his beady brown eyes and I knew right then that we were done. There are some citizens so cemented in their ways that nothing's going to change their mind. Nothing short of a terrorist attack. 'There is no reason for us to be targeted, among the tens of thousands of facilities on Compass. The human boy who blew up the bank was a Blued-Up freak demanding drug money.' Katherine's shoulders tensed. 'Having your metalheads parading around a museum will drive away the very community we wish to help. Bad for morale. No offence.'

'None taken.' Kowalski didn't even try to sound pleasant about it. I've observed it's people deciding what is and isn't a matter of offence who are often the ones doling it out.

'It's taken years of work from Compass, the Alien Embassy, our homeworld and generous donations from a multitude of species to establish this museum. We're the only one of its kind run by my people,' Joreth followed up. 'We've received threats from pro-human establishments before. And yet we're still standing. I won't see its reputation destroyed because of chatterboard gossip. Harmony can't control or protect their own Reapers. What makes you think you can protect us?'

I'd thought the looks he and his staff were giving Harmony – us – had been of cold fascination. Now I realised it was distrust. The House of Suns had already succeeded in driving

384

a wedge between Harmony and the common people. Having an armoured presence, with Harmony's current reputation attached, would do him no good.

Of course, having his building become a smouldering pile of rubble would do him even *less* good.

'You're welcome to scan the building, quickly,' offered Joreth, as if he were doing us the favour. 'But I believe you'll be wasting your time.'

Turned out he was right. Four hours later, the minesweepers, infrared, thermal, subsonic sweepers, bio-hazard detectors and sensor-scanners revealed nothing, as I'd known they would. The House of Suns were too smart to leave their fingerprints lying around. They hadn't launched their attack. But they would. Soon.

'You heard him,' Kowalski said. 'There's nothing to be done.'

'And we're listening to Joreth?' I asked. 'He couldn't find his own arse in the dark. We don't need his permission to investigate.'

Out of uniform and back in our storage unit, Katherine was sitting next to me and wore a loose cream shirt under a grey jacket, a cherry-red scarf slung around her neck. Her hair was wet from a recent shower and smelling of something pleasantly sweet. 'Actually, we kind of do. It's against the Galactic Common's constitutional rights. In case you've forgotten, Harmony isn't too popular.'

'That's nothing new.'

'It is since the terror attack happened. Strong-arming a xeno-museum director isn't going to help much with our reputation. I wish we could force our way in there and insist on installing a full security operation, but it's not going to happen. Until we've got concrete evidence of a planned terrorist attack, our hands are tied. There are other angles we can cover, but not this one. Backs are to the wall, boys.'

'*Harmony* can't,' I said with a smile.

Katherine shook her head. 'No. No lone wolf antics, Vakov.'

'Who said I'd be alone?' I leaned forward, all business. 'Look, you guys can't get in. Bad for PR, I get it. But I can. Let's say they are planning something in the xenomuseum. They're going to have to break in and set themselves up, right? They're too diligent to leave anything to chance with a quickpatch job. We know there's nothing in place now. So, if I'm right, all the materials are still to be delivered. We get the manifesto of upcoming deliveries and trace it back to their munitions storage base, and from there . . .' I squeezed my hands together.

'Okay,' Katherine said slowly, as if hesitant to commit. 'So we just need the museum's delivery schedule. And you understand the risk if you're wrong and get caught? Not just to Harmony, but to you?'

Sitting so close together, I could see the concern lining her face. I wanted to reach out and reassure her. But the runnels of blue stripes along my arm wanted to pull me back. I could almost feel the tendrils worming into my muscles, tearing them apart.

'You'll need me on the other end,' Grim said from his seat. 'Someone's got to make sure you don't do anything I wouldn't do.'

'Oh, good,' Katherine said. 'That's reassuring.'

'I'll be careful,' I promised. 'But we have to do this. Especially with *her* involved.'

'Speaking of which, you might want to see this.' An holographic image grew around us. A figure, clad in a tightfitting suit. Slim, athletic, female. Her face obscured by a space helmet that resembled a black oval, the edges ridged with splinter-like serrations, swept back by the force of an invisible wind.

I recalled the voice on the phone and mentally stitched it together with the image. 'This was taken by a Harmony correspondent early in the Reaper War. Look familiar, Grim?'

'Yeah.' His voice was carefully neutral. 'Yeah, it's her. The Killer Chemist.'

It was maybe the only known image in existence. It was good news. But not the kind I needed right now. 'You said we have to work together,' I said to Katherine. 'Well, this is me trying. We've tried it your way. Now let's get this done. Before that museum is a smoking ruin.'

I couldn't read her. Was she weighing the risks? Weighing the consequences if I fouled this up? Or maybe weighing how much danger she'd be putting me in. If I was caught again, they'd kill me. But only after they got tired of torturing me. And if the Jackal held grudges like I think he did, it would not be for a very, very long time.

'If we do this,' Katherine said, and held up a finger before I could reply. '*If*, then there are some conditions. Understood?'

I made myself nod.

'I need to know you can do this,' she said.

'What do you mean?'

'I mean, what if it's your brother in there? What if it's between you and him, and he's about to plant a bomb?'

There were a hundred things I could have said. The stormtech nuzzled against my inner ribs. Telling me I didn't need Artyom, or Grim or Katherine or anyone else. That they were anchors holding me down. I wished I could shut my eyes and have all the demands on me fade away, but life never works like that.

'I'll do what needs to be done.' My voice sounded hard and rusty. When I'd first agreed to investigate the Reaper deaths and dived back into the world I swore I'd left behind, I knew it might come to choosing between my brother and my loyalty to the Reapers. That this could end with me and my brother

387

staring at each other down the barrel of a weapon. In a world of terrible men, I'd tried to be a good man for him. Instead, I'd hurt him beyond repair. Choosing the Reaper War over my brother was the biggest mistake I'd ever made. No matter how hard I tried to fix that mistake, as a direct consequence of it, I might have to choose taking the Suns down over saving him.

What good do you really learn from your mistakes if you never learn how to stop making them?

I glanced up at the snapshot of Jae Myouk-soon. Turning over all the misery she and her empire of drugs had caused. My muscles swelled and the stormtech gleamed blue all over my body. I was to blame for the situation my brother and I had landed ourselves in. No question of that. But so was Jae. So was Sokolav. So was my father. So were all the Suns. None of us are innocent, after all. And whatever happened to my brother at the end of this bloody affair, she'd answer for it. As would they all.

As would I.

36
Suit Up

The drop-off was in an apartment building located in north Starklands. One of those spacious and opulent penthouses you constantly saw in adboards. Half a dozen bedrooms, elaborate kitchen, state of the art appliances, a private chainship garage. I stared down the vertiginous drop, where the city blocks I'd walked to get to my own apartment had been turned into a glowing circuit board of streets and buildings. Aerial traffic whistled past lazily in the late afternoon sunlight. Harmony used this place as a safehouse for stormdealer informants, spending a fortune and a half to make them feel comfortable. After dumping our bags down, I realised another reason they'd splurged. A gaping chunk of the back wall had been gouged out, leading down into the hollow of the asteroid.

Compass isn't solid rock. Just as planetside buildings have basements and back doors for shipments and secure entries and exits, Compass has a network of tunnels, tubes, pipelines and accessways worming under its rocky flesh called the Hollow. Connecting to buildings and enterprises for deliveries, operative cells, emergency escape rooms, and quick access to spacedocks, the Hollow was a haven for criminals to use for hideouts and dead-drops, and also attracted thrill-seekers who got the smart idea of going on long and illegal expeditions through sectors of the asteroid only explored by drones. Little surprise Harmony had access.

Kowalski had told me to get cleaned up. After a quick scrub down in the jet-shower, I was dressing when I noticed myself in the floor-to-ceiling mirror and barely recognised the feral figure staring back. My hair tumbled down to my jaw. Black, bristly stubble was fast becoming a beard. My body was a series of sharp angles, muscles tight and straining beneath my scarred skin. Even after the shower, I could smell my own sickly-sweet reek. When I breathed I could feel the stormtech stretching with my lungs.

I was about to turn away when I noticed something in my eye. Grit? No. This was *inside* my eye. I pinched the flesh down for a better look. Small, blue tendrils were contorting in the white of my eye and fumbling at my iris like a writing blue sea anemone. I couldn't see them in my vision, but I could feel them like tiny worms squirming and thrashing inside me. Soon they'd crawl into my brain like a parasite chews through rotting cauliflower. I shut my eyes. The House of Suns wouldn't need to destroy the people I cared about; I could end up doing that all on my own.

I'd become what I was in the Reaper War. A savage, uncontrollable monster who only knew how to hurt and be hurt. Back then, I hadn't realised how bad it was going to get. But this time, I'd already walked this path with my body and knew I was in unmarked territory. My urges were less immediate, but more deeply worked into my body, harder to resist in the long run. The stormtech's a jealous organism, and I'd already withdrawn from it once. Maybe now it was taking the necessary steps to ensure I was locked and wrapped up too tightly in its smothering folds to ever tear myself free again.

Don't think about that. Can't think about that. This first.

I walked back into the kitchen. The printer had been

furiously at work well before we arrived. 'We've found you a route in through the Hollow,' Kowalski said, once we'd set up a connection. 'It's how the Academy takes deliveries. Only problem is, the whole museum's rigged up with cams, sensors and top-grade security systems. So you're going in a stealthskin.'

This sounded promising. 'A stealthskin?'

'Yes. They're not cheap, so be careful with it.'

'Since when was Harmony so parsimonious?'

'Since we started dealing with Sector Prone. Printing something that complex will takes hours and a lot of resources. So don't spill anything on it.'

'Oh, I wouldn't dare.'

The stealthskin was a white one-piece with a hexagonal pattern woven into the stitching, splashed with droplets of colour. Several layers thicker and sturdier than an underskin, equipped with textured padding along the elbows, knees, hands and buttocks. When you gripped it you could almost feel it gripping back, like a handshake. I stripped and Grim helped me pull it on. It was like sinking into the depths of cool water before it hardened over my flesh like drying wax. My body was soothed as the gellish substance inside made contact. Grim had to help me smooth it down, working out all the creases until the suit was leeched to me like a second skin. No loose spots. No places where you could even pinch the fabric. It seemed to have its own muscle system, moving in perfect accord with mine, as if designed for my body. I ran my gloved hands over it, grinning at the touch of flexible but firm material. I threw the hood over my face, the suit growing two black lenses over my eyes. A hiss of pressurised air as it sealed to my neck. It lacked the mechanical firmness of my armour, the flexible material unfamiliar against my skin. Wasn't sure how secure something like this could be. But as it charged up, pressuring firmly against my body, I could feel the warm strength coiled inside its nanofibres. Amplifying my abilities, boosting dexterity.

Wrapped up in this cutting-edge suit, I felt a whole new world of tactical agility flooding open before me. My hands and feet were rippling like a light display, before resolving into a mathematical pattern, tipped with thousands of gill-like slits. This thing came with gecko gloves, too.

And as a bonus? The alien plumbing inside me didn't shine through the fabric. Had to invest in this thing.

'It's syncing to your nervous system,' Kowalski explained as an electrostatic pulse crackled along the nape of my neck like liquid bristles. 'It'll conceal you and anything you've got equipped. Try it now.'

I toggled the option on my shib, my body melting abruptly into the background. Grim burst out laughing, as my mouth dropped open. My lenses blinked and a blood-coloured overlay scrolled down my vision. There I was, outlined in a greenish haze in my augmented vision. Just as well. Without the ability to unzip myself out of this suit I'd be royally screwed if I couldn't see my own hands. Cranking the overlay off, on lifting my arm there was a distinct oily smear in the air. 'Not complete invisibility, then.'

'By all means tell Kindosh to pour more funds into science and tech instead of politics, because you want a better suit,' Kowalski said. 'I firmly suggest you don't ruin this one. Be aware it doesn't have limitless energy, but it does self-recharge as long as you're moving, even if it's just flexing a muscle.'

I winked back into existence as the printer finished a weapons harness. I clipped the black straps over my back and torso, the buckles securing tight over my waist and thighs. 'We're sending you in armed, but no casualities,' said Kowalski as I attached my thin-gun and handcannon.

'Now where's the fun in that?' I asked wistfully.

Grim gripped my hand in his as a farewell. 'Take care of yourself, big guy.' He slapped me on the shoulder. 'Make sure no one gouges those pretty eyes out, understand? I've still got films to show you.'

'I'll do my best to keep my eyes ungouged,' I said.

I turned away into the Hollow.

Whoever described this place as a network needed a serious smack upside the head. It wasn't a network. Wasn't even a maze. It was a *labyrinth*. A vertical nightmare of a space-construction site: intersected with a webwork of wires, crane gantries, jutting beams, disused access tunnels, creaking ladders and so many walkways I didn't know which way was up. Superconductor cables and industrial pipes five metres wide and churning with internal fluids plunged in haphazard spirals. There were sporadic glimpses of sulphur-coloured lights in the darkness, but it was the night optic vision built into my lenses that lent me some semblance of guidance. That, and the tactical interface streaming in my shib in the form of a cyan pathway, leading me like a guide rope through the metal jungle. It'd be so easy to take a wrong turn, slip through the cracks and vanish into these infinite depths, knowing freedom was just on the other side of this rock, but with no way of finding your way out.

Inching up through a crumbling access tunnel that dated back to the Construction Era, I found my first skeleton and realised that plenty had done exactly that. Cold, slimy water dripped everywhere. The stink of mould and slime was ripe in the air. It was precarious going as I crawled over a rusty pipe that'd have shredded my skin to ribbons without the suit. When I slipped, I just managed to snag some loose cabling. My falling weight yanked one end out of its socket, my armpits straining as I swung on it like a vine to safety, with a mental apology to whichever restaurant or shop just lost power.

A corona of winking lights beamed above me like stars. On closer look, it was a series of server cabinets. Either someone had something digital to hide, or they didn't want to pay for extra storage space on their property. Whatever their reason, I had to spend a frustrating hour shimmying through suffocating cable ducts, and navigating through stacks of servers, databanks and substrates that crackled with heat and static. It was like crawling through the twitching guts of a whale. The temperature-regulating tubing was broken and I got hosed with a face-full of white, glossy gel. So much for not getting anything on the suit. Sweating, my back and bones aching, I finally pulled my body free into the welcoming chill of the tunnels.

Another hour of crawling through the darkness before I reached my waypoint. Ten metres below was a walkway leading to a door, haloed with a purple-blue outline. Using a beam as a fulcrum, I flicked on stealth mode, my body vanishing as I hopped down and approached carefully. I waited until a tubby woman came through, wheeling a gurney of box-shaped drones of Torven-design. I was directly in her line of sight but her gaze skimmed over me as she waddled by. I grinned behind my stealthskin. One gold star to Sector Prone.

I sliced past and found myself in a darkened hallway. Dull light glared across serried rows of Torven, Bulkava and Rhivik artefacts. Racked up behind chainglass were alien flora, wildlife, history, virtual models of their homeworlds, texts, weapons, gossamer fabrics, suits and armour, and other fragments of their technology and culture.

'I'm in!' I told Kowalski and Grim over the commslink.

'Good work,' Kowalski said. 'It's closed, but that doesn't mean no one's around. Keep us updated.'

I drew on the stormtech. My senses expanded in widening waves until I could hear anything around me. Feet slapping on the pavement outside. Autovehicles slamming by, the vibration echoing up through the walls like sonar. Foosteps and muffled voices in the immediate vicinity. I focused. Drawing tighter. Downstairs. Maybe two storeys down. I detected nothing from the next-door Academy.

It was like listening in for Harvest enemies on the battlefield all over again.

My ocular vision also allowed me to see the floors were crisscrossed with invisible tripwires and pressure pads. Not a problem. I pressed my hands to the tiled walls, feeling the hard suction against my fingers. I don't know how much I weigh, but I'm a big guy, and I doubted these little sticky paws would do any good. But I seemed light as a monomolecular blade as I scaled upwards, going hand over hand. I found myself grinning as I climbed diagonally across the walls, my hands and feet making little sucking noises. I felt like a high-tech animal, wrapped in killer gear light years ahead of the competition. I crawled above the lasers and ghosted past cams and security equipment, sticking upside-down to the ceiling and inching into a room dedicated to alien biology. Skeletons of aliens in various stages of growth, reconstructed with nanofilaments, grinned at me in the pale light. My harness groaned as I grappled around a stone pillar, the buckles tinkling.

The golden glow of subsurface powerlines in my oculars pointed towards the central office. I crawled past podiums for smaller species and incomplete collections donated by visiting aliens hoping to make their mark on Compass. Past artefacts unearthed from archaeological digs, belonging to civilisations yet to be named or discovered. I slipped through a cable duct and dropped silently into the ventricle of the xenomuseum office. It was a high-tech utility hub, the size of a small cruiser-liner cabin, and it was a mess. Gunmetal servers and hard drives were squeezed in countless rows and plugged into a smear of flexiscreens, guts of wiring and coolant tubing spilling out. Lurid red and aquamarine lights winked at me in the gloom. Even in my suit, the heat was unbearable. The projection of an unending virtual world, crammed into this tiny physical space, was complete.

I moved to get to work when I stopped. Sniffed. An excited glow spread through my body, the stormtech rocketing through me in feverish bursts. Even breathing through the suit fabric, the sickly-sweet smell was unmistakable. Like a dog, I followed the scent to some discarded crates. Nothing out of the ordinary, given how much of a wreck the room was, but I began sweating, my hands and feet going clammy. The crates were solid moonrock. You could unload a whole magazine of tungsten rounds into that and barely dent the surface. One whiff of the nearest crate and the earthy, mineral tang knocked me right back to Montenegro's little stashroom. I ran an invisible finger down the sides of another box and sniffed. My stomach muscles cramped. Stormtech. They'd used these boxes to transport stormtech.

'We've found it, guys,' I whispered. I was shaking. Whether with anticipation or fear I couldn't tell. I flipped the crate over and read out the serial number stencilled on the bottom.

Grim punched the number into his search engines. 'If these passed through any spaceport or dock, we'll have a register,' Kowalski said over the metallic pattering of keystrokes.

'Got it,' Grim said in triumph.

My hands tightened around the chest straps of my harness. 'What's the story, Grim?'

'These crates came through the Hovergardens. Spaceport 27B, Hangar Bay 1,' Grim said breezily. 'Now, all we gotta do is narrow down the timestamp, find the itinerary, and we'll have the ship's manifest, which stations it's stopped at, and who owns it. Smooth sailing from here, guys.'

'That can't be right,' I heard Kowalski mutter.

My hands wrapped harder around the harness. 'What is it?'

'There's no spaceport in the Hovergardens,' Kowalski said. The defeat was already evident in her voice. 'They've played us.'

I resisted the sudden urge to take my handcannon out and start laying into the cranking mesh of servers around me. I slumped into a seat, my teeth gritted. 'Another dead end.'

'Hold your horses,' Grim cautioned. Something in his voice supercooled my rage. 'We discovered earlier that the Suns were using Crimson Star Industries as a front, yeah?'

'The compound they used as their old hideout in the Warren?' I leaned forward in my seat, stitching the threads of logic together. 'You mean—'

'The spaceport must be there,' Kowalski cut in. I could imagine her and Grim glancing at each other over the blinking web of data. 'That's how they've been shipping stormtech to Compass. Through their private little spaceport.'

'A spaceport you don't know about?' Grim asked, incredulously.

'Compass is a big place, Grim. Some spaceports get mothballed over the years, retrofitted or reconstructed for bigger ones. Sometimes outright abandoned. The archives don't always keep up.'

'But we searched the place top to bottom!' I said.

'Not hard enough,' Kowalski said. 'We've got a lock on them. Let's move out, before they know we're onto them.'

I scraped off the seat. As I reached an arm out, I realised I'd been immobile for too long and the suit's energy system had guttered out. I was exposed. Time I was long gone.

Then I saw the coil of platinum cabling feeding into the wall from a few strategically placed crates. A box wired up to the operation, familiar-looking knobs gleaming.

Fusebombs.

It'd had been half a decade since I'd witnessed the devastating effects of one of these things but I was never going to forget the immolating blast of heat that fried every photoreceptor in my eye. The acrid stink of smoke. How quickly the explosion spread in burning arcs along the grasslands.

I swallowed and nudged a few server cabinets aside to unearth half a dozen more fusebombs, all rigged up and ready to blow.

Oh hell.

I heard the muffled whine of a thin-gun priming behind my back. 'Don't move. Throw down the weapons.'

A small tightness clenched around my stomach. The voice was muffled by a helmet, giving me no clue who it was. 'What gave me away?' I asked. I heard Kowalski and Grim curse as they cottoned on.

'Motion-detectors in the office. There was nothing on the cams so I almost didn't investigate. Now, get moving.'

I'd have kicked myself if I wouldn't get shot for doing it. I unstrapped the weapons from my harness and let them thunk to the floor. I raised my hands, fingers spread.

'Who are you?' he demanded. 'What do you want?'

'I was in the room when we offered you protection against terrorists. Remember that?' I chuckled without humour. 'You must have been laughing at us the whole time.' I turned around.

'I'm doing what I have to do,' hissed Joreth. The Torven's hand was shaking as he held the thin-gun, the laser targeting sights trained square on my chest. He stared at me through the transparent visor of his spherical helmet. He wore a bright-red suit, the glossy material flame-resistant.

'Explain to me how blowing up your own museum solves anything,' I said.

'Everything's possible with you people, isn't it?' Joreth sneered. 'So idealistic and naive.'

'You can't possibly be part of the Suns,' I said, aware Kowalski and Grim were listening to every word and would hopefully send backup. The alien's face twisted. Bullseye. 'Why do their dirty work for them?'

Joreth couldn't meet my eye. 'I have two daughters. I had to make a choice: blow up this building, or they'd destroy our home with them inside it.'

I flexed my muscles, clenching my fists, rebuilding the suit's energy charge. I wasn't going to stand here and let the Suns get away with this. Not again. Joreth's heart might not be in following through with this, but I know when someone's prepared to do whatever it takes to keep their family safe. Even shooting an unarmed prisoner to keep him quiet. 'We can help you.' I realised the *we* I meant was *Harmony*. 'Protect you. Smuggle you into hiding.'

'No. It won't work—'

'Of course it can work!' I hissed. 'Listen to me. We can have your whole family safely on a lungship tonight, departing to any outpost in any system you want.'

'It should have blown already,' Joreth murmured, as if he hadn't heard a word I'd said.

'Listen to me,' I said, injecting desperation into my voice.

'They must know something's wrong.' Joreth talked over me.

'Listen to me!' I begged.

Joreth's finger tightened around the trigger. 'They might be on their way to my house already.'

'Listen to me!' I yelled, panting hard. They couldn't do this to us. Not again. I spoke fast, aware every second we delayed risked alerting the Suns. 'Think about the message you're going to send. You'll be destroying an alien cultural archive, destroying a symbol of the Common's effort to welcome and

399

integrate other species. On behalf of a terrorist cult who hate their guts. The rise in stormtech? The Bluing Out? The attacks? That's them.' My mouth had turned uncomfortably dry. 'You're a Torven. Your people took decades to integrate into Compass, centuries to fill this place with your valuables. Why would you destroy it all now?'

'None of that means anything if they kill my family,' Joreth said.

'There's another way,' I begged.

'There isn't,' the alien said, almost kindly. 'I'm sorry.'

But I wasn't.

I rushed him. My suit had fully recharged and I clawed at the alien's arm with invisible hands, trying to knock the weapon away. The surface of his suit was slippery, letting him wrestle free, firing twice. Even if I were invisible, at point-blank range he couldn't miss, and both shots punched into my shoulder. I was slammed into the wall with bone-jarring force, my head knocking against something metal. Stars swarmed my vision. I collapsed, visible again, clamping a hand to my bleeding shoulder. Blood soaked my suit as I crawled to my knees, groaning. I felt blue worming up my chest like ivy climbing in fast-forward, circling the injury and smothering the pain. The bullet was popped out as the stormtech welded my flesh together, faster than I'd ever known it.

Joreth watched me with narrowed eyes down the holographic sights of his thin-gun, before lowering the weapon and backing away. 'Joreth, wait, don't,' I begged, still on my knees. My words were swallowed up in the metallic echo of the door slamming shut and sealing me inside.

37

Burning

I reeled to my feet, shoulder throbbing in agony.

'Vak!' Katherine's voice was filled with fear. 'We're coming to get you!'

'Get out of there!' Grim yelled.

'I can't,' I told them, my heart sinking into my guts. No windows. No exit, no way out. The cable duct gaped mockingly above me, at least three metres too high to reach. No amount of stormtech would armour me from the searing heat of a fusebomb explosion. My flesh would melt like wax under a stream of supercharged fire, leaving me a smouldering pile of guts and gristle.

'No! There's got to be something!' Katherine panted. 'Vakov!'

But I was screwed. Fusebombs have a thirty-second countdown. Assuming Joreth had set it off when he shut the door, I was almost out of time.

But my body's survival instinct wouldn't let me quit and the gears kept spinning.

I scooped up my weapons and bundled my body into the largest of the crates. For the first time in my life I wished I wasn't such a big guy as I crammed myself into the rock case. Squeezing the weapons between my legs, I sealed the case shut and gritted my teeth as my injury scraped against the metal, sour sweat dripping down to where the harness buckle was rubbing between my shoulders. How long was I going to be—

There was a flaring, hellish explosion, swallowing up the world in a bone-shaking roar, loud as Harvest artillery fire. My guts leaped into my mouth as the crate went flipping into the air and slammed hard against the wall. My head collided with metal and my mouth filled with blood. I almost bit my tongue in half, choking as smoke seeped in.

I'd survived.

But when I tried to push the crate open, it wouldn't budge. Sealed shut. My eyes were watering from the smoke. I heard the distinct crackle of burning wood and realised I'd locked myself in my own coffin. I twisted in the choking darkness, finding the corners, the crate's weak points. Metal ground against my spine as I manoeuvred myself around, steadily drawing on the stormtech, and pushing against both sides of the crate. Heat built against my skin and I felt my legs, arms and back strengthen, an animal growl tearing out of my throat. I raked in a breath, choking smoke pouring down into my lungs. The next few breaths were going to be my last.

Something gave under my fist. I drew back my hand and punched where the seal would be. The metal groaned as it dented. I punched again, again, again, my knuckles tearing open and bleeding. I swore I felt a bone breaking, but between one blow and the next the stormtech had already repaired it. The seal gave a splintering crack and I tumbled out into a burning inferno. The fire was barely visible through the cloud of smoke. I coughed and heaved as clawed up my weapons. The door had been damaged in the explosion, the tattered remains bursting apart as I powered through. The groaning stairs collapsed under me as I raced down them, sending me flying, almost me skewering on a chunk of rebar. I staggered, choking and spluttering through the roaring blaze. Everything was a fiery red smudge of heat. Smouldering beams collapsing around me, spitting hot wooden shrapnel. Glass and windowpanes shattering in my face. The fire spreading as it swiftly cut off all exits.

There: a slice of daylight ahead, stabbing through the smoke. Not knowing if I was on fire and not caring, I leaped over a burning table and I *hurled* myself at the front door in a great crunch of splintering wood, spilling face-first onto the footpath.

I rolled onto my back, raking in fresh air, too exhausted to move as I watched the xenomuseum surrender to the damage. The walls were already blackening, roof caving in, great sheets of windows shattering and sliding off like cooked flesh off a bone. A scream of tortured wood as beams collapsed. Dark smoke coiling skyward to be sucked up by the air vents. Emergency drones whirled down to stop the blaze spreading to other parts of the Academy, but centuries too late to save anything inside.

I might have found our next lead, but I hadn't prevented the House of Suns from obtaining their victory. They'd destroyed the xenomuseum in their act of planned terrorism. That was its own kind of failure.

I found some reserves of energy to scoop myself up and stumble away. Everything ached. My fist and shoulder were both bleeding. A puddle of sweat and blood had congealed around my feet. I probably had severe burns. But I'd have become a kebab if I'd stayed in that box, so I was going to take my injuries in stride.

And that's when I noticed the crowd staring.

They'd been focused on the burning building. Until I, the lone survivor, came bursting out of it wearing a high-tech suit with weapons strapped to my back. Now, half a hundred people were staring at me with an expression I wasn't liking one bit.

'It wasn't me.' I barely recognised the sandpapery growl that clawed out of my throat, attempting to form words. 'It wasn't me.'

A few looks were exchanged. Fists tightening. Anger building on faces. Someone spat. They'd been primed for this moment by the escalating Reaper and skinnie incidents, by other attacks that looked awfully similar to this. 'It wasn't me,' I choked out again. A chunky ball of stormtech had wedged in my throat and wouldn't go away, my voice turned husky. There was an ebbing in my elbow where I'd been cut getting out of the crate. I twisted it around to examine it. The blood oozing out of the wound wasn't red. It was blue. Splattering to the ground like dye.

Oh no.

'Terrorist dog,' someone shouted to sounds of agreement.

'You people destroyed that bank!' someone else roared.

'No!' I roared, but no one was listening. No one *wanted* to listen. Easier to leap to assumptions then let anything dissaude them. I'd tried to save these people and they were about to turn on me.

'Get him!' someone shouted.

Screw this.

I unslung my scattershot and levelled it at the crowds. 'Get back!' I roared. The crowd gasped. The two men approaching me paused, but didn't back off. I was so focused on them I didn't notice the one sneaking up behind me. He grabbed me by my harness, heaved, and sent me sprawling across the hard concrete, scraping my wounds. Screams erupted as I scrambled for the scattershot, slamming my elbow into the assailant's side before he could attack me again, scooping the weapon up. Another shocked gasp went up. The act of self-defence reading as unprovoked violence, filling the gaps in their minds supported by their own prejudices. I backed up, fresh pain throbbing down my joints, my aim wavering between my assailant and the crowd. It'd be so, so easy to pull the trigger, blowing his skull apart, blood spraying and splattering over the belligerent crowd. It'd teach them not to mess with Reapers. Make these ungrateful bastards respect the men who'd saved their lives in the war.

'I didn't do it,' I said, my voice an angry sob, fighting to regain control of myself. 'I didn't do it, I didn't do it. They did it. They did it all.'

But no one was listening, because mobs only ever see red. I stared down the sights of the scattershot at the crowd. Slowly backing away until I could duck back behind a building. I activated the suit's recharging cloak and my body evaporated into a hazy shimmer. I flattened myself against the cool metalwork, members of the crowd stalking past, their bravery miraculously rediscovered. I shimmied up the walls until I reached the rooftop, then squatted on my haunches along the parapet, chest heaving, surveying the scene of desolation before traversing the rooftops towards home.

38

Stormblood

I've always hated space travel. Being strapped into a military frigate in orbit over a war-torn planet doesn't do much to ease my prejudices. If I thought I could look down without puking my guts up, I'd see the stormy planet of Renchio below. The skies blossoming with artillery fire like little wounds. The clouds crackling with bursts of nuclear ordnance. Our ships have been outfitted with bleeding-edge stealth-tech, so we and the squadron of fighter-ships pass unseen through space as we utilise Renchio's gravity to slingshot to the other side of the planet.

We've spent months tracking the Canine King down, shredding his outposts and smashing his men on the battlefield. With every week, Harvest's grip on Renchio weakens, and his resources with it. Now, we've chased him down to a major Harvest outpost on the outskirts of a city. We break them here, and we'll smash a serious dent in Harvest's control of the planet. If we kill the warlord, it'll be a borderline victory.

The rest of my fireteam sit around me in a corner of the ship. Ordnance, suits and weapons are webbed to the ceiling. The rest of the large military vessel is choked full of fireteams, squads, air-support troopers and miscellaneous Harmony personnel clad in bulky armour outfitted with glowing lights and whirring machinery. In the semi-dark we look like a factory of battle-robots.

This drop is Reapers-only. We're diving face-first into the darkest of Dead Zones. I saw corvettes, fighter-ships and attack drones, artillery being prepped for the operation. We're packing heavy for this one.

I can't wait.

I strain against the reinforced seat harness, too restless to remain seated, knowing that standing up in a storm like this is a death wish. And yet I can't stamp the urge from my mind. The aircraft shudders with sudden turbulence. Strapped tight next to me, Alcatraz's faceplate almost knocks against mine. The holographic readouts around us groan with warnings. 'You seeing what I see?' I ask, tagging a Drop Trooper who's pacing and clawing at his body. His armoured fists slam into the hull, leaving massive dents. He's got a hungry look on his face I'm not liking one bit.

It reminds me of Cable smashing that Harvester's head in until his skull went soft.

And I'm starting to feel the same way. My hands are twitching by my sides. My breathing's gone heavy and fast, like oxygen's in short supply. I'm covered in cold sweat. I'm constantly agitated, an itch in me I can never scratch. Nothing I haven't felt a hundred times already during the war. Only before I could always redirect it. Channel my energy and adrenaline towards our operation with sharpshooter precision. Now, it's like grenades are going off in my body, spraying shrapnel in wild bursts and harming anyone within range. And I'm the one pulling the pin.

When Alcatraz doesn't answer, I know he's feeling the same way. The whole fireteam is. I can smell the stormtech inside them, inside me, growing thicker and more succulent. It should make us better soldiers, shouldn't it? But there's something increasingly wild about my body. Something primal I don't completely have control over.

'I'm not sure we ever had control over it,' Alcatraz says when I share my theories with the rest of Ghost.

Ratchet stops fidgeting with his seat straps. 'What the hell's that supposed to mean?'

'Stormtech makes us addicted to adrenaline. Stands to reason eventually it'll make us do things we don't want to do for that extra kick.'

'They said that would never happen in basic training!' Cable says. 'That our bodies would adapt like any other augmentation.'

'Except it's not an augmentation,' Myra says. The stormtech shivers warm and wet up my chest, like it knows what we're talking about. 'It's alien, and Harmony knows nothing about what it's doing to us.'

'It makes us good soldiers,' Alcatraz said. 'Soldiers who do what no others can. That's why we're on these suicide missions. Marching into Dead Zones, chasing the Canine King, dropping into this battle in the middle of a storm. They're deliberately getting our adrenaline levels to soar. They wind us up, then turn us loose on the enemy, sit back and watch us rack up some serious damage.'

I want to deny it. But it makes too much sense. 'Those Intelligence Officers watching us train,' I say with a sinking heart. 'The post-operation assessments they've been asking us to do. Getting us to wear our armour as much as possible. They're studying us like lab rats to maximise the stormtech's potential. Even if it kills us.'

Fury pours off the others.

'They lied to us,' Ratchet growls. He's starting to shake. 'All this time, they lied to us.'

'We're freaks,' Cable whispers huskily.

'This changes nothing,' Alcatraz says.

'What?' Myra snaps.

'We haven't changed.' Alcatraz looks at us one by one. 'We're still Reapers. We're still family. They can't take that away from us. We're still going to do right by each other. Until we're dirt and dust.'

Slowly, our collective anger dials back down. 'Dirt and dust,'
we repeat, one by one.

'So we go down here and we fight like hell,' Alcatraz says. We
cross our arms over our chests in salute, a tight lump in my throat.
'Not for Harmony. For each other.'

There's that familiar tightness in my gut as we drop out of
orbit and into the planet's gravity well. We plunge through a sky
choked with oceans of boiling clouds. Spears of lightning crackle
down. Sporadic rain spits in rapid bursts across the landscape.
The friendly squadrons scream ahead of us. We shudder in their
turbulence. A siren starts shrieking. White strobes slash through
the blackness, showing snatches of restless Reapers stirring in
their seats. The pilot announces we're fast approaching our drop-
point. I unbuckle and stand with the rest of Ghost, our helmets
sliding down over our faces.

Technicians strap us into the drop tubes; a heavy frame clamps
tight around my back, shoulders and chest, before I'm slotted into
a cylinder. A human bullet in a chamber. My armoured body's
sheathed in metal; the space around me ringed with old-fashioned
white and red lights. The stormtech's burning through me like
wildfire. I'm ready to tear out my weapons and start shredding
Harvesters to pieces.

The interior flares with lights like glowing blood vessels.
Warning icons blink up on my HUD. I'm suddenly spat out of the
chamber and into the air. The wind screams past my helmet. The
world's a dark smudge. Rain hammers against my armour and
faceplate. I straighten my arms and legs, activating my thrust-
ers and burning towards the looming highrise and surrounding
buildings.

Around me, fellow Reapers are lit up in golden outlines,
nosediving through the storm, my fireteam in bright green. Long-
range gunfire streaks skyward towards us. A Reaper next to me

is blasted straight out of the sky, cooked alive in his own armour, careening as he's sent spinning to earth.

In front of me, Ratchet yells down the commslink. He's been hit. He's alive, but his thrusters are dead and he's spinning off-course. I grit my teeth as I push everything my armour's got into full-throttle and charge after him. The sky spasms with lightning and streaks of red gunfire, shedding light on a rushing river beneath us. The ground slams up as I grab Ratchet around the waist, hook my body around his, and brake us both as hard as I can. I crank my shielding so hard I can see a blackness oozing out of my armour like ferro-fluid, cocooning me in an additional layer.

We hit the river hard enough that I black out for a second. My armour tightens around me, sealing against the water. The surface shimmers like mercury above me. Teeth gritted, I kick off the muddy banks, the stormtech lending me the energy to burst through the surface, hauling Ratchet with me. Vision swimming, I activate the emergency override key that Reapers only give to their fireteams. Ratchet's armour unlocks and he pukes out a chestful of water then sprawls next to me. I help seal him back up in armour, extend a hand and haul him to his feet.

We're just in time. Two Harvesters climb the hill, rifles already unshouldered and levelled in our faces. We run together, acting on pure, frantic terror, our bodies supercharged with fury, mud splattering under our boots. At this close proximity, I feel every round rippling against my shielding. A bullet grazes my helmet. I smash into the first Harvester with a loud crunch. His rifle goes off inches from my head, a scream of light in the dark. I break his arm over my shoulder and slam him so hard against the ground he bounces back up. I whip around to see Ratchet being shoved face-first in the muddy water, his visor smashed, suffocating. I tear the Harvester off my friend and he turns on me, slamming his helmet against mine. The world clangs and rattles as I crash backwards through the mud and the Harvester blasts me with a kind of

*military-grade electropole. My body shudders as I'm electrocuted.
I can smell my body hair burning. The Harvest slips and staggers
over in the mud and howling rain, electropole raised towards me.
Dripping with mud, Ratchet leaps on the Harvester's back, stabbing his blade hilt-deep between the Harvester's shoulder blades.
He screams, tottering sideways, Ratchet growling like a frenzied
animal. I dive for the dropped handgun, mud spraying across my
visor. Fingers numb, I fumble it upwards and blast a planet-sized
hole in the Harvester's throat. He splatters and dies in the mud
with a wet gurgle. Ratchet swears, thrusting his combat knife in
and out of the Harvest's back.*

'Ratchet,' I pant.

*'What!' he growls, ripping the blade out and planting it down
again.*

'I think we got him.'

'Oh. Yeah.'

*We take the time to retrieve our weapons and run for the rest
of Ghost, the siege already well in progress. A tangle of platforms
and runways lead to a scattering of soaring highrises that feed
into the mainframe of the central building complex.*

*There're no formations, no attack plans, no strategy in place.
It's little knots of chaos, exploding over into one big tangle of
carnage. Space Battalion Reapers are smashing apart a cluster
of Harvesters blocking the entrance to the compound. Harvesters
perched up on a walkway pour volleys of gunfire down on Reapers
hacking their way up a bottlenecked stairwell. A Drop Trooper's
head disappears, his legs following, plasma fire carving the rest
of his fireteam up in burning chunks. Squadrons of gunships and
fighter-ships are entangled in chaotic dogfights above us, railguns
streaking in furious explosions and lighting up the whole battlefield. They rake the ground with searing plasma streaks a kilometre
long, turning metal into glass, decimating buildings, vaporising
Harvesters and Reapers alike. I dive for cover. A smelter-grenade*

explodes in a furious ball of fire, spraying out what looks like luminescent orange goo. Whoever touches it screams as it eats through armour, muscle, tendons.

I charge, the fighting drawing me in like a gravity well. Somehow, I know how to find the thick of the battle. My HUD reconfigures to the scattershot clutched in my hands. I pull the trigger, tearing mouthfuls of concrete from the walls, blasting Harvesters on the other side. Dust swirls. Rain punches down. I take out a Harvester charging for Ratchet, swerve around to hack at another and sending him smashing sideways. A Berserker tries to send a jacketed slug through my chest, but I'm ducking and weaving, a stray streak of blue blaster-fire searing by my shoulder. I slam my elbow into his jaw, teeth rattling loose, before nailing three slugs into his chest, blood spraying on someone's visor. I'm spinning around. Eyes darting. Hands clenching. Ready for the next target.

The stormtech growls with warning. I jerk sideways, a railgun blast arcing past my neck and erupting a junction box, blue sparks showering out. A Harvester chops at me with his combat knife and clangs against a pillar, wood splinters spraying in my face. Ratchet hacks at him with his blade, gets him down but turns to be overpowered by two more. I rush to help him but a shuddering blast in my back sends me crashing down, my armour clanging against the concrete. A forest of legs around me, helmets knocking, arms reaching for me, trying to claw me up. Hostile faces swarming above me, the glint of knives, mud showering. A boot slams into my face. There, another Reaper about four metres away, in the same position next to me. He turns to notice me just as the blade comes stabbing down, punching through his visor and pinning him there. He goes limp. More bodies slam down between us and he disappears. Hands lock around my legs, more boots against my helmet, scattering stars across my vision. Ratchet is gone, *swallowed up by battle. Bodies piled up around me, grunting, twitching, the world a deafening smear of anger.*

Someone pours engine solvent onto my helmet. It condenses on my faceplate, leaving oily streaks on my chest. Armoured figures slam down on top of me, crushed against me in battle.

I'm in a body pile. We've seen this before, so many times. If the weight of armoured men doesn't crush me, I'll burn alive when Harvesters torch the pile. I struggle, thrashing against others. Legs kicking out, cracking against my visor, stomping my hand into the mud, trying to keep me down. Sweat trickling into my eyes, fogging my vision.

I'm dead.

I'm dead.

No.

I pour all my fury into the stormtech, demanding everything it's got. It goes ripping down unearthed parts of my body and slithering deeper and deeper inside. I convulse, a sudden electricity jumpstarting my body, and I'm tearing upwards, out of the body pile like I'm swimming through it. Fighting my way through it. Fists shattering into helmets, smashing across jaws, clawing at faces. Metal crunches and dents as I reach the edge and grapple with a Harvester, bloody teeth gnashing. I slam my helmet into his throat, hear him wheeze as I throw him sprawling backwards and smashing apart a barricade, splinters showering. I sense a knife being plunged down and grab the Berserker's arm mid-strike. I rip the blade out of his hand and stab him through the chest and out the other side. I kick him backwards, his legs thrashing as he goes spinning over the edge. I chop at a hand trying to claw at me, the arm going limp and it's owner roaring, and I lunge forward and open up his side with a hard slash. I reel out of the way of a blade thrust and kick the assailant staggering sideways and slipping in the mud. I rip out my sidearm as he rears back up to stab me again, blasting him before wheeling around to shoot

413

another Harvester flanking me, the two of them twisting as they go down. Splattered with mud, I burst out of the fray, handgun raised, teeth bared, heart pumping.

I see what's happening.

We've made a massive push for the central building, at the cost of many men. Reapers and Harvesters alike are being cut down around me. Screaming and splashing into the mud. The air's heaving with crisscrossing gunfire. Marble pillars vaporized to ash, metal exploding in glowing-hot chunks. Corridors choked with the crush of desperate men. Entire fireteams of Reapers so desperate to tear down their enemies they run straight into a line of fire, heedless as they're punched full of smoking holes. An injured Reaper is still fighting, refusing to retreat, even as he's swarmed by a squad of Berserkers, cutting him in half in front of his fireteam. Men peel away from cover, preferring to dive into the fray instead of quietly flanking their enemy. A Reaper sprays an autocannon in wild shuddering bursts, bringing an entire concrete walkway smashing down on a dozen Harvesters.

I watch an entire battlefield go insane.

Harmony did all this.

They knew what we'd become.

They lied and deceived and tortured us.

All to make the perfect soldiers.

I look down at the blood coating my hands, a slow horror building in my throat.

I'm exactly what Harmony wanted me to be.

A monster.

We win the battle, but there's no joy. No celebration. We're broken ghosts, staring at the mangled corpses sprawled at our feet. Ratchet's sitting by himself, eyes bloodshot, shoulders slumped. I want to go over and comfort him but I'm afraid of what he might do. What I might do.

414

I've heard the Canine King's been killed. I don't know who did it or how they got him. The mad warlord is just another corpse on the pile. He's gone, and we're left to survive this hell.

We're all running on borrowed time. Our bodies just refuse to accept it.

Reapers prowl the battlefield in a daze. Saws glinting as some try to remove their teammates from the smoking shells of their armour. Others just staring off into the distance, like there's an answer out there somewhere.

There's a commotion beyond the edge of the concrete runway. I frown and scrape off the ledge I'm sitting on, crunch across the spent ammo and broken ordnance. A massive Reaper in armour is stumbling around a muddy clearing piled with the dead. Shovel-like hands twitching by his sides. He's got post-war cravings. He – or his stormtech – doesn't want to let the adrenaline high go, desperate to find a way to reclaim it. It's a feeling I know very well.

Out of nowhere, the Reaper turns and smashes a fellow Reaper across the head. His neck bends at an unnatural angle as he crashes down, dead before he splashes across the mud. My mouth goes dry as he kills another. And another. A Drop Trooper puts up a good fight, but the Reaper knocks him to the mud and kicks him in the side of the head until he stops moving.

He's massacring his own side.

As one, Ghost and a dozen other Reapers run down the muddy slope towards him. When we get closer, my heart drops and lands soggily at the bottom of my guts.

It's Cable.

Ratchet tries to calm him. But the man who carried that refugee girl for twenty kilometres slams his fist into Ratchet's chest, throwing him back into the mud. Ratchet's head cracks against a stone. Gasps and yells ripple along the crowd. Cable reaches down and grabs Ratchet by the neck and lifts him back up. Ratchet's legs thrashing as Cable tries to choke the life out of him.

He freezes.

Because Alcatraz has a pistol pressed up against his forehead.

The sticky circuitry inside Cable reconfigures. Reassesses the threat to his life against the lure of the high. I see his eyes uncloud. He drops Ratchet to the ground.

'You're my brother,' Alcatraz shouts into the pouring rain. More Reapers are gathering. Lightning glints off their armour and faceplates. 'But I will not let you do this. I won't let you kill us. I won't let you betray yourself.'

I swallow. We swore we'd protect each other from whatever the planet threw at us.

I never thought that could include each other.

'Don't make me do it, Cable,' Alcatraz begs. His trigger-hand shakes. 'Please. Don't do it.'

Horror curdles over Cable's face as the realisation hammers home. He sees the broken bodies of the men he called brothers. Only hours ago, he fought with them. Now he looks down at the dripping blood coating his hands, feels the stormtech swirling in his system, hungry for more. The same stormtech swirling inside me, inside all of us.

He reaches out to Ratchet. Ratchet scuttles backwards, his chest heaving, his throat red and eyes bloodshot. Cable freezes. His hand drops. Ratchet watches it drop and looks up at his friend with fear and trepidation. Cable blinks long and hard, delaying reality for one more second. Stares at the gun against his head.

All he wanted to do was find a home and a family after his had been destroyed. A place he could feel at peace in his heart. Feel safe.

'I didn't mean to,' Cable whispers.

'I know,' Alcatraz says.

'I never wanted to. I never . . . I couldn't . . . I don't—'

'I know.'

'Tell them for me. Tell them I fought to the end.'

'I will,' Alcatraz says. A tear trickles down his cheek. 'You're my brother, always. To dirt and dust.'

'To dust and dirt,' Cable repeats. He steps back. Watching with big, gentle eyes, the gathered Reapers around him. Knowing they can't unsee what he's done. That he can't undo what's been done. Instead he crosses his arms in the Reaper salute and takes a long look at the fireteam he fought and bled and laughed with. He turns and walks away.

I try to follow him, but Alcatraz and Myra grab me. 'Let me go!' I roar.

'It's what he wants,' Alcatraz whispers.

'It's not right,' I say. Alcatraz yanks me back. 'It's not right.'

'His last choice, Vakov. Let him have it.'

Tears fog my eyes as Cable sinks to his knees in the middle of the field, watched by thousands of Reapers. Tears trickle down his cheeks, drip down his chin. He tilts his face up to the howling dark, into the pouring rain of his homeplanet. As if searching for an exit, an escape in the cloudy sky somewhere.

When he doesn't find one, my friend sticks his service pistol under his chin and pulls the trigger.

We bury Cable by the cliffs facing the mountain valley, sloping down to curving hills and sweeping grasslands. We bury him in his armour, next to the Reapers he killed. We agree not to remember him in his final moments, but to honour his courage and sacrifice. He was a Reaper until the very end.

We've all seen the alien monstrosity fused for ever into our bodies for what it really is. The stormtech gives us wings, but takes the sky away. It'll help us survive this war, but at what cost? Will I even recognise myself at the end? The things we've done, the things we're going to have to do.

Harmony got the soldiers they wanted. In exchange, we're going to be fighting an unending war of our own. Hell of a price to pay.

I'm sitting by the edge of the cliff with the rest of Ghost. Dawn's beginning to claw its way across the sky. Shavings of light slip over the windswept mountains and rocky hills.

'I wish he could have seen this,' Myra says.

Tears bead in Ratchet's eyes. 'If I hadn't backed away, if I told him it was okay, maybe he'd—'

'No. No,' I tell him. 'This isn't on you. It's on them. It's on this stuff inside us.'

'We've got a choice, don't we? All of us.' Ratchet wipes his nose. 'What if it's me next? Or you?'

How the hell do you answer something like that?

'Cable told me about a word they used on this planet.' Alcatraz talks without looking up. 'It describes someone willing to venture out into the worst storms to help others. No matter how hard or brutal or bitter the weather, they had the bravery and guts to do what needed to be done for the people they cared about.' He rakes in a long breath. 'I don't know the original word. Only the translation. Stormblood.'

He spreads his arms to the stormy sky above, distant lightning forking down as he thumps his chest. 'That's what we are, every single one of us Reapers. We're not fireteam Ghost. We're not Tusk Battalion. We're stormblood. And as part of our new pact, I want you guys to promise me something. If it happens to us, we have the guts to end it. Before we become monsters.'

I close my eyes. The stormtech slithering through me like toxic water, turning everything damp. 'Deal,' I say.

'Deal,' Myra mutters.

'Deal,' Ratchet whispers.

'And on the flip side, if one of us gets killed, we hunt down whoever did it,' Alcatraz says. 'Even if we have to go to the ends of the universe. We do what needs to be done.'

'Deal,' I say.

'Deal,' Myra mutters.

'Deal,' Ratchet whispers.

A rippling echoes soundlessly through the dawning skies, shuddering through my bones. A Harvest dreadnought slams into existence above us. Stark blue with a zigzagging orange streak, it's arrow-shaped design typical of Harvest warships. It's followed by a second dreadnought, its engines burning from warpspace travel, then a smattering of ancillary warships, frigates, and military-class corvettes.

'The bastards already heard what happened to their outpost,' Myra growls.

The stormtech's a biotech bomb, ticking down with every combat encounter. But it's also saved me countless times. Saved my fireteam. Armoured me against the hell that's hammering down on us all.

I could ignore it and die right here.

Or I could gamble again and lean on it until I can't any longer.

I gather the squirming dark monstrosity up, letting it writhe and twitch inside me, fusing its sticky blue threads tighter and deeper into my body.

Alcatraz stands and looks back at the stirring crowd of Reapers scattered around the captured outpost. 'Many of our friends and squadmates are dead,' he yells. 'This planet is dead. They killed it.' He points towards the incoming battle fleet. Reapers pick themselves up, turn towards him in the sunlight. 'We can lick our wounds and mourn. Or we can make their deaths mean something. No one will fight for us. The Common will never remember what we did here today, what we do tomorrow. But we will. Because we're a family, until we're dirt and dust. Are you with me?'

One by one, hundreds of Reapers cross their fists across their armoured chests. A promise. A declaration of undying loyalty. Alcatraz makes an addition to his fireteam name, so it reads as

Ghost Fireteam – Stormblood. One by one, hundreds of Reapers make the same change, the icons popping up in my HUD, until we're all one unit. One family. One shared promise between us all.

The sun glints off Alcatraz's visor as he turns back to us. 'Are you with me?' he asks quietly, my dog tag gleaming around his neck.

'Always,' Myra says with a sniff.

'Always,' Ratchet says, his tears leaving muddy tracks down his face.

'Always,' I croak out, my own tears coming.

We gather in a tight hug. Holding each other against this never-ending nightmare. Then we slide our helmets on, scoop up our weapons and move out, marching with our fellow Reapers into whatever fresh hell's waiting for us. We're all broken, no question about it. But, for now, we're still human, and we're going to make what we do count.

I don't know if the stormtech will let me live long enough to fulfil my promises, but I'm going to fight until my dying breath to do it. That's what a Reaper would do.

I'm stormblood.

Until I'm dirt and dust.

39

Back to Base

I didn't want to watch the news. But it's not like you get a chance to decide what people say about you. There was no footage of me, but plenty of descriptions of *an armed Reaper who threatened a crowd of innocent bystanders* and was now *a suspect in this appalling act of cultural terrorism*. Several very distressed eyewitnesses were babbling that I'd been about to gun them all down. The stories were getting crazier and crazier, prompted by newscasters feigning duty but delighting in the public outrage, exaggerating and distorting the events to boost their ratings, sensationalizing tragedy, their race for the headlines churning nuance and fact into obscene fiction. It would have been worrying enough, but became anxiety-inducing when I remembered the hatred seething from the crowd as they stepped towards me. It was hard not to correlate the events with two recent reports of hate-related crimes perpetrated against stormtech users.

Was it my fault? I'd played into the House of Suns' hands. Seemed impossible not to shoulder some of this blame. That's a Harmony trick: to swoop in, do terrible damage, and then eschew any responsibility.

Kowalski didn't seem to think so when I called her up. 'If you hadn't been there, we'd be none the wiser,' she said. 'We have a lead now, and you're okay. That's all that matters.'

'We need to get over to the Warren,' I told her.

'Got men heading over already. But we can't afford to waste time. You and Grim swing by as soon as you're able.'

Grim helped me strip out of the stealthskin. The thick fabric made a liquid squelching as it peeled from my sweaty skin, like tape being torn away. I noted the inner suit was soaked blue with sweat and blood as I slipped back into my underskin. But besides the stormtech-healed bullet wound, I'd hardly any injuries to show for my work. The bruises, burns and even the fractured knuckles had all disappeared and my body knew what to thank. What to depend on next time. There was a sweet, sticky stench in the air. The stronger the stormtech, the stronger the smell. I could feel my pores clogging with it, the clammy odour caked and plastered over me like a second layer of slimy skin. My body already responding to the arousing smell.

My senses had been sharpening ever since the arena fight, but now everything was turned up to eleven. Every clatter, shout, smell, gust of air was a micro-assault on my body. Too much for my mind to compartmentalise.

I slipped back into my armour, reassured by the solid, hard surface of the suit. The familiar tightness clamped hard over my back, my shoulders, locking around my thighs and legs, the balancing chemicals releasing. The tendrils squirmed and pulsed against my flesh, in my armpits, under the soles of my feet, combating the stormtech writhing inside my inner flesh. I breathed out in slow, controlled bursts, letting my muscles loosen. My body temperature dialed back down. The smell wafting out of me began to lose its potency.

But I still didn't dare remove the armour, still keeping a careful gauge on my body as Grim and I hurried back to the abandoned House of Suns compound in the war-torn Latin Quarter. Standing on the concourse where I'd been held at gunpoint started to dredge the memories back, my body stirring up with it. Not helping.

Kowalski was waiting for us inside.

'It could still be a dead end,' I said as we headed down the halls.

'Don't give them too much credit,' Kowalski said as I removed my helmet. 'We're going to tear the place apart.'

I wasn't so sure what we'd find this time around, given we'd failed on the first try. And then I remembered our simple, singular addition.

We had Grim.

We parked him in the server room, doing his Deep Dive. He was barely ten seconds in before he resurfaced with a result. 'It was buried deep in the mainframe metadata,' Grim told us, smearing the dust off his hands and across the thighs of his skeleton underskin. 'They totally erased any traces of its existence, but forgot to erase any traces of them erasing it. Amateur move.'

Katherine shook her head. 'Our people spent weeks trawling through the mainframe.'

I stepped towards him. 'Grim, what did you find?'

As if in answer, we heard unseen mechanisms squirming beneath our feet and echoing somewhere deep in the compound. Grim sliced between us, following the sound with a childish eagerness. 'If you good people will follow me . . .'

He led us to some mothballed storage unit on the edge of the compound in time to see an impenetrable-looking wall irising backwards. Layer upon layer of armoured latticework, vacuum-approved barricades, and firearm-absorbing barriers peeled back with echoing steel clangs, like layers of metallic fruit, finally revealing a spiralling corridor. Looking at each other, we walked through a cold access tunnel until we faced an armoured door. White block letters gleamed on silver chainmetal.

Spaceport 27B, Hangar Bay 1.

Unholstering our weapons, we glanced at each other and entered. We were standing in the smallest spaceport on Compass; so small it resembled a rudimentary docking bay. One landing pad, one control central office, one row of docking berths, crudely carved out of asteroid rock.

And sitting in the middle of the landing pad was the chainship we were hunting.

Kowalski clutching at my arm. 'We did it, boys,' she said as she turned to plant a kiss on my cheek. 'You did it, Vak.' She turned down to Grim, patting him on the shoulder. 'You too, Grim. Both of you got us here.'

Colour had returned to Katherine's cheeks. Seeing her so happy made me happy, enough to forget, just for a moment, all about the alien strings sawing up and down my guts.

Kowalski gave me another slap on the back before reviewing the sleek, charcoal-coloured chainship. 'Turret-class spacecraft. Older model, by the looks of it.' She gestured at me. 'We'll need to secure the area. If we pull the mainframe, the metadata will pinpoint the—'

'Wait.' I held up a hand. 'Do you hear that?'

Kowalski and Grim just stared. 'Hear what?'

Hear the slow clanking and whirling of machinery warming to life. Hear the dull whine of life-support systems and readouts switching on. Hear the chainship readying for departure.

Our one and only lead was preparing to fly away.

One step forward, three steps back.

I was running before I even realised I'd started moving, helmet folding over my face. I was focused completely on the side hatch that was slowly closing as the chainship lifted off gently on her dampers. I hurled myself inside, pulling my leg through as the hatch hissed shut. 'Vak, don't!' Kowalski shouted down my commslink.

424

'If they get away we'll never find them again,' I said, lying flat on my back in the darkness. 'I'll signal you as soon as I can. I—'

But my transmission abruptly cut off. The chainship gathering speed and velocity as we shuttled out into the deep blackness of open space.

40

Dark Stars

Why did I do that?

I turned the question over in my mind half a hundred times as I lay in the cramped, dark confines. Hard to really break anything down to easy logic when your hormones are fired up and you're running hot on rage. Could have been I was sick of sitting on my arse and watching the Suns run rings around us. Could be the stormtech had given me that little shove forward and I'd taken myself the rest of the way.

Or, it could be I was done with being the hunted. And now, I was the hunter.

I was waiting for the bone-shuddering rumble that would indicate we were entering warpspace. It never came. A Turret-class chainship this small and battered probably wasn't even outfitted with a warpdrive. Couldn't be flying anywhere far beyond the local system, then. Didn't eliminate much, but at least we weren't firing off into deepspace. I don't know how long I waited before I felt the chainship slowing down. External cams would have activated.

There was a small widescreen monitor above my head. I switched it on.

We were fast approaching a space station. The bulk of the station was shaped like a truncated skull, with a greyish texture like it had been dipped in old wax and then rolled in ash. The rest of the station sprouted from the top in a series of spires, corridors and docking gantries forming a jutting crown of black crystal. The skull's eye-sockets were hollowed out, but I got the feeling it was staring back at me.

The ship tilted down towards the jawline, where a hangar was already opening, the blue shield-barrier crackling. My breath steamed hot in my face as the chainship swerved around in a sluggish circle before settling with a jolt. What if they decided to open the hatch? What if they'd picked me up on thermal-scanners? I held my handcannon tight to my chest, listening hard, waiting to be dragged out.

Muffled voices. Feet scuffling metal. Fading footsteps. Clanging and shuttering of metal.

Silence.

I waited for a good half hour before deciding to risk it. I stabbed the emergency opening switch. The hatch opened and I slid out and into cover.

The hangar bay was immense enough to easily hold the scattering of chainships, corvettes and slipships sitting in their drydocks, their hulls scuffed and scarred with age. Rusted chains and hooks dangled from eyeball-shaped apertures in the walls. The House of Suns symbol had been daubed across the utilitarian grey walls of the hangar bay, dozens of them smeared tens of metres high in fluorescent white paint. Subtle.

Behind me, a huge viewport looked out into a sweeping asteroid field. Hundreds, thousands, of broken chunks of primordial rock, swirling past the length of my sight and pockmarked with gaping craters. No matter how often I saw them, I'd never been able to understand how something so vast could be so silent.

I peered past them, but could see nothing. No commercial spacecraft, no flybys, definitely no Compass. We've all heard about those wayward stations and semi-abandoned outposts. Hard to believe I was in one of them now. *No connection* appeared in the upper-right corner of my HUD, as if to confirm I was truly off the beaten path. No way of calling in help if this went sour. But I couldn't waste time worrying about that now.

I slipped out of the hangar and into a telescopic corridor. It was dark and uninviting, the only light coming from blinking terminals and more symbols painted across the mirror-smooth walls. In the darkness, the glowing symbols looked like the mouths and eyes of some midnight predator from the depths of space. I felt the gentle hum of whirling machinery between my feet, the rhythmic heave of oxygen pipes and superconductor cables. Not a smear of dirt nor speck of grime anywhere. It was artificially serene. Like something vital was missing here. A body without a pulse. A great old mansion without inhabitants, wind howling down its empty hallways in the dead of the night.

You know that feeling you get when you know something's wrong, but you can't put your finger on it?

Yeah, that.

This place was infested with that feeling. And it was making me horribly uneasy.

My hands and feet flared up as the stormtech throbbed like a heartbeat. The same reaction as when I'd broken into the Tipei Corporation and discovered the storage of stormtech canisters. But this was gnawing at me like heartburn, all over my body.

I almost didn't want to know what they had stored here.

Almost.

Senses sharpened, I mentally mapped the facility as I slipped into what looked like a dimly lit library. Tight staircases spiralled up past towering bookshelves, the room scattered with dark, brooding decor. The air was perfumed with something sickly-sweet. It took me longer than it should have to realise it was trying to replicate the smell of stormtech. Maybe even the smell of a person infused with stormtech.

Dread knotted in my stomach as I glanced at the onyx walls decorated with artistic impressions of the Shenoi, quotes and eulogies framed in block fonts. Documentaries and reports about the Shenoi played on a loop, the sound muted. Mats had been stretched out in front of teapots filled with hallucinogenic herbs and various chemicals used to crank your mind into hyperaware mode. Some sound-absorbing tech had been meshed into the walls, making the room as silent as a crypt. The ominous feeling I'd had in the corridor returned, only stronger. Like I was somewhere no one should be and surrounded by malevolent information no one should have access to.

I slipped a leather-bound tome off the shelf and confirmed my suspicions. This was the cult's collection of relevant texts. Viklun Ryken's scientific papers were probably here, along with dozens of other works pertaining to the Shenoi. Theories, histories of alien civilisations, possible Shenoi homeplanets, the mysteries surrounding them, articles about the stormtech, collected testimonies from other aliens about the Shenoi. Collected listings about the cult itself, its dogmas, people who had promoted it and founded it, those who had opposed it and how they should have – or had been – dealt with.

I looked up through a layer of shielding that formed the ceiling, straight into the dark canvas of space. Constellations of unfamiliar stars stared back at me, winking in muted colours. It should have been beautiful, but here it felt like I was dipping my head into a dark ocean, teeming with crawling parasites and unknown dangers lurking in the depths.

Because that's exactly what they'd come here to find. This was their place of contemplation, where they gazed up to the countless stars, systems and celestial bodies the Shenoi had once infested like an interstellar fungus. They *marvelled* at it. Respected the aliens' strength and audacity. They came here to wait until the aliens went for round two.

These people were off their rockers. Fundamentalist in every sense, living inside a narrative of confusion and fear they'd created and projected. Luciano hadn't been kidding. They weren't going to be reasoned with. Which was great, because I'd ticked reasoning with these people off the list a long, long time ago.

My hand tightened around my handcannon. Jae Myouk-soon would be here somewhere. Cut off the head, and the body withers and dies. She might be stinking rich and possess a fancy collection of weaponised bio-chemicals, but she'd bleed just like anyone else.

I allowed my body to guide me. Wherever the stormtech was, she'd be. I was walking through a hydroponics chamber when I heard heavy footsteps. I dived under a table just in time to see a series of armed and armoured figures enter the room, with two pairs of armed robots trotting behind them, the decking rattling with the echo of their metal feet. I didn't like the look of the heavy assault rifles they were holding, so I stayed low and slipped through the nearest door.

The stormtech physically *kicked* inside me, like an impatient foetus, desperate to struggle free. Shaking it off, I took a set of backlit stairs up to a vantage point. A honeycombed network of polished laboratories sprawled in front of me, connected by sloping corridors and walkways. In the nearest sector was some sort of processing facility. Figures clad in thick protective suits handled stormtech canisters. Each chrome cylinder was scanned, checked, tagged and inserted through a series of churning machinery before being magnetically sealed in shipping crates. Statistics scrolled in gentle white text across the flexiscreens. Listing where the stormtech would be going on

Compass, which stormdealers would be receiving it, how much it had sold for.

My teeth clenched hard enough to crack. Street drugs like grimwire and bluesmoke were typically processed in dingy dungeons and mouldy apartments that were thick with smoke and littered with dirty workstations. Stormtech had an entire station dedicated to it, as if that made the drug any less evil. It didn't *deserve* this place.

The central area of the laboratories was the largest. Flexiscreens and panels covered the cavernous space like a ring of blue light. Streamlined superconductor cables were plugged into thick sockets, churning with energy. Towers of gleaming surgery equipment were built into outlines in the wall. Tubes as thick as my arm wired up into a vat with a flanged base, tangled with intricate pipework and tightly bound wiring, sprawled over the room like the multicoloured roots of an overgrown tree. I watched a scientist extract stormtech from the vat, blue surging into a hypodermic.

And meshed between the mass of machinery, like fleshy seeds buried within the core of mechanical fruit, were people. Some standing, some strapped to gurneys, some suspended in mid-air by harnesses. Each one filled with stormtech and surrounded by half a dozen suited scientists. In some it was in the infancy stages. In others, they looked like they'd been infected for months, maybe years. Most were twitching in their restraints. Low moans filled the room. Flexiscreens hoisted above each person measured their vitals in bright blue text.

Except . . . they were offering their arms and legs. Smiling as the white-clad scientists emptied stormtech hypodermics into them. They *wanted* to be here and be experimented on.

But the Suns were poisoning stormtech. Surely no one in their right mind would subject themselves to that level of self-mutilation. Unless the House of Suns weren't poisoning this batch. And if they weren't, they were doing the opposite. Enhancing it.

They wouldn't be the first. Stormdealers all had xenochemists and biologists trying to bolster their product to provide more of a kick. The Suns were clearly no strangers to tweaking the stormtech in their favour. If these nutjobs had rigged up an entire space station to house their experiments, they were successful, and had people to show for it.

Still, these guys were a cult, not a military operation. Why did they need an army?

It turned out, not everyone was here willingly. I crept further along the lab, past prison cells and operating rooms containing little worlds of horrors. A man floated in a tank filled with squirming black machinery, cables erupting out of his flesh as the stormtech was funnelled in through a drip feed. A woman with jet-black hair was screaming, her body literally being torn apart, the stormtech ripping out of her like wet, blue stuffing. Four scientists quickly restrained her to a cot as she jerked and howled. More victims thrashed against their restraints, unable to do anything as cables and tubes fused more and more stormtech to their bodies. Others were curled up into a ball, sobbing into the floor. Hundreds of people helpless, suffering as the stormtech tore, ripped, poisoned, mutilated, violated their bodies. Bulkava, Torven and Rhivik were among the prisoners, strapped to tables outfitted with species-specific restraints. To engineer stormtech that was deadly to aliens, they'd obviously needed alien test subjects. A Rhivik had been anchored to the floor with a series of thick chains, a glowing collar clamped around his neck and storms of blue shuddering up his muscle-bound arms. White-hot outrage burned in the alien's eyes as he bashed his head against the chainglass with thudding echoes. A young Torven had been savagely beaten and sealed into a black immobilising suit that was welded to a restraining chair.

It wasn't until I saw the bandaged wounds across his arms that I'd realised he'd tried to kill himself, but the cultists weren't letting a single prisoner slip away from them. He watched, glassy-eyed, as more stormtech streamed into his broken and battered body.

Others were simply long dead, stormtech twitching under lifeless flesh.

It was a stormtech farm. A nightmare factory.

Cold shock ignited from my nipples, carving down through my guts and into my toes. I was swimming in sweat inside my suit. Only the armour and its controlled environment kept me safe. They were running experiments to discover how far they could push the stormtech. How much damage they could stack on a body before the dosage made them collapse or go insane. All the better for them to infect as many Reapers and skinnies as possible. One look at the brutal tests they were running, the gamut of suffering on display, and I knew they were ramping up towards something bigger. Something for which they needed full manipulation of the stormtech. Whatever they were doing, this show of experimental horrors was exactly what the Kaiji had feared.

Lasky stood in front of the cells with a perverted curiosity sketched on his child-like face, making him appear both young and horribly old and rotten at the same time. A playful cruelty you'd see on kids that liked making routine trips to zoos, just so they could throw rocks at the animals and enjoy their confinement. He gleefully surveyed the tortured aliens, some tensing in fear as they noticed him. He rapped his fingers on the chainglass of the Rhivik's cell. The alien, tormented to breaking point, peeled his lips back in a deep, furious growl that echoed hard in my chest. He slammed his head into the glass so hard the wallframe shuddered. Lasky just grinned and walked away.

I was breathing heavily through my nose. Harmony was going to hear about this. *Everyone* was.

From my cover, I watched a door dilate open, a man walking through. He was *bursting* with stormtech. The crawling mass should have torn his body apart, split his skin open, shrivelled his organs into husks. My eyes watered just looking at him. He was in the middle of a diagnostics check when his muscles abruptly locked up. I didn't dare breathe as he scanned the room, as if he'd sensed me. After a while, he shrugged it off and departed.

I found myself moving with him, almost not of my own volition, hugging cover. Every step closer to him made my stormtech pulse harder. He went clattering down a flight of stairs to a raised circular walkway where there were *more* like him, the ravaging blue choking out their natural skin tones. They seemed to be trying to drown themselves with the stormtech – smothering their human biochemistry with the alien organism until they had more alien organic matter twitching inside their biology than human-based DNA. Trying so hard to become like the Shenoi there wasn't a difference. Had to be the ultra-zealots. Probably also the soldiers.

My body tensed the longer I looked. Half of me wanted to hide. The other half was roping me closer, telling me I needed to be like them. Maybe I'd have kept closing in, had a familiar figure not clattered by on the walkway below.

Sokolav.

I tore away from the men glowing with stormtech, hugging the shadows and making sure we were unseen as I swept up behind my former Commander. He stiffened as I parked the business end of the Titan against the back of his neck. 'Next room on your right,' I whispered as I ripped the palmerlog out of his hand. 'Not a word.'

I knew my former Commander too well to give him an

434

opportunity to retaliate. I shoved him into the deserted server room and sealed us inside.

'Vakov? Vakov Fukasawa? Is that really you, my boy?'

'No,' I said, 'the real Vakov died back in the Reaper War. Memory of pre-death is a little fuzzy, but I seem to recall you being *on the other side.*'

The last four words came out as a snarl. Anyone else would have shrunk away. But Sokolav stood solid and firm as a mountain peak. He gave a great, pent-up sigh. 'A great many things have happened since then, Vakov.'

'Oh, I'm sure,' I said. 'Let me tell you what's going to happen now. We're going to march out of here and you're going to explain all these great many things to Kindosh and the rest of Harmony.' I tilted the Titan. 'I'll be there to make sure you don't leave out any details.'

We waited until most of the cultists retired for the night before making our move. My heartbeat threatened to swallow my entire body as I marched Sokolav at gunpoint down the quiet hallways and past the cells packed full of rotting prisoners. I couldn't help but picture myself strapped beside them, operated on until I went insane or Blued Out.

I pulled Sokolav behind a wall while a trio of cultists in scuffed spacesuits walked past. I shoved my weapon under Sokolav's chin, not daring to breathe, not daring to believe Sokolav wouldn't call out to them and sacrifice himself. But his manner was totally languid, and it was starting to gnaw at me.

The cultists disappeared around a corner and I hustled Sokolav through a series of barricades, each taking for ever to open for us, concealing ourselves whenever someone was in the vicinity.

'If only you'd open your eyes, son,' Sokolav said gently.

'Shut it,' I growled.

'You'd see why we do what we do. Why all this is necessary.'

I shoved the handcannon harder against him. 'Just give me an excuse.'

Sokolav fell silent. Sweat slithered down my ribs, my head throbbing so hard I felt the onset of a migraine as we strode into the docking bay with its ring of House of Suns symbols. The chainship I'd arrived in was still sitting in its berth. We were about to climb the disembarkation ramp when a word rang out behind me.

'Vakov?'

I froze. Turned in what felt like slow motion to the lone figure positioned behind us in a spacesuit.

It was my brother.

I don't know which of the two of us was more taken aback. The pounding in my head spilled out to the rest of my body. 'Artyom.'

'How did you find us?' The confusion and dismay on his face melted back into anger, his eyes hardening, hands held tight behind his back. 'I told you what would happen to you if you came here. What's it going to take for you to listen to me?'

'Artyom, there's a way out of this.' I kept my handcannon firmly glued to Sokolav's neck. The old dog would try something the moment I let my guard down. 'Come with me. We go back to Harmony and we make a deal.'

'Are you insane?' Artyom all but spluttered. I noticed that the House of Suns' symbol had been stitched on the shoulder of his spacesuit. 'What, you think they're going to listen to me?'

'No. But they'll listen to me. I'll make sure of it.' I pushed out the words as fast as possible, while I still had the opportunity. 'You give up this place and what they're doing here, help me give up Sokolav, we hold the cards. We can get you out. *I* can get you out.'

Something unreadable rippled over Artyom's face. 'It won't be enough,' he whispered, but I sensed my words taking root

436

in him, growing something past the stubbornness and past the fear.

'It will if we hand Sokolav over,' I urged, feeling a nugget of hope and willing my words to reach him. 'One life for another. You never betrayed Harmony. You're a civilian. You never enlisted. He did. They'll take him over you.'

'Don't listen to him, Artyom.' Sokolav's grey eyes glinted under his mop of hair.

'Shut up,' I growled, aware of the minutes burning away, aware of the many entrances cultists could be rushing through any second.

'Your brother left you behind, dumped you when it suited him.' Sokolav talked over me, as if I'd never spoken. 'But we've taken you in. We adopted you into our family and tore down the lies.'

'I'm your family, Artyom,' I said. 'The only one you've got left.'

'And yet he abandoned you!' Sokolav countered.

'Yes! I did.' Artyom's head snapped up at my confession. 'I abandoned my brother. My own brother. I left you behind like a burden. That's on me. It always will be.' I spoke past the sudden lump of concrete in my throat. My brother stood there quietly, eyes darting back and forth. I slipped my helmet off with a hiss of air and let my brother see me. 'The way out is right behind us, Artyom. Once we're onboard, it'll be over. It won't fix everything, but it'll be a start. We owe it to each other to try. We just have to walk away.'

The words echoed between us. The shadows of distant passing asteroids swept across the spacedecking. The stormtech itched like tongues of wildfire under my ribs, but I refused to unlock sights with my brother.

Artyom's eyes pinned me beneath his matted black hair. 'And you can get me a deal? Let them do a swap?'

Kindosh would, if that's what it took to regain custody of Sokolav. 'I swear it. I'll negotiate it myself, and I won't let them touch you until I'm happy.'

Sokolav's breathing turned shallow. 'Artyom. Think, my boy. Think.' For the first time, I heard genuine apprehension in my former Commander's voice. 'Think very carefully.'

Arytom didn't seem to hear him. The defiance slumped from his shoulders, like an old building finally collapsing. I felt Sokolav tense beside me.

I let go of a breath it felt like I'd been holding for years.

I did it.

I found my brother again.

Together, we could finally put this right.

Artyom unzipped the front of his spacesuit, revealing an underskin beneath as he hiked up the chainship's disembarkation ramp towards me. His face was world-weary and crisscrossed with scars and painful memories. But among them were also the nights we'd shared on the mountain peaks together, the brief fragments of peace we'd shared in a childhood filled with pain. And between all those was the possibility of a future, a chance to put things right.

He reached to push Sokolav into the chainship and I turned to follow.

And that's when I saw the alert transponder in Artyom's hand, blinking the colour of blood.

He darted forward, scything my legs out from under me and slamming my face into the hard metal ramp. Sokolav stomped on my hand until my grip weakened and he could tear the handcannon away. I kicked out at them, furiously twisting out of their grip and scrambling up the ramp. I'd reached the entrance, my fingers inches from the switch that would lock-down the hatch when Artyom tugged me backwards with a grunt, holding me down against the cold metal. The pounding of angry footsteps echoed through the dock as cultists arrived to Artyom's alert. Their smiles were wide and eyes bright as they saw me. Unable to believe their luck, giddy with excitement. Artyom grabbed a fistful of my hair, yanking my head upwards as they came running.

He'd played me.

The cultists swarmed over me like a human net. Grabbing an arm and a leg each and dragging me away. I caught a glimpse of Artyom's face between the seething crowd. Twisted in anger and loathing. Empty of anything resembling the person I'd known. He met my eyes with a disbelieving scoff, like he was disgusted I'd been so gullible, and vanished into the crowd.

And something already cracked inside me completely broke.

41

The Captive

'Put that on.'

I glanced down at the one-piece, dark-blue prisoner's suit dumped at my feet. A ring of cultists surrounded me, the Jackal at their head. His dark eyes watched my every move, the expression unchanged between the time they'd cut me out of my armour and underskin and when they'd dragged me to this metal box of a prisoner's bay. Hideous yellow lighting sleeted down like tendrils of radiation. A dark brown stain had coagulated around a drain grate at my bare feet. Claw and nail scratches on the metal walls. Nothing but madness and misery here. My skin shivered as I looked again at the prisoner's suit, remembering how I'd been forced to wear something similar for over a year when I was a Harvest prisoner. The cult's symbol was stitched on the back and shoulders, underscored with the words *High Risk Prisoner*.

'Put that on,' the Jackal repeated.

I drew my head back and spat in his eye.

The Suns behind him gasped. The Jackal smiled mirthlessly and wiped away the offending blue saliva. Then he drove his knee between my legs with earth-shattering force. The agony swelled up my groin and exploded in my stomach like shrapnel. I folded to the concrete, gasping and half-blind.

'And the Harmony hound barks at last,' he sneered from the other end of a pain-mottled universe. 'He wants to be a dog, we treat him like one. Boys, you know what to do.'

Animal fear and dread eclipsed all rational thought. Clammy hands seized me. Slapping me and stamping on my toes. The light stabbing me in the eyes as they shoved my arms and legs into the prisoner's suit. I tried to bite one, and got backhanded across the face, my head thunking against concrete. Once I was suited up, they activated the suit's neck seal, the fabric leeching tight to my skin. I was hauled to my feet, helpless as they strapped me into a harness with meticulous ease, as if they'd done this countless times to countless prisoners of multiple species. The thick, broad straps crisscrossed my back in an X, clamping tight over my shoulders, across my chest, securing firmly around my waist like a belt, around my thighs and between my legs before locking to a wide buckle in the centre of my back. They sealed my hands in magnetic cuffs and locked them to my chest. A metallic tinkle as they wrapped a steel mesh muzzle around my face, tightening it until it sliced into my cheeks and drew blood. A sturdy chain was tethered from my belt to my muzzle, forcing me to hunch in perpetual supplication. Behind me, the straps were tightened until they were biting into my flesh, a thick cable attached from the back of my harness to a track running along the ceiling. I figured they dragged prisoners through their laboratory like this, to whatever torture awaited them. As a final humiliation, the Jackal produced a spiked dog's collar and lashed it tight around my neck until I could barely breathe.

He made sure I was hunched over and watching as he clapped Artyom on the shoulder. 'You've done well, Artyom. You've truly proven yourself.'

Artyom's face was a dead, blank mask. 'I did what I had to.'

'Oh, no. No, no, no. You didn't. You could easily have let

441

your big brother go. Pretended not to see him. Given him a head start. Maybe even departed alongside him. You didn't. You stood by us. Your loyalty to the cause, to us, made you hand him in.' He leaned in close to me, so only the two of us could hear. 'You see, Vakov? We've been a better family than you *ever* were.'

I lunged forward, startling the audience, a savage growl tearing out of my throat as I tried to smash my head into his. The cable snapped taut, jerking me backwards with spine-snapping force. I seethed in my restraints, my snarling face inches from his. The Jackal smiled as the onlookers of cultists cackled. My body shivered with hatred, the words coming out garbled and furious. 'I'm going to tear your face off and bury you alive.'

The Jackal ignored me and turned back to his audience as he gripped the back of my harness. 'What shall we do with him? Your call, boys. Get creative.'

Half the audience were inching towards me, giving furtive sniffs, hands clenching and unclenching, stormtech-induced mania writhing behind their eyes. I swallowed as a gaunt-faced girl spoke up. 'Dump him in the cell with that Rhivik, the one we've been starving. Let them fight for dinner. That'll be fun.'

'Let's keep him tied up and string him upside-down,' a man with dirty blonde hair down to his elbows and dimpled cheeks suggested. He thrust a slingshiv towards my groin. 'See what parts the stormtech does and doesn't grow back.'

'Why not both?' the Jackal suggested and clapped me on the back. Icy horror grew inside me as they advanced on me from all directions. I jerked back instinctively. They grabbed me and dragged me forward like a bag of trash, my feet scraping concrete, my chains and buckles rattling. 'Hoist him up to this wall,' the Jackal continued.

'You'll do no such thing.' Sokolav stood in the entrance,

hands held behind his back as every eye turned towards him. 'I want a word with our prisoner.'

'You can talk all you like,' the Jackal said. 'But not until I'm done with him.'

'Perhaps you didn't understand me. I'm speaking with him *now*.' I've never heard my former Commander raise his voice in anger. Because when he adopted that steely, authoritative tone, you knew you were going up against more than you could chew. The Jackal's features smoothed over into that smiling, charismatic expression of his. But I knew he'd use our history together somehow, either with me or Sokolav. He departed and his group went out with him.

Sokolav reached out to unclasp the dog collar from around my neck. He dragged out a metal chair for me, before retrieving one of his own. I remained standing. Whatever shreds were left of the man I'd once looked up to, I wanted no sympathy from him.

'You always did get yourself into trouble, my boy,' Sokolav said with a slow shake of his head. 'I didn't believe it when they first said it was you. Didn't think you'd ever work for Harmony again.'

'I guess everyone changes, given enough time.' He'd been a beacon of light, guiding us through the nightmare storm that was churning through our bodies. His cool hand on my shoulder when I was thrashing in my restraints, fighting against the introduction of stormtech to my body. His breath on my neck as he told me I didn't *deserve* to give up. Someone like me had to pull through. 'And now you're working for these psychotic pricks.'

'You don't understand—' Sokolav started.

'Don't you dare,' I hissed. 'You don't know me. You don't know my brother.'

'I doubt that, Vakov. You see, I'm the one who recruited Artyom.'

'What?' I croaked out.

'Vakov, I think *you're* the one who doesn't know your brother,' said Sokolav. 'The day he realised you were going to fight Harvest and he was not . . . it changed him. You knew you were leaving him alone with your father while you escaped. You knew you were breaking your promise and throwing away everything you had together. That betrayal kick-started something in him.'

Sokolav had been one of the few people to know what had gone on at home. 'Don't you *dare* pretend to understand.' I wanted him to hate me, hurt me, give me an excuse to fight back.

'I've never pretended with you, son,' said Sokolav gently. He wore a quiet, sombre expression, like he was watching long-lost events play out in the distance, beyond his control. 'I found your brother miserable, depressed and despising Harmony for stealing you away. He thought you were going to die far away on some bombed-out planet, fighting a hopeless war. The poor soul didn't know how to carry on. He was looking for something that'd take him from here and give him a fresh start. The House of Suns was the answer to that.'

'A bunch of extremist nutjobs, trying to drown Compass in addiction.'

'No, Vakov.' Sokolav was not letting me provoke him. There was that same tiredness in his grey eyes, as if he needed a deep, long sleep. 'You remember my injury at the Battle of Korag, yes? The one that got me sent home with a pat on the back? Lying bed-ridden while newsfeeds spoke about valour and fighting for a cause, I realised that Harmony doesn't deserve to govern our galaxy. Jae Myouk-soon helped me understand the potential of stormtech. Why should Harmony decide who's permitted to use it? Who gives them the right of ownership? The most genetically advanced specimen discovered in human history, and their scientists treat it like a common disease, exploiting it when convenient and banning it when they dislike the results. Their ideas are old-fashioned, out-dated.'

I remembered eighteen-year-old me, sitting on the hard metal chairs in the cold recruitment hall with Artyom. His face still carried bruises from the previous night when our father thought he'd come home too late. I could defend myself. He could not. Posters showcasing Reapers in battle armour and live feeds of Harmony victories were hung up around us. We were both scared and uncertain, and we didn't know if this would be the biggest mistake of our lives.

'Promise me we're doing the right thing, Vak,' Artyom begged me, his hands shaking as they gripped mine. I'd told him we were. I knew we had to be here because if we were sent home, I'd kill my father eventually. Sokolav had seen two dark-haired brothers sitting together and guided us through the procedure, had us tested under his supervision, ensuring we had the benefits that came from being from an underprivileged and troubled household. He'd become the father I never had.

'The best organisms adapt, Vakov. As I did.' He indicated to the stormtech curling up my throat. 'We respect the stormtech in a way Harmony never has. They leaked it onto the market, not understanding the chaos they'd cause, or the good it can be used for.'

'Good?' I yelled. 'There are hundreds of thousands of addicts willing to kill their own families just for a sliver of this stuff. There are *children* who are being kidnapped by stormdealers, shot up with stormtech and forced to work the streets as foot soldiers. Turf wars that are tearing up neighbourhoods. Whole floors *filled* with skinnies turned into empty husks, hurting themselves just to feel something. It started a damn *war*.'

'It's one thing to make a mistake. It's another entirely to continue making them when you know they can be avoided. That's what we're doing. And you know as well as I do that Harmony will continue making mistakes. Which is why we've been planting those deaths on them, helping people see them for who they really are. Do you really think Kindosh cared about stormtech being on the markets until the media pointed out it was her own that were turning up dead? The people won't tolerate their insolence any longer. Once the public discover the potential we've reached with stormtech, the things Harmony never dreamed of, they will listen.'

My old instructor had died in the war. Jae Myouk-soon had simply dug up the bones and twisted them into a pathetic imitation. 'You were supposed to be there for all of us,' I rasped. 'You were supposed to be better than this.'

'I'm sorry, son. You were one of my favourites. I wish you hadn't put yourself in this situation.' His eyes dissected me as a flicker of sombre determination flitted through them. 'But what's done is done. I've chosen my path. You've chosen yours. What happens to you next is out of my hands.'

As if on cue, the rusted doors cranked open to reveal the Jackal, surrounded by his usual entourage. 'Time's up, old man. We're taking him now.'

Sokolav didn't even look me in the eye as they came forward and grabbed me. 'Come, dog.' Every cell in my body ignited with equal parts misery and rage as the Jackal tugged me forward on my muzzle chain. The rail above me rattled, the chain following me as I was dragged out of the metal box and into the steel throat of a corridor flanked by my captors. Artyom attempted to edge away but the Jackal wasn't having it. 'Not you, Artyom. You come along. You watch.'

'I don't think that's necessary—' Artyom began.

'But I do,' the Jackal insisted with a smile. 'It's only fair, given you helped capture our prize.'

So Artyom trailed behind as I was dragged in full sight of the cultists. Feeling hundreds of eyes drilling into me as I waddled forward in the Jackal's humiliation ritual. I rolled my burning shoulders, the harness straps groaning and digging into me. Without the tight confines of my armour, my flesh prickled and shuddered. The itchy fabric of the prisoner's suit chafing against me. My hairs all standing on end, my back prickling with sweat, my body flushed with sticky heat, breath sawing like razorwire up and down my throat. I felt exposed. Vulnerable and filled with dread. I'd spend whatever was left of my life in utter misery, being tortured in captivity.

I'd expected to be tied up in some kind of holding cell. Instead, I was dragged into an office filled with a smoky yellow light. Dark, heavy armchairs and tables decorated the room. The walls were skinned in a forlorn shade of brown, smeared with event-monitoring systems. Tiny, clicking mechanisms perched atop a row of bookcases. Heavy drapes were drawn back from the viewport that peered out into the sweeping asteroid field. Jae Myouk-soon sat behind an antique wooden desk. The woman who had taken my brother from me. She was reading an old manuscript and casually folded it away to inspect me. I took in the pronounced Korean cheekbones, intelligent eyes, dark hair swept up in a perfect bun. Her small frame was almost swallowed up by the highbacked leather chair. If she'd been standing, she'd only have come up to my chest. Her cream blouse, shawl, and pencil skirt looked bizarre in contrast to the scuffed armour worn by the men who'd dragged me here. Sitting above her on a backlit podium was the same black, serrated helmet I'd seen her wearing in the photo.

I was roughly shoved to my knees, still hunched forward. The metallic scrape of the chain being locked in place high

447

above me. Cables were unspooled from the corners of the room and latched to the back of my harness to cement me in place. I couldn't move an inch.

'Good.' She dismissed my escort with a flick of her fingers. Artyom moved to follow, but she called him back. 'I'm told you captured your brother. It's only fair you remain to see the results.'

The Jackal hadn't moved. 'You promised me I'd get to spend time with him,' he said in a low, cold voice.

'I did. That was before you failed in the Pits. Failed tremendously.'

'You owe me for—'

Jae cut him off. 'You are owed nothing, Akira. Only what I choose to give.'

A crack shivered down the Jackal's facade, exposing an animalistic outrage. At first, I'd believed it was embarrassment, rejection in front of others that was his sole weakness. Now, I saw it was also having his authority undermined. He was a quiet schemer from the shadows, manipulating until he had you under his control. Jae saw it, too. Tension strung between them over my restrained body. Eventually, the Jackal bowed his head, his mask back in place. A temporary retreat to fight another day, although he was no doubt imagining sawing my head off with a dull knife.

He departed and left the three of us alone.

'I'd be lying if I said it's not been amusing to watch you scurry around.' Jae inspected me like I was the most bizarre of animals. I smelled her minty perfume as she leaned forward to tap the jaw of my muzzle. My restrained hands shook against my chest with the urge to wrap around her scrawny throat. 'Amusing and annoying.'

'Should have thought about that before you got my brother involved,' I spat through my muzzle.

'Don't be so naive. Artyom joined us willingly, didn't you?'

Artyom said nothing. He didn't have to. 'And what makes you people so sodding special? You're just like any other group of violent nutjobs, spreading fear for power.'

'We're the only ones who see the truth, Fukasawa. Harmony's a parasite. Holding us back in the dark ages when we could be so much more.'

'Did you come about this dawning realisation while poisoning Harvest deserters?'

'I came about this dawning realisation when your people destroyed my home.' Jae's face was expressionless as asteroid rock. 'The Harmony warships swarmed the skies of my homeworld and turned everyone I loved and everyone I knew into meat and rubble. I wanted to know what could possibly be worth so much that entire civilisations would try to destroy each other for it.'

'You think we *wanted* to go to war?' I'd never have defended Harmony once, but I couldn't stay silent at this insanity.

'But a war was had regardless, wasn't it?' She laid her hand just under my collarbone. Her touch burned like dry ice but I was in no position to shake it off. 'And then I found out what the stormtech was and what it could do.'

'So you formed this little band of alien-worshipping freaks?' I asked.

But Jae wouldn't be provoked. 'It seems your brother has all the brains in the family. You're exactly what he said: a rabid dog on a leash.' She traced the stormtech zigzagging from rib to rib. 'You have never understood what a gift this is. How to embrace it.'

I stretched as far as my restraints allowed, trying to shrug her hand away. My knees were already aching and numb. 'Is that what you're doing, as you study and enhance it?' I nodded towards the stacks of leather-bound tomes and readouts, glowing with statistics pertaining to the Shenoi. Maybe I'd die here. But I wasn't going to go down without knowing why the cult was doing this.

'We're embracing what's natural, Vakov. The stormtech heals, enhances and boosts those who are worthy. It sharpens the dullest of minds, nurses crippled limbs back to life, eats diseases out of the human body. It's a *gift*. Harmony wants to take it for themselves, use it for their own gain. Instead, we're giving it to the world.'

'You want to infect everyone,' I breathed. It had never just been about discrediting Harmony. It was a complete and utter rejection of their rule. They wanted to spread stormtech to as many people as possible, while dialling up the distrust of Harmony and any rehabilitation or suppressors they offered.

'We want to advance humanity,' Jae corrected with a vaunted air, her small, fox-like face wrapped with the room's golden glow. 'Why do you think the Kaiji are so much more advanced than we are? Because they're adapting, interacting, exploring, while we're here, rotting.' She gestured to a flexiscreen, winking with orbital data from local galactic regions and celestial bodies. 'We could conquer the galaxy if we embraced stormtech. Our gift could put humanity light years ahead of every civilisation, every species. Imagine what we could build, the problems we could erase. We've pushed its capacity beyond what Harmony could even *dream* of.'

'At the cost of murdering thousands of people,' I growled, 'and potentially murdering millions more.'

'The powerful survive, Fukasawa. As you and your kind have already proved. And power is nothing unless it is used. Tell me, did you enjoy being so drugged out of your little mind you didn't feel a thing as you mowed my people down?' She glanced back at a rotating hologram of Compass. 'No matter. Transhumanism is the only solution. Tens of thousands are already enhanced, their bodies upgraded to their full potential. Why should we hide from it? Harmony is afraid of the inevitable. The House of Suns is not.'

I saw the glaring light of conviction – of madness – in her eyes. She actually *believed* her cult could control and contain the DNA of a galaxy-consuming race of aliens. That the stormtech was just another kind of wetware upgrade that body-modifiers and cyberneticists played around with.

Artyom continued to watch impassively by her side. Nothing I said would convince him to help me now. I was on my own.

'Harmony's made mistakes, but you can't blame them for holding the stormtech back from the public,' I managed through gritted teeth, streams of sweat sliding down muscles that felt as tight as bridge cables. I nodded to the blue ribbons dripping down my legs. 'They didn't mean to create a drug market.'

Jae shrugged. 'Does intent matter if the end result is the same?'

'They've never stopped trying to repair the damage!'

'Apologies don't matter. The way Harmony feels now doesn't matter. They've made their move. Now we make ours.'

I twitched in my restraining harness. 'What?'

'You didn't think those deaths were for nothing, did you? Give us some credit. The stormtech we've been distributing on the market contains a virus, sending the user's body into overload. You've seen as much. Those few terrorist attacks and random killings so far will be *nothing* in comparison to what a good chunk of Compass' population will do once we activate our Surge virus. Remember when you were on the battlefield, eager to tear Harvest soldiers limb from limb? That'll happen with every fifth stormtech user.'

She scraped back the sweaty strands of my hair that had plastered to my forehead with ice-cold fingers. Her nose wrinkled as she inhaled deeply. As if she *liked* the sickly-sweet smell of stormtech wafting out of me. 'It'll be mass hysteria. Harmony will be unable to do a thing.' She reached into the pocket of her blouse and retrieved a hypodermic. 'But we can. We've engineered a solution. We'll shut down the Surge signal and users will emerge from the madness, enhanced by the stormtech. They'll understand there's a way to live moderately with it as a species. Following our example, they'll embrace the stormtech – as we were always meant to. We'll show them the way forward.' She cupped my jaw with a surprisingly iron grip. 'You helped so, so very much when you broke out of that xenomuseum. You and your brother make a fantastic team.'

There was a perfect crack as I headbutted her, hard.

Artyom startled. Jae recoiled, dabbing a hand to her forehead. 'You're going to pay for that, you arrogant little worm.'

This was exactly what the Kaiji had feared: the House of Suns were going to flood Compass with drugs out of some arrogant, screwed up sense of leadership. The sociopaths were doing the Shenoi's work for them. Our asteroid would become another footnote on a long list of fallen civilisations and ravaged worlds across the galaxy. And I could do nothing except sit here and watch it happen. I'd failed my brother, I'd failed Kasia, and now I'd failed Kowalski, Grim and the people of Compass.

A sudden thought struck me, pieces clicking into place and presenting a picture. 'You're immune, aren't you?' I glanced up at her with a mad grin scattering across my face. 'You're like my brother. Your body rejects your beloved Shenoi DNA. You're not just a zealot. You're *jealous*. Jealous of something you can never have. Watching people like me be enhanced by it is driving you insane.'

Artyom stiffened. Jae's face twitched, a crack running down her facade and hinting at the mad machinery powering her actions. I felt her control slip and swerve from her grasp before she promptly regained it. 'I don't need to partake in the stormtech to know its power. Or to show the world what I want them to see.'

My harness groaned as I rolled my stooped back. People will find out how you've manipulated them. They'll find out the truth.'

'People see what they want to see, picking and ignoring what suits them. So far, they've witnessed stormtech-ridden people turn into savage killing machines and drug-addled madmen. Once they know what Harmony has failed to protect them from, they'll turn on them.' She sniffed, as if struck by an afterthought. 'Just like everyone on New Vladi knew what your father was doing to you and your siblings.' Artyom's muscles clenched, but he refused to look at me. 'And that it was your father who hit your mother, her head cracking on the tiles. But it was easier to call her death an accident. People dislike hearing facts that bring them out of their comfort zone. They're content to ignore suffering, as long as it's not their own. It's rather unfortunate you had to learn that particular feature of our species so early on, isn't it?'

My body made an instinctive jerk forward, imagining tearing her throat out. The stormtech was a live wire inside me, and I was twisting and thrashing with its motions. 'You don't understand what you're doing,' I growled.

'Oh,' said Jae slowly, 'we absolutely do.'

Her steely, cold voice triggered something in me. Thinking back to all the military-grade gear and preparations and manifestos I'd skimmed over. 'You're trying to contact the Shenoi.'

'You've got some brains kicking around in there, after all. We've spent years analysing every scrap of researched data, salvaged intel from flyby probes, event-monitoring systems, emissary pods, deepspace expeditions. Now we're ready. We're going to awaken those who left us this gift, Fukasawa. And we're going to do it on Compass.'

453

I felt this ocean of insanity start to drown me in its thrashing depths. 'What you're doing is insane. You're going to commit genocide!'

'Again with the death and destruction. We're uplifting humanity to the next stage.' She stood stiff, chin turned upwards, truly believing she could achieve all this.

'You can't control it!' I roared. 'No one can! It's too powerful, it's not meant to be used!'

'Like I told you, power is nothing unless you use it, as Harmony demonstrated so eloquently when they destroyed our worlds. Now, we destroy theirs, one Reaper and one skinnie at a time.'

'You're a botched abortion of a human being,' I ground out past my muzzle. This was the woman who'd stolen my brother, poured poisoned honey into his ears, indoctrinated him into this world of horror and insanity. 'I've been dealing with your kind my whole life. You're just an evil bully with muscle backing you up. You're a *coward*.'

The steely expression on Jae's face didn't budge. 'If you were any less arrogant, you'd understand. But the only way you educate a rabid dog is by beating it. You wouldn't appreciate what we've accomplished even if you'd seen it.'

'I've seen plenty.'

'Oh, no you haven't. We've been hiding out in Compass for years and your band of war-mongering brutes haven't had the faintest clue where we are. Would you like me to tell you?'

'Actually, I'd rather you drank a bucket of bleach.'

The insult I'd fired at Jae missed her by a mile. She glanced outside the viewport, as she if she could see it floating there alongside the asteroids. 'We're inside the Void Zones,' she continued. 'Entire sections untouched by damage, containing perfectly sustainable living space. And that's where we'll be

454

triggering the virus and initiating contact with the Shenoi, right under their noses.'

My stomach churned as I imagined it. The chaos, the mass hysteria as all Reapers and skinnies and anyone who'd even dabbled in stormtech were turned into bloodthirsty robots, reprogrammed by the sticky alien matter squirming inside their brains, altered by a shadowy cult unknown to the public. Without someone to blame, the public would turn on the easiest targets: the victims. How many of them would they execute in self-defence before Harmony got it under control? Compass would be torn apart.

And then the Shenoi would come along to deal the killing blow.

'You can't do this,' I rasped. I was slipping and Jae knew it.

'Your people took everything from me and left me to die. Look at where I am now. There is *nothing* I cannot do. *Nothing*. And you're going to understand that as you watch it all happen and realise you've failed *everyone*. You'll remember that as the others break you.' She shrugged. 'Assuming you survive this.'

My body was in overdrive, the stormtech zapping in my nervous system like a live wire. Running through her words, the tail end of her speech caught like a splinter in my brain. 'Survive what?'

For the first time, a knife of a smile crossed Jae's face. 'You've been so obsessed with our enhanced stormtech over these last few months. How about a chance to try it out?'

42
Blue Deaths

The door hissed open behind me. The buckles rattling as I strained to glance over my shoulder. Two cultists wheeled a device towards me. It was interlocked with tangled layers of heavy black machinery, two bulbous objects latched to the sides like diseased growths. They heaved and wheezed next to me, as if they were breathing. A series of cables plugged them into the gleaming cylinders of two fresh stormtech canisters.

I knew I'd never leave this station alive. I'd accepted my fate the moment Artyom handed me over. If I was going to go out, it'd be like a soldier. A Reaper. Wasn't about to grovel or beg for mercy that'd never come. But hearing the machine groan and croak next to me, as if excited to be put to use, I felt the blood drain from my face and icy fear rise up to replace it.

'This is some of our purest, most chemically potent product. Normally, it would take you months to withstand something with this big a kick.' Behind me, the two men checked the taut cables holding me for slack, clicking the buckles home, tightening my harness straps until I could barely breathe. Jae pressed her hands together. 'You hurt my men. Killed friends who'd helped build this empire. So you get no such privilege. On the off-chance you do survive, you'll be an excellent addition to our collection of test subjects in the Void Zones.

We could run all kinds of interesting experiments on you for years, maybe decades.'

Tendrils launched out of the tube and snaked towards me like carbon-black fingers. The sharp ends glinting as they jammed into my arms and legs, sniffing out the veins. 'No, no, no,' I whispered as more growths burst towards me. The cables and restraining harness held me like stone. Sweat ran down into my eyes, down my chest. Pinpricks of pain erupted through my body, the machine's wheezing growing faster, more ecstatic.

Jae stepped back next to Artyom. His jaw was clenched tight, hands curled into fists.

'You can't,' I choked out.

'Oh, Fukasawa,' Jae's eyes were so deep and dark they threatened to drown me. 'What did I tell you? There is *nothing* I can't do.'

The tendrils kept coming. Piercing my chest, my thighs, cramming up my nasal passages, jamming below my eye sockets until I was tethered to the whirling machine like a robot to its recharging station. This would corrode my brain, crumble my organs and shred my flesh from the inside as my body struggled to keep up with the relentless assault.

They were going to Blue me out.

Jae flipped the switch. The machine lurched forward into me and a chrome helmet with an open faceplate grew around my head. Ice-cold metal clamped to my cheeks, my forehead, securing me in place. 'This is for every innocent Harvester you killed,' she whispered. Her eyes were wet and shiny like fresh, dark paint. A flicker of the depths of pain behind those eyes, the things she'd had done to her, the things she'd done in order to survive. 'Every bomb you dropped, every bullet you fired, every life you ruined. Harmony will pay for them all.'

No one was coming to save me. Not Grim, not Kowalski. I glanced one last time at my brother, his face cold and barren as a winter tundra. I struggled as the fluorescent blue liquid slowly, slowly gurgled out of the machine and coiled through the shivering tendrils and into me. I jolted against the restraints as the shockwave rolled through. My body already knew something was wrong. The stormtech was mutating, clawing inside me like a live creature. Every attempt I'd ever made to fight it, every mental exercise, every rehab technique, was being torn and shredded apart like wet paper with vicious, alien fingers.

Agony like I've never known detonated in my skull.

Blood was dripping from my ears. I could smell myself: the overwhelming sticky sweetness oozing out of my pores like a skinnie. I gagged as the stormtech inched up my lungs, clawing up my throat. Blue froth foamed from my mouth and nose. The assault burned through every cell, every crevice, fusing the stormtech to the depths of my body. It felt like freezing parasites had begun to take root inside my body, giving birth to slithering infestations, crawling under my skin. I thrashed and jerked against the restraints with bone-breaking force, my back arching, legs shuddering in a seizure. Eyes rolling to the back of my head, the world smearing in a black haze. Choked screams gurgling from my throat. A cascade of fire on every nerve ending. A hundred glass shards jamming into every joint. My bones wrapped in razorwire, shredding my body apart, tsunamis of pain crashing down.

Artyom, blank-faced and stiff, watching me die from the other side of the universe.

One last wave of agony smashed down over me, and I drowned in my own body.

43

Hold the Dark

Most New Vladis believe in the afterlife. Not a heaven or a hell. Just some unnamed landscape where animals roam the endless wilderness and cloudy skies of never-ending light stretch over snowcapped mountains and seething blue oceans, watched over by guardian giants with sad, mournful eyes, their bodies constructed from rocks and animal bones.

Never bought the whole idea. Not really. But there was always a sliver of belief buried in me somewhere. That very far away there existed a quiet, tranquil world tucked neatly away beyond the dimensions of life and death. The valleys trickling with rivers filled with fragments of lost dreams, broken memories and the nameless dead.

Now I knew it was all a lie.

There was nothing here. Nothing but an ocean of darkness and pain. I was just beneath the surface, hooks slowly trying to drag me under. My body was wrapped in a numbing void, all senses and stimuli locked out.

I kicked back. Fought it. But I was barely keeping my head above this sinkhole. The stormtech hadn't won its battle for my body, not yet. But it was close. Every time I fought it, it tried to claw me back, harder each time. It was like being swaddled in syrup. I clenched my teeth, tensing my muscles despite the blistering agony, attempting to shrug off the blue chains wrapping around me. Everything was alien and hollow inside, my body telling me something was terribly wrong. There was nowhere for it to go, so the stormtech kept drowning me.

Something rumbled under me. The stink of oil and burning metal. A golden flash. Metal cladding. Engines churning. I was being taken somewhere by spacecraft.

The stormtech ripped me back with a violent tug. Darkness clenching around me again. No, no, no. I wouldn't let the monstrosity inside my body win. But there was too much churning and sloshing through me. It was like being devoured by an oil slick. Every time I shoved it away, something bigger came swarming in, wrapping wet and tight around my limbs. I was going to die here.

Katherine, Grim, Juvens, Jasken, Saren. My friends, waiting to see me succeed, to find a way to live with the monster clawing inside my heart. Not giving up on me no matter what I did or how I treated them. I hung onto them as my lifeline. Imagining myself tearing free of the layers of thick, wet swaddling around me, crawling towards them. Fighting the stormtech with everything I had.

But what if I did not fight it? *Fight it, and it'll fight you*, Sokolav had told us Reapers. *Draw closer to it, and it'll draw closer to you*. All this time I'd been battling it. Two opposing rips in a never-ending ocean current. Dividing my body. Never accepting the infestation rooted inside me. I'd spent almost a decade fighting Harvest, fighting my own body. I'd run away from my home and father rather than find an accommodation. I'd always picked the easy route. I'd always chosen to fight.

My Reaper brothers and sisters torn apart on the battlefield. Their bodies pushing them towards the onslaught, even as they resisted it. Mindlessly shooting, hacking, tearing. My friends staring at me through the smoke and screams when it was all over. Heaving in their armour. Ash raining down on bloodied faces. Hands clenching with the need to fight and destroy. Hating themselves for it, but unable to stop.

Alcatraz. Ratchet. Myra. Cable. Drummer. Me. Thousands of others.

Locked in an endless war with ourselves. Breaking ourselves apart rather than come to terms with the alien matter squirming inside us.

Except, the stormtech *was* me. Always would be.

Maybe it was time to accept that.

I saw my fellow Reapers. Lost to the chaos of the battle-fields. Buried with their armour across sweeping grasslands and mountain valleys on long-forgotten planets. Coming home broken and lost. Their names whispered by comrades around campfires. Their dog tags worn around the necks of their broth-ers and sisters. Their sacrifices and bravery and brotherhood loyalty etched in the stars and in memory.

Gone, but never forgotten.

I felt them with me now. Part of me, as they'd always been.

Once a Reaper, always a Reaper.

I let myself go.

I lowered all my defences and let the stormtech flow uninter-rupted through the fabric of my body. A glow spread through me like a warm, wet mist. I relaxed, going limp, giving myself over to the stormtech completely. Gathering up all the broken, scattered pieces and merging them into one. Growing me gills to adapt to these waters. The throbbing of my heart boomed in my whole body, supported by an extra, powerful force. I inhaled. Air flooded my body, like the snow-fresh mountain winds of New Vladi, rushing and charging into my lungs.

I'd done it.

Another rumble up my spine. Jolting turbulence. I cracked an eye open and saw the blurry outlines of Hideko, Lasky and the Jackal gathered in the command cockpit of a small transport spacecraft. Crash webbing dangled above me like guts. I was strapped firmly into a plastic seat. I was still wrapped in my prisoner's suit and harness, the muzzle still affixed to my face. Even when on the precipice of death, they weren't taking chances with a Reaper.

A foggy viewport to my right. I tried to look, but a wave of nausea slammed me back like a kick to the chest. Still adjusting. Couldn't rush this. More slowly, I leaned forward. Starklands stretched beneath me. Every building, every object, every individual clear and visible as though projected on a high-def flexiscreen.

Couldn't celebrate just yet. Jae had said they were taking me back to the Void Zones, to be a test subject as they finalised their operation.

I had to get out *now*.

I reached deep into my body and allowed its warm, shivering sensations to cocoon around me like armour, lending me clarity and guidance. I stamped down on my instinct to struggle against my binding straps. Had to free my hands first. I levelled myself upwards, the straps biting hard into my shoulders. The spacecraft was one of those older models in dire need of repair and the metal wall cladding was peeling back in jagged strips. I stretched my bound hands, the chain tethering them to my chest going taut as nanowire, but I latched onto the edge. I pushed down, hard. The metal edge tearing into the meat of my wrists and drawing blood. One wrong move here and I'd slit them open. I reached for the stormtech's wet, slithering pulse. Taking its focus and strength, keeping escape and stealth at the forefront of my mind. Sweat trickling into my eyes and smearing my vision, I pulled harder. Harder. The sharp edge scraped against the cuffs, driving a wedge between the chainlinks as my muscles burned. Dread grew in my gut. Had to glance up, see if

462

the Suns had spotted me. Had to speed up, thrust downwards and break free, no matter how much it hurt.

No. Couldn't lose focus.

The chainlink broke, my hands thrusting downwards, the jagged metalwork slicing a burning gash along my arm. I bit back a scream. With my hands free, I tore the jagged edge clean off the wall. Heart thumping in my chest, I positioned the edge over my neck restraint. Blood trickled from a wound in my neck as my hands slipped on the sweat-slick metal. Clamping down on my panic, gritting my teeth, I sawed a jagged line through the fabric one centimetre at a time, scraping past my jugular.

The fabric snapped. Almost free.

I planted my feet on the hard spacedecking and thrust my body forward. The thick, three-point safety straps biting into my torso, every muscle in my body straining, the stormtech working with me, wrapping around every fibre of my being.

A silent chorus roared in my chest as something inside me ripped apart.

The straps gave with a sudden, violent snap. Soaked in blood and sweat, I staggered to my feet.

Free. I was finally free.

I could have hacked the Suns' throats open and wrestled control of the chainship. I felt the urge enveloping me. I didn't fight it. I didn't cave into it. Instead, I allowed the sensation to crash over me like a wave on a beach, accepting its existence but holding my urges in check until the feeling ebbed away and a secondary escape plan began to formulate in my brain.

Past an emergency barricade for hull breaches was a glowing escape hatch and a series of mottled-white spacesuits with anti-grav protection webbed to the wall. A skyscraper was looming towards us, would be under us in half a minute. I'd throw myself out of the chainship and the spacesuit's emergency override would steer me towards the roof. Wasn't exactly my prime choice, but I wasn't exactly overwhelmed with options right now.

I reached to put the nearest one on when a single word froze me solid. 'You!'

Lasky had noticed the seat was empty. Now, he raced towards me, fumbling for a weapon. I jerked back, scooping up a nearby munitions canister and sending it smashing into his face with a wet crunch. He was slammed screaming to the floor, clawing at his face. His nose was broken, twisted at a hideous angle, several teeth smashed and splintered. 'Get him! Get him!' he screamed like an animalistic child in hysterics, spitting and smashing the decking with his fists.

Hideko screamed at the sight of Lasky. But the Jackal didn't even seem to notice his injured comrade. His gaze latched onto me as he unstrapped himself with frightening speed. I shoved my body into the spacesuit and reached for the emergency hatch with numb fingers, but Hideko was faster. She flipped the ship into a barrel roll. The world spun as I slammed into the ceiling and plummeted back down again so hard I swore I heard a rib crack. Another flip and me and the still-screaming Lasky went smashing into the bulkhead. The Jackal was on his feet and speeding for me, slingshiv glinting in his hand. But he mistimed his lunge and went slipping on Lasky's blood, skidding past us, the hooked curve of the slingshiv missing my eyes by inches. I leaped through the open barrier, stabbing a button to slam it down. The armoured doors began pinching together as the emergency exit hatch slowly peeled open. Wind howled in, fast-freezing my sweat. A pit opened in my gut as the distant streets yawned beneath me.

A scream behind me. Lasky was crawling furiously towards me, his mangled face plastered with hair and blood, twisted in a vicious sneer.

He was so obsessed with tearing me apart, he didn't notice the barricade.

He glanced up just as the armoured barricade pinned him in place, crushing him to the floor. Anger melted into horror and horror melted into agony as the barricade's magnetic seals clamped down. His body twitching as his ribcage and then his spine splintered like rotten twigs.

There's the answer to the age-old question: how do you get Lasky juice?

You squeeze.

I spilled out into open space, spinning in freefall as the Jackal roared my name. The spacesuit used its anti-grav systems and thrusters in small, controlled bursts to guide me down to the hard concrete of the rooftop. I rolled to my back, alive and intact, bloody and sobbing with relief. My bruised body was trembling. Whether from relief or trauma I didn't know and I didn't care. I was alive.

I did it, guys. I did it.

Couldn't afford to sit around, in the likely event the Jackal decided to swing around and finish me off with a railgun. I struggled to my feet, scanning for an exit. I stumbled, pitching over as a hot mass of glutinous stormtech came surging up my throat, splattering wet and thick around my knees.

Make that *barely* alive.

The unfamiliar streets spun around me. Every noise and smell crammed so hard into my skull I was waiting for the moment I'd hear it crack open. My skin was rubbery and translucent as wax, giving me the bizarre notion that if I approached a heat source my flesh would melt and peel off my bones. My bruised arms dangled by my sides like lead pipes. My head pulsed in throbbing waves of pain so deep they knocked me to my knees. My vision was a hazy fog. My insides were clenching so hard it felt like my guts were dissolving in acid, molecule by molecule. My body had suppressed Jae's overdosing to help me survive, but the comedown always swung around, and this time I might not survive it. It felt as if I were already dead, parts of my body slowing and shutting down, while others hadn't realised what was happening.

Go to sleep. Go to sleep and rest for ever.

But the stormtech and my own stubborn pride wouldn't let me.

I had enough sense to tear away my harness and prisoner's suit. Cutting the muzzle from my face was another matter. I netted a dozen fresh wounds and nearly gouged my eye out in the attempt, but the broken strip of steel I'd found eventually cut through the thing and I tugged it off my face. I slipped into an underskin shoved into a broken printer, smelling of someone else's sweat. Judging by the shape, the previous owner had been an alien, but I didn't care. Couldn't care about anything but surviving this nightmare.

I stumbled. Grabbed someone. 'Find Katherine,' I slurred. I was shoved away, slapped against the wall. *Bloody skinnie*, someone spat as the world tilted into stabbing whiteness. I blinked, and I was lying in an alley. Shivering under a blanket of garbage. Freezing wastewater was dripping on me from a broken pipe and I was covered in clammy sweat. My body was still adjusting to the new stormtech, diverting toxic flood water down the sewer pipes of my arteries. I coughed, retching up a sticky glob that was practically fluorescent. I burst into stuttered laughter that morphed into racking, miserable sobs. In the distance I heard the crackle of Harvest gunfire, the dull smack of my father's fists hitting flesh. Felt bruises erupting along my arms like the mushrooming clouds of artillery fire from orbit. Artyom refusing to leave my side when I was sick with fever. Kasia hugging me. My fellow Reapers standing with me in the dawning light.

Someone kicked me out of the alleyway. I snuffled through a garbage disposal for food, soaked up to my elbows in dripping trash. I tried to hunker down in a spaceport shanty, but a group of bored bullies dragged me out to the streets. Punched me a few times before leaving me curled up in a gutter. Blackness came in between blinks. Rain drizzled down. Made myself move before I drowned.

Neon lights from a club stabbing me in the eyes. The guard outside shoved me backwards as I tried to enter. Staggering into an alleyway, sliding to the ground, back scraping bricks. I puked again, lying in my own sick.

Walking. Endless walking. Looking up to see a language I didn't know smudged high above me. People and faces turned into discoloured, nightmarish smears. A hand on my shoulder, quickly starting to melt and drip away. Was I all right? Did I need help? 'Never better,' I said, and threw up again.

I imagined my friends were here with me. Grim urging me forward, Katherine telling me to stay strong, pulling me back up when I sank to the cold, concrete floor. And Artyom, always Artyom, watching me from the end of every alley and vanishing into smoke as I came close.

More walking. Almost hit by an autovehicle. Meandering endlessly through a maze of blurry and dripping back alleys. Heaving, sweating, crying. My skin greyer than New Vladi winter streets after a snowfall. Slowly withering away on the inside.

I took another step, staggered, and my body crumbled. I couldn't move. Could barely breathe. Every limb and muscle had locked up. My head was one planet-sized throb. Panic fluttered like a trapped animal in my chest, quickly swallowed by a warm, fuzzy glow spreading through me.

Go to sleep. Go to sleep and rest.

I closed my eyes.

'Vakov?' Calloused hands rolled me onto my back. A narrow slit of light, eyes creaking open. Someone towering over me and silhouetted against harsh lights. A Torven in a heavy hooded coat. Mugalesh. It was Mugalesh.

'What have you done to yourself, blue one?' she rasped, clothes creaking as she stooped on her haunches next to me. She tsked at the sight of me and hooked me back up, nails digging in my armpits. I wobbled to my feet and somehow managed to take one aching step at a time. I stopped twice to puke. Ropes of blue drool clung to my lips, my insides turning numb. I tried to break away and curl up to sleep. Mugalesh slapped me across the face until the idea of doing that passed.

An eternity later, she pushed me through Grim's door. He rushed towards me, eyes wide, his mouth making shapes. 'Get Katherine,' is all I managed before the blue dragged me under.

44

Second Chance

Flickers of light showed me a white Harmony medclinic, medics and octodrones swarming above me. The hiss of oxygen filters. Someone breathing frantically in my ear. Probably me. I don't know how many times I dropped in and out of consciousness until I stirred fully awake. I was wearing a medskin and attached to a system of whirring white medical machinery that was providing life-support and leeching the stormtech from my body.

The room's visual package had been set to a winter mountaintop. Thick dark pines as old as the galaxy stretched high among carpets of moss and undergrowth, sloping away into mist. The gentle breath of wind whistling over the snowcapped mountain wafted from the speakers, a simulated breeze tousling my hair. The earthy smell of fresh petrichor filled my nose. Somewhere, a dreamy acoustic soundtrack that recalled distant and peaceful landscapes was playing.

White-coated medics came and went. I was to drink as much fluid as I could, to help drain the excess stormtech. My cheeks were still lacerated from the steel muzzle. Didn't want to think about the state the rest of my body was in. My sheets became heavy with blue sweat, needing a routine change every few hours. But I wasn't dead. I wasn't dead. Zero points to Jae, one to me.

Grim was fast asleep in the corner, head sagging against the wall, while Katherine was asleep at the foot of my bed. Her blonde hair sprawled messy and loose around her face. She'd probably been there from the moment I arrived. No doubt the medics had told her to keep out, and no doubt she'd barged in anyway.

I stayed still, listening to the gentle rhythm of her breathing. How long had she waited here, hoping and praying I'd make a recovery?

A lump formed in my throat as everything came crashing down in slow, concussive waves. The friends I'd lost. The Reapers broken and shattered, dying in my arms. The people around me I'd hurt and pushed away because I thought I didn't know anything else, because I wasn't brave enough to listen to their help.

And my brother. The hurt we'd dealt each other because of the hurt the world had dealt us. How I'd failed him in ways I couldn't possibly count. So many brusies and wounds, all tangled up in this mess.

I was a broken man. A poisonous pit that sucked everyone and everything down around me. And somehow, for whatever reason, my friends had seen something worthwhile in me. Something that made them stay by my side in this medclinic, continuing to believe in me, even if I didn't.

Tears welled in my eyes, the lump hardening in my throat as I tilted back towards unconsciousness.

Katherine was waiting for me when I woke up. I could see her body was stiff and her eyes were heavy, but they lit up when she saw me. She wrapped her slim arms around me in a crushing hug, not caring how sticky and sweaty I was. Eventually, she untangled herself and punched me hard on the shoulder. 'What was that for?' I rasped, my throat still raw.

'For leaving us like that.' Her eyes were red from crying. She lifted my arm, where traces of the restraints and needle punctures lingered on my flesh like dissection markings. 'What she did to you . . . if you hadn't come back from that, what would I have done? What would Grim have done?'

'I'm sorry.' I croaked. I noticed I'd been freed of the med-machines sometime during my sleep. Grim was still asleep, still sagging against the wall.

'Even Kindosh was worried about you. Grim's been frantic-ally tracing the routes of every spacecraft leaving Compass. Saren's had search teams searching them out, and Jasken's been pacing and threatening to tear the Suns a new one for hours. And there's an angry Kaiji that won't stop calling and asking about you.'

Juvens. I couldn't help but smile. 'You've all got my back.'

'You're one of us, Vak.' Her hand tightened around mine. 'You're part of the team.'

'That's good,' I said, 'because we're going to need all the help we can get.'

Katherine drew back. 'No. No. No. You're staying right here. The doctors still don't know how your system recovered. You nearly *died*, Vak.'

'Yeah, I'm aware of that,' I said as the stormtech spiralled down my ribs with a newfound vigour. It would take weeks, maybe months to fully integrate into my body, even longer to control it. But I'd learn. I'd learn because there was no other option. 'I'm not sitting here while you go after them.'

'Vak, I will personally strap you down to this bed if I have to.'

I grinned at her. 'You can try.'

But she wasn't kidding. 'The side effects could still be fatal. No one's ever survived a stormtech infestation like that.'

'Which is exactly why I need to help.' I readjusted the universe's itchiest pillow against my back. Like my medskin, it was already saturated with blue sweat. 'I know Jae, and she knows I survived. She'll be expecting us. I saw all the equipment they were using. And this is my brother, my responsibility.'

Katherine placed a hand on my forearm. The rumble of a lungship travelled up from some spaceport below us. 'Artyom is his own man, Vak. None of this is you on.'

'Maybe not. But maybe I can still reach him. I owe it to him to try.' Taking down the Suns would mean consequences for my brother. If he survived, he'd continue to hate me for it. But if I didn't do anything, I'd be damning him to be a part of something he would regret until his dying day. Kowalski knew me well enough to know I'd never forgive myself if that happened.

No more running from my demons. No more pretending I wasn't a part of Harmony. There were only two sides, and my brother and I were on opposing ones. I lifted my arm and watched a trail of stormtech slither up my muscles like smoke. I'd carry this dark gift, along with all the memories and sacrifices that made me who I am, for the rest of my life.

And maybe for the first time, I was okay with that.

Kowalski briefed me about the preparations in place: the squads of Shocktroopers they were assembling, the SSC Battalions being prepped, the tactical plan, the damage control Harmony was installing throughout Compass should the plan go south. It seemed insane, even assuming it all worked out. I didn't know how we were going to repair the damage the Suns had inflicted on Compass. But we had to try.

'We all deserved better,' I told her through my tight throat.

'Who?' Katherine asked.

'Reapers,' I said. 'We stormed into a new hell every day,

knowing what Harvesters, what our own bodies, would do to do us. But we kept at it, because we were doing it for each other. And Harmony lied to us. Used us. We were treated like monsters. So we became monsters.'

'I know,' Katherine whispered. 'That's on us, Vak. And we owe it to you all to try again. *I* owe it to you.'

I gave her a long look. 'You knew about the things stormtech made me do. What it could make me do again. And you never treated me differently for it. You never gave up on me. Why?'

Katherine paused. The simulated wind brushing strands of blonde hair across her face. 'Because I saw you trying, Vak. Even after all you've been through, I saw you wanting so hard to do the right thing, to do right by the people you care about. Even if it hurt, even if it killed you. It showed me the sort of man you are. And I knew I owed it to do right by you, too.' Her hand tightened in mine. 'I'm proud of you, Vak. And I want you to know we're going to do better. Right here, right now. Doing better starts with us.'

I felt the tears beading behind my eyes. 'Vak,' Katherine whispered.

'When Jae began injecting me, I thought I was never going to see you again,' I croaked. 'That we'd never get a real shot at this together. You have no idea how much that scared me. I'm not going to let this go by, Katherine. I swear it.'

A mellow expression came across Katherine's face, as if everything else was melting away, laying bare her bedrock of emotions underneath. There was just her, there. Raw and honest. The person she wanted to become, wanted me to become. I wanted so hard to return it that it ached. My throat closed up as I cradled her second hand in mine, feeling the warmth of her skin. The rest of the world seemed to gently fall away from us, a sudden peace washing over me. One I hadn't realised I'd spent so many hard years searching for. A peace

I thought I've never have again, ever since I buried my sister with my own trembling hands and looked out at the frozen hellhole that was my home, feeling in my heart there wasn't a place for someone like me in the world.

For the first time in years, the future seemed to have hope.

45

Hellbound

Grim almost knocked me over when he finally stirred awake, hugging me with brute strength I didn't know he possessed. He was so happy he kept tripping over his sentences, sometimes abandoning them completely to embrace me again. His eyes were wild and happy as he sat next to me and picked at my breakfast. 'You gave me a hell of a scare,' he told me through a mouthful of spiced eggs.

'I know.'

'I mean, if you'd died, who would listen to my whining?'

I grinned at him. 'Who said I ever listened to it?'

Grim wasn't my only visitor, of course. Shocktroopers, Strikers, gunrunners, Primers and various other Harmony operatives came to offer congratulations, clap me on the back, or just to pay their respects. A few Reapers stopped by, although none from my former Battalion. News travels fast among SSC ranks. Saving Kowalski from the razornade in the Warren had done me a world of favours. I'd asked Jasken to pass on a request of mine to Harmony's chief armourer and he promptly agreed to it.

Eventually, the conversation with Grim turned serious.

'We're going to be forming a co-ordinated assault on the Suns' home base,' I explained. 'Jae's going to be expecting us, forming defence systems against our forces. I need you wired into your technest, ten steps ahead of the Suns, overriding their traps and defences, whatever they throw at us. Any darkmarket tech you shouldn't have, any remote access you shouldn't be using, now's the time to use it.'

'I'm sure I can manage that,' Grim said.

'Don't disconnect for a moment. I don't care if Mugalesh tries to drag you out, you stay in contact.'

'Got it.' He flashed his hacksaw teeth at me, filled with bits of egg and bacon. 'Thank goodness for her, eh? Said you looked like death when she found you in the alley.'

'Felt like it, too,' I said. The stormtech wasn't trying to re-arrange my anatomy for the hell of it anymore, but I still felt its raw power itching through my body like a second musculo-skeletal system. My limbs felt like they'd been reinforced with nanofilament carbon fibre, a latticework of protective armour woven into my flesh. My sense of smell and hearing was so blisteringly strong it hurt. I was probably half alien by now. Maybe more. Blue, rocky scabs were starting to erupt from my skin. Overnight, my body hairs had thickened and grown denser. I smelled more pungent. I could only imagine what other gross side effects my body was gleefully racking up for me down the line.

The bite of the restraining harness clamped around me was a raw memory. The altered stormtech pumping like molten lava into my veins. The trauma had, quite literally, been perman-ently fused into my body. But if you've got scars, it's better to learn to live with them than pretend they don't exist.

'There's no way to stop you doing this, is there?' Grim asked.

'Nope. If I don't make it—' I held up a hand as my friend objected, '*If* I don't make it, Harmony will take care of you. Kowalski will see to it. Will you let her?'

Grim gave it some thought. Then finally: 'If you trust 'em, so do I.'

'I trust Jae and her gang far less, let's put it that way.'

Grim dangled his legs from the bed next to me. Simulated wind tousled his hair. 'I'm scared, man,' he said, serious for once. It wasn't until I saw his hands were shaking that I realised *how* scared. 'I'm so scared I want to puke.'

I raised a small smile. 'So am I.'

'It's the unknown, you know? Not knowing where things are going to land.' He glanced up at me. 'I just don't want this to be the end.'

'It won't be,' I told my friend. 'This is just the start for you and me. We're going to explore every floor of this asteroid together, every crazy bar, every little world, and drink until you're sick and puking again.'

A faint smile traced across Grim's lips. 'How do you know all that?'

'I don't. But I've got to remind myself who I'm fighting for, who I'm returning home to. Otherwise, what's the point to any of it?' I bumped my shoulder into his. 'We're going to make it out of this.'

'That's a promise?'

'It's a promise.'

Walking into Harmony's Tactical Command Centre was a hell of a nostalgia trip.

The sprawling room was lit up in turquoise greens, ultramarine blues and vermillion reds. The reinforced walls were a smear of machinery and glowing flexiscreens. Substrates whined between mirror-smooth panelling that glistened like quicksilver. Tactical command tables beamed with holographic orbital data and incoming updates in electric blues and sunbright golds. On raised walkways, men and women were plugged into circular tactical command pods, pearlescent light from consoles glowing across their faces. The smell of heated machinery, metallic dust and sweat was heavy in the air. Out through a floor-to-ceiling viewport were the tiered levels of the primary hangar bay, the polished decking clustered with ships and frantic with activity.

All bearing a striking resemblance to the Command Centre I'd walked into when I first became a Reaper.

Only difference? Since then, everything had changed.

I stood next to Kowalski as Saren addressed the scattering of Harmony SSC personnel in front of him. Strikers, Shocktroopers, Primers, Reapers and several Sub Zeros stood listening. Their armour was a sea of colours and models, plastered with engravings, rankings, indications of campaigns completed or involvement in certain operations across the Common. Tilted flexiscreens spiderwebbed into multicoloured strands of data: long-range scanners and orbital probes had confirmed the House of Suns' activity in the Void Zones. Harmony research analysts had dredged up ancient schematics of the areas long thought uninhabitable after the war. A three-dee topographical outline of a floor plan was blinked onto the screens in a riot of greens and blacks, spiralling walkways and tunnels carving their way through ancient asteroid rock.

'The Suns must have rigged up a rudimentary life-support system and repressurised the zones,' Saren explained. 'They've fixed the grav-plates and have been siphoning oxygen and power from solar farms for almost a year now. They've been hijacking cargo-haulers, killing the crews and stealing their supplies to sustain the areas.'

A round of murmurs and the slow grind of armour plates against each other. They'd all heard the House of Suns' plans for us non-cultists, and what they'd done to me. Jae had kidnapped and tortured a Reaper, and, by extension, touched them too. Pack loyalty is a hell of a good thing to have at your back.

Saren and his SubPrimers began the tactical formation, allocating his Division into squads, Companies, Battalions. Allocating their attack formations and discussing tactical approaches and battleplans. Those already assigned with a unit departed with their comrades. Battle strategists, weapon suppliers, scientists and mass kineticists whirled around us. Equations and metrics zapping through the air in bright neon reds and blues. Made my head spin just to be in the middle of all this seemingly co-ordinated madness again.

My name was called. I was to be allocated into the Cobalt Squad, Fourth Division, with Saren leading the charge.

There was no telling when Jae would launch her assault, and Harmony wasn't about to let her make the first move. Damage control squads were assembled to deal with the fallout if the House of Suns succeeded in activating the Surge. They were already quarantining infected civilians, supplying them with stormtech suppressors under the watchful care of first-class xenobiologists and medics. Compass was honeycombed and striated with bulkheads and backup life-support systems that would kick in if a floor was breached or required quarantine. Rehab centres were being fully staffed and operational around the clock. Media departments were preparing vid-transcripts explaining the situation to the public.

Wasn't about to say it, but I had an inkling they were wasting their time. If Jae really did succeed in turning Compass into a beacon for the Shenoi, we were all finished anyway. But looking out at the wide gathering that made up Harmony's Special Service Command, I let the thoughts melt away. All these people were going to dive face-first into hell, knowing many would never return home and leaving behind friends, family, loved ones. I told myself to trust in them. Trust that we'd give everything we had to make this work. Because, at the end of the day, it's not machines or power or big ships or big guns that makes a difference. It's people. People willing to fight like hell for the ones they care about.

As Saren delved into some complicated tactical formation, Katherine leaned in to ask if I'd made all the calls. I told her I had.

The briefing ended. Fincher, Harmony's chief armourer, came to inform me my new suit was ready. A blade-thin woman with sweeping dark hair who seemed more in place at the head of a business empire than a grease-spattered workshop. She led me to the armoury on the outermost section of the Station and towards the podium where the armour awaited. *Gunpowder Milkshake* had sent me a new suit. Since Harmony was footing the bill this time, I wasn't about to go for anything but the best. It was a towering beast of black and dark gold plating, so bulky it took a team of several armourers to strap me into it. The helmet had drag-fins and a slick, mirrored curve for a faceplate, glowing with pulsating lights. The inner gel-padding spilled like oily liquid down my back, before forming a resin-like substance that tightened against my body for extra mobility and dexterity. I felt the silicon plating expand with the clenching of my muscles, the close biochemical calibration and hydraulics fine-tuned to strike the balance between mobility and protection. I could feel the composite layers of inner materials, hydrostatic gels, pressure seals, titanium alloy shells, superconductors, microelectric fields, nanoparticle surfacing and shielding, all slotting together like three-dee puzzle pieces, wrapped up and locked with airtight firmness around me. I couldn't stop grinning. I could practically feel the thing snorting like a bull, ready to rampage.

Fincher rattled off some of the perks. Blades hidden in the sleeves. Emergency ejection. Additional magnetic weapons holsters. Kinetically rechargeable nanoshielding – good against bullets and plasma rounds, but not against diamond-edged slingshivs.

Fully armoured, I walked across the scuffed decking towards the utility-cluttered armoury to meet the rest of my fireteam. Led by Saren, it was composed of Kowalski, Jasken and the Shocktroopers from our assault on the Warren – Arya, Kuen and Vanto. Jasken lumbered over in his scarred and blackened gear, lugging a crate of scattershots, handcannons, autofiles, carbines and railguns. 'Planning a good night out?' I asked.

Jasken shrugged. 'Why shoot something once when you can shoot it fifty times?'

'Let's hope our enemies don't have the same philosophy.'

Jasken hefted the meanest looking scattershot I'd ever seen. 'Actually, I hope they do.'

'You *want* them to kill you?'

'No, I want to see them *try*.' He planted himself on a munitions crate, scattershot balanced on his armoured knee. 'Listen, kid. I'm glad you could make all this work. Couldn't have been easy.'

'Just doing what needs to be done,' I said.

Jasken snorted and wolfed down an energy bar. 'I don't believe that, and I'm not sure you do either. But to hell with that, we've got cultists to kill.' He jabbed the energy bar in my direction. 'Want some?'

'How the hell can you eat at a time like this?'

'I always eat before battle,' Jasken said. 'Can't imagine a worse way to go than dying on an empty stomach.'

I collected my weapons from the gleaming racks, strapping appropriate utilities and blades to the magnetic holders on my waist. Quickmatter clips and energy cartridges being slotted in like knuckles cracking. Voices streamed from the speakers, ordering Cobalt Squad to move out. Thudding down the corridor with my fireteam, armed and armoured to the teeth, I was suddenly whipped back to my Reaper fireteam. Us pulling on our armour, trading jokes or insults, moving out to fight on some new, alien landscape. Most of them were dead and buried and I wished more than anything they'd lived to see the future they'd given so much for.

Which meant it was up to me to make it count.

46
Into the Dark

We rode up to the Void Zones in tense silence, all of us outfitted in Harmony's best. Our headlamps cut narrow beams through the derelict tunnels of the Void Zones. The uninviting hallways of exposed asteroid rock were strung up with scaffolding like the weathered remains of an immense whale skeleton, littered with discarded clawdrills, power tools and vacuum-pressurised spacesuits. A gritty blanket of asteroid dust and soot coated everything. Bulkheads were plastered with warning decals, the areas beyond exposed to hard vacuum. One of those abandoned areas of the asteroid that was still under repair all these years after the war had stuttered to a halt.

The wide smears of familiar, ominous House of Suns symbols painted crudely on the bulkheads told us the place wasn't as empty as it appeared. Left little to imagine what had happened to the construction workers here.

Dread tightened in my stomach. *Please let everyone survive this. Please let everyone just survive this.*

Kowalski wore gunmetal-grey armour, bulky and razor-trimmed; she'd swapped out her helmet visor for sulphur-coloured magnifying optic lenses that completely obscured her face.

'You'd think we were on a deserted station or something,' said Kuen. He had hawk wings carved into his helmet, and he peered around with interest as we walked in lockstep. Vanto, a huge brute of a man in bright-red armour, took no such notice and stomped down the silent corridors, his heavy assault slugrifle angled around every corner.

'Eyes open,' Saren muttered. 'The Suns could be lying in ambush.'

'Oh, I hope they are. Let them try and get past me,' Jasken drawled. The spacedecking trembled under his ungainly foot-steps, the skullface etching on his helmet turning him into an armoured ghoul in the dark. He wore a harness pimped out with bizarre grenades and experimental-looking explosives.

We couldn't pinpoint the House of Suns' exact location, but probe scanners placed them in the vicinity of the asteroid's pinnacle, deep in the Void Zones. Our forces were represented as clusters of red dots in the half-completed blueprint of the Void Zones, slowly expanding across my HUD as we headed towards our agreed rendezvous. Jae expected another assault. I doubted she'd anticipate the stealthy approach we were taking.

The massive lifts around us were rigged to transport chain-ships up to the most damaged Void Zones. I shifted impatiently as we climbed in and activated for the top floor, the age-old mechanisms groaning. Suddenly, the stormtech hammered inside me, frantic and fast. I frowned, but the sensation grew as we inched upwards, until it felt like I was attached to an electrical charge.

Then I knew.

'Jae's starting it,' I snapped into my commslink, swapping to the all-units channel. 'She's activating the Surge now!'

Kowalski swore. We'd all known it was going to happen, but had hoped for more time, maybe even to get there before she started.

The lift shuddered to a halt. The lights spluttering and dying as the ancient mechanism groaned and conked out.

Our armour lights winked in the dark. The stormtech was beating inside me, but didn't feel like it was growing now. Jae had pumped me full of the enhanced stormtech she was using for her own men, not the Surge-stormtech she was spreading through Compass civilians. I was in the clear, but my body could still *feel* the ripple effect, like a ghostly transmission on some untapped radio frequency.

'Out, out, out!' I engaged the armour's hydraulics and used the boost to spring the whole four metres to punch through a hatch on the elevator roof. We were in a deep, echoing shaft, simulated wind howling down. My armour lent me the strength to wrench open the rusted door and slip through. I stabbed the emergency override button and the elevator started grinding up again.

I tapped into Compass' frequency as it rose, getting a feed from Starkland's main square. There were two dozen skinnies and Reapers convulsing on the ground. Another dozen were stumbling along the street, eyes turning blue as they threw themselves at people, broke windows, and set themselves to destroying everything in their path. One stumbled into the path of an autocar and went flying, crashing down on the pavement in a blue smear. Someone screamed as a skinnie dragged an old woman by her hair across the street.

'Saren, we have to move!' I said as the others arrived, already moving ahead down the dim hall plastered with more Suns symbols.

'I hear you,' Saren said. Similar affirmatives echoed down the commslink.

I was about halfway down the hall when my body pulsed a warning. I dropped as a dark muzzle aimed towards me and spat three-round burst, crackling past my head and thudding

485

into the wall. The figure poked out of cover, training her rifle on me again, but I'd already bounded forward and driven my slingshiv into her heart. She collapsed at my feet with a thud, yells ricocheting down the halls.

We'd arrived.

My fireteam scrambled around me, weapons primed and readied. The familiar rhythm of sliding into formation, dissecting the battlefield, working alongside my squad, buzzed through me like a long-lost memory as we burst together into an area clustered with a jungle of scaffolding. Two or three fireteams' worth of cultists stared at us down the barrel of their weapons.

The room erupted into chaos. Streams of gunfire shredded wooden beams to splinters, smashed metal into hot red chunks and crumpled scaffolds into gnarled scrap. Multicoloured bursts of gunfire crisscrossed the room in rapid streaks. We slammed into our positions, Arya, Vanto and Katherine performing a wide flank, issuing bursts of suppressing fire and drawing the Suns' attention. The rest split in two: Saren and Kuen, and me and Jasken, each mini-division covering each other. Jasken was roaring insults and taunts, throwing micronades, the room heaving with violent shockwaves and detonating with fiery explosions, frying optic nerves and photoreceptors. Supercharged projectiles sliced past my head, tearing a mouthful of metal from the walls. My armour's shielding rippled in bright blue clouds, a Harvester leaning over a banister and pouring small-arms fire into my chest. I angled my high-calibre autorifle upwards and returned a salvo of superheated rounds, tearing through the scaffolding and through the shooter's face like wet bark. A hailstorm of gunfire clattered on the metal around me, cultists already swinging around to target me. Vanto let rip a burst of covering fire, sending the assailants scrambling for cover, giving me time to tear up through the scaffolding to the next floor. My visor flashing urgent warnings. I ducked into cover, blind firing to give Jasken the time to reach me. A round sparked off Jasken's helmet, knocking him sideways with a grunt. I slammed my shoulder into the cultist who'd done the deed, sending her flailing backwards, before blasting her twice in the head. She tumbled from the scaffold and went smashing to the floor. Panting, I helped Jasken to his feet, already leaning down my autorifle's circular sights, watching for my fireteam, picking off cultists.

Something was wrong.

These people weren't trained. They were barely armoured. It was poor defence. Jae wasn't a soldier, but she wasn't stupid, either. If she'd anticipated our strategy, there was a chance she'd drawn us into a trap.

I called for Grim, but he'd already seen it. 'The room's rigged with explosives!' he said. 'Disabling as fast as I can, but be ready!'

I yelled for the rest of the fireteam to get down. I burst towards Jasken, smashing the two of us to the grillwork flooring as the world above us exploded like hellfire, thunderclaps going off in my skull and shuddering down my spine. The flare was so strong my visor autopolarised. A loose grenade clattered down to explode near a shrieking cultist, turning bone and flesh into a shower of bloody mist. Jae had sent the worst of her men in here to be sacrificed. Poisoned meat for the wolves.

For maybe the first time, I truly understood my enemy.

'The corridors are rigged with death-traps every ten metres,' Grim told me as our fireteam resumed formation, covering each other. 'I'll take out what I can, but watch your back!'

'Same formation as before,' Saren panted, voice muffled by his helmet. 'Keep the commslink clear, always have someone on your flank. Move out. Let's make it count.'

On the schematic, all the other SSC units were slowly carving their way through the corridors, rerouting and doubling back when they encountered traps or blockades. We did the same, moving through telescopic tunnels like the corridors of a lungship, ringed with scaffolds and surface-gear; calling out any hazards and enemy sightings, scanning each sector as we progressed. Jasken suddenly yelled a warning, sending a succession of micronades skittering down the corridor. White smoke gushed out in thick, smothering spurts. Anyone without a helmet would be blind and totally screwed. Cultists emerged from the smoke like armoured wraiths, dark-muzzled rifles already locking us in their sights.

We levelled our weapons, gunfire rattling in a furious exchange of heat and smoke, the fury shuddering in my teeth. The walls and floor buckled and blackened under the munitions. I burst ahead with Jasken, Saren and Kuen at our flank and fired a three-round burst into the smoke, blasting a man in green armour through his faceplate, blood and skull fragments spraying out. Screams and bellows of pain ripped out. Bodies slamming to the floor. Snatches of sun-bright muzzle flashes and glowing visors through the smoke. Blades slashing down, puncturing through armour and through skin. A cultist stumbling sideways, chopped in half by a slingshiv. Molten metal dripping from the ceiling. Beside me, Jasken's scattershot punched devastating slugs into the incoming enemies, ripping out in furious, coughing bursts. A man wearing armour plastered with Suns slogans was whiplashed sideways, a chunk of his chest blown off, his legs thrashing on the ground. The stormtech gave a warning lurch in my chest and I jerked around, saw a cultist with yellow armour fast approaching Jasken from an angle he couldn't see. Too close to use anything ranged. I rushed forward and slammed my armoured bulk into the cultist, crushing him into the wall. The blade that nearly cleaved Jasken's shoulder off slashed harmlessly past, missing him by inches. Teeth gritted, I slammed my fist into the cultist's jaw, using his body as cover from incoming rounds as I kicked him flailing backwards. Jasken timed it perfectly, lining up the scattershot as soon as he was clear, punching a slug in the cultist's head, sending him spattering to the ground.

'Thanks, kid,' Jasken grunted. The rest of the fireteam was tangled up in fights from behind. We pressed our armoured backs against each other. Breathing hard, staring down the corridor through the sights of my autorifle. Jasken hosing incoming enemies from the front with covering fire, me picking them off from the back. A cultist with bones embedded in her armour was wrestling with Katherine, her dripping blade inches from her throat. I sent a three-round burst ripping out, punching through the side of her head and slamming her to the ground. Katherine snapped a frantic nod my way, then spun around to help Saren.

Yells and echoes of gunfire from other fireteams and assault squads sounded around us. I'd forgotten what hell the battlefield really is. No logic. No order. No feats of magnificent bravery. Just you and your friends clawing through a storm of chaos, fighting like hell not to have your head cleaved in two or a hot shell punching through your chest. My body tried to drag me into it, to break from my defence position and lose itself in the bloody whirlwind of the battlefield like it once had. I gritted my teeth, resisting and overcoming my body's urges without outright fighting them. If I broke position, I'd put my friends at risk.

A volley of supercharged rounds detonated off my shoulder. White-hot agony ripped down my arm, speared down my shoulder blades. I gasped for air, swimming in sweat inside my armour. My vision hazy with violent shockwaves. Trying to untangle the horrific cacophony of battle. Vaguely aware of Jasken moving to cover me as my shields recharged.

A cultist in blood-red armour swerved around Jasken's guard and slammed me into the wall. Metal buckled under me, pain stabbing through my skull as my assailant slammed his armoured fist into my jaw. His rifle was jammed between us, going off as we wrestled for it, projectiles the size of a fist punching into the wall around me. Jasken blasted my assailant, but was knocked down by a huge man in charcoal-black armour, the Suns' symbol painted white on his chestplate. Our defences were weakening. Couldn't be swarmed. I gritted my teeth and smashed my helmet into my assailant, skull rattling, sending him stumbling back. I hurled myself clear. A barrage of gunfire went slicing inches above my head as I scooped up a discarded scattershot and aimed at my assailant as he charged me. The scattershot jerked violently in my hands as I blasted chunks of his armour off in smoking scraps, throttling the trigger until I got him dead centre in the chest, crunching against the wall. I swung the scattershot towards Jasken's opponent, barely taking aim before snapping off three rounds into his back, his armour fizzling.

'That was one hell of a shot, kid.' Jasken's skullface filled my vision as he pulled me back to my feet.

The corridor clear, we cut down the remaining Suns engaging the rest of the fireteam before moving on.

I watched Saren and Vanto climb up the scaffolding and run alongside us, tagging incoming enemies. They lit up an incoming squad, their grenades and weapons glowing in my HUD. We focused our fire on a cultist armed with gas grenades and concussion bombs. Rounds ricocheted in furious clatters around us. Heavy, thunking footsteps as a cultist in hulking red armour came barrelling out of the smoke, smashing into us. Metal screamed and crunched. Katherine was slammed to the ground, Jasken half-crushed against the wall. I stabbed our attacker through the hand, pinning him to the wall. He roared and smashed me across the face with his other hand, my head whipping sideways and almost biting my tongue in half. Vanto reared up behind me, blasting him in the head until he slumped down, but the distraction had cost us. A metal thunk at my feet. Concussion bomb. I jerked my head up, an enemy squad charging towards us from around a corner.

'Armour wall!' Saren roared out. Age-old battlefield jargon leaped through my memory as I squeezed between Katherine and Vanto in a line-up, shoulders thrust forward, blades extended, the six of us triggering our armour-lock functions. Our suits shimmered with a red hazy outline of triple-shielding, rendering us near immobile in our armour. I just had time to clench my teeth before the concussion bomb erupted and the incoming squad slammed into us.

Whooopf. The world blared into white-hot fury. Couldn't see. Couldn't see. All sound swallowed up. Felt like a sun had gone supernova inside my skull and spat shrapnel into my brain. The armour-lock had turned my flesh numb. Shapes moving through the whiteness, the world returning in ear-shattering fragments. Helmets smashing into mine, armour plates grinding against each other, blades stabbing down, bloody teeth gritted, eyes wild with battle fury.

We released armour-lock as one. Ears popping, body tingling, I stabbed at a cultist and cleaved half his hand away as he collapsed, but he was replaced with two more. Guns going off at point-blank range, denting my armour in a dozen places. Grenades exploded in furious bursts of red shrapnel down the corridor, shredding fallen bodies apart. Vanto hacked at a Suns' helmet like he was chopping wood, the blade crunching down between the bridge of his nose, the black spatter of brains across his eyes. The muzzle flash of a scattershot roared out, blasting Vanto backwards, almost carving through his armour. Couldn't get a lock on the shooter. Too many of them, over-crowding us too fast. We pulled back as one, spraying cover fire. We'd held, but now we were pinned down. And I've seen what happens when fireteams are caught in a killzone.

I quickly told the rest of my fireteam what I was going to do, told them to be ready. 'Now!' I yelled, getting a running start and leaping ahead on my thrusters. The cultists dodged out of the way on instinct, but I slammed into two of them like an armoured wrecking ball. My skull rattling and the stormtech throbbing, I picked myself up and spun back around, unloaded my handcannon into the corridor, the walls shuddering with echoing blasts. Sandwiched between us, the cultists had nowhere to go as we hosed them from both sides with salvos of gunfire. The heavy, supercharged rounds of my handcannon punching fist-sized holes through them. A cultist with Suns' phrases scrawled along his armour circled like a shark around the scaffolding, ducking my blasts, trying to get up close. I deliberately missed, let him think he had an opportunity. He reared up like a dark wave, but I feinted left, his scattershot blast punching past me, aimed down the glowing barrel of my handcannon and blasted him. His body thudded down as the echoes of the gunshot died out in my head.

The corridor was clear, but wouldn't be for long. 'They're trying to flank us down the side tunnels,' Saren said. 'Move out, quickly!'

But before we could, a barricade slammed down in front of us. Trapping us. We pressed our backs against the wall, Saren and Kuen kneeling down as cultists came screaming around the corner. The walls denting and showering sparks as they ripped out suppressing fire.

'Grim!' I yelled over the armoured thunk of incoming enemies.

'Almost got it!' Grim yelled.

A cultist in heavy silver armour interlocked with black machinery lunged out, the railgun mounted on his shoulder flashing as it vomited out a slug between me and Vanto, splashing metal-eating acid over the barricade. Saren throttled the trigger, tearing through his ankles and sending him shrieking to the floor. More Suns were peeking around the corner, waiting for additional forces before swarming us.

The barricade dilated open and we rushed through. Grim shut it down again as soon as we were clear. We kept each other covered as we pounded down the corridors. The crackle of bullets echoing from somewhere. Saren was about to lead us down another passageway when I called him back. 'It's a trap,' I growled. The stormtech was pulsing in me, my arm hairs raised. 'They wanted us to go this way. Like cattle into the meatgrinder.'

'We don't have time to argue,' Saren yelled, already moving forward again.

'We go there, we'll run straight into an ambush. That's why they flanked us, they knew we'd run this way.' I glanced into the mirrored visors of my fireteam. I thumped a fist against my armoured chest, heaving with the stormtech's frantic motions. 'I can feel it.'

'I'm with the kid,' Jasken grunted behind his skullface helmet. Vanto and Kuen nodded their agreement.

'We can't risk it,' Katherine told Saren. 'We find another route.'

The barrier whined and glowed with heat as the cultists began cutting their way through. 'There's nowhere else to go,' Saren yelled.

'Then we make somewhere.' Jasken kneeled down and primed a micronade on the floor as the barricade gave a tortured groan, bullets spilling out through the opening slit. The five of us formed another armour wall, spraying covering fire, sheltering Jasken with our bodies. Gunfire clattered on the walls around me, grazing my helmet. Vanto yelled and clutched at his chest as a fusillade almost punched through his shields, his armour blackened and guttering with little fires. The barricade creaked higher. Armoured legs became visible beneath. Pipes along the walls bursting, showering oily fluids in hissing arcs, spraying across my faceplate.

'You might want to step back!' Jasken yelled. The words were barely out of his mouth before the micronade detonated, carving open a man-sized hole in the metal. One by one, we dropped into the corridor below.

I glanced up, breathing hard in my helmet. Kuen was the last to come, about to jump down when a barrage of gunfire blasted him backwards and killed his shielding. Saren tried to go back for him, but a cultist swept up behind him and planted his slingshiv through Kuen's chest. Metal slithered out through his back, glistening wetly. He screamed, hands feebly trying to fend off the armoured cultist in front of him, when a second slingshiv went skewering through his faceplate and his body went limp.

Spitting threats of retribution, Jasken lobbed a microgrenade back up through the hole and yelled at us to run like hell, a shockwave travelling up my back as we tore down the halls, rage fuelling the burning in my legs. The edges of my vision merged with the Renchio battlefields. Foreign languages screaming for the murder of my friends. Dirt and mud crunching beneath my feet.

But I was here now, with a new fireteam willing to lay down their lives for mine, willing to walk into hell with me. Like the old one did. Fighting for a future where their sacrifice and courage counted. Ratchet. Alacatrz. Cable. Myra. Drummer. Everything I was, everything that had been done to me, I put into this moment. I let the battle-memory burn in me with a fire that not even stormtech could muster.

We raced into a gently lit hangar bay, easily three-hundred metres tall and twice as wide. A semi-completed arrivals hall for a spaceport hotel lobby near the pinnacle of the asteroid. Scaffoldings ran along the perimeter, the walls still charred ash-black from Harvest artillery. A window bay had been torn open, only the translucent blue shield-barrier holding back the hard vacuum of space.

We kept our weapons up and readied as we swept through. 'No grenades or trap mechanisms in the room,' Grim told us.

'No one on thermal,' Katherine called out.

'All clear,' Saren said.

But my hackles were raised and I didn't hesitate saying so. An exit large enough to drive a chainship through sat open at the top of the metal walkway. We got halfway there before an armoured blast door guillotined down. Magnetic securing bolts the size of a man punched home, echoing like gunshots through the hangar.

'That's a dreadnought-class blast door,' Vanto growled. 'It'd take a warship to punch through that!'

'Watch out!' Grim yelled. Around us, a series of black-barrelled, black-muzzled nanogun turrets thrust out of hidden crevices. Their targeting software was already locked onto us. We ducked down behind a ledge as the soundscape was obliterated, the barrage of rounds shattering the world around us, metal splinters showering out like spears.

'They've got MR-19s!' Jasken roared, our armour scraping as we inched closer together, blaster fire gouging furrows in the sintered regolith all around us.

'Meaning what?' Saren roared back.

'Meaning we're screwed!'

Because the universe has got such a messed-up sense of

495

humour, the shield-barrier at the far end of the hangar began crackling. Dread gnawed through my guts.

'Grav-boots, now!' I yelled. 'They're going to breach us!'

The words were barely out of my mouth before the shield-barrier disappeared and the world was sucked out into space.

47

Trigger Fingers

There's no way to describe the hard vacuum of space. Not unless you've been exposed to it. And the closest description of vacuum is that it's hell. Cold, annihilating, devastating hell. Nothing else makes you realise so precisely that you're nothing more than a few scraps of meat and bone.

Everything not nailed down in the room was sucked out with brutal force. Scaffolds, toolboxes, spacesuits, pylons, work-stations – all cartwheeling and smashing into each other, tearing out into cold space. Metal decking the size of a man ripped from the floor like strips of paper, slicing inches above our heads. The thunder of the nanoguns was silenced, vibrations shuddering up my body as their devastating assault continued, sparks showering, the floors denting. The monstrous beast that was space clawed at us like a starving animal with a bottomless hunger. My balls wanted to crawl back up into the warmth of my bowels. Every muscle flaring up like hard re-entry from orbit. Our grav-boots whining as they glued us fast to the floor. We looked at each other, panting hard and fast in our commslink, caught between getting shredded by warship-class, military-grade nanogun turrets and hard vacuum. It looked like the end.

But I'd already told them of my backup plan. I activated the icon in my HUD – the one given to me by Juvens.

Less than a minute later, a one-man gunship streamed into the hangar. The gunship was shaped like a bullet, the angular edges warbling with tech and ringed with glowing blue lights. Nanoguns swivelled to track the new hostile ship. The gunship's hull crackled with what looked like lightning bolts, the shielding absorbing the assault. Long-barrelled space-cannons oozed out from the gunship's starboard flank like skeletal arms. The hangar flared with brilliant blue-white explosions as a volley of railgun rounds and plasma charges streaked from the gunship. I wrenched my neck up against vacuum, watching the nanogun turrets get blasted away into glistening orange slag and torn out into vacuum as if ripped by an invisible hand. I almost wanted to laugh. Here, the Suns' best ordnance was getting crushed with ease at the hands of an alien species they hated.

Done with shafting the nanoguns, Juvens wasted no time targeting the armoured blast doors that I'd tagged in a golden glow, and giving them a hell of a pounding. He poured an endless stream of furious railgun fire, the metal glowing red-hot as Grim snapped the shield-barrier back into place. We collapsed to our knees as a tsunami of sound came crashing back down and the blast doors were smashed inwards, the bulkheads ripped from their hinges with a shuddering explosion.

'Thanks, Juvens,' I rasped into the frequency. My throat was raw as sandpaper. Must have been screaming. 'You saved our skins. That was a hell of a show.'

The gunship hovered above me like an aquatic creature bobbing in an invisible current as Juvens appeared on my HUD. Surrounded by an array of glowing battle readouts, he was fully armoured and equipped with a sleek black-gold helmet that slipped over his horns like they were metallic scythes. The Space Marshall's smug voice echoed down the commslink. 'That was nothing,' he said. 'Destroying enemy property helps me sleep at night.' The gunship swerved away, slipping through the shield-barrier. 'I'm off to reload. I'll be circling, if you need me again. Don't destroy *all* the cultists before I get there.'

Jasken stumbled to his feet. 'You crazy son of a bitch,' he panted, slapping my back. 'That actually worked.'

But Grim was already warning us of incoming hostiles, the IFF tags on our HUDs blinking crimson. We lost a few seconds checking each other's gear for breaches and damage before jumping through the superheated edges of the bulkhead door, readying our next attack. Burning down the corridor, I couldn't help but glance at what was happening across Compass. Kirribuli was unadulterated chaos. The once-golden sand was streaked with bloody arcs and littered with dead bodies. Skinnies twitched on the ground or chased after others. A young boy screamed for his mother as he ran from two skinnies who were frothing blue at the mouth. Others were straight-up Bluing Out on the streets. A group of people were perched atop the cruiser-liner I'd seen Samantha Wong's body in, rifles barking as they targeted skinnies. Folks were boarding themselves up in shops, fighting for space. Something cracked inside me as a skinnie was cut down moments before she got her hands on a crying girl.

Harmony was trying to get a handle on the situation; tranquilising skinnies in the streets and creating quarantine zones. But it was never going to be enough.

Back in the corridor, we hacked and fought for every inch of space. Enemies ambushed us at every turn. We began making snap decisions and executing crazy battlefield manoeuvres that only the stupid or desperate ever used. We lurched around corners into firing squads or kamikaze bombers, going out in a blaze of bloody glory for their beloved aliens. Grim worked furiously from his technest to disable and spring traps. We broke through bulkhead after bulkhead, navigating the labyrinth of dimly lit tunnels. All the while, my body kept tearing me towards the onslaught, eyes darting back and forth as I dissected the battlefield.

A channel from Ark Squad, Fourth Division, broke into our commslink, his callsign lighting up. 'Saren! This is Ark Leader. We're pinned down on a bridgeway, taking heavy fire.' Screams and gunfire echoing violently in the background. 'Casualties high and about to get a hell of a lot higher.'

'Hold tight, we're on our way,' Saren responded. The callsign corresponded to a waypoint icon, shared with our entire division. Fifty metres ahead, we got to a bridgeway. Below us, Harmony and the Suns fought on similar bridgeways in little worlds of chaos. One was wreathed in smoke, flashes of red and blue as gunfire and grenades were exchanged down the screaming corridor. Another had Ark Squad pinned down by volleys of gunfire. The one below had four Harmony fireteams ravaged and broken. The ones that were still alive were groaning on their backs. The Suns laughed as they moved among the bodies. Taking their time as they jabbed them with slingshivs and electropoles, bullies tormenting a beached turtle. Letting them bleed out slowly before dragging them away.

We swapped for long-range marksman rifles, picking the cultists off level by level. The Suns pinning Ark Squad down whipped around in confusion as a hailstorm of superheated projectiles rained down, cutting them down. 'We owe you one!' Ark Leader said, once they'd peeled out of cover. We advanced together, maintaining pace with the other fireteams as we fought across the bridgeways, the battlefield turning vertical as we exchanged gunfire between the floors. Two at the back, two covering the bridgeway below. Our strategy rippled from level to level, creating a chain of fireteams covering each other's flank. Don't know how it worked, but it did. It was a team effort. Something the Suns would never have; a concept they couldn't wrap their minds around. At my side, Katherine focused her fire on a cultist in grey armour, chiselling away at his shielding until she nailed him in the head, flecks of blue spattering our helmets.

Sweat half-blinding me, I stabbed a cultist through the back of his helmet. For Alcatraz. Dropped him, angling my Titan up and slamming two rounds home into a cultist's chest. For Wong. For all the Reapers that died at the hands of people like these. My body prickled with tension and I spun to see a kamikaze cultist leaping across the scaffolding towards us, heard the whine of the smelter-grenade strapped to his chest. Before I could shoot, a fusillade of red blaster bolts streaked upwards. The torn scaffolding groaned, tilting sideways over the ledge, the kamikaze cultist screaming as he fell in a clatter of metal beams. He exploded into red mist in mid-air, the scaffolding clanging down to crush a squad of cultists on a bridgeway below. Panting, I turned to face Ark Leader. We exchanged a nod of mutual gratitude, each of us returning to our fireteams as we ran through the bulkhead and back into the tunnels.

We heard the heavy rumble of artillery fire echoing around us. 'Juvens wasn't kidding about taking out a few of the Suns,' Katherine muttered.

'Sounds like he's enjoying himself,' I said over a pulse-pounding explosion. The words were barely out of my mouth before the corridor sputtered into darkness and flaring bursts of light from enemy barrels flashed in the gloom, bullets pinging off my armour. Yells as we returned fire, something heavy and wet thudding to the ground. My fingers twitched, my heart thundering. A squad of cultists armed with flamethrowers were charging towards us. Bulkheads locked down behind us. 'Grim!' I screamed down the channel. 'Close the door in front of us. Now!'

The transparent door slammed down. Not fast enough. A cultist had slipped through, a roaring eruption of fire streaming from his flamethrower and enveloping Arya, the crackling heat so fierce I felt it through my suit. Arya's arms flailed and she screamed as she toppled backwards, her suit turned into a blackened shell. The fire whiplashing sideways us as the cultist swerved towards us, but Vanto ducked under the immolating stream, shields flickering as he cut the cultist down. Arya was unmoving, smoke rising from her suit. Only the five of us left.

No time to mourn now. We pressed on in a five-man formation, punching through bulkhead after bulkhead as Grim disabled traps, only to reactivate them when the Suns tried to flank us from behind. Limbs aching and soaked in sweat, I checked the HUD. We were almost there. The next bulkhead led directly to Jae's base.

We were about twenty metres away when chainglass barricades began sealing the entrance, the start of a razorstorm flickering to life. Jasken was already contacting Juvens to help take the barricade out. But by that time, it'd be too late for Compass. There was only one thing to do.

Cut the head off and the body falls.

Explosions rumbled and distant screams swelled as I turned towards the closing barricade.

'Vakov! Don't you dare!' Kowalski snapped. The others turned around towards me, puzzled.

'They'll kill you, Vak!' Grim echoed through the comms. 'Don't do this! Vak!'

But I had to. I couldn't risk throwing anyone else into the meatgrinder. Too much blood had been spilt today. Too many good men and women lost because of my brother and the Suns.

I'm sorry, Katherine. I'm sorry, Grim.

I'm sorry, everyone.

I broke into a run; moving faster than I ever had in my life. Gunfire drowned out my friends yelling my name. I didn't even glance back. If I did, I might stop.

This ended here.

I raced for the narrowly closing hatch winking above me, leaping up the scaffolding and propelling myself up. Lining myself up just right, I stabbed the emergency eject and the armour threw me past the barricade and through the flickering razornade. I landed hard and heavy, rolling to a stop as the gate sealed me inside with the most dangerous woman in the Common.

48

There Will be Blood

I felt the cold first. Freezing, icy cold, creeping to every part of my unarmoured body. I suppressed a shiver, my stormtech spiking as I swept down the hall. My breathing began to slow and I found myself in a half-completed observation deck. The floor was hard, utilitarian spacedecking, but the walls were skinned in pure asteroid rock. The granite-coloured surface had been crudely chiselled back, so the wall looked like overlapping clusters of dark grey spears, about to come raining down. Spacesuits and EVA packs were webbed to metal surfaces. Wrap-around viewports revealed the rough curve of Compass' outer surface. Men were hooked into makeshift battle stations and data feeds trickled down a wall of flexiscreens in bright spasms of colour while secondary screens broadcast the tsunami of chaos below.

Jae wore a vintage dress patterned with bold curlicues, her hair let down in waves. I could hear her conversing with the Jackal through her commslink, checking on progress from some secondary safehouse. She was standing with Sokolav in front of an incongruous spherical box on a tripod, interlocked with whirring black gears and crawling with internal machinery. Twisted streams of cables erupted out of the device like pythons, plugged into a mass of stormtech canisters. The device was all hard, alien edges and I knew, without knowing how, that Jae was using it to contact the Shenoi.

Artyom was standing next to her.

My hands tightened into fists. I should have hated him. The stormtech wanted me to hurt him for the web of lies he'd spun. The grief he'd caused all of us. It wanted me to kill him along with everyone else.

But I couldn't do it. I was not my father.

Artyom might be taller and wider than Jae, but she dwarfed him and everyone else in the room with her presence. I gripped my handcannon hard enough to break it. One shot. That's all it would take. All this could end right here, right now.

I stepped forward. Then I remembered who *wasn't* there.

Hideko's electropole jabbed into my side. My muscles seized up. I tried to fight back but the electrocution came again, the voltage twice as high. My legs lost interest in holding me up and I toppled with a loud thud, my handcannon skidding out of reach.

Everyone snapped around at once. A splinter of a smile appeared on Jae's stony visage, as if she'd expected nothing less. 'And the dog returns to his master.' She was like the mountain ranges I'd grown up around: gentle from a distance, but vast and full of unknown depths and edges that could shred you to pieces.

'Vak?' Artyom was just staring at me. Sokolav's mouth was set in a grim line; as if angry I hadn't escaped when I could.

'Who else?' snapped Jae as two men in armour dragged my limp body towards the centre of the room. They forced me to my knees, one locking my arms behind me so tightly my shoulders ground in their sockets. Hideko smiled at the sight of me in pain. The other guard stripped me of my palmerlog and slingshiv.

A sea of emotions spilled across my brother's face. 'Hey,' I choked out to him. 'How's things?'

'I told you to stay away,' he said. 'Why couldn't you listen?'

'Because he's a fool, like all his kind,' Jae said. 'What did you think you could do in here, Fukasawa? Take on the whole of the House of Suns by yourself? You can't hold back an avalanche with a broom.' She gestured at the flexiscreens. 'Have a good, long look. This is only temporary, you know that. We'll step in with the cure, fix what Harmony could not. There will be blood. They'll fall as we show the world the truth.'

Hideko and her guards murmured a slow, eerie chant of agreement.

'You think you're getting away with any of this? We are coming for you.' I nodded towards the flexiscreens showing Harmony fireteams clawing their way through the hallways. I twisted my face into a wolfish grin. 'What, you Harvesters losing to Harmony once wasn't enough?'

'"We",' Jae mocked as she cupped my jaw. 'You really believe that Harmony is on your side.' Another knife of a smile. 'You tiny, tiny thing. Harmony is not your friend. They are no one's friend. They let you bloody your hands for them. And for what? Revenge? They're a parasite. They destroy everything they touch. They're not coming to save you.' She pitied me. She actually *pitied* me. 'You're alone, Vakov. You've been alone from the day you became a Reaper.'

But she was wrong.

There were people who'd fight with me, die with me. My new fireteam, walking into hell with me to do right by others. The Kaiji who thought Harmony deserved a second chance. Grim, who'd stuck with me even when I'd almost driven him away. And Katherine. Who treated her men like family, who'd seen past the blue parasite twitching through my body, to the person she wanted me to become. All of them fighting towards me even now.

Most of the Reapers who'd fought with me in the war were gone. But their spirit, their courage and sacrifice had remained with me, remained in others, and always would. Jae and her people only understood blind devotion, a faux-unity that stemmed from hatred and a desire to cause harm.

'You're not just a walking disease, Jae. You're not just an untidy afterbirth. You're stupid. And you'll never understand what we have.' The stormtech was boiling like thunderclouds in my chest, swaddling me in an unnatural cloak of heat. My lips peeled back from my bared teeth as I swung up to look at her. 'I can't wait to watch Harmony nuke you and your psycho cult from orbit until you glow.'

Jae didn't flinch. Instead she gave a laconic smile and leaned in to whisper, 'You won't get the chance.'

'If you were going to kill me, you'd have done it already.'

Jae looked surprised. 'Oh, you're not going to die. Not for a very, very long time. I'm told you're very familiar with the torture rooms that Harvest used in the war. I don't think you spent nearly enough time in there. We'll prepare another one. I hope you got a good look at our stormtech experiments on the station, because you're going to get very familiar with them. How long do you think you'll hold out in there? Three months? A year? More?' She smoothed my hair back, gently. 'Maybe we'll hunt down a few of these friends of yours and put their severed heads in there with you for company.'

Hideko jabbed the pole between my shoulder blades. I was sent writhing and spasming on the cold floor again before being jerked back to my knees. Artyom's breathing seemed to get a little tighter. A sudden cold wetness stabbed down into my neck. An immobilising agent. Numbness spread through my limbs, turning them to stone. Within seconds I was limp.

The floor rocked beneath me. Harmony, desperately trying to carve a way inside.

'Should we take him now?' one of the men suggested, kicking me until I rolled onto my back. Crooked yellow teeth gleamed behind a veil of scruffy dark hair that came down to his shoulders. 'Get him tied up on a ship in the meantime. They'll never find him that way.'

'No. Let him see Harmony fall. Pack up what we need and get it to the next base, those dogs might be here soon. They will not get their hands on the databanks.' Jae gave me another smile. 'We have cells and data storages scattered all around Compass, slowly growing into the roots. We're here to stay, Vakov.'

'Don't you need someone to protect you against him?' he asked.

Artyom raised my arm, limp and heavy with paralysis. 'He's not going anywhere.'

The two armoured cultists exchanged a bow, hands clasped into fists. There was a chainship parked nearby, next to an old-fashioned airlock. They began loading most of the canisters and databanks into the chainship's open hatch. Jae turned to Sokolav, laying a hand on his arm. He reached back to touch her, his features mellowing into the brave and loyal man I'd once known. Bile rose in my throat. So that was the nature of their relationship. Sokolav's fingers tightened in Jae's hand before the two drifted apart. He tilted his head to deal me a long, resolute look before sealing his spherical spacesuit helmet and following the cultists into the chainship. My hands shook and I tried to squirm into a sitting position. Nothing. Even if Harmony did get in here, the Suns would slither away with all their research and equipment and continue on somewhere else.

I locked sights with my brother. Pleading for him to do something, anything. He glanced away.

'You actually thought your brother was going to help you.' Jae slipped to his side, hand on his shoulder. My teeth clenched hard enough to crack. 'Artyom has been fully committed to our cause since we became his family, one which wouldn't abandon him. You took a beating and ran away to war. He stayed and faced your father. And now, he's standing up to the evil of Harmony as you never could.'

And the thing was: she was right. My brother was standing with this little snake because I'd run like a coward and let the wolves of the world tear him apart. We were here because I'd failed him.

Yells. Gunfire rumbling through the stone.

On a flexiscreen, a highrise disappeared in a fiery explosion. Dust poured out the broken windows like streams of smoky tears, the hot ruins shedding fire and rubble onto the crowded streets as they collapsed with a great shuddering roar, screams ringing through the speakers.

The chainship winked to life. Ungluing from its berth, the cycling chamber irised open to allow them access to open space, where they'd continue to spread the House of Suns' poison and lies to outposts and stations and habitats all across the Common.

I'd failed.

I almost looked away. A white-hot streak jerked my attention back. A guided Anti-Hull micro-missile, programmed by Juvens to target any unidentified ships making a sneaky getaway. Jae's head snapped around as the missile rammed into the chainship. The hull crumbled like paper as it exploded. Chunks of debris showered outwards, bleeding liquids into space. Sudden streamlined bursts of red plasma fire zapped out from the alien gunship, vaporising whatever was left of the ship and everything inside it.

'No,' Jae gasped, stepping backwards as she watched the man she loved turned to atoms and ash, spilling out into space.

Slowly, slowly, I tested my arm. The drug still had its fever- ish claws hooked into me. But the stormtech was slowly eating it away, coiling its energy inside me in preparation. Heat lashed against my inner chest. 'On the plus side, if there's a hell, you and Sokolav will have all the time you want together. You'll make a great pair.'

Jae turned around. Her black eyes were empty as vacuum. 'Artyom,' Jae said, not tearing her gaze from me.

'Yes, Jae?' Artyom asked.

'Kill him.'

Something in me turned very, very cold.

'What?' Artyom asked, like he couldn't believe he'd heard correctly.

'It's a perfectly simple order, Artyom.' She turned to him. Unblinking, unwavering. 'I don't believe I've ever stuttered. Or perhaps I did, and you didn't understand me.'

'I understood you,' said Artyom quietly.

'Then we are in agreement. It'll be your final step to ascen- sion. You will become one of us.' Jae's voice was as soft and calm as the wind across a Harvest battlefield. She dropped a thin-gun into his hands and stepped back, hands held behind her back. 'Kill him.'

Artyom's hand was shaking as he held the thin-gun between my eyes. The small cold barrel pressing into bone. I looked up past the length of the gun and into my brother's eyes. We were closer together than we'd been since he'd betrayed me to the Suns. His cold breath plumed in the air. I saw the boy who I'd grown up with, who'd walked the midnight streets with me, who'd climbed mountains by my side. The shared memories strung between us like manacles.

No matter what, I'd said, *you're still my brother. You always will be.*

Artyom swallowed. Tears beaded in his eyes and made furrows down his grimy cheeks as he looked at me. His trigger hand wavered, then fell. 'I can't.' His whisper seemed to fill the room. 'He's my brother. I can't. I can't do it.'

Jae nodded in understanding. 'Very well,' she said. Her face was expressionless as she fired six bullets into my brother's chest.

49

Brother

Blood sprayed from Artyom's chest. His legs gave out under him, his body crumpling to the floor. Gasping for air as he clutched at the gaping holes in his chest, right below his heart. His limbs pawing helplessly at the ground as he tried to right himself. But he couldn't. His body shuddered.

'No, no, no, no.' I managed to crawl next to him, holding his hands over the wounds. But there was so much blood leaking out of him from so many places. His breathing turned frantic, more blood bubbling out his mouth and dribbling down his chin. 'Please, don't die, Artyom. Stay with me, stay. Please, please stay. Look at me, Artyom! Look at me!'

He did. His eyes swum in fear, darting back and forth, as if he'd felt himself slipping and was desperately searching for some way to hold on. He shivered in my arms and his hands flopped to his sides. His mouth opened to tell me one final thing, but he made a small gasp and his eyes glazed over. His pulse faded away as his body went limp.

The boy who'd walk with me through the snowfields on winter mornings, who'd climb to the observatory at night to listen to music and stargaze was gone, along with everything he could have become if I'd be a better brother, spreading across this cold, cold floor and pooling at his killer's feet.

A sound of pure anguish tore out of my throat. My body racked with sobs, my vision drowning in tears as I hugged the body of this lost, confused soul. This boy who'd deserved so much better in a world so full of evil and hatred.

'You want to be with your brother? His body will join you in the Blind Room. Traitors have no use here,' came a demonic little voice from far away.

A rage-filled hatred like I've never known, that I didn't realise someone was capable of possessing for another human being, screamed inside my chest. With a sobbing snarl, I swung my fist towards Jae. I punched empty air as Jae daintily sidestepped and I collapsed on my face. Hideko swooped down and punched me hard in the side of my head. I struggled upwards, barely feeling the blow, barely feeling anything. The electropole crackled against my flesh, frying something in my body. I feverishly tried to struggle to my feet, pushing against the pain. Hideko landed another three blows against the side of my head as I got to my knees, then smashed her fist into the side of my ribcage so hard something in me ruptured. Blood poured down my face and I gritted my teeth, internally screaming, desperately trying to claw for Jae. My fingers were inches from her before Hideko kicked me in the jaw. My head whiplashed backwards with a sharp snap, thunking against cold metal as I hit the floor.

The world flashed with sharp, stabbing pain. I watched helplessly as Hideko kicked my brother's body to make sure he was dead. Her face twisted in mock sorrow, hands pressed to her cheeks, her shoulders shaking as she mimicked my tears with little weeping noises. '"Don't die, Artyom. Please."' She cackled with laughter as the world dissolved with tears again. She spat in my face before driving her boot into my testicles. Pain exploded in my abdomen, spraying into every part of me. 'Worm.'

She locked her arm tight around my neck, hoisting me upwards while the other hand jerked my hair back until my scalp stung, tilting my head up towards Jae. I was shaking so hard I could barely see. My grief slowly collapsing me. Everything inside my body going numb and dead, swallowed by a writhing dark nightmare I'd never wake up from.

'Are you listening, Vakov? I hope you are,' Jae said calmly. 'Your little brother died like a mangy dog. But you don't understand true pain. You don't understand what every innocent Harvester felt. But you will. Over the coming decades, we're going to teach you a lesson in suffering.' I wasn't in my own body anymore. I was somewhere far away, watching whatever remained of the person I'd been crumble. Jae started to walk away to the cycling chamber. 'Hideko, strap this little worm into a restraining harness and dump him in a crate with his brother and seal it. Let them have their time together.'

Hideko made a face. 'Artyom's leaking everywhere. It's disgusting. I don't want to touch him.'

'How you do it doesn't concern me. Just get it done.'

Grief still smothering all logic and all senses. Even so, something warm and familiar was trickling through. Feeling in my legs, the stormtech massaging the immobilising agent away. Hideko dragged me by my hair away from my brother. A tinkle as she retrieved a restraining harness webbed to the wall. She cursed, reaching around with both hands to tug the buckle free. She leaned down towards me, trying to loop the straps over my shoulders. Energy born of some mad, animal fury burst through me as I surged to my feet, grabbed her by the back of her neck and brought her face smashing down on the terminal, once, twice, three times, the glass splintering and cracking louder with each smash, leaving bloody stains. She reared back, whipping a burning stripe across my back with the straps. I ripped them out of her hands and scythed her legs out from under her, sending us both crashing to the ground. I wrapped the straps around her neck in three overlapping layers, tightening the buckles until the mechanism threatened to break, then jerked back, my teeth clenching.

Hideko's eyes bulged, her hands clawing at her neck. Her face slowly turning the colour of a bruise. Her legs thrashing against mine. Body jerking back and forth. I stared at my brother's corpse and empty, dead eyes. Called on every untapped nugget of strength in my body and *pulled* so hard I felt my joints straining, my muscles aching. The buckle's edge clawing bloody furrows in Hideko's cheek, the leather straps creaking and groaning, slicing into her neck, her arms shuddering like a flopping fish.

And then they didn't flop at all.

I stood. Jae had emerged from the cycling chamber. Her eyes went wide with horror as she surveyed her dead friend before snapping back to me. I bared my teeth, and for the first time I saw something silently ignite in Jae's eyes. The very thing that she was instilling in so many others.

Fear.

She tore for the desk. Maybe looking for a weapon, I didn't know and I didn't care. My legs were soggy cardboard under me as I surged after her, but blue lanced down my spine and spread to my limbs. I drew on it, letting my grief and anger burn through me.

She clawed up a slingshiv, placing her body between me and the Surge machinery. I wobbled left, her stabbing blow shearing harmlessly past me. I smashed my elbow into the side of her head and kicked her flailing to the ground. I tore towards the machinery, clawing something off the table. But I heard her running up behind me and spun sluggishly, the residue of the drug slowing my reaction. I held my arms up in defence as she slashed downwards, slicing open my left arm. The metal edge of the table jarred my spine as I retreated and she swept forward, slashing open my right arm and nicking bone. She reached out to stab me in the face. I caught her arm mid-strike, the slingshiv's serrated edge inches from my eye. Vision smeared with sweat, muscles creaking, I slammed my elbow into the side of her head. She staggered backwards and I ripped the slingshiv out of her hand, lunging forward.

She didn't so much as gasp as I drove the slingshiv hilt-deep into her belly. Our noses were touching. Chests inches apart. Her eyelashes fluttered with confusion, even as I stabbed her four more times, before twisting the blade up towards her sternum. Hot blood spilled out, spattering the floor. Her black eyes watched me from underneath her black hair, the furnace fire in them slowly guttering out. She was a cult leader, The Killer Chemist. But she was also someone who'd lost her home and everyone she knew and loved.

Heaving, I tore myself away from her. She took one, unhesitant step forward, and crumbled at my feet like a building falling into the sea.

Blue thrummed down my arms and legs as I scooped up the thin-gun and levelled the muzzle at the device transmitting the Surge, blasting it into a smoking pile of scrap.

On-screen, skinnies and Reapers stopped, one by one, looking around as if collectively awakening from a deep, deep sleep. They began collapsing in shock and horror at the things they'd done, the things they'd witnessed. The result stats showed the reports of chaos across Compass waning, dots vanishing.

My shoulders sagged.

It was done.

I lurched over to the second device intended to summon the Shenoi so I could shut it down ...

... and felt something. A thud from the infinite depths of a cavern, echoing in the periphery of my senses like a ghostly shadow. Something too vast and terrible to be understood, brushing against me. My skin turned to ice and my muscles contracted, my breathing becoming slow and deep as if something else were breathing with me.

Slowly, slowly, I looked down. Every drop of stormtech inside my body was being drawn to my torso like magnets. It strained against the front of my body, held there to form one long, uneven shape, pushing out.

It looked like a claw.

I reached up to touch the veins in the asteroid rock, once filled with stormtech, now long mined-out. Compass had once been striated and honeycombed with stormtech, turning the asteroid into a Shenoi body. We'd entered through its pores to live among its organs, building structures between the geometries of its bones.

How many other places across the Common had once been like this?

I glanced past the viewport. The geometries of space peppered with glistening stars and celestial bodies and untapped worlds of wonder. And crawling and writhing among these worlds were horrific creatures of fury and rage, creatures that had consumed galaxies. Creatures trying to communicate.

Well, I had an answer for the vicious bastards.

I picked up the device and brought it crashing down, toppling over the signal booster, then gasped, sinking to my knees as if something had been ripped out of me. Slowly, the stormtech spread back across my body. My breathing returned to normal. I shrugged off the presence like a physical thing.

Then I remembered Artyom.

His body was cooler to the touch. I reached out and closed his empty eyes, once so full of fire and life. I'd brought down a cult, stopped a massacre and killed a tyrant. But I couldn't do the one thing that mattered. I'd been unable to save my brother.

Tears smeared my vision as I held his hand and remembered our last moments before I'd departed New Vladi. *Come back for me*, he'd said as we'd hugged one last time, the snow blowing and whiplashing around us. He'd wrapped his arms tight around me, as if he could stop me from leaving.

I will, I remember saying, biting back tears. *I swear I will*. Dark wind howled across the mountains as we pulled apart. I remembered walking to the waiting chainship and not daring to turn around, because I knew I'd stay if I did.

Would Artyom have left me, if I'd been the one whose body was incompatible with stormtech? Or would he have been braver than me, and stayed? I would never know. All his love, all his dreams and all his mistakes, all his scars and wounds, everything we'd gone through together, was ash and blood lost in the wind.

I blinked. Sat up a little straighter.

No, no. It wouldn't work. It couldn't. The results had been absolute: Artyom Fukasawa's body was incompatible with stormtech.

But what about Jae's altered and improved stormtech?

I was at the desk before I could think it through. They'd packed everything up when they left. There was nothing here. But I couldn't give up. I could almost feel my stormtech guiding me around the bench and between the crevices of the metal grating where a single jar of stormtech had fallen.

I picked it up. How much do you give someone with a hole in their chest? It was crazy to even think it could work. But me and common sense haven't been friends for a long time. I found a hypodermic in an emergency med-pack and filled it with stormtech before kneeling over my brother's body. My hands were shaking. I breathed deep and thought of snow drifting along the New Vladi mountains. The crisp air filling my lungs on the predawn streets. Lending me control.

I injected the stormtech into my dead brother's veins.

Nothing.

Nothing.

I sagged on the floor, warmed by my own blood.

Nothing.

Nothing.

My little brother was dead.

I closed my eyes. Swallowed my tears as I slid my hand over his one last time.

A twitch. A muscle memory.

Artyom's body jerked like it'd been electrocuted, his spine arching as his legs thrashed.

The stormtech was trying to jumpstart my brother back to life.

Artyom slammed down again, gasping and spluttering, his eyes bursting open as he clawed for air. I ripped his underskin open and saw the faintest sliver of blue curling under his chest, followed by more and more, like patches of bright-blue sky opening up as clouds evaporated, until a steady blue stream was cycling through his body. His eyes were wild and confused, entering a seizure. Cold sweat ran down his body as I wrapped my arms around him, rocking him back and forth. 'It's okay,' I whispered through the tears, rubbing warmth back into his body. 'You're okay you're okay you're okay. I'm here. I'm here.'

I don't know how much time had passed before he managed to croak out, 'How?' he rasped.

'Jae's little concoction,' I said.

'I couldn't do it,' he gurgled, wiping snot from his nose. 'This is all my fault. I'm so sorry.'

'It's okay,' I lied, my throat tight as I held him closer. 'You're going to be okay. I'm here. I'm never leaving you again.' As I drew him close I felt something beneath his underskin. I drew it out and held his pendant in my palm. The other half of what he'd given to me on the mountains all those years ago. 'You kept it on all this time?'

Artyom nodded. Something deep in his chest cracked and shattered like a pane of glass, his face dissolving in tears as he broke. 'I'm so, so sorry, Vak. For what I said to you. For how I treated you. I'm sorry. I'm so, so sorry. I'm—' He was shaking and sobbing so hard he couldn't get the words out. He buried his face in my chest, all his sorrow and lies and regret gushing free. Tears trickled down my cheeks as I closed my eyes and crushed him in a hug. Holding him like I had when we'd learned Kasia had died and we only had each other.

Harmony would not let him escape without repercussion. He'd be arrested and tried as a member of the House of Suns, an active participant in their atrocities. I could let him escape. There was an escape pod outfitted with a warpdrive we could leave in together. Never return to Compass.

But we couldn't run from this. I loved Artyom more than anything, but he would have to face the consequences of his actions. As would I. I was not going to run anymore. And neither would he. Because loving someone means you do what's best for them, even when it hurts, even when it scars.

Because that's what being his brother meant.

50

Sleeping at Last

No matter how many funerals you attend, no matter how many times you swear it'll be the last, you know it never will be.

We gathered together in the dimly lit hangar bay. My body was still recovering from the bombardment of damage it had sustained, aches and pains rippling through my flesh like occasional speedbumps. Saren, Jasken and Katherine stood close by to stare down at the bodies of Kuen, Arya, and the other men and women who'd given their lives to protect others. We'd laid them down in their armour with their dog tags. Just like in the war. We bared silent witness as their bodies were encased in gel-padding and sealed up in little memorial pods, each of us carving our initials into the gunmetal hull. Didn't matter that I'd barely known them. We'd fought together in battle, saved each other's lives. Alcatraz taught me that's a bond, a debt that transcends all other debts. One that can't, and shouldn't, ever be repaid.

Reapers crossed their arms over their chests in silent respect. I found myself doing the same. We stood watching as the pods were launched into the dark of space to be slowly swallowed up by the bright constellations of stars. For ever a part of the universe they'd given everything they had to protect. Gone, but never forgotten.

Around me, groups of soldiers of all ranks and Divisions were honouring their fallen, saying goodbye to friends and loved ones with their own little quiet rituals. There was a tally of the causalities, of course. But the stats don't matter. Not when each death etches a little scar in your heart until you're numb. By then, the losses feel innumerable.

Jasken stood watching for a while before briefly resting a heavy hand on my shoulder and then walking off. Saren gave me a solemn nod. I returned it. No one much spoke. We didn't need to. We all knew it was up to us to honour the fallen, to make their courage and sacrifice count. To keep their memory, their fire, alive in our hearts. And to forgive ourselves for not saving them.

That was the part I was never going to figure out.

It ended the same way it had begun: in Kindosh's office.

The place hadn't changed much. Same view of the asteroid. Same coffee-stained desk carved from the same rugged black stone. Same chairs. Same printer. Only this time, Kindosh was somewhat pleased to see me.

'If it was anyone else, I wouldn't believe it,' she was muttering as she sipped her espresso.

I gave her a thin smile. 'Fortunate it *was* me, then.' I'd shaved and combed my hair and wore a new suit of armour. It was a dull dark blue in colour, less battle-hardened and more for everyday use. I clutched the helmet between my hands as I sat.

'I see,' said Kindosh, desperate to plug the silence with some vapid response. 'You and Cobalt Squad are to be congratulated. Admittedly, having Jae Myouk-soon alive and in cuffs would have been ideal, but we're still salvaging data from their operational bases. We've seized control of their station, the one you were taken to in the asteroid field.'

'Any survivors?' I asked.

'Not many. The ones who did are severely traumatised and in very poor condition. We're still making arrests; anyone with known affiliation to the House of Suns is being brought in. The whereabouts of the Jackal and Sokolav remain unknown.'

I was startled. 'Sokolav survived the explosion?'

'Yes. We only found two bodies. There was a spacesuit suit and pair of grav-boots missing from the chainship's armoury racks. He must have slipped back inside through a viewport. I know Sokolav. We'll flush him out easily enough.'

Only, she didn't. Not like I did. Nothing with him was easy or straightforward.

'He survived,' Katherine growled, 'while almost fifty thousand Compass citizens died in that Surge.'

I laid a hand on her arm while Kindosh said, 'Given the circumstances, that's an astronomically low number.'

'Tell that to the victims' families,' I said.

Kindosh looked unfazed. 'Three times as many were injured. Someone was preparing to blow the whole Upper Markets to clear it of skinnies. We were fortunate.' Kindosh looked as tired as I felt, but only for a second. 'We have to minimise the damage and move on, or we'll be swept up in the chaos.' She leaned forward, fingers steepled. 'The House of Suns must still have operational cells. It's going to take us months, maybe years to clear them from the asteroid. To heal the damage they did to Compass and its people? Even longer. Stormdealers are already reorganising, branching out.'

She was right. I'd seen the data-packet they'd released, explaining the general gist of the situation. The House of Suns might not have spread their beliefs, but they had poisoned Compass, just as Harmony had poisoned our bodies with Shenoi DNA. Drug-trafficking was at an all-time high and rapidly climbing. The long-lasting consequences were yet to be seen.

'We're spread thin. We're vulnerable. There's offworld syndicates and species who'll use this as an opening to get rid of us. And then there's the Shenoi threat the Kaiji alerted us to. We have to stay vigilant, gather our allies,' she said. 'I did not survive the Reaper War to lose now.'

'It's not just about winning. It's about how you win.' I levelled my stare at Kindosh until she met it. 'Harmony created Jae Myouk-soon. She fought back the only way she could, because she didn't know any other way. She believed her actions were justified. The House of Suns wouldn't exist without us.' I held up my arm, where long liquid splinters of blue were shooting upwards like glowing arrows. 'We have to change the paradigm. Learn not to make the same mistakes. Or we'll have nothing worth fighting for.'

I'd never trust Harmony completely. They were an interstellar government agency with enough military and scientific power to blast Compass to hell twice over. You'd have to be mad to put unquestioning faith in any organisation of that calibre. But they were also one of the few things holding the stitching of the galaxy together. If I had to bet on something, it'd be them. You learn to work with the intel you're given. Like it or not, they were the best chance we had, and I was going to give them that chance.

If I didn't believe it, who would?

Kindosh took all this in with a slow, deliberate nod. Perhaps listening to me, *really* listening, for the first time. Then her face assembled itself to its usual stoicism. 'Noted. Now, if there's nothing else, I've got a month's worth of Galactic Common meetings to arrange and—'

'There is something else,' I interrupted. 'I want to see him.'

*

Artyom's cell was in the innermost sector of the prison barracks and was roughly the same size as our shared room on New Vladi. Locked behind a crackling electranet, his only possessions were a stained mattress, a stained chair and a stained desk. The cleaning fluid failed to mask the stink of sweat and piss, drilling into my nose.

Compared to my Harvest prison cell, it was a palace.

'Hey.' Artyom wore an orange prisoner's jumpsuit. Fibres running through the thick fabric would seize up if he tried to escape. Licks of blue were faintly visible underneath the jumpsuit.

I held my hands behind my back. 'How you holding up?'

'Could be better.' He looked up. Pain creased the lines of his face. 'You know what's going to happen to me?'

It had been the talk of Harmony. People had taken to looking away when I entered a room, conversations chopped short. Saren told me they'd get over it, but I didn't buy that. I'd been talking it over with Kindosh for hours. Well, more like arguing. 'I don't know,' I admitted. 'Though your death is in your favour.'

'Yeah, there's that.'

'But you were involved in the most serious attack on Compass since the Reaper War. You were given chances to come clean. You ignored them. The Harmony Intelligence Committee will decide what happens to you.'

It didn't need saying that he'd already have been executed if he wasn't my brother.

'Why did you join them?' I'd kept the question bottled up for months now. Sokolav had told me, but I needed to hear this from my brother's lips.

Artyom stared intently at his scarred hands, as if searching for a shred of wisdom there. He looked so thin and frail, like he'd been forced to grow up overnight and the rest of him hadn't quite caught up yet. 'You don't understand how big a gap you left in my life. First I hated you. Then I hated Harmony for stealing you away and rejecting me. Then I hated both. One day, I got tired of waking up alone and checking Harvest correspondent newsfeeds to see if you'd been killed, I started hating the whole world.'

I imagined him sitting alone, watching the smoking battle-fields piled with dead soldiers, leaking red, and knowing I had chosen that instead of him. The rage and injustice forced onto him, spurring him on to force it on someone else. 'They brought injured Reapers back to New Vladi. So drugged out of their minds that their bodies had grown into blue gills, their families grieving over them. But they had *something* to grieve over. They got closure. I didn't. It was like being in limbo. They wouldn't tell me where you were. My own brother, and it was too big a risk to tell me if you were alive or dead or captured. I lost it, Vak. I just lost it. I couldn't swallow the propaganda about stormtech doing what ordinary men couldn't. Remember when Dad would tell us what happened to us was actually our fault? It was like that. Sokolav found me, told me I wasn't the only one feeling that way. For the first time, I didn't feel alone anymore. He said he'd found a source of comfort. It made sense at first. These people wanted answers, like we all do. The longer I stuck around, the deeper and deeper it went and I couldn't get out.' His voice adopted a raw, strained tone. 'I never meant to hurt anyone, Vak.'

'But you did.' The words were glass shards on my tongue. But they needed to be said. 'You hurt people. So did I. So did Harmony. The best we can do is own up to it.'

'Jae told me she'd kill you if I tried to leave,' Artyom whispered.

'She tried anyway.'

'I always said you were too stubborn to die, Vak.'

I raised a thin smile to match his. A brief silence settled over us.

'What happens next?' Arytom asked.

'What do you think?'

'You're staying with Harmony, aren't you?'

'I don't much like them, either. But maybe working on the inside is the way to improve things.' A dreamy instrumental soundtrack was playing from some office down the corridor. Might have been one of the many songs we'd listened to together. 'My advice? Tell them everything. Don't hold anything back.'

'Vak—

'Do it, Artyom. It might be the only way to save your life.'

Artyom's hand brushed the cold metal wall. 'Do you ever think we'll see New Vladi again?'

'One day,' I said, and believed it. One day we'd return to the world of snow-peaked mountains and waterfalls and sweeping pine forests, full of animals and a wild, earthy smell.

I had so many more things to say, but they were lodged deep inside me, and I'd have to break whatever threadbare stitching was holding me together to say them. So I bowed my head in the New Vladi way and turned to leave. Artyom whispered, '*Arigato*, Vakov.' It was the first word of Japanese I'd heard him say in years. '*Domo arigato*. For everything.'

I got halfway to the exit when Arytom called me back. 'Vakov. Kasia would be proud of you.'

Katherine and Grim were waiting for me outside. He bumped my fist as Katherine kicked off the podium she'd been leaning against and slipped next to me. We strode together down the glowing stairs of Harmony Station. She kissed me on the cheek before we headed off. 'How'd it go?' she asked me finally, squeezing my hand.

'He'll live,' I said. 'If Harmony lets him.'

The Kaiji were picking their way up to the main building. The final negotiations of a peace treaty were beginning, as Juvens had promised. Their fleet was coming closer to the asteroid, handfuls of ships parking in dockyard berths designated for their species. The aliens would enter the Common as allies, along with their wartech, space fleets and armed forces for Harmony to call on. It'd take months, perhaps years, of interspecies diplomacy to fully determine the structure of it all, but that wasn't my problem.

Grim was gaping at the big aliens in wide-eyed awe. Juvens noticed, tilting his jutting horns in Grim's direction and baring his teeth. 'I bite.'

Juvens ignored the Ambassadors narrowing their eyes in burning disapproval. The Space Marshall turned to me with a sly, devilish grin, pressing a fist of salute to his armoured chest as he passed. I offered one in return.

We descended to the heart of Starklands, heading for our restaurant. Harmony had set up some sort of major celebratory event, but I wasn't feeling up to it. Never been comfortable in large gatherings, anyway. Hanging out here with my friends was enough for me. At my elbow, Katherine was twirling the vaper in her hand. 'Not going for a puff?' I asked.

'Trying to quit,' she said, finally sliding it into her breast pocket. A trio of heavyweight Shocktroopers in robust armour and carrying their helmets gave us a nod each as we sliced by. I noticed Grim ducking away as they did, as if not wanting to be seen.

'You okay?' I asked him.

Grim squirmed. 'I guess.'

'It's because of Harmony, isn't it?' I asked. He nodded.

'Grim, you saved hundreds of lives,' Katherine said. 'You've got nothing to be ashamed of.'

'It's not about that,' Grim whispered.

Katherine clicked, understanding. My friend doesn't like public attention, and even less when it stems from Harmony. I knew he'd be coming to terms with his new relationship with Harmony. Would be for a while.

Even cleaned up, the streets were still a mess following the outbreak. Casualties were still streaming in. Chatterboards overflowed with calls for missing people. The chaos had touched every floor, every echelon of every sector and class. Nothing's as indiscriminate as random tragedy. The formerly glimmering restaurants and bustling shop squares had been reduced to wrecks of smashed glass and blackened beams by a micronade. Ships had crashed into each other before faceplanting into the asteroid. The damage was steadily racking up in the billions. Spaceports had been shut down, all departures grounded. Communications and trading with offworlders and non-Common alien species were temporarily closed. Flexiscreens flickered with hotlinks and contact information for trauma counselling. Torn posters about uniting together under Harmony fluttered like lost ghosts in the simulated breeze. People still milled about, as if looking for a way to hold themselves together. The never-ending stream of aerial traffic above us had crawled to a standstill.

But that's the thing about people. Knock them down, and they find a way to get back up. Teams of all species were hard at work repairing the damaged property, providing food and shelter and free services. Everyone was doing their best. Floors that had been quarantined yesterday were slowly reopening to the public, reuniting sobbing families under the swaying trees.

Further downtown, orange-domed medclinics had popped up like fungi overnight, dealing with the wave of injured and sick.

Humans and aliens were queued around the medclinics in wide circles like an orbital trajectory. There was an entirely separate line for anyone with stormtech, a battered plastic barrier dividing the queues. I hadn't wanted to believe the broadcast about escalating hate crimes towards skinnies, but now I was starting to see the truth of it.

Slow, fat raindrops drizzled down. The raised glass platforms above us ran with veils of rain and smeared the blinking highrises and aerial traffic into a waterlogged neon stain. In the distance, the once-proud Reaper statue had been desecrated. Sprayed with sinister glyphs, gaping chunks of its body hammered and torn off. My belly was a pit of snakes, the stormtech lashing so violently that I almost didn't hear someone telling me to head to my own line. 'Are you okay?' Katherine asked quietly.

I moved to respond, but suddenly I heard a warbling echo from the trenches of my mind. My arm hairs stood up, body heat rising. A reminder of something far more sinister than anything that had happened on Compass. It had been there ever since I'd gazed into Jae's signalling device. I hadn't told a soul about it. Not yet.

Katherine was still looking at me. 'I'm just afraid we traded one enemy for another.' I swept a hand out at the chaos around us. 'What Jae and the Suns did . . . it's going to ripple. I don't know how we'll fix it.'

'We will,' she whispered. 'It doesn't matter what happens, you won't be alone, Vak. I'm not going anywhere,' she said.

'Neither am I,' Grim said with a wide grin, slinging his arm around my neck.

'I couldn't get rid of you even if I tried,' I said.

'And what sort of friend would I be if I let you?'

Katherine came up to me. 'I promise.'

'Promise what?' I asked.

'That this won't be for nothing,' she told me, cupping my face in her hands until her face filled my entire field of vision. 'We'll make this chaos count. All of it. I promise.'

And you know what? I almost believed it.

Acknowledgements

I never thought I'd get to write this.

It's one thing to write a novel. It's another thing entirely to put it through the gladiatorial tournament that is the publishing process, hoping it'll one day end up on the bookshelf for all the world to read. Something that, in my case, took years of endurance, blood, sweat, tears and alcohol. With every frustrating writing day, trunked project and rejection letter, the odds of writing the acknowledgements page to capstone my debut novel seemed slimmer and slimmer. Now that it *has* happened, I can't pretend it was a solo effort. Many, many people helped bring this book into existence. I'd give you all Rubix caretakers and spaceships, if I could. Alas, you'll have to settle for thanks.

Many thanks go to my absolute legend of agent, John Jarrold. For picking a rough diamond like me out of the slush pile, for answering all my pesky midnight emails, and for putting in a phenomenal effort to get my work seen by the right people. May there be gin in your future.

A world of gratitude goes out to my wise and long-suffering editor, Gillian Redfearn, for giving a debut author that elusive second chance and helping me tell the story I've always wanted to tell. She's spent more time than anyone should in Vakov's head, using her insight, wit and mighty red pen to sharpen his adventure to be as cutting-edge as it can possibly be. Bouncing bizarre ideas off her as we conspire on these books together has been an insanely fun ride. I'm lucky as hell to have someone who just *gets* my work as well as she does. A big thanks to Will, Rachel, Marcus and the wonderful folk at Gollancz Towers, for doing what you do.

I wouldn't be here without my brave beta readers, who read *Stormblood* in its various stages: Jared W. Cooper, G.V. Anderson, Mel Melcer, Spencer Ellsworth, Natailia Theodoridou, and Erin Latimer (who suffered through more of my first-drafts than anyone legally should). Each of them told me what I needed to hear, not what I wanted to hear. Without their feedback, you'd be holding a very different book in your hands.

A tip of the hat to all the amazing authors, editors and artists I've crossed paths with, providing wit, wisdom and plenty of ideas worth stealing. You know who you are.

A shout-out goes to the various mates who kept me sane with encouragement and beers along the way: Adrian Collins, T. R. Napper, Rob Boffard, Derek Kunsken, Alex Shvartsman, Ian MacDonald, Zach Chapman, Alessia and Noemi. A special mention is required for Lyndon Hill. About six years ago now, when I confessed I wanted to publish a science-fiction novel, he told me that very few ever make it, and to keep my expectations in check. He also told me that he'd help me get there, providing feedback and keeping me humble. He kept his promise. Thanks mate, for your unwavering candour and giving me a friend to look up to. Although, you totally deserved your cameo appearance getting shafted (you know why).

To my creative writing teachers helping me hone my craft over the years: Jodie Brooks, Stephanie Bishop, and Meredith Jones, thanks.

A round of applause for the mad bastards over at StarShip-Sofa: Tony, Gary, Ralph, Amy, Lisa, Kelly and Michael. Still not quite sure how we managed to keep our show running over the years, but we got it done. We achieved some insane things that shouldn't be spoken of in polite company. I'll always look back on my time there with fond memories, no small part thanks to you and the incredible cast of authors and narrators who made it all happen.

Further thanks go to Brandon, Mary, Howard and Dan at the Writing Excuses podcast, who dispense weekly writing advice that anyone else would charge for, to good folks at the Fantasy Writers Bar and GFRWs on Facebook for being kick-ass support groups when I needed somewhere to rant.

None of this would be possible without my family. My mother, for the endless patience required to homeschool a hyperactive kid like me, for teaching me to read and instilling in me a love of books, and for introducing me to science-fiction by way of *Star Wars* and *Blade Runner*. My father, for taking me around the world, for never doubting in me for a second, and for always being there for me, even when I didn't deserve it. After graduating university, when I said I wanted to work part-time to write the book I always wanted to write, you never hesitated and supported me every step along the way. I couldn't ask for two kinder, more compassionate and understanding people to have as parents. You're an endless source of knowledge and inspiration to me, and I'd be the shadow of the man I am if it wasn't for you two. Thank you for everything, and a little bit extra.

Thanks, too, to my little sister, Rebekah, being my companion and friend, and always being there to listen to me. I'm lucky to have a sister like you. Here's to many more nights of binge-watching Netflix and arguing the finer points of Marvel films (also, it's your turn to walk the dog).

And thanks to you, dear reader, for going on this crazy little adventure across the galaxy with me. It certainly won't be the last.

Credits

Jeremy Szal and Gollancz would like to thank everyone at Orion who worked on the publication of *Stormblood* in the UK.

Editorial
Gillian Redfearn
Brendan Durkin

Copy editor
Abigail Nathan

Audio
Paul Stark
Amber Bates

Contracts
Anne Goddard
Paul Bulos
Jake Alderson

Design
Lucie Stericker
Joanna Ridley
Nick May

Editorial Management
Charlie Panayiotou
Jane Hughes
Alice Davis

Finance
Jennifer Muchan
Jasdip Nandra
Afeera Ahmed
Elizabeth Beaumont
Sue Baker

Marketing
Tom Noble

Production
Paul Hussey

Publicity
Will O'Mullane

Sales
Laura Fletcher
Esther Waters
Victoria Laws
Hermione Ireland
Ellie Kyrke-Smith
Frances Doyle
Georgina Cutler

Operations
Jo Jacobs
Sharon Willis
Lisa Pryde
Lucy Brem